"HAUNTING."
—*Publishers Weekly*

"A sensitive, original, unpredictable and extremely moving novel."   —*Los Angeles Times*

"Girard's story is an eloquent plea for a renewal of community, for a shattering of the dark forces that drive us apart and make serial killings thinkable. *The Late Man* is the first step in an exciting and rewarding career."
—*Wichita Eagle*

"One of the most stunning and unnerving novels of suspense that I've come across in a long time. A thinking person's mystery."
—*Mostly Murder*

"This is a wonderful novel about three unforgettable people, about grace and love, solitude and hope."   —Andre Dubus

THE LATE MAN

James Preston Girard

AN ONYX BOOK

With thanks to Sharon Lerch

Published by the Penguin Group
Penguin Books USA Inc., 375 Hudson Street,
New York, New York 10014, U.S.A.
Penguin Books Ltd, 27 Wrights Lane,
London W8 5TZ, England
Penguin Books Australia Ltd, Ringwood,
Victoria, Australia
Penguin Books Canada Ltd, 10 Alcorn Avenue,
Toronto, Ontario, Canada M4V 3B2
Penguin Books (N.Z.) Ltd, 182–190 Wairau Road,
Auckland 10, New Zealand

Penguin Books Ltd, Registered Offices:
Harmondsworth, Middlesex, England

Published by Onyx,
an imprint of Dutton Signet, a division of Penguin Books USA Inc. This is an author-
ized reprint of a hardcover edition published by Atheneum/Macmillan Publishing. For
information address Atheneum, Macmillan Publishing Company, 866 Third Avenue,
New York, NY 10022.

First Onyx Printing, November, 1994
10 9 8 7 6 5 4 3 2 1

PUBLISHER'S NOTE

For Barbara

PART ONE

PART ONE

1

Either the deputy didn't know anything or he had orders not to talk, so Loomis turned his collar up to shield his neck against the early morning sunlight slanting through the car window, and pretended to doze.

They headed north, out of the city. There had been a time, six years ago, when he would have known exactly what to expect at a crime scene north of town, on one of the roads along the interstate: a female body, nude, strangled, perhaps beaten or otherwise tortured. And the flowers—four of them, the last time—and the underwear. But that had been six years ago.

The deputy took the exit ramp at 101st Street, going east, then north again, and back east on a narrow dirt road running between deep ditches. Where they stopped finally, there were three county cars, parked at angles, effectively blocking the road, and a board thrown across the ditch, which was muddy from the previous night's rain. Farther along, there were tire tracks cutting across the ditch and more boards had been laid across the lowered strands of barbed wire to allow some vehicle into the field beyond—the coroner's van, Loomis supposed. Despite himself, he felt the first edge of excitement.

He made himself stand at the roadside and wait for the deputy to lead the way, though it was plain enough. Ahead of them was an ordinary field, hilly and wooded, grown a bit wild, perhaps left fallow for hunting. Beyond the fence, hip-high grass rose to a ridge with a single tree at its crest. He could hear birds in the woods he could not see, beyond the hill, and the morning sun, drawing moisture out of the earth, brought with it the crisp hothouse smells of growth and soil and, beneath that, a sharper odor that might have been manure spread on nearby fields, except that it was too late in the year for that. It would be a while before that smell was gone. From now on, this undistinguished place would have a history; farmers would point it out to their visitors, would give it a glance whenever they drove past. Children would explore it by day, avoid it by night. Even after the fence had been set back up and the tracks overgrown again, it would not be the same.

"Is the coroner still here?" he asked, as the deputy walked ahead of him over the board spanning the ditch.

"Been and gone, sir."

Loomis frowned. He liked to see the crime scene while the body was still there. The deputy led him by a roundabout way, following a wandering hedgerow, where there was mostly mud and rock beneath them, explaining, "Sheriff doesn't want the grass trampled down," which might mean that Raines was planning a stakeout. Presumably, someone would remove the boards and restring the wire, back at the road, maybe even smooth out the tire tracks on the road and across the ditch.

Beyond the ridge there was a short, steep slope into a wooded area. They had to cut back through the tall grass again to get there, and when they did grasshoppers flew up in random arcs, like fireworks, striking Loomis on the face and arms, making him feel itchy, though he resisted the urge to swat at them, feeling the unnatural dignity that overcame one in the presence of the slain, who had had all dignity taken from them.

He caught sight of Raines, a dozen yards or so inside the trees, waiting for him, but by then Loomis could have found his own way, following the smell. It was a smell you never confused with anything else after the first time, and it was strong enough to suggest that the body was still there.

Loomis pushed between the trees, but the deputy hung back in the sunlight. Loomis didn't blame him. He still found it necessary to brace himself, still worried a bit about embarrassing himself somehow, though he never had. What he felt when he saw it was a visceral thrill, as if his body had tried all by itself to reverse direction, to rear away from it like a horse. Instead, he made himself lean nearer and say, "Morning, Warren. What have you got?"

Raines didn't say anything, understanding it was just talk. There was no mud in the tree-sheltered clearing, but there was a dark smear at the base of one of the trees, suggesting that something had lain against it. Loomis squinted at what he supposed was the body.

"You're sure it's human?" he asked.

"The coroner says it is," Raines said. "The kids who

found it thought it was a big dog or a deer, and they called the health department. The health department guy had a look and called us. Guess it must have looked human to him. Coroner says he won't even guess about the sex until he gets it in the lab."

"Any clothing? Effects?"

"Not a button."

"Most likely female then."

"Most likely."

Loomis fished his wire-rims out of his shirt pocket and slipped them on, then knelt beside the corpse like a baseball catcher, balancing on the balls of his feet, knees spread, his hands hanging between his legs.

It was like looking at an optical illusion, trying to make it come together into a sensible shape. The limbs had been shortened—chewed by animals, it looked like—but the bones weren't pulled loose and scattered as they should have been. He could see now that it lay on one side the chest pushing out like an animal's. The skin was mostly leathered and that was wrong, too, if it had lain under these trees for very long, but there were also places where it still looked moist, gleaming like patent leather in the half-light. There was an opening that he thought at first glance might be a wound, then realized was the crease of the buttocks, flattened against the crumpled pelvis as the fat inside had turned to liquid and seeped out into the leaves and soil. That helped him distinguish the lower limbs from the upper part of the body, though he still could not quite make out the head and wondered whether the corpse had been decapitated. There were other openings, where flies and beetles went in and out, that might have been knife holes, but Loomis guessed they had been made by the insects themselves, widened perhaps by the body's escaping gases as the bacteria, no longer kept in check by oxygen, had begun turning their host into excrement from the inside out.

He climbed back to his feet and took off his glasses. "Why didn't the coroner take it?"

Raines blinked at the body and then rubbed his eyes, as though he'd just gotten out of bed. Loomis guessed he'd been up most of the night.

"I'm going to stake it out tonight," the sheriff said. "See if he comes back, like he used to. I figure one more night won't hurt it any."

"Probably not."

"The coroner took the jaw," Raines added. "See if we can get a match on the teeth. I got a call in to that anthropologist at K-State, just in case."

Loomis looked at the body again. That was why he had been unable to locate the head. Now he could see the greasy black swatch of what had once been hair, the shallow knob of skull he had tentatively supposed to be a shoulder, which had sunk into the mass of the body. He gazed at the body for a moment in silence, as he might study an artwork of infinite variety.

"She's been dead a long time," he said at last. "What makes you think he'll be back now?"

"It's been moved at least once."

"Could have been animals. The ends of the bones look like they've been gnawed."

"I don't mean just here in he clearing," Raines said. "It's been someplace dry."

"Could be. Did the coroner get some scrapings?"

"Dust and maybe some kind of shavings."

"Any word yet on cause of death?"

"There's some damage to the vertebrae just below the skull. Could be strangulation by ligature."

They were both silent for a moment. Loomis turned over the worn file cards in his mind, surprised to find them still there, sharp and clear: Marty Madsen, Sarah Mosteller, Terry Fillmore, Jeannie Courter. He hadn't thought of any of them consciously in months, yet there was a sense in which they'd never been out of his mind—especially Jeannie, the worst, worse even than this one. He remembered thinking, seeing the Courter body for the first time, *Now you've gone too far; this wasn't necessary.*

"Who do you think it is?" Raines asked.

Loomis chewed at his lower lip, flipping more cards.

"If I had to guess," he said at last, "I'd say Karen Munoz. She's been missing long enough to look like this by now."

"The WSU student?"

"Yeah." Whoever it was, he knew he'd be making a visit later that day, telling some family what they didn't want to hear.

"Too bad," Raines said.

Loomis nodded. That was about all there was to say to that.

"If you're finished here," Raines said, "I'll show you the rest."

There was a path, barely visible, cutting through the trees, disappearing down one side of a mud-slicked gully and reappearing some little ways away, on the other side. Raines stepped carefully down the side of the ravine, ahead of Loomis, looking for dry spots, then gave a little hop to get to the other bank and stopped about halfway up, one knee slightly bent against the incline, waiting for Loomis.

"There," he said.

There was a wad of stiff, yellowed fabric lying just atop the rim of the gully, flattened by the elements amid the scraggly growths of weed and burr. Loomis balanced himself on the bank and fished for his glasses again. Even when they were on, he could not be sure whether he really saw the faded red and blue stripes running along the band of elastic, or whether his mind supplied them.

"Men's underwear," Raines said unnecessarily. "The tag's washed out."

"They'll be Sears mediums," Loomis said.

"I expect so. The flowers are over here. Lilies, I think."

It would have been impossible to spot them without knowing what to look for—some broken bits of yellow blossom, the flattened brown stems nearly melted into the soil, arranged in a circle, or perhaps the points of a crude pentagram. No photograph would show what he and Raines saw there, Loomis knew—something like a face at once familiar and unknown. His heart was pounding in his ears, perhaps from the climb up the gully wall.

"Five," he said, not really needing to count the blossoms.

"Yes," Raines said. "He's kept count."

"So have we."

Raines nodded. "So have we."

Suddenly, balanced precariously at the top of the gully, Loomis felt a surge of something like energy. Could it be joy? He put that thought away, not liking it. But he could remember, all at once, the textures, the feelings, even the smell of the way his life had been six years ago, as though nothing had passed between that moment and this. With it, incongruous but inevitable, because of the connection to that same period of time, came thoughts of Edie, who, like the Strangler, was never far from his thoughts, on whom also he had never quite given up despite the years and the lack of any encouragement.

He frowned, wondering if it could be an illusion, a copycat. There had always been others who knew about the flowers and the underwear, and their numbers had probably increased over the years—the lab guys, their wives, their wives' friends and relations . . .he shook his head again, feeling it was not worth mentioning to Raines. This was no copycat; Loomis was sure of it. This was him.

"I'll want a spot in your stakeout," he told Raines.

The phone rang almost as soon as he was back in his office, and he half-expected to hear George Munoz's soft, unaccusing voice asking, Have you found my daughter yet? But it was Fred Cubbage, the city editor at the *Mid-American*.

"We understand you have a body," he said.

"Isn't the more interesting question whether we have souls?" Loomis asked.

"Ha, ha. What about it?"

"As far as I know," Loomis said carefully, "this department doesn't have any body that you don't already know about."

"We heard it was out in the county."

"Then you ought to be talking to the sheriff's office. I can give you their number."

"Thanks. We've got it. We have information that you're helping them out with this one."

"Really? Where would you get that kind of information?"

"Look, L.J., I'm not trying to worm something out of you. If that's what I was up to, I'd send a reporter."

"What then?"

"Well . . ." Cubbage hesitated, as though reluctant to explain, then said, "I've got a proposition, L.J. I'll be straight with you. We heard it's the Strangler again, and we want to be right on top of it this time."

"Meaning what?"

"Meaning we have someone on the inside, bird-dogging the investigation, shadowing you. But whoever it is wouldn't write anything until it's all over, you see? Stosh would handle the regular police stuff, just like always."

Cubbage waited while Loomis digested that. "You're talking about saddling me with a reporter I'd have to live with every day, like a partner," Loomis said at last.

"That's it. You got it."

"No offense, Fred, but I'm not sure you have anybody over there that I could stand to spend that much time with."

"Well, there's Mickey Goodwin . . ."

"I hope that's intended as a joke."

"Seriously, he's not really that bad, once you get to

know him." Cubbage hesitated, and when Loomis didn't respond, he said grudgingly, "I guess we could pull Stosh off *her* beat for awhile."

Loomis was a little surprised to find that that suggestion made the whole idea seem more attractive to him. He smiled wryly at himself.

"Look," he said, "no matter who you pick, I don't think the chief is gonna go for this."

"As a matter of fact we've already cleared it with him. My boss talked to your boss, and the bottom line is it's up to you."

Loomis gave a soft grunt of understanding. Chief Stanwix and Franklin Rule, the *Mid-American*'s executive editor, were both members of a local power structure that superseded the institutions they ran. When decisions were made at that level, you could never quite figure out what the real agenda was. Maybe the idea in this case was to balance out the bad publicity the chief had gotten when they'd found out Mrs. Stanwix was driving a Lincoln Continental confiscated from a drug dealer. In any event, he and Cubbage were both going to have to live with it. Looked at that way, it made a difference who the reporter was, how the story would be told eventually, quite apart from his own preferences for a companion. He thought a moment, then said, "How about Haun?"

"Sam Haun?"

"Yeah. He covered it before. He knows the cases." Loomis paused, realizing he'd just confirmed it was the Strangler. He'd have to trust Cubbage about that. "Anyway, he did a good job," Loomis said. "And I got along with him okay."

"Well, yeah, but he doesn't do that anymore. He's the late man now."

"What's what?"

"Oh . . . it just means he stays here late and deals with whatever comes up after everyone else leaves. If it's something big, and there's sill time, he gets it in the paper. Otherwise, it's mostly late obits and weather, fires and shootings. That kind of thing."

"That's what Sam Haun's doing now? He got demoted?"

"No, no. It was his own idea. You know his wife and daughter got killed . . ."

"Oh, yeah." Loomis remembered that someone had run a red light up around the university somewhere. In the rain, he thought. The Haun car had been hit broadside, carried through the intersection and smashed into the side of a QuikTrip.

"Anyway," Cubbage said, "he's on vacation right now. Won't be back for four weeks."

"Too bad. He'd be my choice. Stanwix did say it was up to me, right?"

Cubbage grunted, then said he'd see what he could do. After he'd hung up, Loomis leaned back in his swivel chair for a moment, thinking about Stosh Babicki and his own reaction, a moment before, to the prospect of working with her. She was at least fifteen years younger than him. She also wasn't what he would call beautiful, but there was something about her. The guys in the dayroom liked her, which was one of the things that made her good at her job. But it wasn't just the usual male-female thing. They genuinely liked her.

So did he. But he wouldn't want to work too closely with her, not on this kind of case.

Just been too long since you've gotten any, he heard the voice of his first partner, Reyes, say. Probably right, he answered silently. Reyes had been right about most things. He would have said a man needed the physical release, every now and then, without the complications. The problem was, Loomis had never learned how to do that. He and Edie had met in high school, married while he was in junior college, waiting to be drafted. By the time he was on his own again he had been too old to learn to play those games. Probably he wouldn't have been much good at them anyway.

He shook his head, impatient with himself. Time to get back to work. He opened the file beside his desk and pulled out the Munoz folder, spreading it open in front of him.

2

While his son visited the graves, Sam Haun stood by himself at the edge of the gravel cemetery drive, the breeze raising gusts of white dust that speckled his trouser cuffs, and listened to occasional windborne whispers of conversation from the Memorial Day mourners murmuring among the humped marble slabs that looked like coffin lids rising out of the earth. Davy Haun sat motionless on the slab of his mother's grave, his head cocked slightly to one side, as though listening to something. Back at the house, Sam's Aunt Harriet had given the boy a dozen yellow flowers, and he had divided them evenly between mother and sister, inserting them solemnly in the little metal holders at the head of each grave. On his bent neck, just above the collar of his shirt, Sam could see the tip of the scar Davy had gotten in the accident, a tiny arrowhead of puckered skin, could trace in his mind how the rest of the hidden scar ran in nearly a straight line along his spine, veering off just below the right shoulder blade and looping under his armpit.

He looked the other way, to where his uncle, Gerald, was standing at the grave of his own son, Don, smoke curling out into the still air from the cigarette he held before him in one hand, the other cupped below it as an ashtray. Sam wondered what Gerald felt. Gerald had always seemed oblivious to pain, impervious to death. He had worked for a time at the big cemetery at Independence, tending the machinery that scooped out the graves, running the crematorium and putting the ashes and bone—all but the little bit placed in an urn for the family—into green garbage bags afterward. When he was small, Sam had believed that Gerald knew everything, was afraid of nothing, that there was nothing he could not handle. He remembered the times in his childhood when he had seen Gerald gash a hand on a piece of machinery, the blood welling up suddenly and dripping from his fingertips while Gerald had gone on working carefully, unhindered, his only acknowledgment the quick wipe he might give the wound with the rag he carried in his back pocket, to keep the blood off of his work. Lacking a father, not liking the substitutes his mother had found, Sam had made Gerald his model of how men behaved, and what Gerald had taught him, chiefly, was that men ignored pain, went on with their work. He had been trying to do that for the past year, but, now that he thought about it, it seemed to him that he had never been much good at any of the things Gerald seemed to do so easily, at keeping things running or fixing things that were broken. As Sam watched, Gerald bent forward and straightened the tiny flag that stood at the foot of Don's grave, pulled a couple of weeds the trimmer had missed, then straightened again and took a drag on his cigarette, looking back at Sam expressionlessly.

Sam turned away, found Davy looking at him, too, and gave the boy a little wave, pointing toward the car that was parked slantwise on the side of the humped road, the passenger door hanging open. As Gerald slid into the driver's seat, Sam gave his son a boost by the seat of his pants, helping him crawl up into the middle.

"How long is four weeks?" Davy asked.

"Not long," Sam said, although he remembered it as an eternity from his own childhood. "You'll have a good time in Malden. I loved coming here when I was your age."

"Okay." Sam heard in the boy's unconvinced response an echo of his own fatalism—the quality Clare had called passivity.

"Your dad and my boy Don used to spend the whole summer barefoot," Gerald said to Davy.

"Where is he now?" Davy asked.

"Don? He's dead, son." Gerald's words carried a weight of inevitability, as though he might be speaking of someone of his own generation.

At the exit from the cemetery, Gerald turned right, toward the new highway that would take them to Independence and the bus depot, and Sam wished they could drive back through Malden, across the one-lane bridge over the river that edged the town, so that he could point out things to Davy—the field where an outdoor movie had been shown every Wednesday night in the summer, the water tower that Don's friend Jody had climbed one night, the river itself, where he and Don had seen the water moccasin. But it was out of the way, and he supposed that things had changed in the intervening years. Of course, the river and the water tower were still there; probably the field was, too, though he doubted that the traveling movie came anymore.

Davy twisted suddenly beside him, raising himself onto his knees to look back through the rear window. "Bye, Mom," he said. "Bye, Debbie."

The bench in the alley behind the bus depot was partly filled by a family of black people: two heavyset, elderly women, a stooped man in a brown sweater and wire-rimmed glasses and a slim teenager clutching a narrow plastic suitcase. Sam nodded when they glanced his way, then moved past them to the sidewalk to wait by himself. In the buildings across the empty street, curtains hung out over the sills of half-open windows in the upper-floor apartments, to catch a nonexistent breeze, but the shops along the street were all closed for the holiday.

"When you get back to Omaha, Melvin," he heard one of the black women say, "you be sure to tell your mama how much we enjoyed having you with us." Her voice had an odd, threatening edge to it. Sam hadn't known what to say to Davy when they had parted a few minutes before. He hadn't wanted the last thing he told him to be a lie he would remember the rest of his life, so he hadn't said anything at all about coming back for him. Finally, he had simply knelt while Davy had thrown his arms around his neck, clinging with a tenaciousness that belied his outward acceptance, and then had disengaged from him gently, saying only, "I love you. Be good for Gerald and Harriet."

The bus arrived suddenly, with a roar, the door slamming open with a sigh of compressed air, the driver swinging down with one long, practiced move to take their tickets, and Sam stood back, letting the black family say its good-byes to Melvin. Inside, there were seven or eight people scattered among the stiff seats. Sam ducked his head and looked for a place as near the back as he could find, behind all the others except for a long-haired boy with the scruffy look of the '60s about him, who sat by himself at the very rear. From where Sam sat, he could see the purplish white hair of an old woman who leaned into the aisle as she read, balancing her book on the armrest. Two seats straight ahead, the top of a soldier's duffel bag leaned against the window.

Then the drive came hurtling through the open door and into his seat, and the doors hissed shut while the engine roared, and they were in motion, grumbling through side streets, slowed by turns and stoplights, looking down through green-tinted glass at cracked sidewalks, the tops of parked cars, deserted sand-strewn intersections, until the bus nosed its way onto the big road that led north to the highway and gathered speed. There was a stretch of filling stations and hamburger drive-ins, then the dark length of pavement running between the football stadium and the big cemetery where Gerald had worked, where Sam's father was buried.

Driving the other way, a short while before, his uncle had surprised him by asking whether he wanted to stop and visit his father's grave. Sam had declined, but he still wondered what had made Gerald ask that, whether it had been something in his own demeanor. Perhaps it had been Gerald's oblique way of asking why he hadn't approached Clare's grave, standing off by himself while

Davy paid his respects. If Gerald had come right out and asked—something Gerald would never have done—Sam had no idea what he would have said. He had not intended to keep his distance that way, but when they had arrived at the graves he had too strong a sense of Clare's presence, an irrational apprehension that she would know what he was up to. So it was guilt, he supposed—not about what he planned to do, but about what he risked doing to Davy in the process.

Still, it was odd to think of visiting his father's grave after all these years. He almost wished he had now, out of curiosity. All that grave meant to him, really, was endless, scratchy summer afternoons, forced by adults to stand impatiently, pointlessly, beside a small curved stone with its American flag and the anchor symbol etched beneath the familiar name that attached to no one he had ever known: Robert Patrick Haun, 1919–1944, USN. A young man in a photograph, looking vaguely like himself, only happier, more confident.

Clare had been dead nearly a year now—more than a fifth of Davy's life. Would he too grow into a sullen teenager, fidgeting beside the twin graves with no real memory of the people who were buried there, only fixed, idealized notions of the long-lost mother, the little girl who had once been his big sister? There might even be three graves by then. Or more—for surely both Gerald and Harriet would not live that long. Would Davy, grown, bother to visit any of them at all? Who would bring him?

There was a scraping sound behind him, and Sam looked backward, between the seats, to see the long-haired youth lifting a backpack from the rack above his head. Painted on the side, in orange Day-Glo letters, were the words THE CALIFORNIA KID IS ON HIS WAY! The pack was so old and worn that Sam wondered if he were still on his way to whatever he had had in mind when the words were painted. Perhaps, like Sam and Clare, who had begun their life together in the era he evoked, he had never had any particular destination in mind, only the adventure of going. Although Clare, it appeared, had had some goal in mind after all. That's what the journals he'd read in the year since her death seemed to indicate. Not a goal she could have described, perhaps, but one that she had been disappointed, anyway, in not reaching. It was still not entirely clear to him what had disappointed her about their life together; he could only guess, from what he read in the journals, that it must have been himself.

The last two years of her life had been filled with clues he had missed: the weight she had lost so easily after years of failed diets, the new clothing and jewelry she had bought, the books on sex—he had found them stacked in the corner, beneath her side of the bed, titles like *How to Be Good in Bed* and *How to Make Love to a Man*, and had assumed foolishly that he was the man she had in mind, even while seeing no evidence of it in their lovemaking. Then, too, there had been the therapist, the lithium, the tears and the dark moods she could not explain to him. And of course the journals themselves, which she had kept compulsively and made him promise never to read. It had all been there before him, obvious to anyone, but he, a reporter, a professional observer, had not seen it, had been stupidly surprised to find it out after her death.

He wondered often whether Franklin Rule had any idea how carefully Clare had documented their affair. Susan Rule had sent him a card of condolence after Clare's death, but he and Frank had not exchanged a word since then, except for what came up in the normal course of their jobs. Which was very little anymore, since Sam had talked Cubbage into letting him work the late desk for awhile, partly, at first, to avoid even having to see Rule, though of course that was not the reason he had given Cubbage. Now, though he had no real desire to go back to reporting, and had rather gotten to like the late-night rhythm, the solitude, the easy sameness of the job, he regretted the lost opportunities to study Rule in his natural habitat.

On the other hand, with Davy in preschool, working nights had given him the time he needed to read the journals, and to think, to begin to plan. It had taken him nearly a year to read them—it had been slow going at first, as he adjusted to learning the truth, and he could only read and digest so much at a time—but he was nearly finished now, as it had long been clear that the answers he sought would not be there, that he must find them out for himself. Margaret Kerns, the counselor Merow had talked him into going to, whom he still saw out of some compulsive sense of duty, had encouraged him to read the journals, saying they substituted, to some degree, for the conversations he would have had with Clare, had she lived. Of course, Margaret also told him he was asking the wrong questions of them, questions about Clare and Rule instead of about himself. The distinction didn't seem that clear to him. Surely, in asking what Clare had needed that he could not give her, what she had found in Rule that she could not find in him, he was asking about himself as well. In studying Rule, it seemed to him that he was learning about himself in reverse, as though studying a photographic negative. Margaret wanted him to let go of all that as soon as possible, so he had stopped saying anything about it to her. "You have to get on with your life," she liked to say. It seemed to him that that was what he was doing. Indeed, he had looked forward to this vacation with a great deal of impatience.

Not that he quite knew yet what his final plan would be, what specific action would result. He had ideas—seducing Susan Rule, undermining Rule's position on the newspaper somehow, costing him his job or his reputation. They all seemed equally improbable at this stage, but that was normal when one was working on a big new story, when it might lead in any direction, when any sort of outcome was possible. He was used to working that way, and he had confidence in his own ability to find the correct path, the way that would lead to the round, satisfying conclusion, the place where things made sense finally. He was well aware that if he tried to explain his intentions to anyone, especially his counselor, they would sound bizarre, melodramatic. He would seem to them like some crazed phantom of the opera, living only for revenge. In fact, he did not think of himself as a very emotional person, the sort to swear a vendetta and then devote his life to it. That was not how it felt to him at all. He thought of himself as essentially reasonable—or at least rational—a man who normally eschewed violence and passion, always finding a way, with the fatalism he saw now in Davy, to make the best of things, to recognize what was and to accept it.

But there were some things that could not be accepted, losses one could not simply write off and go on from. Rule had not killed Clare, but it seemed to Sam that he might as well have. For he had destroyed Sam's memory of her, or their marriage, their life together. Sam had tried to find a way to live with that, to go on, to do his best for Davy. But there had come a point, just after Christmas, when he had been watching Davy play with some toy he had gotten, and he had imagined, despite himself, the two who were not there, who would never be there again—Debbie with her own toys beneath the tree, Clare sitting in her wooden rocker with one or the other of them on her lap—that he had realized suddenly that this could not be borne, that it would never go away. This must be dealt with, he had thought; something must be done about this. About Frank Rule.

That was when he had begun thinking of approaches, considering the avenues by which Rule might be attacked—his wife, his fortune, his career, his reputation. At first it had been only idle speculation, tinged with skepticism, but then gradually he had begun seeing ways that might be possible, and a point had come, as it did with any big project, when it was time to focus, to concentrate, to begin pulling the threads together and see what one had, where it led. Four weeks, of course, was not a great deal of time, but it was what he had, and he was used to working on deadline; indeed, it was the way he worked best.

It had been necessary to clear the decks, remove all

distractions. To make the phone stop ringing, he had paid the bills that had been accumulating. He had had a plumber in to unclog the basement drain that prevented him from doing laundry at home, and he had taken the car in to have all the things fixed that he had been neglecting, so there would be no breakdown in the middle of things. It would be waiting for him, back in Wichita, along with the silent house. For it had seemed necessary to get rid of Davy for awhile, too, to allow himself to think only about his project, about Frank Rule. Hopefully, it would only be four weeks, as he had said, and then everything would be over, the project successfully concluded. The problem was—as he was too rational not to admit—that he really had no idea how it would all come out, how much things would be changed in his life be then, how much damage he might have to accept for himself in order to damage Rule. That was why he had not been able to promise Davy that he would come back for him, why he had not been able to approach Clare's grave, or Debbie's. He had tried to do the best that he could for his son, under the circumstances, to provide for him the foster home he himself had known as a boy, that had been in fact the best home he had known then.

What do you do with your anger? That's what Margaret Kerns asked him, over and over, dissatisfied by his dismissals of the question, his insistence that it wasn't a matter of anger. I will do with it what I always used to do, before Clare, he said to himself now—save it and use it later, when I have a better opportunity. That was what he had done with the bullies in the countless new schools, with the abusive men his mother had sometimes thrown him together with. He had learned to turn away and to watch, to avoid seeming threatening or judgmental, to put everyone at ease, to wait for whatever opportunity might arise. It was not a quality he had liked about himself, but it had seemed necessary, before Clare. After she had come into his life, bringing safety as he thought, he had expected to have no more need of that way of living. He had said none of this to Margaret Kerns, for it had been obvious to him by then which truths she wanted to hear and which ones she didn't.

North of U.S.–54, the land flattened and the wind came up, though he could tell it only by watching the trees along the highway's edge, which bent toward the bus as it passed, then whipped upright again. No sound of wind penetrated the bus, but he could feel the pressure against the side and see it in the driver's hunched shoulders, the way he leaned slightly, balancing against the wind.

As darkness grew outside the windows, the little lights flicked on, showing him more of the bus's interior, by reflection, than he seemed able to see directly. Soon after the dark came rain, audible as a distant rumble above the thick ceiling, although the water on the windows ran silently as a dream of drowning. After a time, tiring of his reflection looking past him, he flicked off his own light to watch blurry forms loom and fade along the road, imagining trees, fence posts, rain-hidden farmhouses, dark portals leading into other worlds, fantastic creatures populating the dark.

Imagining, he dozed and dreamed of things he forgot

as soon as he awoke, startled, to find the bus stopped. It was no longer raining, and through the windows beyond the aisle he saw the top half of a low white building like a tiny cafe, although the sign on the window said DEPOT. The California Kid blocked his view, moving past on his way to the front. He was no boy, Sam saw; they might be contemporaries.

"Where are we?" Sam asked him.

Their eyes met briefly, without connection.

"Twenty-minute stop. That's what the driver said."

The air outside was muggy, soaked with spent rain. There was no wind at all, and he was sweating before his foot touched the gravel.

Inside was a cafeteria line of sorts, sandwiches in triangular boxes and bags of chips. A bald man and two teenage girls, wearing white aprons, grunted irritably as they dispensed the packaged food and cans of soft drinks. The passengers spaced themselves warily among the tables, as they had on the bus.

"Many of the people in the southeast corner of the state have Italian or Polish names," a voice said from beside him. Sam glanced that way, thinking for a moment he was being spoken to, but saw a small boy munching potato chips while a tall woman, her back to Sam, lectured matter-of-factly, her own sandwich lying untouched on the paper plate in front of her.

"It was a mining region once," she said, "although the mines are almost played out now. They used to call it the Kansas Appalachians. And that's why our name is Bonfiglio." Her voice cracked on the last word and she dabbed at her face with a handkerchief. While she wept, the boy's eyes wandered, indifferent. The woman reminded Sam of a junior-high science teacher he had had, who had once worked as an emergency room attendant and had come away with the knowledge that there was no such thing as a painless death. "The best you can hope for," she had once told the class, "is to pass out from the pain and to die before reawakening." He had always thought that she meant this somehow to be a comfort to them.

An unseen jukebox rattled to life and a high, thin voice began singing:

> *Sweet dreams of you*
> *Every night*
> *I go through*

The song was one he liked, but now it made him feel suddenly nauseous, and he tossed what remained of his food into a metal can beside the door and stepped outside, where the air seemed to have lightened somewhat. The glow of lights from the tiny town made the sky feel near, just overhead, like a lid. Walking past the long window, he caught a glimpse of himself: a thin man in a dark suit that looked dull about the cuffs and a bit baggy, as if it belonged to a slightly larger man. Perhaps he had been a slightly larger man before Clare's death.

"Cuckold," he said aloud, saying it to hear how it sounded. It sounded funny to him, a funny word, the way it sounded to most people. "Cuckold, cuckold." It no longer hurt at all—or rather, whatever pain there was was muted, familiar, like the pleasant pain of muscle ache, with its accompanying sense of earned strength, of justification.

The depot door opened and he closed his mouth and moved toward the shadow cast by the bus as the tall woman and the boy emerged behind him. The bus rumbled to itself, stinking of steel and plastic, its side flaps hoisted like awnings above the caves that held the luggage. Sam closed his eyes, trying to imagine a breeze against the sweat-damped parts of his body, and caught a faint odor of the grain and pastureland lying somewhere in the darkness beyond the tiny circle of lights. I'm so tired, he thought, surprised by the discovery. If I could lie down in that darkness, where those smells come from, I could sleep forever.

He stepped deeper into the darkness beyond the rear of the bus, watching as the other passengers straggled across the strip of gravel from the depot, and for a moment he considered not getting back on, staying there, finding some other way back to Wichita, doing something else entirely, as though he might give up that easily the one thing he had thought of for the past six months. It reminded him of the way he had postured, in his existentialist days, back in college, making a choice of everything, telling others it was always theirs to choose, that things were not really forced on them, as they supposed. Now, it seemed to him, this was more true for him than it had ever really been, and he frowned for a moment, thinking of Davy and the responsibility that was the flip side of liberty.

More of the little lights had been turned off inside the bus. He watched through the tinted window as another bus arrived, discharging sleepy, confused passengers, some of whom found their way uncertainly into seats on Sam's bus, stumbling and clattering in the aisle as they tried to move quietly, and the two drivers lazily negotiated the transfer of luggage in the circle of light outside. At last the side flap slammed down, the door hissed and the bus growled to life, the lights of the depot giving way to a seamless blur of countryside.

This part of the ride was oddly familiar to him, for it reminded him of traveling these same roads with his mother, in the junky old cars she had owned, mostly going back and forth to Malden, whenever she had found it necessary to leave him there, mostly in the summers, but not always.

It was the summers he remembered best, a jumble of timeless childhood days from which only a handful of moments stood out in his memory, intertwined, like a collection of flashlights illuminating a twisting path along the riverbank, where he had lain in wait in the darkness in the endless nighttime games of commando he and his cousins had played, roving in loose alliances, flashlight beams for gunshots, killing and capturing, dying and being reborn. He remembered the pleasure of waiting in the darkness, unseen against the cool earth, listening to the stealthy movements of the others in the brush around him. He had been good at the game, unafraid of the night, keeping his flashlight darkened until it was needed.

A daylight moment he remembered also involved the river. It had been hot and he and his cousin Don, roaming the riverbank on their own, had dared one another into entering the dark waters, leaving their clothes hidden among the gnarled roots of trees clinging to the steep bank, and clinging to those roots themselves as they eased their way into the water. He could remember even the surprise he had felt when his feet hit the mud, which slid at first between his toes and up around his feet as if he might sink down into it forever, but then became a cold, luxuriant support, an unexpected place to stand; he had supposed the river was bottomless, had expected to have to hang onto the looming branches. But after the first shuddering touch of that bottom, when he had curled his toes instinctively, fearing the touch of twisty things that lived down there, he had found it not only bearable but pleasant. At first he had simply stood still, letting the cold water run over his body, his arms floating just beneath the surface like hidden logs, the slow current pulsing at his neck, not quite touching his chin. When he had tried a testing step, feeling for how the bottom sloped, he had found it nearly flat. Don, who was older but shorter, had stayed near the bank, his arms spread on the water for balance, frowning as he felt for any sudden drop-off.

But there had been none. Gradually, the slippery bottom had become familiar to them, a thing they trusted, and they had moved further out into the water, heads straining to stay in sunlight, the brown current reaching Sam's chin and lapping occasionally at his mouth, so that he spat back a flat, metallic taste not unlike what came from his aunt's faucets.

It had been silent under the arching trees. For some reason, they had not spoken, sliding carefully in the mud. The breeze that moved sluggishly in the bushes on the banks had scarcely touched the water at midstream, and the sun had marked it only here and there, in speckles that floated on the brown surface. Now and then a dragonfly had hummed nearby and was gone as quickly; a leaf might have rattled softly and dropped without a sound to the river. All the unseen things that filled the nighttime banks with noise must have been sleeping.

Then Don had pointed soundlessly, his mouth and eyes making circles of surprise above the water. Sam had turned to see, moving slowly against the water, the way one moved in a dream, feeling trapped. At first he had seen nothing but shadows and sunspots, but then the wake of his turning had cut something sleek and straight that knifed across the current toward him. He had stopped, his eyes drawing to the point of movement, focusing hard, as though he might seize the thing with his sight and cast it away. Then he had seen the undulations of the body, its manufactured waves against the slow rolling of the water on which it rode, behind the diamond-shaped head that clove the surface smoothly like a prow, nearly on a level with his own eyes.

He had stared, unable to move, rooted to the river bottom by the inexorable rhythms of water and serpent. Don, too, had stood motionless, the two of them waiting, but it had been Sam the wavering arrow aimed at. Between his eyes and the snake's head had lain a jagged golden circle, a pool of sunlight gleaming like burning oil on the brown water. The closer the snake came, the more his eyes had drifted into that hole of light between, the more frozen he had seemed, he and the snake tumbling together toward the floating sunlight.

His consciousness had run ahead of him, like a snake on the water, toward that blinding rendezvous.

Somehow, at that last moment, as the snake's head had moved into the circle of sun, he had seemed to rise out of himself, above the river, so that he was looking down at himself, his cousin, the serpent—not with his eyes but with some other unknown sense, in which the brown river water had the faint odor of old rubber left in the sun, and the snake itself was like an acrid flume of smoke from a newly struck match. He believed he remembered seeing the brown diamond-shaped lacings along its body, that he could have counted the scales. He had been no longer frightened then, only curious to see what the threatened boy—the other boy, himself—would do. At the last moment the snake had drawn its head back slightly, perhaps seeing the obstacle for the first time, and its body had compressed along its length, an absentminded coiling, ready to strike along the water's surface. It had drifted that way for a moment, riding its own wake nearer the boy's face, and then it had veered off suddenly to the side, seeming to slide across the current, and had darted somehow between the two cousins, finding its way downstream. As it passed, Sam's head—my head, he thought now, reminding himself—had disappeared beneath the brown water, and Don, freed from his own stasis had plunged suddenly toward him to pull him back. After that there had been only the blackness of the water and then a fluttering of dark and light, like wings beating across his face.

He remembered awakening later in his aunt's house, being fussed over, and sometime later his mother telephoning from somewhere, the arrangements that had been made for a new apartment, a new job, a new father . . . those were the parts that lost themselves among one another. It was the river and the snake he remembered, the vision he had had of himself disappearing beneath the brown water. Had he talked about it with Don later? He could not remember that, and Don had long since disappeared, too, in Vietnam. Still later, in high school, he had been told for the first time flatly, authoritatively, that there were no water moccasins in Kansas, and in the years since he had come to accept that he must have been mistaken, that it had been some other kind of snake, something harmless.

It had always been important to him to know the truth about things, to understand what had really happened, to be able to report it accurately, yet it sometimes seemed to him that there was little in his personal memories, in what he knew of his own life, that had the weight of fact, as though he were standing on some shifting river bottom, squinting into the sun, trying to distinguish the portentous from the ordinary. Even his memories of his mother were like those of the weather—sometimes a long, sunny time, or a time of dark and cold, sometimes nothing, echoes thrown back by the wind that no longer moved. And now, thanks to Rule, his whole life with Clare, nearly his entire adult life, had become a mystery to him as well, something he was not sure he had ever really understood.

Lightning flashed outside the thick window, and he came back to himself, feeling something cold on his cheeks. Touching them, bewildered he thought for a moment that the moisture he found was raindrops, then realized, astonished, that he had been crying. He sat still, listening intensely to the hum of bus silence, trying to determine whether he'd made any noise, attracted any attention to himself.

Another burst of lightning showed him bowed trees beyond the road's edge and grain tossing like seawater breaking over rocks. There was no rain at all, no sound even, but he saw in that glimpse that the world had grown wild outside the bus; some furious wind battered unnoticed at the tube of stale air they rode in. He pressed his forehead against the glass, wanting to see, and stared into the greater darkness that settled in after the lightning, in which he could barely make out fields and hillsides chopped by ravines and clumps of cottonwood, gathered by no apparent design into fields bordered by ragged hedgerows and wandering gullies. Scrub pastureland, laced with brush and clumps of cottony weed, alternated with rectangles of grain that here and there sprawled through the near fence, merging with roadside lawns of waving goldenweed.

He thought again, wistfully, of being outside the bus, in the night and the wind, by himself in the flat open country running between highway and sky, in the spaces broken only by clumps of prairie trees guarding scattered farmhouses, their lost lights floating in the dark like fallen stars.

He sank back in the seat, away from the window, and closed his eyes. Perhaps some freedom like that awaited him, at the other end of the four weeks. Perhaps he and Davy would come out all right, together.

But it was not something he could count on, just as he had never been able to count on his mother coming back for him. As he had learned never to count on anything, except, for awhile, Clare's faithfulness.

3

Loomis fried a couple of hamburgers for supper and ate them with his feet propped up on the foot of his bed, in the easy chair by the window. It was growing dark when he left the apartment and took the interstate north, the way he had driven every night after work for four years, when he had been living just outside the city with Edie and Marcie.

Beyond the lights of the city, the big road swept into a long curve, falling down and around a bright service area and then into the darkening countryside beyond. It was a road that had always seemed different to him by daylight. In the dark, there were mysterious bridges that came up suddenly in the middle of a curve, sheeted with ice in winter, and bottomless bends swooping out of sight into valleys he could never find by day. There was one high crest, just before the exit he wanted, where the road peaked and then fell away sharply, gray concrete turning abruptly to spangled blacktop, invisible when it rained, so that he had often had to steer a middle course down the long incline between the scattered reflector posts set at the edges of the ditches.

Raines had given him the entrance drive to a farm-house on the other side of the woods from where the body had been found. The drive forked just inside the gate, one branch running toward the house and the other curving sharply away, behind a row of trees and over a small hill, running directly into the woods, where it circled a secluded pond. The road petered out a good fifty yards from the spot where the body lay, but it was just possible the killer had come that way, or might now if he visited his victim.

Loomis found a place where he could pull completely off the road and still watch both the house and the entrance to the driveway, a hundred feet or so from where he sat. According to the deputy who patrolled this area, the house was rented by a childless couple in their early thirties. The husband worked nights in the city; the wife stayed home and did some gardening. Through the trees, Loomis could see the light from a large window toward the front of the house, some of which filtered also through the back screen, making a glow that showed him where the rear of the house was. The front porch light was on as well, but the porch was mostly hidden from him by the trees.

He checked in on the radio and then turned everything off and made himself comfortable, sitting with his back to the passenger door and his feet up on the seat. He slipped his holster off and stowed it in the glove compartment, leaving his jacket draped over the seat back. There was a full moon, with thin clouds blurring the stars, but it was dark under the trees and there was a wind moving among them, making them whisper. Loomis sat in the darkness and stared at the house, thinking of nights like this when he had slept in the farmhouse he and Edie had owned the last four years of their marriage, only a few miles away. More often, that last year, he had sat up late trying to see how to fix what was going wrong. But he had not understood it then, would not have believed it if he had. He had believed he was protecting the two of them from the world he lived in, had believed that they could be protected from it, and would not have understood how he could be blamed for that. When Edie had moved out, not long after the Courter killing, he had told himself that she had held his job against him, that she had not been up to being a cop's wife. What he had really meant, he knew now, was that that was a period when he had not been quite up to being a cop, when the job had seemed futile to him, when he had hidden it from Edie not to protect her but because he had been ashamed of what he did, and what he could not do.

Those were the times when he would awaken at three or four in the morning thinking he could almost see the killer's face, afraid he had cried out in the dark, and then would get up and go to the living room, try to settle himself enough to go back to bed. Other times he had lain awake in the dark, thinking not of the killer so much as all the things that seemed to threaten Edie and Marcie, all the things he could never protect them from. He remembered one night in autumn, when there had been a first touch of winter in the air, and he had gotten up from the couch, where he had been sleeping because of some fight, and gone to the hall closet in the dark and pulled down blankets, one for Marcie and one for Edie. What he remembered now was the small, identical sounds of pleasure each of them had made in their sleep at the added warmth as he covered them, and how he had felt that that was the most he could do for them, the closest he could come to keeping them from harm.

Yet they were both alive, even without him, and others weren't. Thinking of George and Elena Munoz, or of Sam Haun, he knew that he ought to feel grateful for that, but instead what he felt was more like a perverse kind of envy, not at what had happened to them but at their ignorance beforehand, at their being taken by surprise, not knowing what lay ahead until it was behind them. It was part of his job not to be surprised that way, not only to know everything that might happen—how easily it could happen, how quickly—but also to know everything they would need to know after it had happened—how to get the body released to a funeral home, how to recover any personal effects. He had not gone inside the Munoz house that morning; he and George had talked on the front porch while Elena had stayed inside, her slight form moving past the shaded picture window now and again like a ghost. Yet he knew that the living room was filled with the tiny bears Elena collected—statuettes, pictures, trinkets—and he knew too that one of them was missing: the pendant she had given Karen, that Karen had been wearing when she disappeared. Elena Munoz would go on collecting bears, but no matter how many she accumulated, her collection would always be incomplete, short by one. That fact made Loomis more angry, somehow, than did the simple fact of Karen's death.

He thought of the other parents—John Mosteller,

who still called him occasionally, drunk, demanding action; the Fillmores, who had turned Terry's room into a kind of religious shrine; the Courters, whose ties to their daughter had been broken long before her death, who seemed irritated by being forced to care about her again, once it was too late. He was lost in those thoughts when headlights lit up the treetops at the far end of the road, and then rose over the hilltop like twin, cold suns. He hunched down in his seat as they approached, but before they reached that far they went out suddenly. He blinked at the darkness, and it took him a second to work out that the car had turned into the drive to the farmhouse.

He fumbled with the radio, reporting in a whisper to whoever was on the other end, then clicked off without waiting for a reply, dragged his holster out of the glove compartment and slid out as noiselessly as he could, shrugging into the holster while he made his way gingerly over the uneven ground between the trees, heading for the house.

By the time he got close enough to see the front porch and the circle of gravel in front of it, the car was nowhere in sight. He started to go on, inside the side yard, but just then a tall, thin man, balding in front, with a neatly trimmed beard, hopped onto the end of the long porch, apparently having parked his car out of sight beside the house, and paused to straighten his collar with one hand before advancing to the door. In his other hand he clasped a greenish bottle of wine. He knocked softly on the door and it opened almost at once. As soon as he was inside, the porch light went out.

Loomis stood for a moment in the great darkness, feeling foolish, partly because he knew that Edie was seeing a man she had met while taking a course at the university—a sociology professor named Guy Nyzer—and he imagined Nyzer, whom he had never seen, as looking something like this bearded, balding man. He moved out into the open, skirting the gravel parking area to get a look at the other branch of the road. The full moon over the trees made him think of old were-wolf movies, but he didn't smile. He went back to the car long enough to check back in and squelch the alarm, then pushed through the trees again and crossed the gravel driveway, feeling invisible in the moonlight, liking the feeling, and entered the deeper darkness of the trees on the other side. Once he paused and looked back, hearing the woman's laughter from the farm-house, clear but distant.

Just over the top of the little hill, looking down through branches at the black hole of the pond, he stood still, trying to see how it might have happened, how he might have brought her this way, the two of them walking silently in the dark. Twenty yards farther along, following the twin ruts by feel, they would have come to the pond itself, where there was a tiny, half-finished cabin.

Had it been there, or beside the pond, or farther along in the trees? When it had finally come down, had she cried out or pleaded, or simply been silent, hope-less? Sometimes he saw them one way in his mind, sometimes the other. Sometimes he imagined the whole thing happening in silence, neither of them say-ing anything.

And what did he think about it, how did he feel? What was it like to be him? Sometimes Loomis felt that if he could answer that question he would know who he was, would know his name. Inside his own head, Loomis supposed, he was not evil, perhaps not even wrong. Nobody thinks of himself as the bad guy, Loomis had learned; practically everyone is a victim, in his own mind. That was how criminals thought of themselves—people who were just trying to get even, imagining grievances against their victim, or their parents, or the opposite sex, or powerful people, or the universe. The funny thing was that, after you'd been a cop for awhile, you started to sympathize with that point of view. You, too, began to feel that you were way behind, that you had a right to do what was necessary to catch up, to get even.

What would it have been like, the first time? The first one must have been like a change of state, a rite of passage, Loomis thought. After that, you would be different from everyone else, and you would know it. Sometimes Loomis could imagine it so clearly that he was swept with guilt and remorse, the knowledge of something hard that would have to be lived with from now on, to be hidden from everyone, so that there would always afterward be a guarded part of himself; he would be forever alone. Loomis closed his eyes in the dark and rested his hand on the butt of his revolver, reminding himself of who he was. Probably the killer didn't feel that way at all, he thought; more likely he treasured his secret, thought of being different from everyone else as being better.

When he went back through the woods to the road,

past the house, the living room light was out and another window was lit, further back. He caught a glimpse of movement there, but then that light went out as well, and the whole house was dark except for the faint glow from a nightlight somewhere deeper inside, a patch of gray on one of the front windows that was barely distinguishable from the darkness.

He awoke in the dark apartment, trembling, feeling as though he had just cried out, although the apartment was silent. The dream he had awakened from left him feeling as though there were someone or something there with him in the dark, something powerful and full of rage.

He had been with Edie and Marcie in the hallway of some building downtown. It might have been the city building except that there weren't as many elevators. There were only two and one of those had been on the ground floor, too far to wait for. They were in a hurry to get on the other one, to get out of the building, but he hadn't known why. When the elevator came, he had pushed all the buttons, spreading his hands to do so, certain in some secret, nonsensical knowledge that that would make the elevator go more quickly to the bottom, without stopping. And it had seemed at first to work. The pointer over the door, tracing an arc like a sunrise, had swept inexorably toward 1. But when it stopped, the door had opened to daylight on a different world, flat and featureless, but completely covered by naked people who seemed also blind, crawling over one another like worms, coupling by accident, without purpose or desire.

Edie and Marcie had tried to go out, not seeing what was there, but he had prevented them somehow, slapping at buttons to make the door close. And when the elevator moved again, it had gone impossibly further down, and he had seen that the dial over the door went all the way around now, a circle like a clock, and that the pointer was moving to the lower half, where the numbers were negatives, in red. The elevator had seemed somehow to hang by a thread, as though about to plunge downward.

But then they had stopped again. In fact, they were no longer in an elevator, but in an ordinary room with a single wooden door, no furniture or windows. Edie had begun moving toward the door, taking Marcie with her, and Loomis knew that he must stop them, that once outside they would be lost, no way back, but he had not been able to make himself move or speak. And then they were gone, out the door, and he had been left by himself, wanting to follow, but afraid of the open door, terrified of what might come through it next.

He rolled out of the bed, crouching, naked, and groped for the chain of the reading lamp beside the window. The apartment was empty, but he made sure. He turned on the glaring overhead light—a bare bulb in a ceiling socket—and went into the tiny kitchen, walking barefoot on gritty linoleum, and turned that light on as well. Back in the other room, he checked the closet and the dark place behind the beat-up desk opposite the bed, and tugged at the deadbolt on the door to make sure it was solid. His revolver was lying in its holster on the chest of drawers inside the closet, and he rested a hand on it momentarily, but then left it there and shut the closet door.

He slumped into the chair beside the open window and peered out at the sidewalk below, partly hidden by branches, and the blank brick wall of the building across the street, the full moon floating in the narrow rectangle of sky above. There were no windows, no lights but the moon in any direction—only the glow of the city itself rising like smoke into the sky above the treetops.

He wasn't ready to go back to bed yet, to chance another dream, so he got up and went back to the kitchen to get a can of beer from the little icebox. In the chair again, he balanced the cold beer can against his naked thigh, partly just to feel the dull pain of it, and glanced at his watch lying on the desk. Four-fifteen, not long until dawn. He sat up and finished the beer.

When he stood up again, the breeze from the window reminded him that he was naked, and he glanced that way, but made no move to cover himself, only turned off the reading lamp, so that the apartment was as dark again as the world outside. Darker, for he could now see the first hint of morning light in the sky above the city. He stepped to the window and listened to the silence of the empty streets, wanting to feel the breeze again against his body, but everything was still now, there was nothing, no feeling but the trapped heat of the apartment, his own dampness, the floor against his feet and a familiar, centerless ache that he supposed was with him always but that he rarely noticed.

He looked at the full moon and thought again of old werewolf movies, of the foolish things that had once frightened him, and then of how easy it seemed to be for them, the real killers, the ones who killed strangers and were so often never caught. He thought of the cooler air moving out there in the darkness of the city streets, and felt a sharp envy, a hunger to be out there, to be moving, to be the one doing things instead of the one waiting to react.

He looked at the bed, thinking that if he didn't get back to sleep he would be groggy and useless all day long. But instead he stood by the window in the dark, not moving, barely breathing, his eyes fixed on the gray sidewalk below, as if waiting for something down there to move.

4

In the long mirror behind the bar, Sam could see himself and the other men spaced out along the row of stools, none of them sitting together, the curling smoke making their faces waver as they stared open-mouthed at the TV above the mirror, where a stripper on the Carson show was narrating a videotape of her ejection from a baseball game.

"That one guy had hold of my chest," she said. "He had one of my chests in a kind of wrestling hold or something. Do you see that silly grin on his face, walking along holding onto my chest?"

The men in the mirror, strangers to Sam, nodded in agreement. Good's was the bar where newspaper people congregated. He had not been there in more than a year, but it seemed a good place to start, on the fringes of Rule's world, the way he might approach any undercover story. Unfortunately, however, there was no one there this evening who seemed likely to be of use to him. Mickey Goodwin was at the far end of the bar, playing what was possibly the last true pinball machine in Wichita with Brad Stintz, one of the assistant wire editors. Some of the other, younger people in the place might be reporters or editors who had joined the paper during the past year, when he had not been keeping track of such things. Once in the door, Sam had decided to have a beer before going on to the newspaper itself, where he hoped to have the library to himself.

Now the pinball machine went *pop! pop! pop!* as one of them hit a replay, and Mrs. Tyrone, wiping glasses behind the bar, jerked her head up and screeched, "I ain't tradin' no goddam beer for those, and I'm closing in twenty minutes." One of the men at the bar said, "Language, language," in a deep voice, and everyone laughed. Mrs. Tyrone gave the speaker a shy smile.

Sam slid his change in tiny circles in the pool of water fed by the glass rings on the polished bar. On the TV, the stripper was telling Carson about how she had been stripping ever since she was thirteen, sometimes working several shows a night.

"When I get out in front of that audience, I get that old entertainment urge," she said. "It makes it all worthwhile."

Sam tried to remember feeling that way about one's work.

"Fucking Goodwin," someone said, and he glanced in the mirror to see that Stintz had joined him. "He takes all the fun out of pinball," Stintz said, sliding onto a stool. "You want to play poker?"

Sam shook his head, bemused to find Stintz talking to him so casually, as if they'd been together there just the night before.

"Gotta have seven guys, anyway," Stintz said philosophically.

Somebody down the bar yelled, "Hey, Mrs. Tyrone.

What kind of wrestling hold is it called where they get hold of your tit?" Mrs. Tyrone said, "Language, language," and everybody laughed again.

"I gotta get out of this business," Stintz said. "It's gonna kill me."

Sam studied the wire editor's face in the mirror. He was four of five years younger than Sam, but was prematurely gray and looked older.

"You don't get that old entertainment urge anymore?" Sam asked.

"It's okay for the reporters," Stintz said. "They run around, get their exercise. But those VDTs, man, they're making us blind and sterile. I read about it on the wire."

"Maybe you could do something else."

Stintz took a drink of beer, belched silently and then said, "Shit. After you been around this place five years, you've had your chance."

"I switched to something else," Sam said.

"Sure. You can always move down," Stintz said, then gave Sam a quick, sly look, to see whether that offended him. "Anyway," he added, "you could do anything. You were their blue-eyed boy."

Sam rolled the expression around in his mind, examining the truth of it. Yes. That's what he'd been once. Their blue-eyed boy. Or rather, Rule's blue-eyed boy. It was Rule who had brought him there from Topeka, after reading the Sunday magazine piece he had done on survivors of the New Left at the state universities. He took a sip of his beer and found that it had grown lukewarm.

Artie Plamann, one of the city desk clerks, appeared in the mirror on the other side of Stintz.

"You want to play poker?" Stintz asked him.

"Nah. I got no money. I spent it all on wine last night. Me and Foster." He waved a finger at Mrs. Tyrone, and when she brought him a beer he handed her a folded five-dollar bill.

"What do you call that?" Stintz asked.

"Well, that's it, man. That's all I got. I gotta eat on that till payday."

"What we ought to do," Stintz said, turning back to Sam, "we all oughta go out and get laid. What do you say?"

"You got the girls, man?" Plamann asked, causing Stintz's head to swivel back the other way before Sam could figure out how to respond.

"Shit, no. I was counting on you. You're the young stud. You're always talking about this babe and that babe. I figured you could set us up."

"Did I tell you about this friend of mine," Plamann said, "this photographer, out at the university? He takes pictures of the girls. I mean, they pay him to take photos of them in the nude. Or with just . . . you know . . . little skimpy things on that you can see through. It's a kind of fad. They get a set of pictures, different poses, to give to their boyfriends. My friend, he gets fifty bucks, plus he keeps a set of negatives."

"Now you're talking," Stintz said. "You got the names of some of these chicks?"

Plamann gave him a pained look.

"These are respectable college babes, man. They already got boyfriends," he said. "Didn't you listen to what I said?"

"I guess I went to the wrong college."

"But just think about the blackmail possibilities," Plamann said.

"Your priorities are all fucked up. You know that?"

The Carson show ended and the late news show came on. During the teaser, the anchorwoman said something about an unidentified body, but before Sam could catch any more of it, Stintz shouted, "Turn it off! Get it off!"

Mrs. Tyrone came over and gave him one of her looks, drumming two fingers on the counter.

"I'd think you'd want to see the news," she said finally. "It's your business."

"I hate the news," Stintz said. "It's the bane of my fucking existence."

"What was that about a body?" Sam asked, after Mrs. Tyrone had moved back down the bar.

Stintz made a face, but didn't say anything.

"I heard Cubbage say something about the Strangler," Plamann offered.

"The Strangler?"

"Yeah. You know, the guy, five, six years ago . . ."

"Yeah. I know." Sam stared at himself in the mirror for a moment. "They think it's the Strangler?" he asked Stintz.

"How do I know what they think? Fuck, I hate shop-talk."

Sam slipped off the stool and walked to the pinball machine, where Goodwin was still hunched over, his elbows cocked above the flippers, his tie thrown back

60

over his shoulder, playing off the replays. He stood for a moment, not saying anything, watching the ball carom from bumper to bumper. When it slid down the long center slope, toward home, Goodwin deftly caught it on one flipper and hurled it back toward the top, grunting "C'mon, you whore," under his breath. He noticed Sam then and added, "Hi," not taking his eyes off the machine.

"What's the story on this body they found?" Sam asked.

Goodwin straightened slightly and looked directly at Sam, then glanced back and punched belatedly at one of the flippers as the ball rolled home.

"If you want it, you got to get in line," he said.

For a second, Sam thought he was talking about the pinball machine.

"I'm just curious," Sam said. "I covered the Strangler killings before."

"I know. I read the clips."

"So you're on the story?"

Goodwin turned halfway back to the machine and punched up the next ball but didn't shoot it yet. "Well," he said. "I figure, it's either me or Rule's girlfriend." He regarded Sam speculatively, as though expecting him to contradict that.

"Rule's girlfriend?"

"Stosh Babicki."

"Oh." That was another thing he hadn't kept track of during the last year. Of course Rule would have another one by now. He looked back toward the bar but decided he didn't want to go back there. Instead, he left

Goodwin frowning behind him and pushed through the door to the outside.

He stood in the dark at the edge of the parking lot for a moment, trying to get a clear picture of Stosh Babicki. She was one of the new ones, but one he knew slightly; she had come to the paper during the year before Clare's death, right out of college, he supposed, although now that he thought about it she seemed a bit older than that. She sat at the desk next to Merow's, and he had the vague impression that they were friends. He wondered if people in the newsroom had spoken that casually of Clare as "Rule's girlfriend," when that had been the case.

He thought about the Strangler, that whole period of time when the killings had been happening. What had the last girl's name been? Carter? Courter? That was when he had been the blue-eyed boy for sure, full of his job and full of himself. But that last killing had shaken him, had even shaken the cops. It had been different, though the cops had seemed to have some reason for thinking it was the same guy.

Back in the car, he drove toward downtown, the wind coming through the window blowing the smell of the beer he had drunk back into his nostrils, making him feel slightly tipsy, though he wasn't, and reminding him of other nights in that former life, cruising the city at night, feeling good, listening to music on the radio, on his way to the police station, or heading back to the office, or just driving aimlessly, full of energy, as though everything that passed by him in the dark—the city streets, the cars and people—were less substantial than himself, things provided for him so that he might do his job. Now he was just another of those in the dark, and that was all right with him.

He approached the newspaper building from the rear, to see what cars were still in the back lot. The executive slots along the wall by the back door, where Rule parked, were all empty. He saw Merow's car in one of the customer slots, but didn't recognize any others. Most of the parking lot was filled with the pickups and vans driven by the nightside pressmen. He found an open place along the railroad spur that separated the lot from the row of warehouses fronting on the next street over, where winos slept under sheets of cardboard in cold weather, and sat in the dark for awhile, still remembering that other time—the grieving parents, their names long faded from his memory, the detectives, especially Loomis, who had been in charge and who had grown increasingly gloomy as the killings went on. He himself had spent much of the time collecting bits of detail, sense impressions, bits of dialogue, like a detective gathering evidence, against the day when the final story would be written. But that day had never come, for him or for the police. It had all just dribbled away in a succession of Kiwanis Club meetings and county politics and visiting dignitaries, with no new murders, until finally the unsolved killings had somehow become old news.

At the back of the building he rang the bell and turned his face toward the TV camera, waiting for the guard to buzz him in. Sometimes, standing here this way, he imagined the guard not recognizing him, refusing to buzz; Sam thought that if that happened he might simply turn and walk away, never come back. But the buzz came, as always. Inside, he found the long first-floor hallway deserted. The old elevator moved slowly, balkily, clanking and whispering to itself, hesitating for a couple of heartbeats at the top, bouncing slightly, before the door slid open on the bright, nearly empty newsroom.

Merow sat at the city desk, his hands behind his head, talking with Kelly Jo Greenleaf, the nightside copy girl, in her tight blue jean cutoffs and faded, armless sweatshirt. They both glanced at Sam as he came out of the elevator, and then Merow said something and Kelly Jo gave a squeal of laughter and headed off toward the photo department, giving Sam a nod.

"Your first week of vacation and already you're back in the office," Merow said. "I can't say I blame you. I'd forgotten how easy this job is, sitting around and listening to the monitors and flirting with Kelly Jo."

Sam perched himself on a corner of the big desk.

"I heard something on TV about a body."

Merow gave him almost the same speculative look Goodwin had given him, but without the hint of malice in it. Merow was a short, round, nearly bald man, and he wore glasses with round lenses that made his eyes seem large and comical. Without the glasses, Sam knew, those eyes were unusually bright and clear, his gaze direct and unsettling, and Sam sometimes wondered whether he really needed the glasses, except to hide his eyes. In this new age of electronic journalism, while others his age complained or even retired prematurely, he had become the newsroom's de facto computer expert.

"I heard it might be the Strangler again," Sam said.

"Yeah, that's what I heard, too."

"What do you think?"

"I try not to. It only gets you in trouble around here."

"Seriously."

Merow shrugged. "All the honchos came out of the news meeting this afternoon looking like a bunch of kids with a secret," he said. "You know, excited but trying to be solemn and professional. I hate it when they get like that, when they start trying to play newspaper instead of staying in their offices where they belong. But I suppose that means there must be something to it."

"You didn't hear any details?"

"What I heard was that Joe Lee picked it up from somebody at the sheriff's office. Not for attribution. It's out in the county somewhere, and they're leaving it there for awhile, for a stakeout."

Sam nodded. "Yeah. He used to visit them sometimes. Has there been any traffic about it?"

"Scrambled. On the sheriff's band. Nothing on the police band."

"That in itself . . ."

"Yeah."

A young reporter, one of the interns who'd come in for the summer, approached the desk diffidently to ask Merow a question. Sam stood up and looked out the big windows behind the desk while they talked, not listening. Three stories down, on Douglas, the cars moved slowly, bumper to bumper, like twin currents of a sluggish river. To the west, beyond the railway underpass, where the brighter lights of downtown began, groups of young people roamed the sidewalks, many of them wearing headphones, some on skates, shouting back and forth to one another and to the slow-moving cars. No sound came through the thick glass. He wondered whether Merow had any special access to Rule's personal computer files. Not that he'd be likely to share if if he did, even with a friend like Sam.

"You seem interested," Merow said. Sam looked around to see the reporter was gone. It took him a second to remember what they'd been talking about.

"It's just funny for it to pop up again now, if it really is the Strangler. I guess I kind of feel like it's still my story. Just a reflex."

"It probably could be your story, if you wanted it," Merow said.

Sam shook his head. "I'm done with all that," he said. "Besides, the younger people have the inside track now." He hesitated, then said, "I suppose it would be either Stosh Babicki or Mickey Goodwin."

"Those would be the logical choices," Merow agreed. "Babicki probably has the edge."

"Could be. She's better than Goodwin, and she is the police reporter. She knows the turf."

"And I hear she has an in with Rule."

Merow leaned back in his chair, his lips pursed, and studied Sam for a moment.

"Don't get the wrong idea about Stosh," he said.

"What's the wrong idea?"

"That she's sleeping her way up the ladder. She isn't. She's a good reporter. This thing with Rule . . ." He shook his head. "She's young. Everybody makes mistakes."

"I guess so. Still, it can't hurt."

Merow gave him a sour look. "Yes, it can," he said. "It can keep people from taking her seriously." He shrugged. "But there's no talking to people in love. As a very great philosopher once said, 'You can't always get what you want, but if you try real hard . . .' "

"Yeah, I know the rest of that," Sam said. He stood up and found that one foot had gone to sleep, and he had to steady himself with a hand against the desk while he twisted the foot inside his shoe, bringing it back to life.

Kelly Joe came back out of the photo shop and gave them a sly, sidelong look as passed, as if she suspected they were telling dirty jokes. Even with the floppy sweatshirt, it was obvious she wasn't wearing a bra.

"So you like working the late shift," Sam said.

"It has its compensations."

"Kelly Jo must be at least thirty years younger than you."

Merow ignored that. "Don't you find that sitting around with nothing to do, listening to these monitors, has kind of an aphrodisiac effect?" he asked. "I find myself sitting here, watching Kelly Jo sashay back and forth, looking so fresh and innocent, and all I can think about sometimes is throwing her over one of these desks and fucking her eyeballs out."

Sam laughed, genuinely shocked. "You're a happily married man," he said.

"That I am. That I am. But it doesn't mean you have to give up your fantasies. You just have to give up acting on them. I'm sure Pat has her fantasies, too. By the way, you going to the party?"

"What party?"

"Rule's annual summer wingding. It's two weeks from Saturday."

Sam stared back at Merow for a moment, understanding what he was really asking. Neither of them ever went to those parties; for the past several years, in fact, the two of them had gotten in the habit of holding down the newsroom together that night, while everyone else slipped out early. In fact, it had been on that night a year ago that Clare and Debbie had died, the first reports coming in over the two-way monitor as they had sat chatting, much like now, at the deserted city desk. It was Merow's oblique way of asking him what he was going to be doing on that night, perhaps of offering to keep him company again.

"I don't know," Sam said. "That's still a long time off. And I am on vacation."

Merow nodded, watching him through the thick lenses. Sam had never been able to find a way of asking Merow whether he had known about Clare and Rule. He still couldn't.

Instead he asked, "What would you do if Pat acted on one of her fantasies?"

Merow smiled. "I'm not sure. I guess it depends on the circumstances. But I know what she'd do, if I were the guilty one. she'd cut my balls off. She's said so, often enough, and I believe her."

"You're saying there might be circumstances where you could accept it?"

"Sure. Anything's possible. I'm not saying I'd like it."

"Do your fantasies ever involve Stosh Babicki?"

"Now you're getting personal. Is this for publication?" Merow shook his head and laughed. "No," he said.

"Getting to know somebody can play hell with your fantasy life."

Sam nodded. He understood that. Not letting yourself get to know them would be important. He wondered how Rule managed that.

The library file on Rule didn't exactly disappoint him because he wasn't really expecting it to have as much information as there would be on, say, the president of one of the local banks. It was only a place to start, to pick up leads. And there were a few, scanty as they were. He and Susan had been married twenty-three years, with no children. Had that been choice? If not, whose problem had it been? Could Rule have had a child with some other woman? Certainly the opportunity had been there. Sam had already thought of building a dossier on those other women, at least the ones connected with the newspaper; the possibility of a child gave that an added edge. Apart from women, Rule's private enthusiasms appeared tepid and unpromising. He enjoyed cooking. He played golf and racquetball. Nor did the clips reveal anything from his past that could be used against him. Sam made a list of the newspapers where Rule had worked before coming to Wichita, going back to his father's newspaper in a small town in Minnesota. The libraries in those places might have more interesting information, and it was always possible that there would be those who remembered Rule and who might be willing to talk about him.

It was all standard stuff, but by the time Sam left the building he felt reasonably good about the beginning he'd made, the sense of having gotten started on a task he was familiar with. Outside there was a smell of rain in the air again. He turned on the car radio, but could find only country music and talk shows, and turned it off again. North of the center of town, the streets were black and deserted, overhung by old trees that made tunnels leading away from the city lights, where the kids cruised. His house sat in the middle of a block that butted up against the river at one end, in a neighborhood nestled in the river's bend, a remnant of what had once been a fashionable area.

He parked the Lynx halfway up the gravel drive, in the night shadow cast by the garage, hulking out of the trees at the rear of the house. The backyard had grown wild at the far end, where a rusting fence, hidden in the overgrowth, marked the slope of the riverbank. There was a small patch of level yard, just in back of the house, but even that was shaggy now, unmown; the swing set near the house had begun to rust during the last year and weeds had sprung up through the bottom of the sandbox. Davy, when he was home, seldom played out there anyway. The two of them stayed inside mostly, watching TV or reading—Davy his Sesame Street books, Sam the journals he had inherited.

Now he sat in the armchair, turning on the lamp beside it, but he didn't pick up the journal that lay atop the short stack on the floor beside him—the final one, which he was nearly finished with. He would have to read some of it before he went to bed, in order to have something to tell his counselor at their regular meeting tomorrow. but the original avidity had long since faded; it all seemed tedious and futile to him now, and there was rarely anything anymore that was able to hurt him.

He had gotten used to the world of the journals, in which Rule's presence was all-pervasive and Sam and the children hardly seemed to exist, except in an occasional passing reference. He had even gotten used to Clare's accounts of the good times she and Rule had together, the private jokes they shared, the little gifts he had given her. Once those had been the most painful kinds of things to read about, but now he felt only impatience with them, a sense of having been through that already, wanting something new, as though the journals were a sort of pornography whose effect became dampened with exposure, requiring new twists, new variations on the enduring theme. In fact, the journals covering the last couple of months read more like a love story gone wrong; there were extended sections in which Clare seemed to keep on with the writing— and with the love affair itself—as doggedly and reluctantly as Sam did with reading about it.

The passages that interested him most now where the ones that seemed to him to provide glimpses of Rule as he really was, as even Clare could not avoid seeing him at times.

There was one he found himself thinking about frequently, from the February before the last, fatal summer. The affair had been going on nearly three years by then, and Clare had been going through one of her bad times—bad enough that even Rule had realized something was wrong, and had proposed that they get together and talk about it, straighten things out. Clare had welcomed the opportunity, but the meeting hadn't turned out that way. There had been no talk—not of the kind Clare had hoped for anyway—and when she had realized that she could not really talk to Rule about her pain and confusion, she had gone to bed with him almost resignedly, as though there were nothing else she could do. Afterward, Rule had told her he wanted to give her a massage. It was a minor skill he took pride in, like the cooking, and when she had demurred, he had pushed her onto her stomach—playfully, she thought—and begun giving her one anyway. She had tried to relax and enjoy it, taking it as his way of trying to make amends, to show his concern. But then, without warning, he had pressed the weight of his body onto her and begun entering her from behind, almost roughly. When she had tried to squirm away, he'd said, "Just settle down now," his voice rasping in her ear as if she were some misbehaving child, and had gone ahead as though it were his unquestioned right. When she'd complained later, he'd acted mystified, saying, "I thought that's what you came for," and then added, "Why don't you have a glass of wine before you go? It'll calm you down." Later, at home, she'd bathed and then waited up for Sam to come home from work, and then, ignoring his tiredness, she'd pulled him into bed and made love to him determinedly, almost as aggressively as Rule had done to her, doing all the things he most liked.

Sam remembered that night. It was one of the few points in the journal that he was able to match up to his own experience. He also remembered what had followed it, how she had been so depressed in the following days that she had finally become too ill to go to work, though she had still insisted on going. Finally, thinking it was the flu, he had forced her to call in sick, and had called in sick himself so that he could sit beside the bed, talking to her until she drifted off to sleep. When he had gone in later, to check on her, he had kissed her lightly on the forehead and she had awakened suddenly, and had clutched his hand and said, "You're my true friend, aren't you, Sam?"

He had said, "You bet," and kissed her again, and she had begun crying, and then after awhile had fallen asleep again. He had sat beside the bed for a long time then—foolishly, it seemed to him now—trying to figure out why she had said that.

It seemed to him now a moment that, if one of them had taken advantage of it, could have changed the course of things, changed things between them, perhaps somehow even prevented the deaths that followed. But it was a moment that was never mentioned in Clare's journals.

5

"No pendant," Kreider said. "No nothing. Just like the others."

Loomis sat in the chair in front of the coroner's assistant's desk, his arms crossed. Kreider half-sat on the edge of his desk, fumbling with papers.

"Munoz," he said. "She was the one who disappeared from Roxy's, right?"

Loomis nodded. "That's where she was seen last," he said.

"It's kind of like the Courter case . . ."

"It isn't like the Courter case," Loomis said, more harshly than he'd meant to.

Kreider pursed his lips, giving Loomis a glance over the tops of his glasses.

"Well, you know," he said, "we haven't had a chance to really look at the body yet, apart from the teeth. So we don't actually know what was done to her."

"I don't think it was anything like that," Loomis said, softening his voice, then shrugged and rubbed at his eyelids with the fingertips of one hand. "Anything on the scrapings yet?"

Kreider searched momentarily for another sheet of

paper, came up with it. "Nothing much. Some dust, some little plastic curls consistent with a trunk floor mat, traces of coal dust . . ."

"Coal dust?"

"That's what it says here."

Loomis was silent for a moment, pondering that, but it meant nothing to him.

"You know," Kreider said, "whenever I think of Courter, it's that tree limb I think about. We had it sitting in there in the lab for a month, wrapped in paper. I wish we could have told for sure that she was dead before he did that."

"She was," Loomis said.

"How the hell do you know?"

"I just know." After a moment, he added, "You go over these things so much, you start thinking you can see everything that happened, how it happened. I used to wake up at night . . ." He shook his head. "She was dead by then," he said. "When I think about it, that's how I see it."

"Very scientific," Kreider said. "You ever think you did it?"

"What?"

"You ever get to thinking you're the one you're looking for?"

"Where do you come up with a bullshit question like that?" Loomis asked, but it had touched a nerve. Kreider smiled, unoffended.

"I was thinking of the Boston Strangler case," he said. "You ever read that book about it? The cops were going nuts. There were thirteen killings, I think it was, and the guy left absolutely no fucking clues; he was invisible. At least we got the underpants and the flowers. They never would have got him if he hadn't confessed. Even when they finally knew who he was, they couldn't have proved it without the confession. Every crime scene was like a picture with nobody in it. They could see everything else, but they couldn't see him. You said you used to wake up at night? Some of them were dreaming about it, like they'd been there, like they knew what happened. Pretty soon, I guess, you know so much about the case, and nothing at all about the guy who did it, you start looking like a pretty good suspect to yourself. I think some of those Boston cops, after awhile, they were obsessed with getting him mainly because they wanted to prove it wasn't them that did it."

Loomis frowned.

"They dreamed about it?" he asked.

"That's what I read."

"How was it yesterday?" Ron Binkley asked.

Loomis yawned, the lack of sleep last night beginning to catch up with him.

"Not too bad. I just talked to George, the father. He'd been expecting it, I think. He was calm."

Loomis had found Binkley and his partner, Danny Davidson, sitting at one of the round metal tables in the city building cafeteria. They'd be checking out the prostitutes while Loomis himself backtracked over the leading suspects from six years before, those who were still around.

"You know," Binkley said, "when we get this guy, it's gonna turn out he's crazy, and they'll stick him in an institution somewhere. Maybe even cure him and let him go."

"I don't know," Davidson said. "Did you ever think that maybe some of these guys aren't crazy at all? Maybe it's just something they do, like a hobby."

Loomis and Binkley exchanged a look.

"I don't follow you," Loomis said, playing the straight man.

Davidson put down the sandwich he was eating, frowning seriously. "I mean, maybe it's just something they've found out they like to do, even though they know they shouldn't. Like gambling, you know? More like an addiction."

"You don't call that crazy, man?" Binkley asked, his voice rumbling.

Davidson sat back slightly in his chair, misunderstood. "I'm just trying to imagine it from their point of view, that's all," he said. "It's like Binkley here, and his candy. What are you charging out at these days, Slim?"

Binkley, a former college lineman who had probably not been below two hundred since he was in junior high, grinned and shrugged. " 'Bout two-eighty, I guess."

"He knows that shit's gonna kill him," Davidson explained to Loomis, "but he keeps poppin' the quarters in that machine, snarfin' up those Twinkies. Our guy could be kind of the same way. Not necessarily a raving psychotic, is all I'm saying."

"Folks do like to think a killer is someways different from them." Binkley said. "You remember that Y-chromosome bullshit?"

"It's like the werewolf," Davidson said.

"Say what?"

"The werewolf. You ever notice, he's always just a regular guy, not a bad guy? Hell, he's almost the fuckin' hero. I mean, anybody can be the werewolf, if he gets bit. 'Even a man who is pure of heart,' and so on."

For some reason that he couldn't explain to himself, Loomis didn't like the idea that both of them had been thinking about werewolves. He set down his empty coffee cup, positioning it neatly on the ring it had already made on the tabletop, and looked soberly into Binkley's round, black face.

"Your partner's nuts," he said. "You have an insane partner."

Binkley grinned. "He's everything I never wanted in a wife," he said. There was a touch of pride in his voice that made Loomis feel vaguely jealous. As captain of detectives, he had no regular partner. He could have had a regular assistant if he'd wanted one, but he didn't.

"Look," he said, "when we catch this guy, he's going to turn out to be an evil little creep who's that way all the time, not just when there's a full moon."

Davidson nodded, unruffled.

"You could be right," he said. "He could be more like the vampire, just pretending to be normal. We could be talking about a vampire here."

Sam was coming up the back steps, after his appointment with Margaret Kerns, when he heard the telephone ringing in the front room. He went through the house, not hurrying, and picked it up, expecting to hear only a dial tone. But it was Georgia Earle, one of the city desk clerks.

"Sam? Fred Cubbage wants to talk to you." Then he was listening to Muzak, which in turn was shattered by Cubbage's too-loud voice. Sam imagined him shouting into his speaker phone from across the little office. "I know you're on vacation, Sam, but I need a favor."

"What kind?"

"It's this new Strangler killing. We've got a chance to do something really different, really good, but it's got to involve you. Would you be willing to come by the office and talk about it?"

There was a small stirring of excitement, but not enough to deflect him from his main business. Still, he hated to turn Cubbage down flat. He temporized by asking, "Are you sure it's him?"

"I talked to Loomis. He as much as said so, off the record."

Sam hesitated. It was more tempting than he would have thought, to have it offered to him this way. "I don't . . ." he began, but Cubbage interrupted him, his voice echoing from the speaker phone.

"I'll give it to you straight, Sam. This is a pet project of Frank's, something he set up with Stanwix. We have a chance to get someone inside. But it's got to be you."

He felt an odd little chill, the kind his grandmother had once said meant that someone was walking on your grave. "You mean Rule said it has to be me?" he asked.

"No. Loomis did. He doesn't want Goodwin. I asked him who then, and he said you. He said you did a good job before."

The praise from Loomis was flattering, but it was the involvement of Rule that interested him. How much personal prestige would Rule have invested in this?

How much would he be counting on it? "What about Stosh?" he asked.

"She'll still be covering the day-to-day police stuff. You'll probably want to get together with her, coordinate things."

"If I decide to do it, you mean."

"Don't jerk me around, Sam. You're not gonna stay on the late desk forever, are you? And you owe me something for that."

That argument meant little to him, but he said, "I'm willing to talk about it."

"That's all I ask. Can you come by after lunch?"

In fact, he drove to the newspaper during the noon hour to find his old Strangler file, which was in one of the archive files in the library. He also got copies of the clips, which seemed somehow less substantial than he remembered: only a dozen standard news stories, plus the two longer write-throughs he had done—the lead story on the Jeannie Courter murder, and the story tying it to the killings of Marty Madsen, Sarah Mosteller and Terry Fillmore. The names came back to him like those of people he had once known slightly, from a distance, but had had a special interest in, like the head cheerleader or the star quarterback in high school. Even the newsroom had been different then. There had been pots of rubber cement, photo zincs, the rattle of the teletype, the woody copy paper and the old tan Smith-Coronas. He was surprised to find that he missed all that, though he'd paid little attention as those things had vanished, one by one.

Reading over the Courter story, he remembered his

frustration at not quite understanding why the police were so sure that murder was linked to the others, and the anger of the police themselves at the unnecessary brutality, as if the Strangler had violated some rule beyond the crime of murder.

Sarah Mosteller, the second victim, had been beaten, but not that badly; she had not been tortured. It had been possible, despite the bruises, to tell that she had died of strangulation. With Courter, it had not been so clear. There were half a dozen injuries, besides the strangulation, that could have killed her.

There was a row of four mug shots of the victims above the headline of his tie-in story, and he studied them for a time, recollecting each of them individually, as well as he could: Marty Madsen, the first, mousy and hardworking, who had disappeared somewhere between her downtown job and the Towne East shopping mall, where she had been headed after work, according to her co-workers; Sarah Mosteller, looking haughty and untouchable in a posed yearbook photo, who had vanished between acts of a concert at Century II, the big auditorium and convention center, wearing the gown she had bought for the occasion; Terry Fillmore, the one Sam had always thought looked most likable, most genuinely attractive, who had disappeared from the downtown library at night, returning a book; and Jeannie Courter, the one who didn't fit, about whose disappearance the least was known. She was the oldest and the plainest—not nondescript, like Madsen, but severe, judgmental. On the other hand, despite her looks, she was also the one who had been most sexually active, had lived closest to the edge of things. There

had even been some rumors that she had been a part-
time hooker, but as far as Sam knew, that had never
been confirmed. The night she was murdered, she had
simply left her apartment on foot and never returned.

Her photo reminded him now of a picture he had of
Clare, in a box somewhere among baby books and other
random photos. Taken by one of her friends, between
tennis games, it had shown her with a sweat-soaked
headband, her skin glistening, her unsmiling jaw
slightly clenched. When he had first seen it, he had
known without having to ask that she had lost the previous match, and that she would refuse to leave the
court without playing another, and winning. Her gaze,
like Jeannie Courter's in the photo before him, had
been fixed inward, on a world she shared with no one
else.

When he finally saw Cubbage, he surprised him by
agreeing to take the assignment without having to be
persuaded. He could tell it bothered Cubbage a little,
in fact, as though the city editor suspected he had
some other agenda, had no real intention of ever writing the story in question. It was an assignment that
would give him the freedom and flexibility of being on
vacation, but would also allow him to drop by the newspaper whenever he liked, without anyone wondering
why he was there. And it was something Rule cared
about, apparently, a chance perhaps to do him some
small injury.

More importantly, something he had first thought of
the night before, learning almost simultaneously of
Rule's latest "girlfriend" and the return of the Strangler,

had begun to take more definite shape in his mind. It had not really occurred to him previously that Rule would continue as he always had, after Clare's death, and that that in itself might present an additional avenue by which to get at him—and a peculiarly appropriate avenue at that.

He told Cubbage he would wait in the lunchroom downstairs until Stosh got back from the city building. He was sitting in a back corner, nursing a cup of coffee, out of sight of the entrance, and he saw her come in, in the mirror on the cigarette machine, before she spotted him. When she did, she smiled and approached his table.

"Want some coffee?" he asked as she sat down.

"No, thanks. I'm getting hay fever early this year, and the caffeine aggravates it." She fidgeted with her purse a moment, looking for something, and Sam took a sip of his own coffee, finding that it had gone cold. She extracted a pack of cigarettes from the purse, studied them for a second, and then put them back in the purse unopened. She gave Sam a mock-guilty look then and said, "I'm really excited about this. Not just the story, I mean, but working with you on it. I'm glad you decided to . . . come back." She smiled.

He could see what Rule saw in her. Her face was full and intelligent, and her slightly crooked smile made her seem a bit out of control, revealing more of herself than she intended. She wore a high-necked dress of some loose, wrinkled material that made her seem invitingly soft as well, decidedly female.

"Why do you care?" he asked.

She blinked at the challenge in the question. "Because you're good," she said simply, as though it were obvious.

He pursed his lips, not saying anything.

She leaned an arm on the table in front of her, the fingers slightly curled, almost reaching toward him, and asked, "Do you remember when I interned here?"

He shrugged. There were half a dozen interns every summer.

"It was three years ago, the summer just before the off-year elections," she said. "You wrote a story about an ice cream social the county Republicans held."

He nodded, remembering troupes of high-school girls in pep-club uniforms and sashes bearing the names of their candidates, elderly women at folding tables selling elephant jewelry, sleek candidates with smiles nailed to their faces and fat old men huddling over drinks to tell dirty jokes.

"What about it?" he asked. "There couldn't have been much to it."

"That's just it. Anybody else would have written three 'graphs and let it go at that. But your story ran across the bottom of the front page."

"It's a Republican newspaper."

She shook her head and said, "The reason I remember that story is because Fred pointed it out to me at the time. He said that's the kind of thing I ought to try to do, in every story. I still think about that whenever I'm working on something I don't think amounts to much."

He made a sour face. "Did Cubbage tell you what he meant?"

"He meant the way you always tried to make things come alive, even on a nothing story."

Sam grunted, reminded of the old irony. His goal had always been something slightly different from Cubbage's formulation: to make the reader see what he saw, feel what he felt. In the case of the Republican gathering, to make them see how self-serving and venal it all was. But even a couple of the Republicans had written him letters in praise of the story, thanking him for it.

"So I gather you're nor pissed off," he said.

"Pissed off? At what?"

"At not having the Strangler to yourself."

"Oh, no. I didn't really expect to."

"Why not?"

"I still have to cover the regular police stuff. I figured they'd bring someone else in for this. I thought it was going to be Mickey Goodwin."

"Why not give it to you and let someone else cover cops for awhile? You think he's better than you are?"

He saw a quick flash of anger in her eyes. "No," she said, "but he's the top GA. At least while you're not working."

The flattery was beginning to irritate him.

"Actually," he said, "I think it would have been Goodwin, except that the cops don't like him. Because of the way he covered the union stuff, I imagine."

Stosh studied him for a moment. "Do you think he's better than me?" she asked.

Sam, watching her face, which appeared to conceal so little, revealing the anxiety with which she awaited his answer, tried to picture her naked, with Rule, to imagine that same face contorted with passion, but he couldn't.

He shook his head. "You're a better reporter," he said. "But people think he's a better writer because he's clever with words. Most journalists think that's what good writing is." Before she could say anything, he added, "We need to talk about how we're going to do this."

"You're the boss," she said. "Tell me what to do and I'll do it."

Her submissive tone suddenly made the image come clear in his mind, after all—the darkness of nipples and hair against the white skin, the swell of hips. It came so suddenly, bringing a surprising arousal, that he looked away, feeling as though his thoughts must be transparent to her.

"First, we'll need to meet with Loomis and get our roles sorted out," he said.

"Do you know him?"

"I used to. From when I covered the first four killings. I don't know whether he'll remember me or not. There were a lot of reporters around then, and he was preoccupied."

"Okay," she said. "I usually get to the city building at ten. If you want to meet me there tomorrow at that time, we could see him together."

"Fine." They talked for awhile longer about how it might work, what information they might share, how often they ought to meet, finally deciding that most of it would depend on Loomis, how he chose to handle things.

As she left, he watched the curve and sway of her

hips beneath the skirt, thinking how long it had been since he had felt the press of any flesh but his own. It was a definite possibility, he thought. She was something of Rule's, something he presumably valued. And he had the feeling he could do it, though he had never done anything like that in his life before. He wondered if Rule had ever had it done to him.

He ate supper by himself, at a restaurant he and his mother had once gone to, when he was in high school, and then drove around for awhile, circling the downtown area to avoid the crush of cruising teenagers, keeping to the darker streets. Driving, he found that the encounter with Stosh, his speculations about her, had left him feeling edgy with a mix of loneliness and desire that was always just beneath the surface of things, but that he had mostly been able to keep at bay in the last few months.

It was something more than mere horniness. What he yearned for, when he let himself give way to it, was the reassurance of flesh, a kind of reassurance he had grown used to in the years of his marriage, but that existed for him nowhere now, for it was specific to Clare.

At home again, he stripped out of his clothing and lay down on the bed, turning on the little fan that stood at its foot. This was the simplest way to take care of it, to keep it from becoming the pervasive, self-pitying ache that could bring him so quickly to the brink of depression. The trick was not to think about Clare, for that inevitably involved thinking about Rule, and he could too easily wind up in the midst of some voyeuristic fantasy which would leave him feeling worse than before.

He reached out one hand, enveloping his erection, his eyes turned toward the drawn shade on the window nearest him, and experimented with thinking about Stosh, recalling the image he had had of her and Rule earlier that evening.

He remembered how he had imagined her, but it brought little true arousal now. He worked at filling out the scene, imagining context, saw her removing her clothing piece by piece, while Rule watched, expectant. Even with Stosh, it was Rule that was troubling. He banished him from the scene, saw Stosh sitting naked before a vanity mirror, her arms up, doing something with her hair, her buttocks flattened against the fabric of the stool she sat on.

For some reason, that less explicit image brought him back to arousal. He let out a long shudder, felt the sweat beginning to build on his forehead, beneath his arms, between his legs, despite the fan. He imagined coming up close behind her, putting his hands on her shoulders, her waist, for some reason unable to see anything of her in the mirror in front of him, willing her to turn around, but not until the right moment, when he would be ready for it, when the sudden revelation of the imagined mystery would turn it into the old familiar story, no mystery at all. He was nearing that point. Now he thought, tentatively, of Rule being somewhere nearby, in another room, knowing what was happening but unable to do anything about it, forced to listen. What would her expression be when she turned around? Fear? Resignation? Surprise? He did not imagine gratification, anything pleasant. He did not want anything like that.

Then, in his mind, she turned around toward him, pivoting in his arms to bring herself against him, all breasts and thighs and brush of hair, but it was Clare, after all, not Stosh, his own fantasy betraying him, and her expression was one of indifference, mild annoyance. Rule was waiting for her somewhere, impatient, and she was willing to put up with Sam to get to her own pleasure.

His lips curled back and his breath became ragged. It was too late to stop; there would be pain either way. With a kind of mental brute force, he pictured her spread-eagled beneath him on the bed, tried to force her features into a look of humiliation and disgust, but her face would not come clear now, and even her body began to seem insubstantial. Desperate to finish, he reached out in his mind for other images, photos he had seen, and what came, unbidden, was the photo of Jeannie Courter, the terrible one the police had shown him so long ago, the dark unrecognizable face above the white body, mottled with bruises and cuts and burns, the twisted limbs, the dark gash of her crotch, as if she had just given birth to something monstrous, and in that instant, though he would have stopped it then if he could, came a tiny burst, not so much an overflowing as a tearing, a feeling of something separating inside him or of something that had wrung itself dry.

He lay gasping, hearing the diminishing sobs of his own breath only distantly through a ringing in his ears that made the silence around him seem sudden, as if he had been crying out in pain only a moment before, so that people for blocks around might have heard him. At last, he stumbled out of bed, his body covered with grit and sweat, and went to the bathroom to shower. Beneath the cool water, feeling better, he reflected that this was the single moment, the moment just afterward, when everything was as close to being all right as it could ever be again, when he genuinely wanted nothing to do with Stosh or with Clare or any other woman, when he could nearly be at peace with all that, even with Rule. But he knew that there was never any way of holding on to that moment.

6

Stosh, running late and a bit breathless from the climb up the metal staircase, stopped just inside the door from the parking garage and scanned the city hall lobby, looking for Haun. Some older ladies had set up a charity booth inside the big glass doors at the front and were selling giant chocolate chip cookies shaped like clowns and teddy bears, and the people who usually moved briskly through the sterile lobby, from the doors to the elevators and back again, were mingling and browsing, caught by the sharp, sweet odor that made Stosh's mouth water, reminding her that she'd slept late again and skipped breakfast.

She caught sight of Haun then, lounging with his hands in his pockets in front of the newsstand near the hallway that led to the city offices. With his back to her, he looked drawn and slight, not quite the imposing figure she had once thought him. She had had something of a crush on him then, when she had first come to work on the paper, although she was sure he was completely oblivious. That thought brought a surprising twinge of nostalgia for the girl she had been then, less than two years ago. Probably Haun's feelings about her had changed as well in that time, if he thought of her at all. Something about him, maybe the way he had looked at her during their meeting in the lunchroom, told her he knew about her and Frank. But then, she supposed everyone in the newsroom did. Frank, inside his glass office, might believe that they had kept their secret from a building full of journalists, but she didn't.

As she watched him, Haun glanced up at the clock above the elevators, then began to turn away from the newsstand, probably starting to look for her now, but then he paused, his attention caught by something else. She followed his gaze and saw Frank emerge from one of the elevators and walk quickly across the lobby and out the door, ignoring the cookie stand and the little crowd around it. When she glanced back at Haun, she saw that he had stepped back behind the phone booth at the side of the newsstand, out of sight, and was watching Frank with an intensity she could almost feel, his body bent forward slightly, focused, like a basketball player about to spread his arms and rise onto his toes to guard an opponent.

She supposed Frank had been up to meet with Chief Stanwix, something to do with the special assignment Haun had been given. Once again, despite what she had told Haun and despite her genuine belief that he was the best person for the job, she felt a small pang at having been left out of that. Still, she would undoubtedly have a part of it, an opportunity to work with both Haun and Loomis.

"Want a cookie?" Haun had come up alongside her, holding out one of the chocolate chip teddy bears, wrapped in cellophane. "I'll split it with you." He folded back the cellophane and broke the cookie at the neck, handing her the round head and keeping the slightly smaller body for himself.

"Thanks," she said. "I missed breakfast. I don't think I want that much, though."

"Save the rest for lunch." He smiled and something in his look caught at her for a moment, but then was gone. She had thought, talking to him the afternoon before, that his eyes were opaque, that she could not see behind them to what was in his mind. It seemed to her that she had caught a glimpse of it, just now, but that it had faded away as quickly as the dream.

She smiled back, then broke off most of the cookie and stowed it in her purse. "Let's go," she said.

The police station was on the top three floors. Sally Dowd, the desk sergeant, a large woman with short hair and shorter nails, sat in a glass enclosure opposite the elevators. She nodded at Stosh and then eyed Haun with frank curiosity.

She introduced them and asked Sally to see if she could get Haun a place in the parking garage, letting her know that it was something the chief was involved in. While Haun filled out the papers, Stosh wandered over to the dayroom entrance, to see who was in.

She liked the atmosphere of the dayroom, the cops in their white shirts and shoulder holsters, pecking at their typewriters with beefy fingers. There were some who would square their shoulders and strut when she came in, while pretending to be oblivious of her. There were others, mostly the older ones, who would tell her dirty jokes in a halting, almost courtly way, using euphemisms that seemed funnier to her than the jokes themselves. The dayroom was something like a newsroom, though in some ways it was a world apart. For one thing, there were far more women in the newsroom. For another, most of the reporters were graduates of faraway colleges, putting in their time in Wichita on their way to bigger things; most of the cops had grown up around here and done a year or two at the local university or a nearby junior college. All in all, she preferred the dayroom—perhaps because it was the only place in town where she could count on finding an intelligent conversation about basketball. She thought the cops liked her, too, for the most part, and they didn't know anything about her personal life.

One of the younger detectives, Jerry Majors, spotted her and came over to the door. "Your boss was just up here," he said.

"Up here? You mean the detective division?"

"Yeah. He was talking to Binkley and Davidson, back there." He jerked a thumb in the direction of the interrogation rooms at the rear. "He had an appointment," Majors added.

She didn't know what to make of that. It sounded like a formal interrogation, and one conducted in privacy, not at a desk out in the open.

"What are Binkley and Davidson working on?" she asked.

"They're working with Loomis."

"You mean the new body?"

"I didn't say that." But then he couldn't resist adding, "Would that make headlines? Or would it?"

"I suppose it would," she said, not sure exactly what he had in mind. Frank as a Strangler suspect?

Someone touched her on the arm and she jumped, then laughed. It was Haun.

"Where next?" he asked.

Loomis's office was on the next floor, down the hall from the elevator and around a corner, as isolated from the rest of the department as it was possible to get.

He glanced up as they came in, then did a double take at her face and said, "Uh-oh," so that she realized she was frowning. She changed it to a smile.

"Captain Loomis," she said, "do you know Sam Haun?"

"It's been awhile. Hi, Sam." The two shook hands but didn't say anything else. Loomis looked at her expectantly; she had apparently been put in charge of this first meeting. Loomis had his jacket off and was wearing his wire-rims, which made his face look scholarly, even soft. His body, with the coat off, looked oddly compact, despite his size.

"You ought to wear your glasses more often," she told him, enjoying his pained look. He had not needed glasses until a couple of years ago, and his dislike of them was well known; he put them on only when he had to.

"You're after somebody this morning," he said, dropping back into his swivel chair and motioning to them to sit down. Haun took the straight-back chair against the wall, leaning back slightly and clasping his hands together in his lap. She sat in the bigger, more comfortable chair facing Loomis's desk.

Opening her purse to take out her notepad, she found the uneaten part of the cookie.

"Want some of this?" she asked Loomis. "They're selling them in the lobby."

"Yeah, I noticed. Thanks." She broke off a large piece and handed it to him, and he devoured it in a single bite.

Putting the rest back in her purse, she thought, Now we've all shared the same cookie, like some kind of communion.

"You know why we're here," she said.

"In a general kind of way."

"The Strangler case," Haun said.

Loomis gave him a slow sidelong look, then looked back at Stosh and said, "That's not the case I'm currently working on. Not for publication. Officially, I'm helping the county with a murder that just occurred."

She nodded.

"The four girls," Haun said softly. "Madsen. Mosteller. Fillmore. Courter. Have those cases been reopened?" There was something formal about the way he spoke the names, as though he were invoking higher powers, reciting a magic formula. Oddly, Stosh thought, the recitation seemed to have something like that effect on Loomis, who sat up a bit straighter, his expression growing somber. She understood that those names were familiar to both of them in a way that excluded her.

"They were never closed," Loomis said. He frowned and asked, "Are you two a team? This isn't exactly what I expected."

"I'm still on the regular police beat," Stosh explained. "So I'll be doing daily stuff as we go along. Sam will be working with you, however the two of you work it out."

"I see." Loomis looked down at his desk top for a moment and then looked up again and said, "It's a little awkward. I don't want to have to keep thinking about what I've said to one of you that I can't say to the other, so . . . I think it might be better to deal with you one at a time." He gave Stosh a quick apologetic smile. "What you say to each other is up to you, I guess, as long as I don't see anything in the paper that's not supposed to be there."

"What if I come up with something on my own?" Stosh asked. "I mean, something you've told Sam on background, but I get it somewhere else?"

Loomis cocked an eye at the ceiling for a moment, then said, "I'm not going to tell you to check everything with me because I know you won't anyway. But . . . hell, I guess it depends on what it is. I can't promise you I won't get pissed off if the wrong thing breaks."

"I'll keep that in mind," Stosh said.

"But I'll believe you if you tell me that's what happened," he added.

Before Stosh could react to what seemed to her a surprising vote of confidence, Loomis picked up a sheet of paper from his desk and said, "This is for publication. We have a female body two miles north of town, just off a county road that runs parallel to the interstate. The body was found by two boys who live in the area. I can get you their names if you need them. The victim has been identified as Karen Munoz." He paused, letting Stosh catch up, then added the age and address. "She was last seen the evening of May 7 at Roxy's downtown. She was a junior at WSU . . . or would have been, this fall. Planned to major in social work. She lived with her parents. She was the youngest of seven children, the only one still at home."

"Cause of death?" Stosh asked, her voice catching

annoyingly. She too was the youngest of seven, the only girl, and she could not avoid a sudden memory of the way her parents had looked when her oldest brother, Danny, had died.

Loomis shook his head, appearing not to have noticed. "The body was in very bad condition. We're still waiting for a final report from the medical examiner."

"You're sure it's murder, though."

"That seems pretty likely. She had no car, so someone had to drive her to where she was found. Also, there were no belongings with the body, no clothing."

"Evidence of sexual assault?"

"Again, we don't know yet. Given the condition of the body, we may never know."

"Barring a confession," Haun said.

"Yes. Barring a confession."

Stosh took a deep breath and said. "You questioned Frank Rule this morning. Was it in connection with this case?"

Loomis blinked and looked at her in surprise, then said, "Not me."

"Binkley and Davidson. They're working with you, aren't they?"

Loomis gave a slow smile. "Somebody downstairs is maybe just a little too eager to talk to a good-looking reporter," he said.

She didn't react to that, hoping she hadn't gotten Jerry into trouble. Loomis shrugged and said, "Detectives Binkley and Davidson are indeed assisting me with a part of this investigation, and they did indeed talk to Franklin Rule earlier today. That's about all I can say about that; actually, that's about all I know at this point. Mr. Rule is free to tell you whatever he wants about it, but if I were you I wouldn't make too big a thing out of it. A word to the wise."

"Is he a suspect?" she persisted, feeling that the last thing she could do, particularly in front of Haun, was let it lie. She would have liked to see Haun's reaction to this, but didn't allow herself to look at him.

"That depends on what you mean by suspect," Loomis said. "This is a fairly broad investigation, covering a lot of routine bases at this point. In one sense— the sense you probably mean—there are no suspects yet. But in another sense—hell, there are about fifty-thousand guys out there who are suspects. Including Franklin Rule, the mayor and the police chief."

"I've wondered about the chief," Stosh said.

Loomis grinned. "You and me both, kiddo."

She snapped her notepad into her purse and stood up. "I'll leave now so you can tell Sam all the good stuff," she said.

Loomis stood up hurriedly, caught by surprise. "Speaking of good stuff," he said, "you got any more of that cookie?"

She bought another cookie for herself on her way out, and then ate it at her desk, missing the conversation she would usually be having with Merow, who was sub-bing for Haun on the late desk. Her mouth was full when the telephone rang, and she let it ring an extra time while she chewed and swallowed, finally grabbing it before it could cycle back to the switchboard. It was Frank.

"Come in for a few minutes?" he asked.

"Sure."

In his office she closed the door behind her, though they could both be seen through the long window that looked out over the newsroom. She always felt as if they were on display there, everyone watching them, though she supposed few people really cared. Nevertheless, she sat down in the big chair in front of his desk, letting herself slump, to be a little more hidden.

"Hang on," he said. He punched a couple of keys on his terminal, watched the screen for a moment, as though to make sure it was really doing what he had ordered it to, and then swiveled around toward her. He was wearing his neutral office face.

"I just wanted to make sure everything was squared away on this Strangler thing, with you and Haun. Is the arrangement all right with you? We haven't had a chance to talk about it." He leaned back in the swivel chair and put his hands behind his head, raising his eyebrows questioningly.

"Sure. It's great," she said. "I'm glad to have a chance to work with him. I'm glad he's back to reporting."

Frank gave a wry grin. "Well, we'll see," he said. "We can damn sure get somebody to do obits and weather for a lot less than we pay Haun. Anyway, I wanted you to know it wasn't my choice."

"What? You mean Haun?"

"Yeah. We left it up to Loomis, and Haun's the one he asked for. I guess because they knew each other before. I just wanted you to know."

She felt herself blushing slightly. "Haun's the best one for the job," she said. "I didn't assume there was anything else to it. I didn't expect . . ."

"I know," he said. "But some would." She knew he meant that some had—some of the other newsroom women he'd been involved with in the past. She wasn't exactly jealous of them; after all, their relationship had grown out of his telling her about that part of his life. But she didn't know who any of them were, either, and she didn't want to know.

She had hoped that he might be leading up to telling her something about why he had been at the police station, but apparently not. He got up and walked slowly around his desk toward her. His approach could still make her feel a small rush of excitement, and she became more intensely aware of the window and the newsroom beyond. He went past her, made a pretense of studying one of the pictures on his inner wall, then turned and walked back, ending up directly behind her. She didn't look around, but his presence there was like the heat from a radiator, warming the back of her body. When he touched her at last, as she had known he would, resting a hand on her sleeveless arm, below the level of the window, she shivered involuntarily, and then felt absurdly angry with herself, with the certainty that he had felt it, that he was too aware of his power over her.

"You shouldn't do that here," she said, her voice betraying her by cracking slightly.

"Do what?" He patted her arm in a neutral, comradely way, and went back around to the desk, perching a hip on the edge of it. It was a pose he favored, particularly when meeting with the senior editors on some big, breaking story. He wore a black vest over a silver tie that matched his prematurely gray hair, which always seemed carefully, attractively tousled—unlike her own, she thought, which was simply unruly. She knew he liked to see himself as slightly rakish, still the boy reporter, but she also knew he would have looked out of place, a bit too immaculate, sitting at a desk in the newsroom.

"Was that it?" she asked, making a move to get up.

"Well," he said, lowering his voice. "I also wanted to let you know that Susan's going to be out of town this weekend." He glanced at the photo of Susan that sat on his desk, and so did she. His gaze was absent, distracted, as though he didn't really see what he was looking at. He had told her often that he loved Susan, but she had never seen any other evidence of it. It was something she felt a great deal of ambivalence about, so she preferred not to examine it too closely.

"Is that so?" she said.

He grinned. "I could fix supper for us," he said, as though that were a major inducement.

She laughed. "Maybe," she said. That was part of the game they played. She never said yes; it was either no or maybe, though both of them knew that maybe usually meant yes. Somehow, it was an important part of their relationship that he would never be sure that she was coming until she arrived at their meeting place, near the package pickup at Sears at Towne East. And there had been a couple of times when she hadn't shown up, partly just to see how he'd react, to see whether he thought of her as obligated. So far he didn't appear to. In fact, he had been so accepting, so nearly indifferent, that that in itself had bothered her. Sometimes she felt that she wouldn't have minded his being a bit more possessive, a bit less politically correct about respecting her autonomy. But that was another thing she felt ambivalent about.

"Something wrong?" he asked.

She hadn't realized she'd been frowning. She shook her head. "No," she said. "I guess I was thinking about something else."

"Well, that's flattering." He looked down at some papers on his desk, and she thought this might be the moment to ask him about his meeting with Binkley and Davidson, but before she could say anything, he looked up with a smile and said, "You know the party's coming up."

She nodded. "I'll be there." She always made a point of attending gatherings that Susan was involved in.

"No maybe about that," he said wistfully.

She smiled. He was beginning to fiddle with things on the desk beside him, a clear sign that the meeting was over. She took a breath.

"I saw you at the police station this morning," she said.

He was perfectly still for a second, then slid off the edge of the desk and went around behind it and sat down, putting his hands behind his head again, a posture of ease, though it seemed to her he did it consciously this time.

"Did you? I didn't see you."

"I was just coming into the lobby as you were going out. One of the detectives told me you'd met with Binkley and Davidson." She hesitated, then said, "I understand they're working with Loomis on the Strangler case."

He pursed his lips. "Find out anything else?" he asked, as though it were a story about someone else she was working on.

"Well . . . I did ask Loomis about it later. He wouldn't tell me anything, but he said you were free to tell me about it, if you wanted."

Frank gave a sudden laugh, infectious enough to make her smile in return. "This is the problem with being involved with a reporter," he said.

"Is it a problem?" she asked.

"Not really. Except . . . I guess I need to know: Are we talking now as reporter and editor, or reporter and source?"

She shrugged. "You tell me."

"All right. All right. Here's what happened. I'll leave it up to you." He paused for a moment, collecting his thoughts. "There is someone who has a grudge against me. This person has caused me problems of various kinds over the years. It isn't the first time I've been reported to the police as a possible suspect in some crime, usually sex-related, and of course they have to do their job, so they question me about it."

"What do they ask you?"

"Well, in this case, they just wanted to know where I was the night this latest girl disappeared. So I took my appointment book with me, and showed them I'd been out of town on that date, at a meeting at corporate headquarters. They said thanks and I left. That's really all there was to it."

She thought about it for a moment. "Couldn't you sue this person for harassment or something?"

"I suppose I could. But . . . it's not that simple. Other people would be hurt."

"I don't understand. Is it someone who has a grudge against the paper?"

"No. It's personal." He was silent for a moment, his face growing sad. "Stosh," he said, "you know the kind of man I've been, the things I've done, before I met you. Of course, I've made enemies."

"Oh." She felt stupid for not having understood sooner. A husband, probably. She closed her mental notebook and stood up.

"Think there's a story in it?" he asked.

"Sure. But not one we can use."

"Yes," he said, smiling sadly as if he regretted the fact. "That's about the size of it." His smile brightened. "See you at the party," he said. "If not before."

Back at her desk, she found herself trembling slightly. Despite what was between them—maybe because of it—it had taken some courage to ask him about his visit to the police station. She recalled a dream she had had—an ordinary performance-anxiety dream, really—not long after she'd started to work on the paper. She hadn't known Frank at all then, really, except as the remote, powerful figure to whom everyone in the newsroom answered. She couldn't remember any of the detail of the dream now, only that he had been in it and that she had been frightened of him— enough so that the mood of the dream had hung over her for a day or two afterward, and she'd consciously avoided running into him in the office. She wondered now whether some residue of that dream, a lingering sense of danger, might not have had something to do with the way she responded to him later, when he had begun confiding so much to her, wanting her friendship and approval.

She began riffling through her notebook, finding the stuff Loomis had given her, preparing to write the story on the Munoz killing. May 7, a Saturday, was the date the girl had disappeared. She stared at her own scribbles for a moment, then got up and went to the cubicle across the hall from Frank's office.

Dotty Engle, his elderly secretary, smiled up at her, looking vaguely confused, as she had ever since they'd replaced her typewriter with a computer terminal.

"Dotty," Stosh said, smiling back, "I'm doing a piece on Frank for the corporation house organ. Can you check something for me about an appearance he made, back in early May?"

The first streetlights were just beginning to glow weakly when she pulled into the parking lot at the apartment complex. She hadn't really been troubled much by hay fever so far this summer, but now she could feel the first itching in the corners of her eyes and in the roof of her mouth. If she could ignore it until she got inside, she thought, the air conditioning would keep it at bay. She always tried to put off antihistamines as long as she could; they made her feel slow and groggy, at a distance from the world. She locked her car hurriedly and, just in case, pulled a wad of Kleenex from her purse along with the house key as she climbed the steps from the parking lot.

At the door, she fumbled for a moment, getting the

key into the lock. There was a sneeze coming for sure now, but she tried to stifle it by pressing her tongue hard against the roof of her mouth, resisting the temptation to rub at the itch, and tears squeezed from the corners of her eyes, blurring her vision. Despite her efforts, the sneeze erupted as she was turning the doorknob, and she turned her face the other way, trying too late to cover it with the Kleenex.

"Gesundheit," someone said.

A man's form appeared at the top of the wooden stairs, the same way she had come, with the parking lot lights behind him, so that she couldn't make out his face. She bent her head to one side and blinked back tears, trying to see, and at the same time took an instinctive step backward toward the door, clutching behind her with one hand for the knob, while she held the tissue to her face with the other, her purse clamped awkwardly beneath her elbow. She tugged the keys loose from the door, keeping an eye on the man, who had paused at the edge of the porch, but when they came loose at last they fell from her grasp, bouncing away from her on the concrete.

"I'll get them," the man said, and she recognized Haun's voice. She released her breath, surprised to find she had been holding it, and that triggered another, unanticipated sneeze. She wasn't quite quick enough to turn her head away from Haun, who threw an arm up in self-defense.

"I've got to get inside," she told him hoarsely. She stooped to pick up the mail from the carpet inside the door, then added, "Sorry for sneezing on you."

"I've been treated worse."

She went ahead of him through the living room and into the kitchen, turning on the lights and the air conditioner, vaguely nervous. She didn't often have visitors, especially co-workers.

"If you want something to drink, I've got fruit juice and diet 7-Up," she said. "I could make some instant tea or coffee, too."

He shook his head, following her into the kitchen and standing just inside the door, looking unsure of his welcome.

"Sit down," she said. "I'm going to have some grapefruit juice. Sometimes it seems to help the hay fever."

He took a seat on one of the chairs at the yellow kitchen table, clasping his hands on the tabletop in front of him. She got her drink and stood leaning against the sink, sipping it, her sniffling under control now.

"So?" she asked.

"I thought maybe we ought to touch base again. I mean, about sharing whatever information I get from Loomis."

She shrugged. "I thought Loomis pretty well scotched that," she said. "I don't think I want to know anything I can't use in a story. I might get it on my own, and then not be able to use it because you'd told me. It might be better, like Loomis said, if we just work separately."

Perhaps she said it more angrily than she'd intended, for the look of distress that crossed Haun's features seemed to mirror the disappointment she'd felt herself, realizing that she wouldn't be working closely with the two men after all.

"But I'm willing to discuss it," she said, back-pedaling. "If you think there are things that wouldn't be a problem, that could help me on background . . . or if there's some way I can help you . . ." She took a couple of swallows of the grapefruit juice. It was unsweetened and if she took too much at once it made her shudder. When she looked up again, Haun was staring at her.

"What?" she asked, a bit startled by the focus of his attention.

He shook his head and looked away from her. She realized that the initial apprehension she had felt on the porch, not knowing who he was, had not entirely waned, and how like the dream of Frank it was, the same vague fear. She felt annoyed with herself.

"Listen," she said, "one thing I would like to know. Did Loomis say anything about Frank after I left?"

He hesitated, then shook his head.

"Because I asked Frank about it," she went on. "He told me someone gave his name to the police, someone with a grudge against him. I think it must be someone he had an affair with, or maybe her husband . . ."

"Did he say that?"

"Not in so many words." She hesitated, realizing belatedly that she was assuming Haun already knew about her and Frank. What if he didn't? But Haun didn't say anything or change expression, only waited for her to continue.

"He told me all they wanted to know was where he was on the night when Karen Munoz disappeared and that he showed them his appointment book, which showed he'd been at a meeting at corporate headquarters." She hesitated, then added, "But he wasn't at any meeting."

"He told you he wasn't?"

"No. I checked it with Dotty."

Haun gave a faint, incredulous smile. "She let you see his appointment book?"

"I made up a story for her. Anyway, he wasn't out of town at all in May. On May 7, he was at a seminar at WSU from seven P.M. to ten P.M."

Haun nodded, pursing his lips. "Do you think Rule makes a good suspect?" he asked. He didn't sound skeptical; he sounded genuinely curious.

"No. Of course not. But why would he lie about it?"

"Well, actually, he didn't. At least, not to the police."

"What do you mean?"

"I mean he only lied to you. He told the police he was at the WSU seminar. He never said anything about any corporate meeting."

She frowned, confused. "I thought you said Loomis didn't tell you anything."

"He didn't. But he's letting me see whatever I want, and the first thing I looked at was the report on Rule. Everything he told you was the same as he told the police, except for where he was at the time."

"I don't understand that at all. Why would he lie to me about that?"

Haun studied her for a moment, then said, "Maybe he's just uncomfortable telling the truth to a woman."

She felt herself flush. Haun's expression was bland, unreadable. "That's a shitty thing to say," she said. She hesitated, then added, "This is really none of your business, but the fact is, no matter what his reputation might be, Frank has always been completely honest with me. About everything."

"Really? How do you know?"

She started to flare up again, but then realized that it was a good question and that Haun wasn't asking it rhetorically, wasn't taking a jab at her. He really seemed to want to know how she knew that. And that made her realize that there wasn't much she could say except, "Because I know." What it came down to was that he had told her so many personal things, so many things she was sure he hadn't shared with anyone else, that she had to believe him.

"He's never had any reason to lie to me," she said.

Haun appeared to turn that over in his mind, as though examining it for flaws. She found herself wondering how they had so suddenly gotten around to talking about her and Frank, and why Haun seemed so interested in that. What was somehow more disturbing was that his interest clearly wasn't prurient or gossipy. If anything, it seemed professional, analytical, as though he might be working up a story on the subject, as though it had something to do with his job. She wondered if he knew more than he was telling her.

"Maybe he wanted to make sure you didn't look into it any further." Haun said at last. "His real alibi doesn't completely exonerate him, after all. He still could have been in the area. I don't think the police take him seriously as a suspect, and he probably knows that. But you might be inclined to look into it more closely, as you obviously have. So he gave you what he thought was an ironclad alibi."

Stosh considered that. "Why exactly do you think he wouldn't have wanted me to pursue it?"

"Because of the nature of the report, probably. Haven't you wondered how it was that this report came through so quickly?"

"What do you mean?"

"Well, the investigation's barely under way. The victim's name hadn't even been released yet, as you know. You wrote the story yourself, this afternoon. Yet, according to him, some citizen had already come forward to link Rule to the murder."

"Loomis said . . . well, he implied that there were lots of interviews going on already."

"Sure. Of known offenders. Former suspects. People whose names are in the computer. There aren't any new suspects yet."

"You mean Frank had already been named by someone in connection with the stranglings, back before." She tried to remember whether he had said anything about when the vindictive report had been made. She couldn't remember that he had.

"That's right." Haun studied her for a moment, as though debating whether or not to say anything more, then said, "Binkley and Davidson are running down the hooker reports."

"Hookers?"

"In a thing like this, every hooker has a candidate," Haun said. "I don't imagine that we're talking about a common streetwalker, of course, from South Broadway.

This is probably the kind of girl you take out to dinner first. My guess is, you can't even get her number unless you belong to the Petroleum Club. But that kind gets busted, too, occasionally."

Stosh felt the taste of the grapefruit juice rising in the back of her mouth.

"So," Haun said, "this particular woman was picked up by vice at one point, a few years ago, and she talked about some of her clients, including Franklin Rule." He made a face, speaking the name, and then, as if he could not keep from talking, said, "The police were somewhat interested in what she reported to be some of his . . . preferences." He looked away from her then, as though embarrassed.

Stosh cleared her throat and said, "It was several years ago?"

"Three or four years."

It began to make sense to her, and she felt relieved. She turned and poured the rest of the grapefruit juice into the sink. Of course he would be embarrassed to have her know all this, that there'd been a time when he went with prostitutes, that that's how he'd been involved in the Strangler thing. He'd told her a lot of other things he was ashamed of, about the other women, but those had been conquests, not purchases; men were supposed to be sensitive about distinctions like that. The implication about peculiar sexual preference piqued her curiosity, but she wasn't going to ask Haun to elaborate. She'd never noticed anything of that kind herself—certainly nothing she would have linked to the Strangler. She became aware that Haun was staring at her again, with a look that seemed oddly hostile.

"You don't think much of me, do you?" she said.

He blanked his expression, looking surprised. "I'm just irritated with myself," he said, "for bringing all this up. I didn't intend to mention it."

"It wasn't part of the background stuff you were talking about?"

"No. It was just supposed to be for my own information."

She frowned at that, remembering he'd said that the first thing he'd looked at, given the opportunity, was the report on Frank, just as she probably would have, just as she'd checked Frank's alibi with Dotty, as though Haun, too, had some personal interest in Frank. Then some things she'd heard and forgotten, some vague allusions Frank had made, suddenly came together in her mind.

"My god," she said. "Your wife."

Haun smiled as though pleased. "Did he tell you about it?"

"No . . . no." She made an equivocal gesture with her hands. "I mean, he never told me any names."

"Then that was well done," Haun said. "You're a better reporter than I thought."

"When was it?" she asked. "How long ago?" She realized it was a clumsy thing to ask, but she felt flustered, and that was what she wanted most to know.

"It was going on when she died," Haun said. "She'd written all about it in her journals. I didn't know anything about it until I read them afterward."

"Jesus."

Unnervingly, his smile widened a bit.

Clare Haun's death had been the summer before, just about a year ago, around the time when she and Frank had become involved. Surely it had been just before, not just after? She couldn't remember and didn't want to ask. Of course, she and Frank had been friends—not yet sexually involved—for some time before that. It shocked her to think he had still been seeing Clare Haun during that same time when he had been meeting her platonically, telling her all about his past affairs. And how had she gotten the idea, as she had, that he was not involved with anyone then? Had he said so, or was it just something she had assumed because she wanted to? A darker thought intruded: Had Clare Haun's death been the catalyst that inspired the change in their relationship? She tried in vain to remember some sign of grief, of his having been on the rebound.

Haun was watching her as though he knew what she was thinking. And perhaps he did. "I know how it must have been," he said. "You were just friends for a long time. You'd have supper together. Sometimes he'd cook for you at his house when Susan was away, everything completely innocent. And then he started confiding in you about his past relationships with women, telling you how ashamed he was of all that, but that he'd come to accept the way he was. He told you that he was so glad to finally have a real friendship with a woman, for a change. And then after awhile he confessed to you that he was beginning to feel differently about you."

She stared at him, unable to say anything.

"It was that way with Clare," he explained. "It's all in

115

her journals. I imagine it's pretty much the same each time."

She felt suddenly weak, and wanted to sit down, but felt that she had to stand and face what Haun was saying.

"With Clare, it started in Atlanta," he went on quietly. "Several of us went for an investigative reporters' convention, and the newspaper let us take our spouses along. Maybe that was Rule, part of his plan. He's good at arranging things in the background, you know. I suppose you do know. Anyway, he flew in one night and took us all out to dinner, and he spent the whole meal talking to Clare, entertaining her, being charming, soliciting her opinion on things. I didn't think anything about it. We used to visit him and Susan sometimes, play bridge, that kind of thing. We were all friends. So I was pleased. Clare seemed to be having a good time, and she was kind of unhappy right then, because of her job and some other things. Rule paid attention to her, made her fit in, made her laugh." He paused, his gaze turning inward. Stosh waited, her stomach churning.

"Then later on, back here," Haun continued, "he managed to run into her one day, downtown, and they had lunch together. He told her how much he had enjoyed talking with her in Atlanta, that he valued her friendship. They began having lunch together more or less regularly. She became his confidante. And then she began going over to his house for supper sometimes, when Susan was gone and I was working on some project or other. She kept that from me because she didn't want to betray his confidence, he was telling her such personal things." For the first time, Haun's voice took on a slight edge of sarcasm. "It was two or three months before anything actually happened between them. He's a patient man, very good at what he does."

She turned away, faced the sink. It had occurred to her that, even though Frank could not have known Clare was going to die, he had been getting a successor ready.

"I'm sorry," Haun said behind her. "I probably shouldn't have said all this. But when you guessed right about Clare and him, it just all came out. I haven't talked about any of this to anyone but my counselor, up to now. I suppose I must have thought you'd be uniquely qualified to understand. It was presumptuous of me. I'll go now."

She turned around again. "No," she said. "It's all right." It wasn't of course, but she couldn't really blame Haun, under the circumstances. Although she did, she realized. It seemed to her he had just dismantled the entire structure shoring up her self-respect, enabling her to go to work each day and still see Frank, and had made her see herself as a fool, one in a long line of fools. At this moment, she very nearly hated Haun, though she knew that would fade. It was her feelings about Frank she was more interested in, and she couldn't quite get a grip on them yet. It was all too big, too sudden.

"I'll be going," Haun repeated. He gave an apologetic nod and went out the door.

For a time she moved about the kitchen, needlessly straightening things, rinsing glasses she had already rinsed and moving them from the sink to the plastic drainer, a great emptiness building up in her gut. If she hadn't figured out about Clare Haun and Frank, or if she hadn't spoken the thought aloud. If Haun had never stopped by, if the Strangler hadn't reappeared . . . She shook her head. It wasn't Haun; all this, if it was true, had been lying in wait for her. She would have learned it sooner or later.

It made her feel diminished, as though she were a less substantial person than she had thought. She made herself stand still and look around at the kitchen, trying to see it as Haun had seen it, to see what kind of woman it showed her to be. But all she saw was the half-dead plants on the window ledge above the sink, the magnets on the icebox, beer caps and basketball mascots, the insurance company calendar depicting a harbor in Maine. It meant nothing, said nothing. She thought of the Dr. J poster on the wall of her bedroom—almost an antique now—and wondered why she kept it there, instead of on the living room wall with the European travel posters she'd accumulated. It seemed to her suddenly that the things that might help explain her to others were the things she kept most hidden. Not even Frank had been in her bedroom.

After that first time, in his car, when it had all been like some silly, adolescent adventure, a matter of seeing what it would be like to do something like that, they had simply gone back to meeting at his house, as before, but with the addition of sex, as though that were nothing. They had both behaved, in fact, as if nothing really important had changed, and it was only now, perhaps, that she began to understand that it had, inevitably. But how much had she changed? She wasn't sure she knew, and was a little afraid of finding out.

She found herself standing in front of the open icebox, staring sightlessly at what was within, and closed the door, at the same time giving a loud moan of frustration that made her laugh at herself. She knew what it was she had wanted from Frank originally—the same thing she had thought he wanted from her: friendship, honesty, a sense of belonging. She was less sure about why she had agreed to go to bed with him, and even less sure about what it was she wanted from him now. When she had understood what Haun was telling her, the first thing she had felt was a great fear that she would be forced to let go of it all, to let go of Frank, to salvage any self-respect. Now she felt a duller kind of fear, that she might find some way of talking herself out of that, of continuing herself the deception that Frank had begun.

She shook her head angrily and flipped off the light switch, heading down the hallway to the bathroom. Running the water, peeling off her clothes, watching herself in the mirror, she thought of what Haun had said about the prostitute: the kind of girl you took out to dinner first. Frank had never taken her out anywhere; he said it was too risky. But he took her to his house, which seemed to her riskiest of all. What did it mean? If Haun were right, could she believe anything Frank had told her, even his liking to cook? Could all of it, every detail, be part of a well-honed strategy?

Sitting in the tub, soaking, she smiled crookedly, thinking that, if so, it was a perfect strategy for seducing a reporter: the appearance of handing out deeper truths, confessing the real story. The agonized and embarrassed way in which he had told it to her, his apparent relief afterward at having got it out. Remembering, she found it hard to believe that it hadn't all been spontaneous, that he had done it before. Could she be that gullible? No wonder so many female reporters ended up as crazy middle-aged ladies, she thought, wearing strange hats and smoking cigars and shocking the interns with their language. For some reason, imagining herself that way made her feel better for a moment.

She decided, under the circumstances, to allow herself a single cigarette, holding it in cupped hands above the water, the half-shell ashtray balanced precariously on the bathtub rim. Could it be Haun who was lying, or in some way mistaken? Certainly, there was something dark and vaguely threatening about Haun, something that had already bothered her before his revelations. Perhaps his grief had done something to him; how could it not have? She took a long drag, thinking hard, trying to see how Frank could be exonerated, then shook her head. If Haun was lying, he had made a supernaturally shrewd guess about the way she and Frank had begun, the things he had told her. She could not think of any way Haun could have known about that without having heard it from someone who had been there. Even Merow, who knew about the affair and who was Haun's friend as well as hers, didn't know that much about it.

Sometime later, sleeping fitfully, she had a dream about being with Frank at his house, but with everyone else there as well, all the newspaper people, even Clare Haun, whom she had never met. In the dream, it all turned out to be some sort of practical joke being played on her, something completely innocent, and everyone laughed to see how genuinely worried she'd been about it all, how sad. She laughed with them, filled with a vast, liberating relief.

7

As soon as Binkley and the man he was questioning had left the interview room, Loomis stood and turned on the light, making the window he and Haun had been peering through turn into a mirror again.

"That's not him," Haun said matter-of-factly.

Loomis grinned. "Oh, really?" Well, you're probably right, but they surprise you sometimes." The young man they had been observing was a graduate student at the university, Robert Goldescu. He had been picked up by campus security guards while apparently trying to open a back door at one of the women's dorms. He claimed he had seen someone else trying to get in, had chased the other man away, and then had been making sure the door was locked when the security guard had showed up. He was tall and ungainly, and watching him squirm on the undersized chair in the interrogation room had reminded Loomis of himself, at teachers' conferences at Marcie's grade school, pretending also to be innocent, normal.

"What was all that about Baltimore?" Haun asked.

"When he was in college there, he was found early one morning taking a shower in one of the girls' dorms.

Just stepped out of the shower all of a sudden, stark naked, while a couple of girls were in the john. He claimed he'd been staying overnight with a girlfriend, hadn't realized anyone else was there. But he wouldn't name the girlfriend and no one came forward. I guess they had enough doubt that he wasn't actually prosecuted, but they more of less forced him to drop out of school, and he came back here and enrolled at Wichita State."

"He comes from here?"

"Yeah. In fact, when he was in high school, there were a couple of complaints about him. One girl said he tried to force her into his car, but he claimed he'd just been joking around. Then another girl said he was following her, spying on her. He denied that. It was during the time the Strangler was operating, and there were a lot of reports of that kind about a lot of guys."

Haun thought for a moment, then asked, "What kind of person you think he is?"

"Goldescu?"

"No. The Strangler."

Loomis gave a grunt of mirthless laughter. "I think he's an asshole who kills people."

"No, I mean in real life, when he's with his family and friends. Or do you think he's a loner?"

It was the kind of question Loomis and the other detectives had asked endlessly of themselves and others, never really getting any satisfactory answers.

"There are profiles," he told Haun wearily. "Odds are supposed to be pretty good that he's either a student or working class—maybe some kind of skilled trade, like a plumber. He's got to be somebody with a flexible schedule, somebody who's usually up late."

"Like me."

Loomis shrugged. "A reporter might fit, except these guys usually aren't white-collar. Cops fit the profile better." He paused, expecting Haun to smile, but Haun only nodded, digesting the observation. "But," Loomis went on, "assuming it's the same guy as six years ago, he's getting a little old to be a student now, unless he's a grad student like Goldescu. Actually, the reason I rule Goldescu out, in my own mind, is because he's so tall. Somebody somewhere would remember a guy like Goldescu, at the library or at Century II or at one of the bars. Nobody ever notices our guy. The old lady who might have seen him, Mrs. Hardesty, didn't remember much about him, and she would have remembered him being that tall, I think."

"He must make some kind of impression on the women who go with him," Haun said, "unless he just uses brute force."

"Unlikely. Yeah, you're right. What I figure is, he's not much to look at, but he's got some quality that women like. Either he seems nice and harmless or else he's got . . . what do they call it? Magnetism. Charisma. Something like that. He's one of these guys that can tell a woman to get in the car, and she does, without hardly thinking about it. Like some guys were born to order women around." He hesitated, thinking about that, then modified it, adding, "Some women, anyway."

"And he knows which one," Haun said, with an intensity of interest that surprised Loomis. "He recognizes them when he sees them."

"I suppose so. We don't really know whether he tracks them or acts on the spur of the moment. There are good arguments both ways."

"Do you think you'll recognize him, when you meet him?"

You mean *if*, Loomis thought, but he said, "You always think that. Sometimes it even works out that way."

Later, driving west on Harry Street, toward the river, bound for the day's first interview, Loomis told Haun, "I grew up around here. Over near the river."

Haun glanced at him, not saying anything, then looked out dutifully at the bars and hardward stores, liquor shops and mom-and-pop groceries.

"The west side never changes," Loomis said. "Except sometimes nowadays you see a sign in Vietnamese. 'Course, nowadays, when most people talk about the west side what they mean is all the fancy new neighborhoods farther out." He sighed. "Some of these stores I think are exactly the same, haven't even been painted," he said. "I feel like I might see myself anytime, running down the sidewalk." He laughed. "How did I get to be an old man so quick?"

Haun was silent for a moment, then said, "You're probably still eligible to be the Junior Chamber of Commerce Young Man of the Year."

Loomis grunted. "That's a great comfort," he said, then added, "You know, I think this guy broke up my marriage." He felt Haun's sudden interest, his gaze turning toward him like a light turning on in the car.

"This guy we're going to see?"

"No, no. The killer."

"How do you mean?"

"Oh . . . Edie . . . my wife . . ." He shook his head, wishing he hadn't brought it up. He knew he had a kind of instinct for interviewing, for leading people into areas that revealed things about them—he did it almost unconsciously—and sometimes, as now, it led him into places he himself didn't want to go. "It was just something about this case that was the final straw," he said reluctantly.

Haun didn't say anything for a moment, clearly waiting for him to say more, then said, "You were under stress."

Haun was a professional interviewer, too, Loomis reminded himself. "I guess so," he said.

"You must have been working lots of hours, hardly ever coming home."

"Yeah. That's true."

There was another long silence and he knew that Haun knew he was evading the issue.

"When you were home," Haun asked at last, "did you talk about the case or not?"

Loomis was surprised by how close the question came to the heart of the matter.

"Hardly at all," he admitted.

"When you've got a job that's not like other people's jobs it can be hard to talk about," Haun said. "Just because there's no common ground. People who don't do it don't really understand what you're talking about. So there's a tendency to just clam up."

Loomis nodded.

"And if you're doing your job all the time." Haun persisted, "So that you didn't really have anything else to talk about, that could create a communication problem in a marriage, I imagine."

Loomis sighed. "I think that's kind of how Edie felt about things," he said.

Haun was silent again, staring out the window, apparently satisfied with his analysis.

"But that wasn't really it," Loomis said, not quite sure why he wasn't able to leave it at that. "Edie understood my job. That's not why I didn't like to talk about it."

Haun's head swiveled back toward him, his gaze unruffled, unsurprised.

"I know," Haun said. "It was because it was ugly and scary."

Loomis stared ahead at the street, swallowing, remembering. Ugly and scary. That was it exactly. And humiliating, because there was nothing he could do about it. He—whoever he was—was out there somewhere, and nothing led to him, nothing kept him away. He took the ones he wanted, out of crowds, out of the ordinary moments of their lives, when they should have been safe. Edie had lived with his own fear and humiliation as long as she could, and then it had driven her away, maybe without ever really understanding why, for he himself had only begun to understand what had happened to them when he had found that the pain of separation was mixed with relief, as though he would not have to worry about them once they were gone, as though the things he feared were somehow connected to himself.

"It was scary," he agreed. "It still is."

* * *

The old three-story corner house had probably been the home of some civic leader, back when civic leaders had lived in the southwest part of town, maybe in the previous century. There was a big L-shaped porch with thick railings of wood and stone, and ornate Gs carved into the stone beside the steps, but the screen of the front door bulged out and there was paint flaking from the walls. A row of black mailboxes gave the apartment numbers, but no names.

Loomis paused inside the narrow hallway, letting his eyes adjust to the gloom, while Haun studied the metal numbers nailed to the nearest doors—a 1 and a 2, opposite one another. The No. 2 door, on the left, was set in a wall that appeared to be newer than the rest of the structure, as if a large open room had been closed off. A staircase with broad, flat banisters, incongruously wide, rose away from them at the far end of the hall.

Loomis knocked at the No. 1 door. It opened almost immediately, just far enough to permit them to see a bald, wrinkled head with a cigarette dangling from its lips.

"Kirby Banks?" Loomis asked.

A brown-spotted hand materialized below the head, took the cigarette from the lips and jabbed with it, making a palsied, darting motion.

"Over there," the man said, but the second word was cut off by a rough cough, surprisingly deep, and the hand withdrew.

"Thanks," Loomis said, but the door had already closed. He knocked on No. 2. After a few seconds of silence, he knocked again. He had just begun to turn away when he heard footsteps approaching. The door opened a few inches, like the other one, but this face was much younger, narrow and wide-eyed.

Loomis slipped his badge out of his jacket pocket and let the man look at it for a moment.

"Are you Kirby Banks?"

The man nodded, not opening the door any further.

"I'm Captain L. J. Loomis, Wichita police. This is Sam Haun. I'd like to ask you a couple of questions. May we come in?"

The round eyes stared for a moment, taking only a quick glance at Haun. "You got a search warrant or something?" The voice was high-pitched, slightly wavering. It made him seem vaguely adolescent, although it said on his sheet he was thirty-one.

"I just want to talk to you," Loomis said.

Banks smiled suddenly and swung the door open wide. He was slender but well muscled beneath the tight white T-shirt and blue jeans. The smile transformed his face, making him look open and friendly, but the eyes were watchful, a con's eyes.

"Guess I seen too many movies," he said. "'Course you don't need no warrant just to talk." He nodded past Loomis at Haun, who slid in behind and took up a post against the wall.

The living room reminded Loomis of his own, except that it was larger and less cluttered—not from greater neatness but from scarcity of belongings. There was a padded swivel rocker in one corner, tilting slightly to one side, with stuffing peeking out of the seams along the arms. The sofa slumped beneath the drawn shades of a picture window, its cushions sagging in the middle, and there was a pillow propped at one end and a rumpled blanket on the floor in front of it, as if someone slept there. A tiny black-and-white TV sat on a straight-back chair a few feet from the sofa, its cord pulled taut to reach the nearest plug.

"I was just taking a nap," Banks explained.

"How long have you been back in town?" Loomis asked.

"I've lived here all my life. I'm a native."

"But you've been away for awhile."

The smile wavered for a second, returned.

"Yeah, that's right. I was living in Colorado."

"Where in Colorado?"

Banks gave a sheepish smile. "The state prison."

"You were convicted of sexual assault?"

"Well, yeah, but on a prostitute. It wasn't really . . ."

"You did five years?"

"See, she stole some money from me. I was just kind of taking it out in trade." He grinned a Haun, who stared back.

"Do you remember being questioned about the death of Terry Fillmore?"

Banks frowned earnestly, as if trying hard to remember.

"I don't remember the name," he said.

"It was about six years ago, before you left for Colorado."

Banks shook his head.

"You recognize the name Karen Munoz?"

He shook his head again. His expression was mildly apologetic, the look of someone trying to be helpful but failing.

"Do you read the newspaper, Mr. Banks?"

"Oh . . . was she killed?"

"You know about that?" Loomis asked.

"No, I don't know nothing about it. You . . . you just said it was in the paper." He seemed to grow agitated as he talked, as if his own words annoyed him. "There's lots of people get killed," he said. "It's terrible. I'm for the death penalty myself. But I only went up the one time, and that was just 'cause of that whore that robbed me. And I didn't even hurt her, really. It don't hurt a woman, you know. Not really. I mean . . ." He ran down, glancing at Haun as if for support.

"Do you ever hang around the university?" Loomis asked. "Visit the bars in that area?"

"I work construction. When I can get it."

Loomis frowned. "That's not what I asked. Do you ever . . ."

"I mean I got nothing in common with college kids," Banks said.

"You do go out with girls?"

Banks smiled almost bashfully. "Sure."

"Where do you meet them?"

"Oh . . . around. You know."

"At the library?"

Banks laughed. "Do I look like the kind of guy hangs around a library?" he asked. Then his expression grew thoughtful. "I remember that library stuff," he said. "That's what they wanted to know about that other girl. Was that who you were talkin' about, the one that was at the library?"

"Terry Fillmore."

Banks shrugged. "I don't know no more now that I

did then," he said. "I don't see why anyone would think I was hangin' around a library."

Loomis nodded. "Can you give me the names of some of the girls you've gone out with recently?" he asked.

Banks blinked his bland expression turning wary. "What for?"

"Just routine."

"I don't know all their names."

"Just the ones you do know."

Banks looked down at the floor, and chewed at his lower lip. "There was a Jennifer," he said finally.

"Jennifer who?"

"Beats me. I never asked."

"You mean she was a prostitute?"

Banks shrugged.

"Are there any girls you've gone out with since you've been back in Wichita who weren't prostitutes?"

Banks squinted at Loomis as though trying to remember, then shook his head, smiling with faint embarrassment.

"I know it's illegal," he said. "But . . ."

"You're on parole, aren't you?" Loomis asked.

"A man's gotta have an outlet," Banks said. "That's human nature."

Loomis moved a hand dismissive in the air. "I'm not your parole officer," he said, then asked, "Exactly how long have you been back?"

"Uh . . . since November. I came here right after I got out."

"You have family here?"

"No, not anymore. But I had a job lined up. Besides, it's my hometown. Where else am I gonna go?"

Loomis nodded and looked around the room, wondering if the rest of the apartment was equally bare. He reflected that it didn't take much to make a man a suspect in this kind of crime. How many lonely, misfit men were there, living in apartments like this—men like Banks? Men like Haun and himself, for that matter.

"I tell you," Banks said, "I didn't kill no girl."

Loomis looked back at him for a long moment. Banks returned his look, earnest, sincere. "You mind if I look around a little?" Loomis asked, breaking the moment.

He was rewarded once again with the wary look that peeked through occasionally. Banks was a man with something to hide, although it might not be murder. "What if I say no?" Banks asked.

"I guess I could come back later with your parole officer," Loomis told him.

Banks made a sour face and shrugged. "Help yourself," he said.

Loomis glanced at Haun, who roused himself to follow. There were two other rooms, a tiny bedroom with a single, pillowless twin bed, and a surprisingly large kitchen. They stepped through like visitors in a museum, not touching anything, Haun with his hands in his pockets, looking bored. Squeezed between the bed and one wall was an unpainted chest of drawers. A pile of dirty clothes lay in the open door of a closet at the foot of the bed. There were a couple of pair of men's shorts, with orange stripes around the band—not the killer's brand.

The kitchen sink was full of dirty dishes, and a skillet full of greasy water, with some flatware soaking in it, sat on the stove. Newspapers and magazines were piled on the little table, leaving only a narrow strip at one end, where the dishes from Banks's most recent meal still sat, unrinsed. An empty Hamburger Helper box, its top torn off, stood on the floor beside the overflowing wastebasket. There were two doors at the back corner of the kitchen, one of them padlocked. The other one, Loomis could see thorugh the glass, led to the narrow backyard and the sagging two-car garage whose entrance faced the alley.

"Where does this go?" he asked, putting a hand on the locked door.

"Down to the cellar."

"Can I see it?"

"You'd have to ask the manager. He lives over in 1, across the hall."

"You don't have a key?"

Banks smiled apologetically.

"Why is it locked?" Loomis asked.

Banks stared at the padlock as though he'd never wondered about that himself.

"I guess he don't want nobody going down there," he said finally, frowning.

"You park your car in the garage?"

Banks gave a startling bark of laughter.

"Nobody gets in there but the manager," he said. "Got his precious car in there. Won't even let me put my bike in." He paced to the other end of the kitchen, suddenly full of nervous energy, then turned toward them again with an amazed smile.

"What kind of bike?" Loomis asked. "A motorcycle?"

"No, a bike. A bike. With pedals, you know. Helps me keep in shape."

"Where is it now?" Loomis asked. "I didn't see any bike out on the porch."

"It's . . . uh . . . I got it being worked on. Derailleur was slipping. Couldn't keep it in gear."

"Where do you ride?"

"Wherever. There's bike paths along the river. City finally did something for the working man, but they won't keep the skaters out. Those creeps, they make you run off the path. Think they own it. Bunch of fuckin' punks. Cops ought to do something about that." The charge he had gotten from complaining about the manager seemed to have changed his mood, made him more assertive.

Loomis walked back into the bedroom. This time he noticed something under the head of the bed and bent to have a closer look. It was a flat metal lockbox, padlocked.

"What's in there?"

"Personal stuff. Papers."

"Can I see?"

Banks stared at him for a moment as though coming to a decision.

"I don't think so," he said with a nervous smile. "I think I'm gonna draw the line there, Cap. I guess you could come back with Mr. Delmas, or get a search warrant or something, but I don't care. A man's got a right to some privacy."

Loomis nodded. for some reason, Banks's defiance made him doubt that there was anything important—to

Loomis, anyway—in the box. Even if there were, there wouldn't be by the time he could make a legal search.

He and Haun walked around the house once before going back to the car. The building jutted out at the rear corner, to accommodate the basement staircase, and there was a slanted cellar door, also padlocked, opening onto the side yard.

"What do you think's in that box?" Haun asked.

"Drugs or porn, most likely. Maybe both."

"Why do you think the cellar's locked up?"

"Security," Loomis said. "Otherwise, someone could get into Banks's apartment by going through the cellar."

"You don't think there's anything down there?"

"The furnace. I don't see one on the first floor."

Haun nodded and stared at the side of the house for a moment. "My aunt and uncle have a cellar with a slanted door just like that," he said.

"When I picture the Strangler," Haun said, "I see him mainly as dark. A dark man."

They were back in the car, heading north on I-35, out of town. Loomis had promised to show Haun the sites where the bodies were found.

"You mean black?"

"No. I don't even mean a dark complexion. I guess I mean his clothes; I see him dressed in black. But more than that." He shook his head, dissatisfied. "And he seems quiet to me," he added. "Knowing. Confident."

Loomis pursed his lips. "I think you're going to be disappointed when we catch him," he said.

"Are you sure you'll catch him? Maybe he's . . ." Haun stopped and Loomis grinned.

"Too smart for us?" Loomis asked.

"Or maybe just very good at what he does," Haun said.

"Well . . . I'm pretty good at what I do," Loomis said, then added, "I hope he thinks he's too smart for us."

Haun was silent for a moment, then said, "They don't always get caught."

"No. Not always. Maybe some of them are too smart for us. But most of them are just punks, like Kirby."

"I actually kind of . . . I don't know. It's not that I liked him, exactly, but there's something kind of appealing about him. You know?"

"Sure. That's why I think he's a fair suspect. Not that we've really got anything on him."

There was another silence, and then Haun said, "They were all found north of town, except for Jeannie Courter. And she was different in several other ways, too. But you guys were always convinced it was the same killer. How come?"

Loomis hesitated, then said vaguely, "Same MO, really, despite the differences. He might have been interrupted or something, forced to leave the body where he killed her. We're pretty sure all the others were killed someplace else, that he keeps them awhile and then uses this area up here for dumping them."

Haun shook his head. "It was more than that," he said. "She didn't look like the others, didn't dress like them. She was older, a different kind of woman. There was talk she was turning tricks. And he did things to her . . . you say he could have been interrupted, but, Jesus, look at what he did . . ."

Loomis hit the brake hard, coming to the stop sign at

the bottom of the exit ramp, making Haun rock forward and back, shutting him up. The road, 110th Street, was really only a dirt section line, connected to the interstate for the convenience of the farmers whose land it ran through.

"Look," Loomis said, letting the car idle, "there's one big thing you don't know about. It's the one thing we know about and the killer knows about and hopefully no one else does. You see what I'm saying."

"It's a secret," Haun said, smiling faintly.

Loomis smiled, too, in spite of himself. "It is," he said. "If I tell you . . . I'm gonna tell you, but you've got to keep it to yourself. You can't tell anyone, even Stosh . . . especially Stosh. If this would get into the paper, we'd be fucked. Also, it could produce copycats."

"I get it," Haun said. "You want me to swear or something?"

Loomis shook his head. "This is it," he said. "The guys leaves flowers and a pair of underwear with each body. Men's underwear, Sears mediums. It's even stranger than it sounds. According to forensics, the underwear is always brand new, never been worn. Sometimes you can still see the fold marks."

Haun digested that. "What kind of flowers?" he asked.

"It varies. It's the number that's important. There was a single white carnation near Marty Madsen's body. At that point, if it had been some kind of wildflower, we probably wouldn't have noticed it, but it was out of place there. Then there was a pair of tulips next to Mosteller and three roses with Fillmore."

"And Courter?"

"Yeah, except . . . they were wildflowers, something he probably picked right around there. And he left them right on the body. The others had been away from the bodies—farther away in each case, in fact. That's why they weren't in the photos you've seen. Except for Courter, and in that case you'd hardly notice them if you weren't expecting them." He glanced in the rearview mirror, saw an old pickup truck coming down the ramp behind him, from the interstate. He swung out onto the dirt road. "But she had four of them, plus the underwear," he said. "That's why she fits."

"And there were five with Munoz?" Haun asked.

Loomis nodded. "Lilies."

"What do you think about the underwear?"

"I don't know. Everybody has a different theory. The profile says he was probably abused as a child, so the underwear could have something to do with that. The shrinks say it and the flowers could be some kind of personal symbolism, something to do with the person he really wants to kill, which of course they think is probably his mother. The girls are just substitutes."

"What are the other theories?"

"Well, Davidson thinks it might be some kind of joke."

"A joke? I don't see it."

"Neither do I. Maybe you'd have to think like these guys to understand their humor. Or like Davidson. One of the other detectives thinks it's just something crazy to keep us guessing, distract us. And there's another school of thought, that it's a statement of what he thinks of girls. Use them once and throws them away. Except that he doesn't really use the underwear. I don't know. I used to think if we could figure out that part we'd have him, but it just goes around in circles when you think about it, so I quit."

He eased the car onto the shoulder and stopped. There was nothing particularly distinguished about the Mosteller site. It was in a flat stretch between two hills, with no houses around, no trees to speak of. The hills hid the area from traffic, except for cars coming along 110th Street, and anyone working there at night would have had ample time to spot approaching headlights.

Loomis led Haun about forty feet into the unfenced field, then stopped to get his bearings, looking for the rock the tulips had been lying on, a dozen yards from the body.

"Over here," he said. "The flowers were on that big rock there. The body was right about here. He just carried her out here and dumped her right in the open like this."

There was a wind lowing through the shallow valley, rippling the surface of the field, and when Haun said something Loomis didn't quite catch it.

"What?"

"I said, he doesn't just dump them. He poses them."

Loomis thought about that, then nodded. That had been true with Mosteller and Fillmore, anyway. Mosteller had been left spread-eagled, her arms spread wide, her feet toward the road. Terry Fillmore had been left on her knees, her face in the dirt, her buttocks thrust into the air. Assuming it was done on purpose, Loomis supposed they might represent sexual positions, perhaps those favored by the killer. but the other three hadn't been that way. Madsen, contrary to what Haun said, had simply been dumped; Courter had been left hanging from a tree by a length of wire—maybe, it occurred to Loomis, the killer had left her there because he felt he couldn't improve on that—and Munoz's body was too far gone to tell. But maybe that, in itself, could be considered a "pose."

"He's like a perverted artist," Haun said. "The opposite of an artist, I mean. Instead of giving life to lifeless things, he turns life into dead matter."

"It's easy to start giving these guys too much credit," Loomis said, thinking that Haun was beginning to take a lot more interest in the case than he's seemed to have originally. "It doesn't take any great talent to do what he's been doing."

"No, that's true," Haun said after a second's hesitation. "But it takes the will."

"You're going to like this guy better than Kirby Banks," Loomis said. "I mean, you're not going to like him at all, but he's more what you're expecting."

They were at a trailer park south of town, and the address Loomis was looking for turned out to be a plain white trailer with a black Chevy Nova parked in front. There was a small wooden shed at the far end of the structure, and single tire tracks in the dirt leading into it suggested a motorcycle. Otherwise, the unadorned trailer seemed out of place among the tiny fenced gardens and shiny metal trim of the surrounding mobile homes.

The man who answered the door was a big man, bigger than Loomis, with a handlebar mustache that he obviously took pains with. He didn't look happy to see them.

"John Carlock?" Loomis asked.

Something slammed against the bottom of the metal screen door, making Loomis's hand twitch automatically toward his holster, and he found himself looking into the snarling face of a Doberman. The dog's paws slashed at the screen, making it bulge.

"Get back, damn it! Yes, I'm John Carlock. Who are you?"

Loomis showed his badge and identified Haun by name. The deal was that Haun could come along as long as no one objected. If there was a problem, he would wait in the car. Carlock didn't even give him a glance.

"You want to come in?" he asked with a touch of sarcasm.

"Yes, if you can control that dog."

"I control everything that belongs to me. Wait." He disappeared into the trailer's interior, and the dog watched them through the screen, making a low, continuous growl. It looked to Loomis as though it wouldn't take much of a lunge for the dog to go right through the screen, but it seemed content with guard duty.

Carlock came back with a length of bright silver chain. He attached one end to the dog's collar and twisted the other end two or three times around his right hand, then went back into the trailer, pulling the dog with him.

"Come ahead," he said.

Inside, Haun stayed near the door, although he didn't

appear overly concerned about the dog. His gaze wandered around the inside of the trailer, the way a cop's might, looking for the odd detail that might tell him something about the man who lived there. Loomis straddled a kitchen chair, the back between his legs, and faced Carlock, who had sprawled in a massive leather armchair that took up nearly one entire end of the narrow living room. The dog sat, poised but restrained, beside the chair, and then slowly sank to a lying position, still alert, keeping up a low rumble which Carlock made no attempt to quiet.

"I'm investigating a series of assaults on women," Loomis said.

Carlock laughed. "I get all the pussy I can handle without having to strong-arm anyone for it," he said.

"We have reports that you prefer it rough, though."

"Women like it rough. The women I go out with."

"Not all of them. A couple of women have told us you scare them."

Loomis expected him to ask who the women were, but he didn't.

"Fuck, that's part of the fun," he said. "Like riding on a roller coaster. They like it. They just think they shouldn't."

Loomis took a notepad from his jacket pocket, the movement making the dog rise back up stiffly on its front legs. He flipped a couple of pages, as though searching for something, although in fact he didn't need to refer to it.

"What about this business of shoving your penis down a woman's throat and cutting off her air until she blacks out?" he asked. "Do they like that, too?"

Something happened in Carlock's eyes, but when he spoke it was in the same flat, good-natured voice.

"You'd be surprised," he said. "Suffocation is a rush, a high. It's a scientific fact. I've got books . . ."

"Yeah, I've heard that. If it's so great, do you let them suffocate you, too?"

"No," Carlock said. "Because my trip is being in charge. That's my fantasy, see? And being suffocated by a woman wouldn't fit in."

"And what if the woman doesn't like your fantasy? Maybe she has her own trip. What do you do then?"

Carlock moved his head very slowly to one side, keeping his eyes on Loomis, then taking a quick glance at Haun and back again. For a moment, his face had the same look that was on the Doberman's. Then he shrugged.

"Nothing," he said. "I call her a cab and that's the end of it. That doesn't happen very often, though."

"You sure you don't slap her around a little bit first?"

Carlock rolled his head back briefly, as though he were stretching sleepily.

"I don't know what anybody's told you," he said, his voice slowing and softening, "but if I'm hit, I hit back. Everyone's got a right to self-defense, don't they? Has anyone filed any charges against me?"

"Not so far. Your name has just come up here and there."

"Well, then."

Loomis went ahead and asked him about the dates in question, ran the girls' names by him, looking for a re- action. If there was anything there, it wasn't close to the surface, and the alibis were ones that would be easy to check. He closed the notepad at last and put it away, saying, "We may be back."

"You like listening to me talk about my sex life?" Carlock asked, grinning.

Loomis stood up and the dog gave a sudden lunge, jerking Carlock's arm out straight, but his grip held. Loomis surprised himself by not flinching.

"You know," he said, "if that dog got loose and came at me like that, I'd have to kill it."

Carlock stared back at him for a moment, then glanced away with an angry expression.

"You can't come in a man's house and kill his dog," he said. "I don't care who you are."

"You could always file a complaint afterward," Loomis said.

"Okay. Madsen left work late, after dark, on her way to Towne East to do some shopping before she went home, but she never got there. Mosteller went with her boyfriend to a concert at Century II. At intermission, she went to the john and never came back again. Fillmore drove to the main library at night to return a book that was almost overdue, and her car was found in the parking lot there. Nobody ever saw her again. It's the way he plucks them out of the middle of things that gets me. None of those three girls was the kind to go off with someone they didn't know in that kind of situation. That's what the parents always say, but with those girls it was true. And Munoz was the same way. She's downtown with a bunch of her girlfriends, and then the next thing you know she's disappeared forever." Loomis was sitting in his armchair by the window, his fist wrapped around a can of beer. Haun sat on the edge of the bed, holding his own beer in both hands, between his knees, his shoulders hunched forward.

"All but Courter," Haun said. "Courter's different."

"Well, if you mean that she was the type that would go off with someone she didn't know, yeah. Fact is, we know zip about where she was, how she disappeared. She hung out in a lot of odd places . . . "

"Binkley says she was a writer," Haun said.

"Yeah, she was enrolled in a writing course at the university. I read some of her stuff. Not bad, kind of depressing. All about lowlifes, hookers and druggies and like that. She seemed to know a lot about all that, and she wrote a lot about prostitutes, so maybe that's why people said she was hooking. We never actually had any evidence of it, just rumors. The places she liked to hang out . . . maybe it was just to study the people, for her stories. She was kind of a loner, which is unusual for a woman her age. Didn't seem to have any close friends, no roommate. Even her parents didn't seem to have much to do with her. The people in her building said she liked to go out in the middle of the night all by herself, sometimes on foot." Loomis sighed. "In other words, she was a cop's nightmare. We're not even sure what the last time was that anybody saw her alive. We've got her on campus at noon and then maybe in her apartment around eight P.M.; one the neighbors thought they heard her come in or go out. Her car was still parked in front of her apartment, down on South Terrace, when her body was found out west."

"The flowers and the underwear are the only things

that really match," Haun said. "If it wasn't the same killer, it'd have to be someone who knew about that."

Loomis let his breath out in a long sigh, and then belched involuntarily. He didn't like to think too much about there being more than one of them.

"Someone close to us or someone close to the killer," he agreed reluctantly. "Maybe a pair, like the two guys in L.A., but working separately. Or maybe someone on our side, so to speak."

"Have you tried running down everyone who knew about the flowers?"

"We know who they are. Mostly cops."

"Well, yeah, but what I mean is trying to trace who else could have found out. It's been awhile. People talk, especially when a story . . . I mean a case gets old." He thought a moment. "Did you guys do all the lab work, or was Dr. Eckert involved?"

"We took some of it to the university," Loomis admitted.

"Which means grad students, maybe. What's Goldescu in?"

"Aeronautical engineering."

"He could have a friend in forensic science. I don't know. I'm just thinking that we've gotten some of our best tips from out there sometimes. Off the record, or course. But the university isn't a great place for keeping secrets." He paused, then said, "Courter was connected to the university. So was Munoz."

"I thought you didn't like Goldescu," Loomis said.

"I don't. Actually, I don't like any of them so far. Banks is pathetic. Carlock's too obvious. He's not as tough as he tries to act."

"Our guy isn't necessarily tough," Loomis said, "except with women." He regarded Haun for a moment, then said, "You're starting to get into it, aren't you? Thinking like a cop."

Haun looked back at him blankly, surprised by the observation. "Not really," he said. "I mean, it's interesting, sure, but . . . I'm not personally involved with wanting to catch him. Don't get me wrong. I think that would be a good idea. But it's your job, not mine. I'm just trying to understand."

"That may be the more difficult job," Loomis said.

"I know."

There was a little silence, then Loomis asked, "You'd really be happy just to know who he was, why he does it, that kind of thing, even if he was still out there? You'd be satisfied with that?"

Haun thought about it and then nodded slowly. "It's the way I have to think," he said, "in order to see clearly. I'm the guy with the camera. You're the guy with the gun. You have to feel the way you do, to do your job." He hesitated, then asked, "How would you feel if you knew who he was, but you couldn't do anything about it? It'd drive you crazy, wouldn't it?"

For a second, Loomis thought Haun meant that literally, not only as a figure of speech. "I wouldn't be happy," he agreed. "Still, it'd be better than not knowing at all. At least I could keep an eye on him."

"You wouldn't try to do something anyway?" Haun asked. "You'd stick to the law? Knowing he was going to keep on killing?"

They looked one another in the eye for a long moment, and it was Loomis who looked away first. He was good at staring down people like Carlock, but there was something in Haun's eyes he had to look away from—not a challenge but a greedy kind of interest that made him feel uncomfortable.

"I don't know," he said. "That's hard for me to imagine. For that matter, I can't imagine how I could know for sure who he was and not be able to do something legal about it."

Haun nodded, dropping his gaze. "Yes," he said, as though he'd lost interest in the topic. "It's unlikely." He lifted his beer can, found it empty and set it down again.

"There's more in the icebox," Loomis told him.

Haun stood up. "What I really need," he said, "is directions to the john."

"Outside and down the hall, the other way from the stairs."

Haun went out the door, pausing first to scan the apartment, as if memorizing it.

There was something strange about Haun, Loomis thought, some private agenda. Maybe that was why he had invited him up to the apartment, a place where few of his colleagues had ever been. Maybe that was it—just that Haun was an outsider, someone who'd go back into his own world eventually. Or maybe it was that they had something in common—two men living alone, after having lost their families. But that wasn't quite right; Haun still had his son. Apparently the boy was off somewhere, staying with relatives. Loomis frowned, thinking that Haun acted as though the son, too, were dead, as though he were all alone, though when he tried he couldn't put his finger on anything Haun had said or done to give that impression. Maybe he was mistaken.

He looked around at the tiny apartment, seeing it for what it was—just a place to sleep. Maybe he'd never really needed or wanted any more than that. Still, sometimes, usually at three or four in the morning, he felt a kind of desperation about it, imagining himself growing old, becoming a pathetic old man, living out of tuna cans and sacks of fast food, growing a beer belly, not caring about the holes in his clothes. A lot of cops who ended up alone like that wound up swallowing a gun barrel.

He thought about moving, every now and then, but he seemed to have too much inertia. Once he had gone so far as to look at other apartments. That had been because of the time he'd taken Marcie roller skating.

It had been an enthusiasm of hers at the time, maybe still was. They'd gone out to a place at the south edge of town, and then had stuck close to each other, not knowing anyone else. But then the "change partners" skate had been announced and they'd each lined up obediently with their own sexes on opposite sides of the rink. He had watched Marcie be chosen, almost at once, by a boy about her own age, and had been pleased, because she had been one of the first girls picked and because he found that he felt no jealousy about it. Also, he had assumed she'd pick him at the next whistle, so he wouldn't end up standing alone by the railing. But another girl picked him first, a girl about Marcie's age, perhaps thirteen, just as the edge of puberty. He had been simultaneously embarrassed and flattered and, circling the slick floor awkwardly, the girl's tiny hands in his own, he had glimpsed Marcie with yet another boy, frowning back at him. When the next whistle had sounded, he had found himself in a dilemma, self-conscious about choosing some younger girl, yet, feeling Marcie's eyes on him, unable also to select anyone nearer his own age. Finally, he had simply skated off the floor and made himself invisible.

He had realized two things: that Marcie was growing up, becoming a person with a social life of her own, and that she was simultaneously becoming aware of him in the same context. For those reasons, he had spent a day driving around town with an earnest young woman from a rental agency who had promised to find something "super" for him. He had followed her silently and obediently from one townhouse complex to another, all of them looking the same to him, climbing spiraling staircases cut in rough wood, to apartments with sliding glass doors and the chill of central air conditioning, sunlamps built into the bathroom ceilings and sometimes mirrors over the beds, initial anticipation turning gradually into a kind of randy tedium, so that after awhile the only thing he had found to interest him was the rump of his guide, twitching beneath her tight skirt as she led him up the countless stairways.

Something inside him had resisted the thought of bringing Marcie to such a place, having her think of him there, among such people—the young singles haunting the swimming pools and party rooms, their sleek red and black cars under tarps in the parking lots; the solitary older men like himself, keeping out of everyone's way, slipping in and out with their small grocery bags; the divorced women in their groups by the wading pools, watching each other's children splash and fight with one another, their eyes sliding his way behind their dark glasses as he walked self-consciously behind his young guide. Better to have her think of him as he was, in a place that suited him.

Haun came back into the room and went straight to the kitchen, getting another couple of beers out of the icebox, and handing one to Loomis as he went back to the bed to sit down. "Has your wife remarried?" he asked.

Loomis shook his head, a little surprised that the question didn't bother him, coming from Haun. "There's a guy she sees," he said. "A professor." It embarrassed him to say that, but only because he supposed Haun would read more into it, more pain, than he actually felt. "Actually," he said, "Edie and I have a pretty good relationship, pretty friendly. I can see Marcie, my daughter, anytime. It's all very . . . relaxed. There never was the kind of nastiness you hear about, custody battles, that kind of thing."

"An amicable divorce," Haun said. "Did you know it was coming?"

"What? The divorce?"

"The breakup. My counselor says most men are caught by surprise by things like that. Unless it's them who initiate it, of course."

It interested Loomis that Haun was still seeing a counselor a year after his wife's death, and that they talked about breakups, divorce. Why would that be? "I knew something was happening," he said. "I knew things were going bad. I didn't know what to do about it, but I can't really say it surprised me. I guess maybe it surprised me a little that it happened so quickly, once things started rolling. How easy it was, I mean."

"Easy?"

"All I mean is, once you get past a certain point, it all has a momentum of its own. It's easiest to just keep going."

"You would have liked to turn it around?"

"Sure. But it's hard to discuss anything when you don't really understand what's going on."

"Were there things you didn't know about?"

Loomis studied him for a moment, thinking he knew what he meant. "There wasn't any infidelity involved, for either of us," he said. "But there are always things you don't know about, aren't there?"

Haun nodded. "And they don't tell you," he said. "They want you to figure it out on your own, to be sensitive enough to know what's wrong. And if you can't, they hold that against you."

Loomis was surprised by the bitterness in that. He thought about other survivors he'd known who'd been angry with the dead, feeling guilty about issues that hadn't been resolved. That was most often the case with the families of suicides.

"Sometimes they don't know what's wrong themselves," he pointed out.

"But they still expect you to do something about it, to save them from it," Haun said. The words were belligerent, but his voice had fallen back into its normal tone, measured and reflective. The words were even a little imprecise, slurred by the beer. "You know," he said, "those women's magazines, they have all these articles on commitment. But it's only the man they're talking about. You ever notice that? they're like business magazines, like how to look for the safest investment in a man. And being prepared to cut your losses and run if it goes bad. The women, I mean. The men are supposed to be committed."

Loomis pursed his lips. "I don't read those magazines," he said. "I do read men's magazines occasionally, and I don't think I'd want to be judged by what's in them."

Haun nodded, staring at the opening in his beer can as though there were something fascinating inside that he could not quite make out.

"Yeah, you're right," he said. "I'm a little drunk." Then he grinned. "What kind of magazines do you think the Strangler reads?" he asked.

8

It was still early for someone used to working the late desk, and the beer had made him hungry, so Sam drove north from Loomis's apartment, thinking of getting something to eat at one of the drive-ins on the edge of the downtown area. Stopping at the light on Maple, he realized that this was the same intersection where Mrs. Evelyn Hardesty, an old woman driving home from a friend's house, had glanced at the car beside her to see the young woman in the passenger seat give her a stricken look and mouth the word *Help*. She hadn't done anything about it, thinking it was a joke of some sort, young folks making fun of her, but that had been the night Sarah Mosteller had disappeared from Century II, and Mrs. Hardesty had come forward later. Even under hypnosis, however, she had been unable to supply a useful description of the driver or the car.

At the concert, earlier that same night, another young woman had been approached by a man who asked her to come hold a rear door open for him so that he could load some of the musicians' instruments into a van. She had told him to wait for her fiancé, who was in the john, but the man had simply shaken his head and walked away. Later, no one could identify him among the workers at Century II. The woman he had approached described him as looking "just like a million other guys." She had thought he might have had a light mustache, but wasn't sure.

Following Loomis around, Sam had come to appreciate how apt that phase was: "just like a million other guys." How many men there were, in truth, scattered about the city, who had the appropriate background, the necessary psychological makeup. The Strangler was not necessarily a dark mystery after all, not an alien. He was probably someone more familiar than that, someone who, starting with the same potential so many seemed to have, had found a way to release it, to let go of the restraints most people took for granted, were scarcely even aware of.

There were enough facts known about the Strangler to cover barely three pages of the notebook Sam had begun. It was well established that he had type A blood, but there was still some technical difficulty with a more precise match. Some of the bodies had been covered with dust and tiny plastic fibers, suggesting an automobile's floor mat, perhaps a trunk mat—but that was from six years ago. Beyond that, there was a lipstick cap found near Marty Madsen's body—not the type she used, and perhaps having nothing to do with the killing—a bloody heel print in the mud near Jeannie Courter's body and—though he hadn't known it before today—the flowers and the underwear.

Loomis had also given him a list of the girls' missing belongings—clothing, jewelry, the contents of their purses—things he hoped the killer might have kept.

There had been a bear pendant Karen Munoz's mother had given her, the aviator watch Marty Madsen had worn, a handful of other things that might be identifiable. One item had already turned up: the book Terry Fillmore had intended to return to the library the night she disappeared had been found in the outdoor book drop a week later. It seemed to Sam a fascinating detail, but Loomis pointed out that someone might simply have found it and returned it.

The light changed and he drove on, turning east at Douglas to join the flow of young people in their cars along the main drag, the night lights of the downtown buildings gleaming dimly above the muted headlights, and was swept along with them under the railroad bridge and past the newspaper building, its third-floor lights burning brightly at the last edge of downtown before the long stretch of darkness where the cars accelerated briefly before emerging into the next pool of brightness at Grove. There, green-reflectorized signs with arrows pointed north to the interstate, the direction he and Loomis had driven earlier.

There was a drive-in there also, catercorner from the high school he'd attended for a couple of years, when his mother had lived in Wichita. He walked the wheels carefully over the short, steep entrance ramp, remembering scraped car bottoms. Inside, standing in line with jostling, wise-cracking teenagers, he found himself looking unconsciously for familiar faces.

The girl at the counter was named Doris; the name was stitched on her blouse, just at the place where her left breast began its slope. She had large, round breasts, and he found himself watching how the fabric of her

157

buttoned uniform blouse tightened and gapped as she moved. Despite her wide-hipped, buxom build, she was very short, and had piled her hair high on top of her head, perhaps to give herself stature. She was about the same age as the copy girl Kelly Jo, perhaps even a year or two younger. The dark eye shadow made it hard to tell.

He got his order and took it to one of the tiny tables by the side window, feeling self-consciously adult but liking the fluid atmosphere, the invisibility possible within the shifting crowd, preferring that for the moment to the dark car with its burnt-out dash lights.

Since Clare's death, he had found that he liked to be alone in this way—in the midst of life and movement with which he was not himself engaged; perhaps it had always been a part of him, only now becoming more pronounced. He had found that the county zoo, out at the northwest edge of the city, was nearly ideal, and he sometimes drove out there in the mornings when the crowds were small. The presence of the animals, the absence of people, of any threat of human interaction, was just what he wanted at those times; it made him feel safe, content. He could sit for an hour or more on one of the concrete benches, not looking at anything in particular, listening to the animal sounds and the rustle of wind on the surface of the nearby lake. During a counseling session once, Margaret Kerns had told him to close his eyes and think of the place where he felt most happy and at peace; the early-morning, unpeopled zoo was what he had thought of, though he had not told her that, not wanting to have to try to explain it. He had pretended to have difficulty thinking of anything, and then had described an empty beach at sunset, the sounds of the waves and the seagulls—all images he had acquired from movies and television. He had never been to a beach like that.

He looked at Doris again and saw her stretching to place an order into a clothespin hanging above the grill, the uniform pressing tightly enough against her hips to show the outline of her bikini panties. Turning around again, she smoothed her blouse against her stomach absentmindedly, so that the fabric pressed and defined her breasts.

It occurred to him that it might be in this distant, casual way that the Strangler selected his victims, that it might easily be him sitting at this tiny table, appraising this girl named Doris with hardly even a tremor of real passion, his thoughts filled with the necessary detail of the project—how to isolate her, then how to secure her attention, her interest, her acquiescence. And then there was all the rest of it to think of, especially the flowers. The Strangler, too, would have his tentative plans, his fallback options, his deadlines. Surely there had been failures, times when the prepared bouquet had to be thrown away—and perhaps other times when an opportunity presented itself and the necessary props were not at hand. That might even explain Courter, the difference in the flowers, the unusual ferocity. Maybe there had been some special, personal dimension of Courter, something that had overwhelmed his normal caution, impelled him to take her even when he was unprepared. Sam remembered mystery novels he had read in which only one of a series of victims was the true victim, the one the murderer really wanted to kill, all the rest distractors. But if that were the case, it would surely have been foolish to stop with the real one. And why start up again suddenly after six years? It couldn't be anything that simple, that rational.

Still watching Doris surreptitiously as he finished his food and nursed his soft drink, he remembered how he had also studied Stosh, sizing her up in much the same way. That thought troubled him for a moment. What was the difference? His interest had not been primarily in Stosh but in what she represented to him—Rule. But wouldn't something much the same be true of the Strangler? Surely the identity of his victims was irrelevant to him. Surely he was also striking out, through them, at something else, something they represented to him, to which they seemed to provide an access he could find no other way.

He got up, feeling edgy now, and left the drive-in, avoiding the traffic on Douglas and driving north a few blocks before heading back toward the river and home. He hadn't noticed that it had grown overcast, but now it began to rain lightly, little more than a mist, though it made the streets wet, reflecting the light from the street lamps, and made the cars glisten as their tires whispered over the damp concrete. The moist wind swirling now and then inside the car, between the open windows, made him feel better, and he drove more slowly, feeling himself relax, begin to grow sleepy.

He stopped for a red light at the odd Y-shaped intersection where Central split in two, looping along the smaller branch of the river, and sat for a moment, no other traffic around, just himself and the dark car, rattling softly as it idled. In front of him, beyond the streaked windshield was one of the big apartment complexes that curved along the river, across from the older neighborhood where he lived. He remembered with a kind of dull surprise that that was where Stosh lived. It began to rain harder, and a strong gust of wind came through the front seat, spattering him with water and making him roll his window halfway up. Headlights swept the nearest parking lot, then blinked out, stopping in one of the covered bays at some distance from the nearest building. His light changed and he turned into the curve, driving slowly along the edge of the lot. A woman—not Stosh—was moving from one patch of lamplight to the next, in and out of darkness, in and out of the rain, making her way from her car to her door.

Watching her disappear and reemerge, he wondered if this might not be more the Strangler's style after all—locating the time and place, and waiting for whatever victim came along, not caring who it might turn out to be. Perhaps Loomis and his men should not be looking for a person at all, but rather for a likely spot, something like a watering hole in the jungle, where the lion might come to drink with the zebra, and then lie nearby in the tall grass and wait. He slowed nearly to a stop, watching the woman pause at a door and then disappear inside. He let out a long breath and accelerated, heading to the river bridge.

At home, he found he had left the back door open and rain had come in through the screen, puddling on the kitchen floor. He closed the door, not stopping to wipe it up, and went into his bedroom—not the one he and Clare had shared, but the one that had been

161

Debbie's. Sometimes, in the dark now, there was something frightening to him about the other, and he often preferred to sleep here.

He didn't turn the lights on, but sat on the edge of the narrow bed, listening to the silence of the house, the rustle of the rain outside the half-open window, feeling himself alone, disconnected. It would be a good night to sleep, but he didn't feel ready to sleep. He didn't feel like doing anything else, either—not turning on any lights, not going to the living room to watch TV or to finish reading the journals. He could name the things he didn't want to do, but not the thing he desired.

Suddenly it seemed to him that his notion of taking Stosh away from Rule was absurd, foolish. He probably could not do it, and even if he could it probably would not bother Rule much. Why should it, if he chose his women so casually, so indifferently? He frowned, realizing that that was the Strangler he had been thinking of, not Rule. Surely, in fact, Rule was not indifferent at all; surely he chose women for something in themselves that he recognized, that responded to him. Surely the loss of Stosh would be a real loss to him, as no doubt the loss of Clare had been.

Sam lay back, his feet still on the floor, his eyes staring into the dark. For a long time he had thought of Rule and himself as being opposite, at the two ends of a pole. But now the Strangler—the dark man, as Sam had begun to think of him—had confused things, insinuating himself somehow as the third point of a triangle. Which of the other points was he nearest to—Rule, who also took his pleasure where he found it, without regard for the consequence to others, or Sam, who was evidently prepared to use a particular woman who happened to be appropriately situated for his purposes? He had grown interested in the dark man, he knew, despite his original intentions—but what was it that interested him really? By hunting that quarry—with only a camera, as he had told Loomis—did he expect to learn more about the more serious quarry he hunted? Or was it that he needed to study the dark man to learn his aptitudes, knowing he would need some of that ruthlessness to finish the job he had given himself? He had an odd, incongruous vision suddenly of Stosh and Davy huddled together, frightened, as though threatened by a common peril, himself. And of course it was not incongruous; it was apt. He understood that he could have no illusions about what he intended, that neither of them deserved whatever pain he might cause them, that if he were to proceed he must find some way, as the Strangler presumably had, to give himself permission to cause that pain, to act without remorse. And what of Rule? Would that make him different from Rule, or the same? He fell asleep imagining the triangle—himself and Rule and the dark man—as a forking of two paths, much like the place where the street branched within the loop of the river, and trying to see where each path led, what victim awaited him at the other end.

9

"That's the wife," Jerry Majors said.

Following his nod, Stosh saw a woman sitting in one of the uncomfortable grade-school desks along the rear wall of the day-room, staring at a cup of coffee that she made no move to touch.

"The guy was driving home from work, going through the intersection at Hillside and Murdock and, *bing*, a bullet comes right through the window on the passenger side, never even touches the car, hits him right in the side of the head," Jerry tapped the side of his own head, to show the spot, closing one eye as he did so, as if feeling some of the pain himself. "He went over the center line and hit a pickup truck. Lucky nobody else was killed." He gave a massive yawn, covering his mouth.

"Late night?" Stosh asked.

"Stakeout."

"Something interesting?"

He squinted at her and said, "First off, there's no such thing as an interesting stakeout. Second, the last time I told you something I got my ass chewed by Captain Loomis."

"You mean ... when my boss was up here? I didn't tell Loomis you told me anything."

Jerry shrugged. "Maybe he gave everyone the same going-over, and I just felt guilty. Anyway, there's some kind of pressure coming down not to talk to anyone about you-know-what. They're goin' around askin' everyone if they might have already let something slip, who they might have told it to. Regular interviews."

"Internal affairs?"

"No, not like that. More like, 'We're not gonna do anything to you. We just want to know.' Of course, everybody's clamming up. Like me, right now."

Stosh nodded. "But you can talk to me about this shooting," she said, nodding toward the woman on the bench.

"Sure. Why not? I don't know anything about that."

"What do you think about it?"

He made a face. "I think it was probably some kid fooling around with a gun, got lucky."

"You mean unlucky."

"Yeah, that's what I mean, all right."

They both glanced at the young woman who was so suddenly a widow, then away again. Jerry shook his head.

"She's got a kid at home," he said. "The husband worked at a muffler shop. Not a whole lot of money, I guess."

Stosh nodded.

"It'll turn out to be some kid," Jerry said. "And they won't do anything to him. Guy might as well've got hit by lightning."

"What can you do?" Stosh asked.

"Take away the guns, for starters. Sometimes it seems like everybody in this fucking town carries a gun, pardon my French. You remember that thing downtown, the woman with the boyfriend and the husband?"

Stosh shook her head. "What happened?"

"Guy's driving along, sees his wife and her boyfriend in another car. This is right downtown, Douglas and Topeka. Middle of the day. They're all stopped at a light. He gets out, pulls his piece, starts shooting at them. The boyfriend jumps out of his car, pulls his gun out, returns fire. You can see this, can't you? Everybody ducking down inside their cars, people on the sidewalks don't know whether to shit or go blind. Pardon me. Anyway, the next thing, the woman jumps out, she pulls her gun out of her purse, she starts blazing away, too. I don't remember now which one of them she was shooting at. Nobody hit anybody."

"Like those two real old guys," Stosh said.

Jerry laughed. "Yeah, that old-folks apartment house over on Hydraulic? Empty their guns at each other from about six feet and never touch a hair. What were they arguing about?"

"I think it was a woman." They both laughed, making the woman look up, so that they sobered quickly, and Jerry went back to his desk. Stosh stayed where she was for a moment, getting up her nerve, then walked over to where the woman sat.

"Can I get you some more coffee?" she asked. The coffee cup was still full, but had obviously gone cold.

The woman looked at her, and then at the coffee cup as if it had materialized in front of her at that instant.

"No, thanks," she said. She touched the cup tentatively. perhaps just to see if it was real, then put her hands back in her lap.

Stosh eased into the chair next to her, putting the notepad on the desktop. "My name's Stosh Babicki," she said. "I'm with the *Mid-American*."

The woman looked up again, and then held out one hand. "I'm June Crandall," she said. Her hand was so tiny it made Stosh feel large and ungainly.

Stosh's mind went blank. She suddenly had no idea what to ask the woman. She saw herself as a TV reporter, asking "How do you feel?" and thrusting the microphone forward. It would all take five seconds, no conversation, no real engagement. But perhaps that was what the readers wanted, to know how it would feel to have someone, and then to have him disappear suddenly, without reason. Stosh understood that; what she lacked was the ability to pretend that this woman would be able to answer such a question in a sentence or two. What would she say if someone asked her how she felt about Frank now? She couldn't even explain it to herself.

"I don't really have anything to ask you," she said at last. "I just thought . . . if you feel like saying anything, if you want to talk I'm here."

The woman frowned. "I can't think of anything to say," she said. She sounded apologetic, afraid of disappointing. "I'm not sure what happened," she added. "They told me to wait here."

Stosh felt a chill of apprehension. Could it be the woman didn't know her husband was dead?

"You don't have to say anything," Stosh told her, now wanting just to get away. "If at some point you feel that you want to make a statement, if you have something you want to say, you can call me." Hurriedly, she fished a business card out of the side pocket of her purse and handed it over. The other woman looked at it for a long time, then seemed to remember what it was and put it carefully into her own purse. Someone called June Crandall's name from the other side of the dayroom, making her jump, so that the coffee sloshed on the desktop. Stosh grabbed the cup to keep it from sliding off.

"Would you come with me, please?" It was a black policewoman, impossibly young and looking far more nervous than June Crandall, who got up calmly and followed her out the doorway into the hall.

Stosh sat where she was for a moment, feeling as though she had failed some test, learned something about herself she would rather not have known.

"Stosh." It was Jerry again, beckoning to her from the front desk. She got up and walked over to him.

"It was a woman," he said in a low voice. "About two blocks away. Some kids were teasing her dog and she fired a couple of rounds over their heads, to scare them off."

"Is she in custody?"

"Nah, not yet. They'll probably go for negligent homicide, but everybody knows it was an accident, and they'll bargain it down to discharging a firearm in the city limits, something like that. Or else she'll get suspended on the other charge. She won't do a day."

"That doesn't seem fair."

Jerry shrugged. "It's the bad people we're really after, not the stupid ones. The jails are full enough already."

"But somebody got killed."

"Like the lawyers say, not every harm has a remedy."

She had a cup of coffee in the city building lunchroom and was feeling better by the time she ran into Loomis in the hallway.

"You have a minute?" she asked him.

"Sure." But he stood where he was, not moving toward his office, indicating that he wanted to avoid a lengthy interview.

"I just wanted to check on the murder investigation."

He shrugged. "I haven't got anything new for you on that. The physical evidence is still being processed. We're still questioning people."

She thought about asking whether the department was really cracking down on leaks, and why, but decided not to take the chance of getting Jerry's ass chewed again.

"Where's Haun?" she asked.

Loomis nodded in the general direction of his office. "Going through the files."

"He must be in hog heaven."

"The main thing he's finding out is that police work is boring as anything else."

"How are you two getting along?"

"Oh, just fine." There was something in the way he said it that told her he didn't want to be asked about that, that made her feel like an outsider. It was something she was familiar with, having grown up with older brothers.

"Well," she said, "I guess there's nothing more for us to talk about."

He didn't say anything, only waited politely.

"Guess I'll go have some lunch then," she said, and as soon as she'd said it, felt stupid and self-conscious, thinking it must have sounded as though she were angling for an invitation, or for him to join her. She felt flustered, but realized that saying anything to counter that impression would just make everything worse. So she turned away, hoping she wasn't blushing visibly, and hurried to the elevator.

"See you later," he called after her.

Back at the newspaper, she had trouble shaking the feeling that she'd made a fool of herself, both in the abortive interview with June Crandall and the encounter with Loomis. It was as though, having learned about Frank, she was no longer competent to deal with anyone, just staggering along from one gaffe to another. Fortunately, there was a lot to do to keep her from worrying about things. There'd been a train derailment up north, with a poison gas leak, and three whole towns had been evacuated. Cubbage seemed intent on repopulating them by sending most of the newsroom to the scene; he asked Stosh to spend the afternoon in the office, taking up the slack on general assignment.

And there was a lot of slack, but it was mostly telephone stuff: tracking down a rumor that the city manager had been offered a job in a larger town, finding out about a trip that one of the local high school choirs was going to be making in the fall, putting together a story detailing all the activities the park commission had planned for kids the rest of the summer.

"I need to do this every now and then," she told

Cubbage at one point. "It reminds me how much I like the police beat."

At midafternoon, she finally took a break, going to the lounge on the second floor, which was empty, and allowing herself a secluded cigarette. It looked like this thing with Frank was going to have her smoking full-time again soon.

She found herself in the curious position of believing what Haun told her while still, in another way, not believing it, continuing to imagine that it might be some sort of misunderstanding or lie. She realized that this was not a rational way of looking at things, that this doublethink itself was an indication of how far out of her control things had gotten. But she couldn't seem to find her way back to any sort of stable ground at the moment, and was leaning on work and cigarettes until a decision point came along that she couldn't avoid.

One thing she had been considering—as tempting as it was improbable—was that both Frank and Haun might be telling the truth. That would be possible if Clare had been special to Rule, just as she was, had been the only other woman he'd revealed himself to. The fact that he had made no reference to the affair with Clare, even omitting the name, lent strength to the idea. Of course that would be the one he found it most difficult to talk about. It wasn't a particularly flattering scenario—seeing herself as a kind of rebound replacement for someone else who had died—but it was preferable to the other way of looking at things. wherein she and Clare both were only the last two in the long line of pushovers. Thinking about it, she nearly persuaded herself that Frank had given her little hints about a special woman, one other who had been different.

Eventually, she knew, she would have to ask him about it—ask him specifically about Clare Haun, and what Sam Haun had told her. But she didn't know when that would be. She wasn't ready for it now, that was certain. In fact, she had no idea what she'd say or do the next time she saw Frank, and was avoiding him because of that uneasiness. He was becoming a frightening figure again in her mind, much as he had been after the long-ago dream.

She sighed and stubbed out the cigarette. It was beginning to look as though this weekend would be one of the rare times when Frank waited in vain at the Sears package pickup. She couldn't see herself going to meet him there unless something happened in the interim to make things clearer to her, and she couldn't see that happening without talking to Frank. Maybe she would be able to work up to that, but not yet, not today. Walking back up to the newsroom, she had the disagreeable feeling that she had somehow become a passenger within her own life, waiting to learn what her destination would be.

The rest of the afternoon, she kept expecting Frank to call her, but he didn't. When she glimpsed him occasionally, in his office or across the newsroom, he seemed engrossed in other things, utterly inaccessible to her. When Cubbage finally told her to go home, she went down alone, in the empty elevator, filled with pity and loathing for herself.

The door opened on the first floor to reveal Haun

lounging against the opposite wall. She nodded, embarrassed, and hurried past him, expecting him to get on the elevator. Instead, he turned and walked beside her, toward the back door.

"On your way home?" he asked.

She nodded. "It's been kind of a crazy day."

He looked blank for a second, then said, "Feel like a beer over at Good's?"

She started to shake her head, but Haun said, "Please. I wanted to apologize for the way I talked the other night. I'm not quite sane yet, I guess. I'm seeing a counselor, the whole bit. I just wanted to tell you you shouldn't pay too much attention to what I say."

She watched him looking straight ahead as he spoke, not looking at her, and then she surprised herself by saying, "Actually, a beer sounds good right now. I'll meet you there."

She hadn't been to Good's since her first year on the paper—what she thought of wryly as her "single" days. Someone had told her that the place was actually named "The Good Tavern"—there was no one named Good—but its patrons had begun calling it Good's, and the name had stuck. If it was true, they had even changed the sign out front. Haun got there ahead of her; she found him sitting in the booth farthest from the door, beyond the air conditioner whose hum covered all conversation. It was early yet and there were no other customers. It seemed odd to her to be there in the daytime, with sunlight filtering through the splits in the window curtains, the jukebox and the pinball machine silent. It reminded her of a campus tavern where she'd gone to study sometimes, back in college, in the mornings when it had been deserted. When he saw her come in, Haun got up and went to the bar, bringing back a couple of draws.

"So how's it going?" she asked. "Anything you can talk about?"

He gave her a tiny smile. "You mean about the Strangler?"

"Yes, but . . ."

He nodded. "They're still doing interviews, re-checking old suspects."

"There seems to be some kind of crackdown among the cops themselves," she told him, wanting to sound as though she too knew something about what was going on. "Everyone's clamming up about the case, and I was told people on the force are being interviewed."

Haun looked pensive for a second, then said, "Loomis told me a cop could fit the profile they've drawn up. Maybe they're getting desperate."

"So Loomis hasn't fallen in love with anyone in particular."

"I beg your pardon?"

She laughed, pleased to have puzzled him. "That's something they say," she explained. "When they're sold on a particular suspect, they say they've fallen in love with him."

"Ah. I know what you mean. They talk about liking this guy or not liking that guy. It confused me for a while because most of these guys aren't very likable." He laughed.

"So how about you? Have you fallen in love?"

He shook his head. "I like them all," he said, "but I haven't found Mr. Right." His smile faded and he said,

"You know, there are an awful lot of men out there who could be the one. The right profile, I mean. The right background, the whole thing."

"Gee, that's a comforting thought."

"I fit," he said offhandedly, sitting back in the booth, seeming neither proud nor dismayed by the observation. "All it really takes is to be a male living alone, a little bit crazy, with something against women. There are a lot of guys like that."

"Do you have something against women?"

His smile returned, but there was something disconcerting about it now. "You don't dispute the part about me being a little bit crazy," he said. "Don't you think a psychiatrist would say I probably have some anger?"

"You said you're seeing a shrink. What does he say?"

"She. It's a woman." He laughed softly. "Maybe that proves the point, though." He was silent for a moment, then added, "She isn't really a shrink. She's just a psychologist, at the university counseling center. Merow put me in touch with her."

"She thinks you're angry at all women? Not just Clare?"

"Well . . . she keeps reminding me that Clare isn't all women."

"She's right about that."

"Oh, I know." The topic seemed to bore him. He was silent for a moment, as though casting about for something else to talk about. She took a sip of beer, conscious of a new tension between them that kept their eyes from quite meeting. She looked toward the bar, the long mirror behind it, the far wall where the pinball machines stood and, finally, almost surreptitiously, at

Haun, who, to her surprise, was now sitting patiently, watching her, as though waiting for her to finish her inspection of the place.

"Tell me about Clare," she said impulsively. She had been thinking quite a bit about Clare since Haun's revelations.

"Who?" he asked, and then smiled and shook his head. "It's impossible to describe the people you know best. To me, she was just . . . Clare, that's all."

"Well, what did she look like?"

He squinted, as though that might help him see her better in his memory. "Well . . . she was short. A little shorter than you, I'd say. She had dark hair, blue eyes. Not bright blue; sort of dark blue, almost purple sometimes. There was something kind of Mediterranean about her, although her family was German on both sides. She was in good shape, toward the end. She worked out." He made a face and took a swallow of beer.

"You didn't like her working out?"

He gave her a wry smile. "It wasn't me she did it for," he said. After a moment, he said, "I always thought of her as a shy person, but most people wouldn't have thought so because she was also very outgoing. She'd get everybody talking, you know, organize games, be the center of things. But she was really shy. I can't . . ." He seemed to search for words, and give up. "I can't explain it," he said.

"What did she do?"

"You mean her job? She worked at a private employment agency. She went there looking for a job herself, and they hired her to interview people. I guess that in

176

itself tells you something about her. She had a way of making people want her."

"So you worked different shifts? The two of you?"

"Yes. And the kids spent a lot of time at the sitter's." He gave a little impatient shrug and said, "Let's talk about you for awhile."

She pursed her lips, wanting to press on, having grown interested in the interview,, but then shrugged and said, "I had a very normal upbringing. Nothing worth talking about."

"Is that so? What kind of a name is Stosh?"

"A boy's name, actually. It's the Polish version of Stan. I had six older brothers, and I used to try to hang around with them, act like a boy, you know? So my oldest brother, Danny, he was so much older than me he was more like an uncle, really, he started calling me Stosh, kind of as a joke. So everybody called me that from then on. Except my parents."

"What do they call you?"

"My real first name."

He waited for her to go on, but she shook her head and said, "I don't tell."

"Must be good."

"I guess. But it never seemed to fit me. I was glad to have the nickname. If you really want to know, you can find out from personnel. Frank did." She'd forgotten all about that until just now.

"No kidding." Suddenly Sam seemed genuinely interested. He might have been someone who was writing a biography of Frank and had just found another little bit to put in it.

She sighed. "He acted like it was a kind of joke on me. Said it was his old reporter's instincts coming out." She shrugged. "On the other hand, I checked out his alibi, so I guess we're even."

"You know, he was never really a reporter," Haun said.

"Sure he was."

Hank shook his head. "Only while he was in college, for one summer, on his father's newspaper. He covered high-school sports. In the summer. When school was out. Get it?"

She tossed down the last of her beer, feeling called upon to defend Frank. "Whatever else you may think about him." she said, "he is a good journalist. He's a pro. You've worked with him enough to know that."

"You want another?" Haun asked. Without waiting for her response, he got up and went to the bar, coming back with two full glasses. "I promise you that I will never look up your real name," he said, sitting down again, then added, "Unless I have to write a story about you, of course."

She laughed, a bit troubled by something in his tone, but then she raised the glass he'd brought her in a mock toast. "Fair enough."

After another beer or two—somewhat more than she'd intended to have—they decided to get something to eat. The hamburgers at Good's were notoriously bad, so Haun suggested a Chinese restaurant where he and Loomis had eaten recently. She insisted on going home and changing first, and Haun followed her to her apartment and waited outside for her, almost as though he were afraid of going in there again. Freshening up, putting on a summer dress that revealed her shoulders, she felt as though she were going out on a date. Sliding into his car, she thought, Is that what this is now? For a second she had a strange fantasy of Sam rescuing her from Frank. Did she need rescuing? She wouldn't have said so two days before, but now the idea seemed to make a weird kind of sense. She wondered what Sam thought was going on between them. Probably just collegiality, a couple of reporters having dinner together, the way he and Merow might. That thought made her feel good, safe. The other thing suddenly seemed distant and comic, a product of the beer.

At the restaurant, somewhat to her surprise, Sam resumed the conversation about Clare, becoming almost expansive, as though he had been waiting for someone to tell all this to. Perhaps he had. He told her his counselor discouraged him from talking about his wife, insisted on his talking about himself. What he told her now was that Clare had dated his roommate in college, but the roommate had stood her up one night and she had come by the apartment, distraught, looking for him, and she and Sam had ended up spending the evening together, just talking, becoming friends. Apparently they had been no more than friends for a long time after that, though it had been a clandestine sort of friendship, kept secret from the roommate, whom she'd continued to date and who had continued to treat her badly, finally dumping her. She'd come to Sam for consolation, and they'd spent a long weekend together, just the two of them, and by the end of it they'd been lovers.

"She still makes excuses for George," Sam said, and then blinked and said, "I mean, she still did, long after we were married." He paused, then added, "The point of the story is that there's a sense in which I was always second choice, and her first choice was someone who treated her badly. My counselor likes to remind me that I was the one she married, but there's no question she was on the rebound. Who knows what would have happened if my roommate hadn't dumped her?" He shrugged, not seeming all that troubled by the idea. She guessed it was something he had thought about a lot.

She was thinking about her own history, about how many friendships she had had with guys, back in school—having grown up surrounded by brothers had made it seem easy. But she'd had few romantic relationships. That part had been hard. Still is, she thought.

She felt a touch of envy at the way Sam and Clare had apparently managed to combine friendship and romance, at least for awhile, and also a touch of anger at them for letting it get away, for failing to appreciate what they had achieved.

It was dark by the time they left the restaurant, and darker still inside Sam's old car, whose dashboard lights were burnt out. The motor made an odd ratchety sound, and the whole car smelt of oil, making her uneasy about her clothing.

"You should have seen the car I drove before this one," he said. "I paid eighty-five dollars for it. It was a

'58 Plymouth station wagon with no heater and a cracked front windshield. It also had a window that wouldn't roll up and bald tires all around and a transmission that slipped. And it used so much oil that I used to carry around a case of cheap oil in the back and put three or four quarts in whenever the light came on."

She laughed.

"One year," he went on, "we lived in a duplex just off Hillside, and the street we lived on slanted, so that it was uphill to the stop sign at Hillside. In the winter, when there was snow on the street, I'd stop at the stop sign and then I wouldn't be able to move, but I could never tell whether it was the bald tires spinning or the transmission refusing to kick in." He was silent in the darkness for a moment, and she guessed he was smiling at the memory. "Or course, if the weather was really bad, it wouldn't even start. I was working nights, so I didn't go in until two-thirty or so, and you could usually get a gas station to come out and jump it by then. The worst part was getting the kids to the babysitter in the morning."

They stopped at a light and she was able to see his face, which was expressionless, studying the traffic while the engine clicked and rattled, obscuring the evening street noises. After a moment, the light still red, he turned right onto Thirteenth, heading west toward her apartment.

"Clare would get up and feed the kids," he said, "and then she'd get me up when she was ready to leave for work. I'd always been up till three or four the night before, so it wasn't easy, and I was usually in a lousy mood, growling at everybody." He gave a startling bark of laughter. "I'd finish dressing the kids and drive them to the baby-sitter, so I could come back home and sleep for another couple of hours."

His voice ran down as though he'd lost the thread of what he'd meant to say. She turned her face to the window, not saying anything, thinking for some reason of the semester in college, after her brother Danny had died, when she had seemed to lack any will and had stayed in bed all the time, hiding under the covers, not getting up for class, hardly getting up to eat.

"The winter," Haun said. "That's what I started to tell you about. In the winter, we'd pile into the car, the kids and me, hoping it would start, and that we could get enough traction. And the snow would be blowing through the open window, and the kids would be crying." Something changed in his voice and Stosh glanced at him but couldn't read his expression in the darkness. "There were times it wouldn't start," he said, "or I couldn't get it going for one reason or another, and I'd walk them over to the baby-sitter. I did that once in a blizzard. I mean a real blizzard, snow blowing sideways, the whole bit. It was six blocks with snow blowing in our faces and sub-zero temperatures, ice freezing on our faces. At one point I actually thought about knocking on someone's door and asking for help." His laugh was like a gasp of pain. "I was carrying Davy, but Debbie had to walk beside me, and my feet hurt so bad I wanted to cry, so I know hers did, too. And she was crying—both of them were crying. I suppose, by the time we got there, all three of us were crying. The baby-sitter's husband offered me a ride back, but I turned it down. That was my punishment, see, walking back again by myself." He was silent for a moment, perhaps waiting for her to say something, but she didn't.

"The kids both hated that baby-sitter," he said. "They would have walked back with me, if I'd let them. But I had to get back home so I could sleep for a couple more hours and then get up and watch soap operas until it was time to go to work again."

He had pulled into the parking lot at the apartment complex. He stopped the car near her door, the motor running.

"You want to come inside for a minute?" Stosh asked, partly to break the mood he seemed to be sinking into.

At first she thought he hadn't heard, that he was too much caught up in his thoughts of the blizzard, the children, the life he had lived then, but after a moment he said, "I guess so," and he put the car in gear, coasting into a nearby parking slot.

Inside, she led him to the kitchen, turning on lights as she went, and then switched on the radio beside the sink, not liking the silence. The radio was tuned to a station that played mostly oldies. "You want some coffee?" she asked him.

He shook his head and looked around distractedly as if he couldn't figure out now why he had come up with her.

"I would really like a cigarette," she said.

"Sorry. I don't smoke."

"No, I have some. I'm just trying to quit. One of my

rules is that I can't smoke when I'm with someone else."

"I won't tell."

"Thanks. You're a big help." She was debating whether to take him up on that or not when Sam suddenly took a step toward her. She felt a rush over the surface of her body, an expectation of being touched, but he reached past her to the radio, turning up the volume slightly.

"I haven't heard that in years," he said.

She leaned nearer, standing beside him at the sink, intensely aware of their arms barely touching, trying to pick the words out of the lush music.

> *Love*
> *Brings such misery and pain.*
> *I guess I'll never be the same*
> *Since I fell for you.*

"A sad song," she said, and turned toward him, found him looking past her with a faint smile on his face, which deepened as he caught her glance.

"Melancholy songs always make me feel good," he said.

"Aren't you going to ask me to dance?" she asked. She felt suddenly breathless, unsure whether what she felt was anything more than the moment, the drinks they'd had. How easy it seemed, suddenly, the notion of swapping Frank for Sam, how much sense it made. Surely things like this were never that easy and sensible, though.

He looked at her in surprise, and there was one of those moments when she thought she could see the person he really was looking out of his eyes. There was a kind of fear in there, she saw, and she supposed he had just realized how the tenor of the evening had changed, was wondering what to do, perhaps how to flee. For a second, she fully expected him to back away from her, to begin making an awkward exit. But then he opened his arms to her woodenly, his half-smile not fading, and she stepped into them, taking both his hands in hers and pulling his right arm around behind her, encircling her waist.

He looked past her as she moved against him, getting him moving, though the little kitchen was too small and they only swayed, nearly motionless, between the table and the sink counter, their hips brushing the hard surfaces as they turned, and she felt surprising comfortable, despite his own obvious awkwardness, letting herself settle against him, not clinging, not holding tight, only touching, his slender body surprisingly solid after all, not ghostly and intangible as she found she had half-expected.

She thought for a second that he was murmuring something in her ear, but then realized it was the radio, still singing:

> *I guess I'll never see the light.*
> *I get the blues most every night*
> *Since I fell for you.*

"Anastasia," she said softly.

"What?" He leaned away from her slightly, puzzled. "That's me. I'm Anastasia."

He stared at her for a second longer, then suddenly kissed her on the forehead, his lips warm and unexpected, seeming to warm her whole body, and she wound both arms around him, pressing herself against him, and arched her head back to catch his lips with hers, holding him, that way for a long moment, and then releasing him.

He seemed stunned, unable to move or to speak. She reached for his hand again, but this time he did pull back.

"It's too soon, isn't it?" she asked. "I should have known better. You're thinking of Clare, aren't you? I'm so sorry. I guess it's just . . ."

"No," he said. "I was thinking about Rule."

It was her turn to feel stunned, as though she'd been slapped. She stood still, feeling the blood in her face as he shook his head and then turned away from her, going out through the living room to the front door. After a moment, she made herself follow.

At the door, he turned and looked back at her. "I'm sorry," he said. "I guess I shouldn't have said that, but it was the truth. I wanted to tell you the truth." He ran a hand through his hair, looking lost. "I'm no good at these things," he said. "I've always known I wasn't.'

"No," she said, not knowing exactly what she meant by it, only wanting to reassure him, and herself as well, to recapture something she had felt between them— maybe not what she had thought it was, but something good, which she felt she had clumsily crushed.

"He's never been here," she said. What she meant for Sam to understand was that there was still so much of her life that had nothing to do with Rule, that she had kept for herself. But she heard how it sounded—like a plea or an explanation. The kind of thing, perhaps, that Clare might have said, if she'd had the chance.

"I'm sorry," she said stiffly. "It's the drinks. I'm not used to drinking so much."

He gave her a forced smile. "It's not you at all," he said.

She didn't understand that, but she shook her head, denying it. "I'm going to have that cigarette," she told him. "Please don't leave." She went back to the kitchen and found her purse. Her hands trembled as she lit the cigarette, but when she had taken the first deep draw she felt herself steady, become more herself again.

Sam was standing in the hallway with the door half open, his hand on the knob. He had waited, as she asked, but he was still on his way out.

"Maybe if I'd found out about it and she hadn't died," he said, "we could have talked it out. Maybe I would have gotten over it. Or maybe we would have split up. At least it would have been resolved one way or another. Or maybe if she hadn't kept the journals, if I hadn't found out and I could have just mourned her, without all the rest." He shrugged. "You see how it is. I have to find a way out of all this. I know you don't understand what I'm talking about, but I wanted to tell you what was going on."

"I do understand," she said. She went to him and

took one of his hands in both of hers, and he didn't pull away this time.

"The problem," he said, as though he hadn't heard her, "is that Clare was my wife, but she was also my best friend. Maybe I could have stood losing the wife, if only the friend hadn't gone, too. It leaves me with no one to talk to about it." He smiled and shook his head.

That was just how she'd felt when Danny had died in Vietnam, as though she'd been left all alone, as though no one else in the family really counted. She wanted to tell Haun now that she would be his friend, that he could talk to her, but it seemed suddenly too facile, too self-serving, almost less true than it would have been to tell him she loved him, had they ended up in bed, which she realized might well have happened. Love is easy, she thought, appalled by the discovery. You really have to know someone to be friends. She remembered thinking that she and Frank had been friends, she realized that what disturbed her most deeply about the things Sam had told her was the possibility that she might discover that had never been true.

Perhaps her face revealed something, for Sam peered at her suddenly, his expression softening, and then wrapped his arms around her, hugging her tightly, oblivious of the lit cigarette she held away from him in one hand to keep from burning him.

When he let go, he looked at her again, his eyes searching for something, as if to see whether her expression had changed, and she thought for a second he was going to say something, but he didn't. He only gave a small shake of his head and turned away, going through the living room and out the front door, closing it behind him, leaving her standing by herself in the half-lit hallway, still feeling the pressure of his arms, wanting it back.

PART TWO

PART TWO

10

Sam sat in the darkness, the engine off, the radio murmuring to him as distantly as the lost voices of memory. "Baby, baby," it said, "Baby don't leave me, all by myself."

He wasn't listening to the radio; he was staring at the opening in the trees beyond the road, where the woman in the jogging outfit had disappeared a few moments before, leaving her little gray car hidden in the darkness beside the road.

His black Lynx sat on the other side, some distance behind hers, in its own pool of darkness. Just as he had been about to get out, attracted by the cool wind blowing along the river, the other car had come up behind him, grazing him briefly with its lights, and stopped.

He hadn't noticed whether she'd locked the doors or not. If not, it would be simple to get in, hide in the back seat, wait for her return. That was a common enough scenario in simple rape cases, but unlikely for the Strangler, because of the difficulties of later getting rid of both the woman and the car, and the danger of leaving his own parked here, perhaps to be noticed by the police who patrolled the park occasionally. The dark man would be clever enough to get her into his car.

He imagined kneeling in the darkness beside the woman's car, letting the air out of the tires, his head bent close to the stem, so that the hiss of escaping air would drown out the *thrum* and *whir* of insect sounds from the woods and the river. Instead of gloves, to prevent fingerprints, he would have covered his fingertips with a light coating of airplane glue, and he could feel the crust of it, crinkling and tightening as he worked. The glue would have been purchased at some hobby shop, along with a simple makeup kit and some other, innocuous items—nothing that would be remembered. All that would be necessary for a disguise would be a bit of coloring to darken the skin, heighten the cheek bones, and perhaps a small but noticeable chin scar, something to focus the attention.

Standing in the darkness beside his own car, he watched the woman come out of the woods, breathing hard, her arms flapping to a stop against her sides as she finished her run. When she bent over at the waist, her hands on her knees, he could see her every movement clearly somehow, even the sweat glistening on her face and neck, beneath the hair tied up tightly on the back of her head, the swell of breast and hip beneath the baggy running suit, as though there were a dark light shining on her there, illuminating her for him alone.

He saw her notice one of the flats, her head jerking to one side in disgust or anger, her hands on her hips, and he was back inside his car, the engine running, the light on, coming around the curve slowly, going past her

THE LATE MAN

a bit, as though he would drive on, then stopping, pulling the car over, getting out and walking back toward her, the gravel crunching under his feet, feeling as though his own body were ablaze in the darkness.

And when she saw him something happened to her face, a flickering expression that suggested for an instant she knew who he was, what this was all about, as though all that followed were a pretense on both their parts, for then he said, "I noticed the flat tire. Do you need help changing it?" and she said, "There's two of them. I don't know what to do."

He could change one of them and then take the other tire off and take both flats to a service station to be fixed. That's what he told her, and she thought about that and agreed. And after he had changed one tire and removed the other—the gleaming jack hoisting the car effortlessly, the nuts sliding off and on so easily he could have used his hands instead of the tire iron—he carried one flat to his own car, opening the trunk, and she followed him, wheeling the other behind him, and when he opened the passenger door for her, she slid in without hesitating, as though that, too, had been agreed to.

Riding in the car, heading west, she spoke once but he didn't hear what she said because he no longer had to listen, to account to her for what he was doing, and because, too, there was a roaring in his ears, like the roaring inside a seashell, and so he said nothing at all, and after awhile she said something else, spoke twice more, but he still heard nothing, made no response, and so she was silent then also, even when they went past West Street and under the interstate bypass into the dark country beyond the last possible lights of any gas stations that might have fixed her tires.

The place they ended up at was a gigantic ditch, a flood control project, a place where he could drive up and over the lip and down into the flat, grassy slough, hidden on all sides by the terraced levees from everything but the sky. Turning off his lights, getting out, he went about his business for a moment, setting out the things he had prepared, nearly ignoring the woman who remained in the car, silent. There was a blanket he spread out, mashing the clumps of Johnson grass, and a paper sack that held the plastic cord he had bought at a sporting goods store—a lanyard, really, with a little metal loop at one end for a referee's whistle—and the new unused underwear and the plastic bag with the tiny red flowers he had found along the riverbank behind his house.

When everything was ready, he went back to the car and opened her door and waited for a moment, and she got out finally, not saying anything now, and he took her elbow lightly in one hand and steered her toward the blanket, and then stepped back away from her and said, "Take off your clothes."

He could not read her look then—perhaps it was abstracted, as though he had interrupted some reverie—but she began stripping away the jogging clothes as though they were of tissue paper, seeming to tear them from her body, casting them into the darkness that surrounded them, and she knelt on the blanket, and then his own clothes were off, so that he felt the night breeze for the first time against his skin, and he looked out across the slough, at the ridged slopes and the darkness beyond, and had no sense of anything but the silence, or the roaring in his ears, which was nearly the same thing now, and then he knelt beside her, pressing her back gently onto the blanket and covering her with himself, her legs parting at his touch and himself sliding between and then all the way in, without fumbling, as easily and mysteriously as the jack had slid beneath her disabled car, and the same easy, rhythmic movement until there was a lifting, a lifting, and it was done.

And then everything was clear and cold, and what remained was not pleasure but duty. Putting out one hand in the darkness beside the blanket, still holding her body against the earth with his own, he found the paper sack and inside it the lanyard, and brought it up slowly, his face buried against her neck so that he himself could not see what was coming, only raising himself quickly at the end, to bring his hands together and grasp the two ends of the cord, pressing it down against her throat.

And that was where everything froze, the moment he could not see beyond, could only feel himself rising in breathless flight above his own body, from where he looked down upon himself, his pallid form gleaming against the dark square of blanket on the grass, hiding the smaller, stiller form beneath it.

He came back to himself in the car, still at Sim Park, and found that the wind had come up strongly. He could see dimly the movement of the trees against the gray night sky, and there was no moon anywhere. And what about the body, then? he thought. What about the two flat tires in his trunk, the car sitting on the jack with its empty rims? He glanced that way now and saw that the car was gone; the woman had returned from her run and vanished, unnoticed.

From where he sat, there was no light in any direction—even the glow of downtown was obscured by the trees rising along the river—and the wind and the pounding of cicadas among the trees masked whatever city noises might have drifted to him. His senses felt unnaturally acute, as though he could distinguish the sound of each separate insect, determine the movement of each leaf in the dark. He could see the wind moving through the weeds in the pasture at the edge of old Cowtown, back along the riverbank, making a watery motion that flowed up the slope to the riverbank, and, in the pit of dark formed by the bordering river and the cottonwoods, he could imagine that the asphalt road was only a rutted path through an unfenced prairie of the tall grass that grew wild nowhere now.

He could imagine the Cheyenne camping there, in the shelter of the circling trees, beside the river. He tried to picture their squat tepees dotting the pasture slope and felt an unaccountable pang of loss, although, as far as he knew, he was no part Indian. In some of those buffalo-hide homes, he supposed, captives would have lain alone or with their masters—sun-flushed, rough-handed white women taken from the settlements, their past lives burning forever behind them. Some of them, later, given the chance of rescue, had chosen to remain. For some reason, the thought of that brought a chill, making him shiver.

He shook his head, impatient with himself. Time was running out, his deadline approaching—only a week until he was to pick up Davy—and he had done nothing. He had allowed himself to be distracted, by Stosh, by the Strangler, and neither had led him anywhere useful, though both remained obstinately in his thoughts, confusing him when he tried to think clearly about Rule. He had begun to lose interest in the investigation, though he could not shake his interest in the dark man himself. But the sad, angry, pathetic men he had watched Loomis question, in apartment houses, hotel rooms, now and then at the police station, were so far from the powerful figure of his imaginings, the man who was in every way the opposite of a victim, that he had begun to feel it was all futile, as futile as his notion of revenging himself on Rule. He had not seen Loomis for three days, had called in sick one day and then just not shown up after that. No one seemed to notice, although it was also true that he wasn't answering his phone and it had rung two or three times in that span.

Driving back to Malden to pick up Davy without having done what he had intended would be a bitter defeat, an acknowledgment that Rule had won, that Clare had chosen correctly after all. And maybe that was true; it was a possibility that had always lain in the darkness at the back of his thoughts. Now, as it pushed closer to the light, it brought with it that other possibility he'd considered—Plan B, as he thought of it—the one that had kept him from promising Davy that he'd return for him. Instead of pricing makeup kits, looking for flowers or braided lanyards, he had lately, with the same sense of make-believe, the same apprehension as to how near it might come to reality, begun studying the labels of nonprescription drugs, considering how best to seal the cracks and openings of his old garage, investigating in his customary, methodical way all the painless ways of dying.

He started the car now, taking a deep breath, imagining the odorless fumes filling his lungs with a blessed darkness, but finding instead a damp smell in the air, as though rain were coming. In the glow of his lights he saw a frost of dew, or perhaps of condensed breath, on the inside of the windshield. When he turned on the defroster, the burst of air flushed a huge mosquito from one of the vents, big enough that it might have been a wasp or hornet, except that it made no buzzing sound. It skittered along the slanted surface of the windshield, finding no purchase on the wet glass, until he flattened it reflexively with a yellowed newspaper he fished from the floor on the passenger side.

Then he sat for awhile longer, looking at the brown smear on the windshield, the crumpled legs, thinking with some envy how easily and quickly death might come, how odd it was to think the universe would care more about the death of a human than that of a mosquito. None of us is really any more safe than that, he thought. He considered the five dead girls, his cousin Don, his stranger father, the man Stosh had written about who had been shot while driving home, all the graves in all the little country cemeteries, the hidden grave of Debbie's hamster in the backyard and Debbie herself and Clare, beneath their marble lids. Now that they were all dead, were they any more real than the woman in his fantasy a few moments before? The dead girls had been memorialized on the front page; most who died were put in little boxes of type somewhere in the back, and in either case they disappeared, vanishing into tomorrow's concerns. All the obituaries he had written in his months as late man had been the most infinitesimal part of the whole. There was this steady, daily emptying of the world, and yet the world remained full of people, frustrating each other with their carts in supermarkets, crowding the bike paths along the river, shattering the solitude of the zoo, filling the world with noise and inappropriate laughter. And yet each of them, incredibly, was loved, would be missed by someone, as he would be missed by Davy and Gerald and Harriet, perhaps even by Merow; that was the real mystery, it seemed to him, the thing he could neither escape nor understand. He had a comic vision of mosquitoes gathered around the smear on the window, weeping and complaining, as though it had never occurred to them that anything like that could happen, as though it must mean something.

Banks's car was gone, but that was okay. It was the manager Loomis wanted to talk to this time.

His name was Joe Puckett, and he turned out to be a bent, shriveled old man who talked in a whisper—emphysema, Loomis guessed. The hand that opened the door, just a crack, held a lit cigarette.

"Some kind of trouble?" he asked when Loomis showed him his badge.

"I'd just like to chat with you a little bit about one of your tenants. Kirby Banks."

"He in trouble?" It didn't sound as though the possibility surprised him.

"Not exactly. I talked with him a couple of weeks ago

and I'd just like to check a couple of things. It's routine."

"Routine," the old man said, nodding, as though that were the punchline of some familiar, not very funny joke. But he pushed the door further open and turned away, leaving it to Loomis to follow him.

Despite the little air conditioner chugging on its highest setting in one of the windows facing on the alley behind, the living room seemed close and stagnant, steeped in the fossilized odor of burnt tobacco. It was cluttered with furniture whose frilliness and relative congruity seemed to echo the one-time presence of a woman, though the discoloration and worn places, here and there, seemed to suggest that the woman, whoever she had been, was as long gone as the uncounted cigarettes whose ghosts also lingered.

Puckett sank heavily into a slightly cockeyed armchair just beneath the air conditioner, letting go of a walking stick Loomis had not noticed before, so that it fell against the side of the adjacent lamp table, within easy reach. Two or three magazines—*American Bass Fisherman* was one of them—lay piled beneath the lamp.

Loomis sat down on the sofa, catercorner from Puckett, and leaned forward slightly, letting his elbows rest on his knees.

"What do you think of Kirby?" he asked.

Puckett shrugged, not quite returning Loomis's gaze. He looked ill at ease, a man not used to company.

"Don't think nothin' about him," he said. "He pays his rent on time, doesn't make a lot of noise."

"You never had any trouble with him?"

"No."

"He said you wouldn't let him put his bicycle in the garage."

"Well, that's true. But there wasn't any trouble."

Loomis nodded. Actually, that contradiction fit with what he felt about Banks—that he was a man who would avoid confrontation, smile at being rebuffed, then nurse the grievance in private, letting the anger out only indirectly, talking to someone like Loomis himself.

"You mind if I ask you why you wouldn't let him keep it there?" he asked Puckett.

The old man coughed out a burst of smoke, then said, "Not up to me." He blinked, his eyes watering. "The guy up on the second floor rents the garage."

"You don't keep your car there?"

He shook his head. "Got no car."

That was more interesting, because it could mean Banks had lied. On the other hand, it could also be a simple misunderstanding on Banks's part. There were often these little discrepancies that turned out to mean nothing. Still, it was best to make sure. He didn't want to push too hard at that topic, though; a man like Puckett would clam up if he thought the questions were coming too near himself. He'd go on with the routine stuff for awhile, then circle back to the business of the garage and the bicycle.

"Kirby keep to a pretty regular schedule, does he?" he asked.

The old man shrugged again, and then fidgeted in his chair, looking uncomfortable. "Far as I know," he said.

"I don't keep track of 'em, you know. I ain't no fucking housemother. I just collect the rent, take care of stuff."

"Did you happen to notice whether he goes out at night a lot?"

"Yeah, I guess so. He's a young guy. If I was young, I'd go out at night. I hear his TV sometimes."

"What?"

"His TV. I hear him playin' it at night sometimes, when I'm comin' down the hall. So sometimes he don't go out at night."

"Does he have visitors?"

"You mean women?" Puckett shook his head. "Not that I ever noticed. They ain't supposed to have women in overnight. I tell 'em that when I give 'em the keys. 'Course, if they do, there ain't a hell of a lot I can do about it."

"I didn't necessarily mean overnight," Loomis said. "Just anytime."

"Not that I ever noticed," Puckett repeated.

Loomis sighed. He was fishing and Puckett knew it. Might as well go the whole nine yards. "You ever notice anything unusual about him?" he asked.

Puckett shook his head, clearly bored, and gave another painful cough.

Loomis stood up. "Okay," he said. "Thanks for your time."

Puckett reached for his walking stick, rolling slightly on one hip, getting ready to heave himself to his feet, but Loomis held out a hand. "Don't bother to get up," he said. Puckett sank back down.

Loomis put his hand on the doorknob, then turned back as though he'd just remembered something else he wanted to ask. "Where does Kirby keep his bike?" he asked. "I didn't see it outside anywhere."

Puckett jabbed a thumb toward the rear of the house. "Coal cellar," he said.

Haun's voice came back to Loomis as clearly as if he had been in the room, telling him how the slanted door reminded him of his uncle's house. It had nearly clicked then, but it had gotten away. "Coal cellar," he repeated softly. "You don't heat this place with coal, do you?"

Something in his voice made Puckett turn cautious. "No," he said. "There's a gas furnace down there now. Used to be a coal cellar."

"That's the one that has two doors—the slanted door outside and the door from Banks's kitchen?"

"That's right."

"So he's got keys to those padlocks?" Loomis persisted.

"'Course he does. How else he gonna keep his bike there?" Puckett was agitated now, frightened of the new intensity in Loomis's questions. "He takes care of the furnace for me," he said, "so I don't have to go up and down them stairs. That's in exchange for keepin' his bike there. The owner don't mind. It's just a . . ."

"So you don't have the key?" Loomis said.

"The key? Sure I do. I got all the keys, keys to everything. I just don't never have to go down there is all. Like I said."

Loomis hesitated for a second, considering the legalities. Was the cellar part of Banks's rental, under his control?

"Did you promise him you wouldn't go down there?" he asked Puckett. "Was that part of the deal?"

The old man peered at him blankly, one eye blinking in the stream of smoke from his cigarette. "Why would I do that?" he asked.

Loomis nodded. "So you could show it to me," he said.

"What . . . well, sure. You mean right now?"

"If you don't mind.'

The old man obviously did mind, but was wary of refusing. After a second's hesitation, perhaps hoping Loomis might reconsider, he grasped the walking stick and levered himself up out of the chair, then went into his kitchen. Loomis heard metal rattling in a drawer, and then Puckett came back clutching a fistful of keys on a metal loop.

"I'd like to go in through the outside door, not through the apartment," Loomis said. He guessed that all he needed was Puckett's permission, but it was better not to push his luck.

Puckett shrugged and led him slowly into the hall and out the front door, leaning on his stick, then down the porch steps and around the side of the building.

Loomis helped him lift the heavy door, revealing a short flight of concrete steps going down into darkness. Puckett hesitated, obviously hoping Loomis would go down by himself, then made a face and went ahead. Halfway down, he reached somewhere over his head to flick a switch, and a dim light bulb came on. With the old man taking it a step at a time, they descended into a damp, vaguely sour smell, suggestive of mold or spoiled food.

The cellar was smaller than Loomis had expected—nothing like a full basement. To his left, at the bottom of the steps, was a flight of rail-less wooden stairs leading back up to the door at the rear of Banks's apartment. The walls were rough and porous-looking, with lightning-shaped cracks that let in moisture, judging from the stains, although it seemed dry now that they were standing on the dusty concrete floor. Spider webs latticed the wooden ceiling. At the rear, covering nearly the whole back wall, yet looking incongruously slim and modern and clean in that setting, was the furnace.

Loomis squatted and pinched some of the dust from the floor between two fingers, wondering how many decades it had been since the cellar had actually held coal, whether there would be any way to match this dust to the coal traces found on Munoz's body. He studied his fingertips, looking for tiny black specks, but saw none.

"Where's the bike?" he asked.

Puckett looked around. "Beats me," he said. "Maybe behind the furnace."

Loomis stepped quickly to the rear of the furnace and ducked his head to peer behind. There was a passage perhaps three feet wide between the furnace and the sidewall, leading to a slightly wider open area behind. Squarely in the middle of that space sat a bicycle-sized object, covered by a green sheet of plastic.

"Can I look under that?" Loomis asked Puckett, who had come up behind him and was craning his neck to see.

"Don't know why not."

He edged into the open space and lifted one corner

of the plastic sheet just enough to reveal a rear tire with a blue fender. The bike stood on a large square of cardboard, torn roughly around the edges, apparently one side of a large carton.

The cardboard interested him, but he could not say why, only felt that there was something wrong about it, something that wasn't clicking yet. Not for the first time recently, he wished that Haun were along, studying everything with his restless, unemotional gaze.

"I'd like to move the bike," Loomis said.

Puckett merely shrugged and backed away to give him room.

He lifted the plastic again, to keep it from tangling in the wheels, and rolled the bike forward, off of the cardboard, taking care not to step on it. Then he squatted and felt for the glasses in his shirt pocket.

The only markings on the cardboard were numbers, stamped in red ink. It appeared clean apart from the tracks of the bicycle wheels. Here and there, around the frayed edges, there were smaller bits of cardboard that had torn loose, some a bit darker than the rest. When he picked up one, about a third the size of a fingernail, he found that it was dirtier than the large piece, flatter and older-looking. It might have been stepped on, he supposed, or more likely was a remnant of an earlier piece of cardboard. Then he saw what was wrong—not the cardboard but the floor beneath it and around it. Except for those fragments, the concrete had been swept clean in all directions, as far as the sides of the furnace. He ran one hand along the base of the furnace in the dark, feeling cold grit, and then held his breath as he stared at his own fingertips. The tiny black specks sparkled like bits of glass in the half-light.

"I'd like to lift the cardboard," Loomis said, finding it hard to speak, even to breathe, as though the air in the cellar had grown thin. He glanced up at Puckett, who merely shrugged again, watching now with naked curiosity. Loomis balanced himself on the balls of his feet and carefully raised the sheet enough to peer beneath it. He didn't know what he was looking for, exactly, but what he saw was a whitish, oblong area, like a residue of white dust outlining a lopsided circle, perhaps six inches across. He sat back on his heels, wiping his hands on his pant legs. Would it look like that, he wondered, if someone used bleach to try to get rid of a bloodstain? That thought made him realize that he had been smelling the faint odor of ammonia since he had knelt down. And, beneath it, was there not just a lingering hint of something else, something much worse? Perhaps he was imagining that part. He wanted very badly to find out what the lab guys would say.

"I'd like to use your phone if I could," he said to Puckett, standing up.

Some of the older guys had gathered in the little breakfast nook off the kitchen, away from the main part of the party, to talk shop. Cubbage was there, as well as Tom Coplik, the wire editor; Paul Paretski, who covered county courts; Jim Gandy, one of the older sports writers, and Ted Lueck, the assistant managing editor in charge of special sections. They'd commandeered a platter of the little barbecued sausages, a vat of melted cheese and two big bags of tortilla chips from one of the tables in the dining room, and they were chowing down in earnest while they talked.

Stosh stood indecisively in the doorway. The kitchen behind her was as crowded as the living room and den beyond, and the little gathering in the breakfast nook looked like a haven of quiet to her. She had spent most of her time at the party so far trying to avoid Frank, trying to look as innocently like everyone else as possible, to not appear too familiar with the place. She had come partly, as always, out of fear that her absence might seem suspicious to Susan, who must surely to suspicious by now of most of the women who worked at the newspaper. But now, as always, in the crush of the party, she realized how unlikely it was that Susan would notice anyone's absence.

She had come partly for another reason, which she was now realizing had been equally foolish: the hope of seeing Haun, having a chance to talk to him, find out what he was thinking about her, about what happened at her place. Of course he wasn't here; he and Merow were famous for avoiding these parties. What she wanted to find out was whether he'd been avoiding her lately, as she suspected. She hadn't seen him anywhere, at the newspaper or the city building, since the night at her apartment.

It bothered her more than she would have thought, partly because she'd already begun feeling shut out by the partnership Sam and L.J. had formed. Far from working with them, as she'd first expected, she'd found herself completely isolated, relegated to the daily routine. Her concern that she might find out something sensitive on her own—the rationale for keeping her and

Haun's work separate—seemed laughable to her now. Even Jerry Majors wouldn't talk to her about the Strangler case anymore.

Now, from across the tiny room, she saw Cubbage grinning at her, perhaps because she had had some comical expression on her face, or perhaps because he assumed she had been listening to what someone else had just said, for most of the men were laughing at something.

She longed to go into the room, sit down at the little table, share the chips and dip and laughter with them, but was suddenly, vividly aware of her sex and age, afraid that to do so would be to alter the character of the gathering. She had done that too often with her brothers—and often enough on purpose—not to know that it could matter.

She turned away, feeling once again, illogically, abandoned, and edged between the bodies in the kitchen, finally emerging onto the little landing that separated the kitchen from the den. In front of her, three wide carpeted steps led down into the crowd and the party; to her right, a dozen feet along the half-lit hallway, was the door to the downstairs bathroom. At that point, although you could not see it from here, the hallway itself jogged right, opening onto the staircase that led to the upper level, where the bedrooms were. She went along the hallway, past the closed bathroom door and stepped up onto the stairs, stopping at the third one and turning around again. Anyone entering or leaving the bathroom might glance her way and make out her form there in the dark, but otherwise she was safely hidden from the rest of the party.

She leaned against the wooden railing, her arms crossed, wishing she had brought her cigarettes and an ashtray with her; the patio off the kitchen had been deserted, and she might have gone out there to smoke, but when she had come in it had been raining lightly. Now footsteps sounded above and behind her, along the upper hallway—someone coming back from the upstairs bathroom, probably—and then came softly down the stairs behind her. She shrank against the railing, waiting for whoever it was to go on past.

But he didn't. Instead, he pressed against her from behind, his arms encircled her waist. She gave only the faintest of starts, recognizing the smell and feel of him at once, and feeling also a not unpleasant mix of fear and excitement well up inside her.

"Looking for someone?" Frank murmured in her ear.

"Anyone could come out of that bathroom door at any moment," she said in a low voice.

He kissed her on the back of the neck and then withdrew his arms. "I know," he said. "I just saw you standing there and . . ." She felt him shrug. "Here we are, like so many times. It just felt . . . right. Normal."

She shrugged her own shoulders, freeing herself, and took a step downward, half-turning to look at him. For a moment, she felt an indistinct echo of the dream she had had, of Clare and herself in this house, with all the others around. "Susan is right in there," she said. "So is most of the newspaper."

He stepped back and studied her. "You've been avoiding me," he said. "Not just when you didn't show up that weekend, but even at work. I can tell. What's going on?"

She stared back at him, momentarily confused by the accusation, surprised to see what looked like real distress in his eyes.

"I wondered if maybe it's become a problem for you," he said. "Or maybe there's someone else. I wouldn't blame you. But I'd like to know. I've never wanted to be a problem for you. But I do need you."

She swallowed, feeling unexpectedly guilt. "I've . . . I've just been confused lately," she said. Had the setting been different, it would have been the moment to ask him about Clare Haun, about the things Sam had told her. But it was not something that could be talked about on a stairway at a party. "We need to talk," she said. "Not now. When we have more time."

"Yes," he said eagerly. "I know that. That's what I want, too. A chance to talk, get things straightened out. You know, when I don't see you for awhile, I start getting . . . you know. The way I used to be. I stop liking myself."

If everything had been a lie, then this was a lie, too, but it didn't feel that way to her. At this moment, it was far easier to believe that Sam was lying—or had just misinterpreted things—than to believe that Frank was deceiving her, had been deceiving her so elaborately for so long. She put out a hand and touched his, clutched his fingers tightly for a moment in the half-dark. "When?" she asked.

"Tomorrow night. Susan has her arts council meeting and they always go out to Café Chantilly afterward, for espresso and all that. She never gets back till midnight."

She hesitated at the idea of coming to the house

when Susan was in town. But there might not be a better opportunity for a long time, and she felt suddenly desperate to be alone with him, as though it were a single chance that might slip away forever.

"It'll be safe," he assured her. "Just a couple of hours, long enough to talk."

Someone appeared in the open space at the bottom of the steps, and the two of them stepped even further away from each other. It was Jane Cornell, one of the dayside copy editors. She tried the knob tentatively, pushing open the bathroom door, and then noticed them standing on the steps just above her and gave a start.

"Hi, Jane," Frank said quickly. "Having a good time?" His tone was just right, not guilty but not too jovial either, as though Jane might have interrupted an important but innocent conversation.

She became appropriately flustered. "The food's wonderful," she said. She gave Stosh a quick nod and hurried through the door.

"Okay," Stosh said, feeling shaky and wanting once again to get away from him until they could be alone together. "What time?"

"She'll leave at seven. I'll be at the mall at seven-thirty."

"Seven-thirty," she said.

He stepped past her, took a quick look along the hallway, put one hand on the knob of the bathroom door to hold it shut and then put the other hand behind her head, drawing her to him long enough for a quick kiss, then releasing her and the doorknob and hurrying back to the party.

Stosh stood by herself for a moment longer, then took a breath and went back along the hallway to the kitchen, crossing it once again to the breakfast nook where the old guys still sat and jawed. This time she went straight on in.

"There was a story going around back then that Morrison killed his wife," Lueck was saying. "Hey, Stosh. Try some of those little wienies. They're good." The other men smiled and nodded, then looked back at Lueck. Stosh edged around behind their chairs and seated herself on the broad windowsill that looked out over the patio. Unlit Chinese lanterns hung here and there in the trees, looking forlorn in the mist that streaked and blurred the window.

"What I heard," Paretski said, "was that that guy— who was that big guy that used to be in charge of county maintenance? Farley, Harley, something like that?"

"Turley," Coplik muttered.

"Turley. I heard he cleaned it all up. Morrison and his wife used to get drunk and have these big fights. I mean physical fights, knock each other down, throw things. You know, Morrison, he was just a little guy. Anyhow, I heard he knocked her down the stairs or something and she died, and he called Turley, 'cause Turley owed him for something or other, and Turley brought a couple of guys over and they cleaned everything up and made it look like she just fell."

"Turley always acted like he knew where the bodies were buried, like no one could touch him," Fred observed.

"That's probably the best story I know of that never got in the paper," Lueck said.

"Shit," Coplik said. "What about when we had the goods on the county assessor, and old man Springer pulled the plug on it, 'cause it involved so many big advertisers?"

"Bullock resigned over that," someone said.

"Yeah, well. Bullock was a self-righteous asshole. You and I stayed to fight another day, right?"

They all laughed. Paretski looked at Stosh and gave her a wink. She felt a surge of pleasure. It was all right after all, her joining them. Sometimes it seemed to her that this sense of fitting in, this easy acceptance, was all she really wanted.

Except for Frank, she thought, beginning to feel sure about that again, as though awakening from a spell that Haun had somehow cast over her with his own grief. She understood that Frank could never really be hers; she'd never let herself lose sight of that. But she needed someone to be there for, and when things were okay, Frank was better than a husband or a boyfriend—less demanding, less intrusive. When things were right, everything was okay except the secrecy. That was all she ever minded—the lack of sharing, apart from their few moments together. And also, she had to admit, the old, not-quite-shakable sense of doing wrong, or betraying a woman who had never harmed her. She felt that if she could have been granted any wish, it would have been to have Frank with her right then, his arm casually around her, as the two of them sat and talked with these other men, their colleagues.

She frowned, understanding at once that what was

mainly wrong with that image was that Frank wouldn't fit into it. Should he really come in and sit down, with or without her, all the others would stop telling their stories, would drift away one by one. Not just because he was their boss. It was something about Frank himself, perhaps something he couldn't help, maybe couldn't even understand.

Frank sometimes spoke as though he enjoyed this sort of camaraderie, but in fact she'd never seen him do anything to encourage it, except with her, those evenings they'd first spent talking over coffee at some late-night restaurant. Had it really been her companionship he'd wanted then? She found that the chill of Haun's view of him had come creeping back once he was out of her sight, unable to touch her. Why couldn't it be true Frank had wanted that, too, as well as the rest that had happened between them? Apparently, she had needed more than that herself, for here she was.

She thought of what Merow would say to that, how he would quote to her his favorite Rolling Stones lyric. But maybe it worked the other way around, too: If you always got what you thought you wanted, maybe you never got what you needed.

11

The big front doors of Rule's house opened onto a kind of foyer, or perhaps an enclosed porch, whose walls were of the same brick as the exterior of the house, and whose floor was the same pink marble as the front walk. Sam thought of it as a kind of air lock, a transition between outside and inside, perhaps some remnant of earlier times, larger houses, a place to greet callers without actually letting them in.

That was where Sam stood now, in front of the smaller door that was the entrance to the house itself. He had awakened that morning feeling calm, nearly serene, as though he had decided during his sleep what he would do. He had spent much of the rest of the day preparing the car and the garage, working with an unhurried satisfaction he associated with household jobs from his old life, when Clare had been alive—mowing the lawn, replacing a light switch, all the little things husbands did. Today he had worked out an efficient way of running a length of hose from the Lynx's exhaust into a window vent, sealing it all off with black electrical tape, then had carefully disassembled it again, needing the car for the other small errands remaining to him.

This was the last one, dealing with Rule and with Stosh. Putting gas in his car earlier, he had begun to see that Stosh and Rule were like the two sides of a complicated symmetrical debt, one that he owed and one that was owed to him.

He was still amazed by how close he had come to succeeding in his intended seduction—something he had never really believed himself capable of. And apparently he wasn't, for he hadn't been able to carry it off. It hadn't had anything to do with his thinking of Rule, as he had told Stosh, knowing that that would drive her away again. It was true enough; he had been thinking of Rule all evening. When did he not think of Rule? But it hadn't been what had made him want suddenly to flee, to get himself away from her. It had had something to do with the way she whispered her real name to him, a gift for which he had not asked, the kind of gift a child might make to a new friend, as though trading him that for the secrets of his own that he had told her so calculatingly.

So he felt now that he owed her something, some recompense for the deception, and for her name. And the one thing he could think of to do, which might in some way settle the other score between Rule and himself, was to sever her from her bondage to Rule. He understood well enough that he might not be able to do such a thing—he had only a half-formed notion of what he would say to Rule when he saw him—and that Stosh might think it interference rather than aid, that she would most likely want him to do no such thing.

But it seemed to him that it was the right thing to do, if he could manage it. More than ever before in his life, he felt that he was running on instinct now. When he had come out this evening, even the surprising weather had seemed somehow to confirm his change in intentions, as though it were a kind of orchestration behind his life. He had found the city lying under a black lid of cloud, gusts of wind blowing up from every direction, prying loose the flotsam of the neighborhood and scattering it along gutters and sidewalks. Everywhere there had been a kind of invisible motion in the world, the clouds themselves swirling and scrambling overhead, a nightmarish kaleidoscope of grays and blacks in which he had felt oddly at home.

The cars of his co-workers, crowding the narrow, curbless Eastborough roads, forcing him to park nearly a block away, had brought him up short; the others at the party hadn't figured in his plans. The thought of a houseful of people he knew, lying between himself and Rule, was momentarily intimidating. So he had sat inside the car for awhile, all his lights out, watching the others come and go in twos and threes. Sometimes, he noticed, the big doors stayed open for an extra moment, throwing light out onto the black wet grass, as though someone were holding them open, and he wondered whether Rule was waiting just inside, greeting everyone who came in. That, too, needed some thinking about.

The rain came and went, now a slapping of heavy drops on the roof, now a mere mist that streaked the window, turning everything beyond into shadows that seemed to move with some unintelligible purpose.

What he knew was that, having come this far, he could not drive away again.

What set him in motion finally was seeing Stosh's car go by, nosing its way into an open place up ahead that someone else had just vacated. He had sat still a moment longer, watching her move quickly along the road and up the sidewalk into the lighted haze of the big house's windows, and then opened his door and got out. He had stood for a moment in the dark, enjoying the touch of rain on his skin, and then walked slowly toward the house, directly across the wet grass, through the shifting darks and grays of the trees along the road, the morning's serenity falling over him again, so that by the time he reached the door he felt ready for whatever awaited inside.

Opening the inner door now released a burst of music and chatter and the arrhythmic clink of china. The door bumped against someone on the other side who moved away and then turned to peer at him.

"Hey, Sam. How you doin'? Long time no see." It was Van Torkelson, the chief photographer, shouting drunkenly against the background of voices.

"Hi, Van. Is Rule around?"

"Uh . . . sure, somewhere." He turned and looked around the big crowded room, stepping back so that Sam could enter. The place was a seamless mass of people juggling tiny plates, napkins, squat tumblers while they talked and laughed. Torkelson gave Sam a sloppy, apologetic smile. "Don't know. He was right here awhile ago."

Sam nodded and pushed his way on in, keeping to the edge of the crowd. There was bland, formless piano

221

music coming from somewhere, as well as the mixed smells of barbecue, pineapple and burning mesquite.

He circled toward the kitchen, pausing as little as necessary to return greetings. In fact, there seemed to be as many strangers as acquaintances there—people, he supposed, who had come into the newsroom during the past year, when he had not been paying attention. Nearing the entrance to the kitchen, he paused and stepped back against the wall, craning his neck to peer through the opening.

To his surprise, the kitchen was almost empty—no one but a couple of the younger female clerks picking at some dish beside the stove. As he watched, Rule appeared suddenly from the rear of the house, nodded to them and then strode on across the room and out the side door, toward the den. Sam stepped back, to let him get out of sight before following. He felt himself grow wary, as though Rule were some quarry he was tracking in one of those long-ago riverside games, or as though he were the dark man Loomis hunted.

As he began to step out into the kitchen, Stosh emerged from the same direction as Rule, and he stepped back again before she saw him. She looked flushed, Sam thought, and he wondered if they had just made love quickly in one of the bedrooms upstairs. He thought she seemed more upset than pleased by whatever had happened—her face reminded him of the tennis-match photo of Clare—and it firmed up his resolve to rescue her. She disappeared through another doorway at the far end of the kitchen, past the big copper-colored refrigerator.

He waited a beat longer, then crossed the kitchen

himself, the way Rule had gone, past the entrance to the hallway and down the short carpeted steps to the den, and back into the press of the party. Mickey Goodwin loomed in front of him, waving a half-glass of some bright yellow liquid.

"Hey, Haun," he said, "catch the Strangler yet?" He grinned and glanced around like someone expecting appreciative laughter.

"Hi, Mickey," Sam said, going past him.

"Don't sweat it," Goodwin said, his words slurring. "You can always be late man."

Sam, half-listening, understood belatedly that the other reporter was trying to bait him. It was such a feckless thing to do, under the circumstances, that he paused, nonplussed, and looked back at Goodwin. Then he saw that Goodwin had made an unintentional pun. I haven't caught the Strangler, Sam thought, and I'll soon be a late man indeed.

That made him smile and brought a frown to Goodwin's face. For a second it seemed to Sam that he saw Goodwin as he was, in a kind of pitiless light that had shone around him all the dark day. What he saw was a man of craft without art, ambition without aspiration. Would it be better to have been like that, after all, not knowing what one lacked, what one really needed? Or perhaps Goodwin did know; perhaps that was what accounted for the hostility that always emanated from him, disguised as humor.

"Why'n't you take a picture?" Goodwin asked belligerently. "It'll last longer."

Sam, seared by his own thoughts, shook his head and turned away again, pushing on through the crowd.

Halfway across the room, he spotted Rule perched on a high stool at the bar in the corner, leaning back on his elbows, watching the party with what might have been postcoital pleasure, self-satisfied, his jacket unbuttoned, his tie awry. Sam slowed and moved sideways, picking up a drink from a round table beside the wall and sipping it. It tasted like nothing but melted ice.

He was nearly at Rule's side before Rule became aware of his presence and looked around. His smile then seemed spontaneous and genuine.

"Sam! What an honor! I thought you never came to these things."

"I wanted to talk to you," Sam said, but the welcome disoriented him for a second.

"Fred told me you hadn't been around the office much since you started on this Strangler thing. Still working the late shift, even with the cops, eh?"

Sam nodded. "Strangler's hours," he said.

Rule smiled appreciatively. "Any breaks?" he asked. "Off the record, of course."

"No. I don't think they'll catch him."

Rule gave him a troubled look. "Really? A lot of work for nothing, if they don't."

"That's the cop biz," Sam said.

"And the news biz, too," Rule said. "If only people knew." He looked out over the party and shook his head, then looked back at Sam expectantly.

Sam understood that this was the moment—probably the last possible moment—to say whatever it was he was going to say. He had trusted that when this moment came he would know what that was. Now, he was surprised to find that he did. "There's something I've been wanting to ask you," he said. "For a long time."

Rule raised his eyebrows, indicating polite interest. "Ask away."

"I wondered whether Clare ever told you that she kept a journal."

Rule stared at him for a beat longer, his expression still bland, perhaps not sure he'd heard correctly, and then he gave a quick grimace, like a man who has made a small but irritating error, and looked out across the crowd again.

"A journal?" he asked.

"Yes. A lot of loose-leaf notebooks, actually. They were all stacked in our bedroom closet, but I never paid any attention to them." Sam was suddenly bemused by his own conversational tone, as though this were a scene he was watching from somewhere nearby, in his reporter's way, off to the side of things, and he shook the feeling off, wanting to be within himself. "I could have looked at them any time," he said, "but I never did until after she died. I guess you could say that was bad timing." He took a swallow of his drink, not tasting anything.

Rule took a drink, too, as if in response, though he was still looking away from Sam, intent on something in a far corner of the room. Sam guessed it might be Susan, but he did not look to see.

"I've just about finished them," he told Rule. "The last entry is the day before she died. I know that because I looked ahead."

"Sam," Rule said, then seemed unable to find anything to add.

"She wrote in great detail about everything," Sam said, feeling an unwanted tug of self-pity and putting it savagely away, knowing that the effort, perhaps the anger, would show on his face, but not caring.

"I didn't know," Rule managed, his voice soft, controlled. "I didn't think you'd ever know. I didn't intend . . ." He shook his head, his own control cracking very slightly, and looked down into his drink.

"The best-laid plans," Sam said. "No pun intended."

Rule looked at him in surprise, perhaps alarm.

"We shouldn't discuss this here," he said.

Sam shrugged. "It'll have to be here. It's the last opportunity."

"Why?"

Sam ignored the question. "Anyway, it's not really Clare I want to talk about," he said. "I just wanted to get your attention."

Rule frowned. "I'm not following you."

"I want to talk about Stosh."

"Stosh?" Rule had regained some composure, but now his eyes grew wary.

"I want you to leave her alone," Sam said quietly. Because of the crowd noise, he was leaning quite near to Rule now, their heads no more than a foot apart. "There must be plenty of them out there, for a man like you," he said. "That's what you told her and Clare, isn't it? It's not as if you really need this particular victim. You can throw her back."

Rule stared at him for a moment, then took a large swallow of his drink and said, "I don't think you have any right to talk to me this way." He seemed to be trying to take control of the situation, putting on the face he wore at the office. But it seemed frayed at the edges, a mask put on hurriedly, slightly awry.

"Any right," Sam repeated, genuinely puzzled by the phrase. "I don't think that makes any sense. If we start talking about rights . . ." He shook his head.

"I mean, it has nothing to do with you," Rule said. Then continued, talking quickly, in a hoarse whisper, "Actually, if you want to know the truth, the other thing really had nothing to do with you, either. I hope you can believe that."

"Of course it had to do with me," Sam said in his normal voice, not so much arguing as correcting a mistake, the way he might in some news meeting. "You might like to tell yourself it didn't. Maybe you have that much of a conscience. But the simple fact is you can't fuck around in someone else's life and then pretend it has nothing to do with them." He smiled and shook his head. When Rule didn't say anything, he added, "Whether you like it or not, there is always going to be something between us, something you owe me. With Clare dead, you can't ever pay it back. But let Stosh go and I'll call it even."

Rule cleared his throat. "She's not a prisoner," he said. "I don't control her, as you seem to think. It's up to her as much as me."

Sam shook his head. "I know that lie," he said. "Clare understood what was going on better than you probably think. She didn't quite understand how you did it, and I don't either, really, but I know you take away their power to choose somehow. And all the time you pretend that everything is up to them, that they're actually making all the decisions."

Rule gave him a pained smile. "That's a little bit crazy sounding, Sam," he said. "If I can speak frankly, I think you need some help. Though I can understand how you feel."

Sam shrugged. "I suppose I am a little crazy," he said. "And I know I've built you up a little in my mind, given you too much credit, the way I did the Strangler. But still . . . there's truth in it, too. There's something to it. You can't talk me out of that."

"The Strangler?" Rule gave a sharp laugh that seemed partly contemptuous, partly bravado, and started to say something, but Sam waved it away.

"Just leave her alone," he said. "That's all I want from you."

"That's all you want," Rule said, shaking his head in mock amazement. He looked away again, then looked back, his eyes narrowing. "Is there something between you and Stosh?" he asked. "Is that it?"

The question caught Sam by surprise, stopped him for a moment. He didn't know exactly how to answer it, and felt himself suddenly, unexpectedly, on the defensive. "Just leave her alone," he repeated, but he could hear the conviction draining out of his voice.

Rule's eyes narrowed, focusing like those of an animal sensing that its prey has been wounded. "Listen," he said, "if there's something going on . . ."

Sam turned away, retreating, knowing he could not trust himself to say more, could not be sure now that what he had said was anything like what he had intended, or that it would make any difference. He held one hand up behind him as he walked away, palm toward Rule, a stop sign against whatever else he was going to say. He heard Rule call his name once, softly, but that was all. He kept walking, did not look back.

When he stopped, he was in the dining room, on the edge of the crowd, by the glass doors that opened onto the patio. One door was slightly ajar and there was a breeze coming in through it, cooling the crush of bodies; outside, it looked as though the rain had stopped, and someone had even lit a couple of the lanterns hanging from the ornamental trees in back, although there was no one out there at the moment. Sam pulled the door far enough open to slide through, then closed it behind him, dampening the light and noise from within. The few drops he felt were only leftover rain, from the branches of the trees. He moved into the shadow, out of the lantern glow, and found himself in a place where he could see into three rooms—the dining room, the kitchen and the little breakfast room off the kitchen.

Someone had cranked open the narrow breakfast-room window to catch the breeze, and Sam saw Stosh sitting on the broad sill just inside, resting her chin on her fists like a little girl. He stepped nearer the window, knowing he could not be seen by those in the light beyond the glass, and saw that Cubbage, Coplik, Lueck and a couple of others—all the older guys—were sitting around the little table shooting the breeze, while Stosh listened.

". . . the worst. Absolutely the worst," Coplik was saying, his voice a deep rumble that seemed to make the window frame vibrate.

"I've got one worse," someone said. It sounded like Jim Gandy. "When I was up in KC, covering courts, there was this case where a guy was charged with torturing his stepson to death. The kid was seven or eight, something like that. Part of the testimony was that, at the end, he was lying in the middle of the living room floor and . . . he was badly injured, you know, broken bones, cigarette burns, the whole bit. And he said . . ." Gandy fell silent for a moment, as though having to clear his throat. "He says, 'Daddy, I want to die.' And the stepfather steps on the kid—steps right in the middle of his stomach—and then he says, 'So die.' And the kid died. Right then. Just like that."

"That's . . ." someone began, but Gandy interrupted him.

"The thing about it was that this was the mother testifying. She'd watched the whole thing and never raised a finger, and she told it in court like she was telling about a movie she'd seen."

"You remember Gil Sterkel?" Cubbage asked.

There was a silence, a couple of faint murmurs. Sam looked at Stosh and saw she was frowning, that the name was unfamiliar to her. Sterkel had been the nightside wire editor when Sam had started on the paper. He'd seldom spoken to anyone, never joined in the repartee around the rim, had just done his job and then gone home, a quiet, ordinary-looking man—Sam remembered thinking he looked more like a clerk than an editor. One night during Sam's first six months on the paper, Sterkel had gone home and hanged himself. In the bottom drawer of his desk at the office they'd found a kind of scrapbook he'd been keeping for years, of wire stories the newspaper hadn't run because they were so disturbing, mostly dealing with the abuse and murder of children—stories of people running over their own kids in their own driveways, locking their kids out of the house as punishment, leaving babies alone to drown in a bath or to die of starvation. Sterkel had been childless, unmarried. Sam thought about what it would be like to hang, why anyone would choose that way of doing it.

Inside, Cubbage was recounting one of the stories from Sterkel's scrapbook, about two children who had frozen to death in a backyard treehouse where their parents had been making them live, in winter, as punishment for some small offense.

"Hey," Coplik said, "you remember the baby under the ice, that thing that Haun covered?"

Sam took a step backward, a sound halfway between a growl and a sob rising from his throat. He looked at Stosh, saw her head lift slightly, her eyes move to the speaker.

"Sam?" she said softly. For a disoriented second, he thought she knew he was there, was calling out to him, and the softness of her voice, the sadness he heard in it—or was it pity?—pierced him like a shaft of the ice that had splintered and refrozen along the creek bed that day, the wind he could feel now on his face and hands.

"There was a wreck on the interstate out north of town," Coplik told Stosh—for surely everyone else in the room knew the story. "There'd been an ice storm and everything was covered about half an inch thick. You couldn't go over twenty miles an hour without chains. Anyway, this young couple, their car had smashed into a cement bridge railing and they'd both been killed. When Sam got to the scene, along with one of the photographers—who was it? That kid, Fernandez?—anyway, they found out that there was supposed to be a baby in the car, too, but it wasn't there, and so everyone was looking for it. So Sam and Fernandez, whoever, joined in, walking along the creek under the bridge. Finally—I guess it was a good fifty yards from the bridge—they found this place where the ice had broken and then refrozen. They called the cops over and when they broke through with their shovels they found the baby in the water underneath, not a scratch on him, drowned. What they finally decided was that the baby went right out the door when it sprung open, slid along the creek till it came to a place where the ice was thin and fell through and drowned, and the ice refroze over the top."

The last words came distantly. Sam had walked away from the widow far enough that he could not hear what response was made, could not see Stosh's reaction if he had been looking that way. Debbie had been less than a year old herself then, Davy not thought of yet. He had been unable to tell Clare about it, had not taken the paper home with him that night, so that she wouldn't read the story he had written. He had not slept that night, for fear of dreaming, and had gotten up when Clare did the next morning—a thing he'd rarely done then—and sat groggily at the kitchen table watching her spoon squashed bananas into Debbie's mouth, as though only by watching, by seeing for himself, could he be sure that nothing really had happened to them, the three of them, only to the world outside.

There had been a time when he had tried to think

what it would be like, the sudden noise, the screams perhaps, then bursting out of the warm car and into the silent cold, that long slide in darkness, the stars spinning bright and sharp overhead, the world giving way beneath one, and then that final surprise of water and death. Thinking of it now, he found that he was breathing heavily, had come clear around the house to the front, as if fleeing, and that it was raining again, colder than before, though that might only be the cold he remembered, which he supposed had been lurking somewhere in his mind ever since that night.

Away from Eastborough, Sam drove west on Douglas, toward downtown and the river beyond, toward home. In the car, he felt himself grow calm again, more like himself, the self he seemed to remember having been once, that he did not even realize was missing except in these occasional moments by himself in the car, driving the city streets, as though he might be going home from work, to Clare and Debbie and Davy. In that moment, the things he had said to Rule seemed silly and melodramatic, almost embarrassingly futile. He had nothing to do with Stosh's life, or with anyone else's anymore.

Sometimes he felt to himself like one of those children raised by wolves, no longer quite human or animal, trying clumsily to be a wolf but not having the anatomy for it. Or perhaps it was more the other way around—more like the animal treated as a small human, the pet dressed in miniature clothing, taught to shake hands, given its own bowl and chair. He gave a grunt of laughter. Surely, after all, the Strangler was never a confident man like Franklin Rule, not the dark man he had imagined, but only a man like himself, an uncertain man, unable to conduct his affairs by daylight, a man like all the pathetic men Loomis had introduced him to. Following the dark man only led him back in a circle to himself.

He stopped at a red light and rubbed at the inside of the windshield with his handkerchief to clear the frost of his own breath from the glass, not wanting to turn on the defroster. He was at Hillside, the road on which, a year ago and twenty-odd blocks to the north, Clare and Debbie had died. It was actually another three days until that anniversary, though it had been a Saturday like this, the night of Rule's party, and rainy. All that was so much a part of this consciousness that he rarely thought of it directly anymore, only when something reminded him, as now, and then it all seemed newly surprising, impossible.

Now he peered northward through the drizzle, imagining the intersection as it would have looked on that final night of his old life, the police lights pulsing through the rain, a solitary cop in a yellow slicker waving a flashlight to divert traffic, a couple of firefighters washing down the pavement with a hose, helping the rain wash the residue of gasoline into the gutters, tiny bits of wet, broken glass flickering here and there like fallen stars against the concrete.

He felt for an instant that if he turned north he would come to that same scene, be back in that moment that held his first fears and his final hopes, before everything had changed forever, before he had stood by their graves and then gone home and looked into

Clare's journals. Even if he could reach back to that moment, would there by anything, after all, that he could do? Before he could decide, the moment passed, the light changed and he drove on, crossing Hillside, heading into the glow of the city beyond the haze of rain.

The only sharp light was the beacon atop the newspaper building, once an aid to aviation, now meaningless. He thought of himself and Merow, that long year ago, sitting warm and dry beneath that beacon, in the deserted newsroom, imagining themselves free, content, safe, in that last moment before the voices had begun crackling on the monitor beside the city desk, the dull voices of a thousand newsroom nights, reporting minor fires and dead animals and prowler reports, no different from all the others, only this time reporting a 10–48, an injury accident, enough to make them half-listen, Merow and himself, not stop talking yet, then changing to a 10–40, fatality, and the two of them becoming silent, Merow reaching for the microphone to dispatch a photographer, making some small, familiar joke about sending Sam out into the rain. And then the numbers—the voice of some cop at the scene, halting and whispery in the rain, juggling his notes, turning the wet paper this way and that in the dim light of the car, or beneath a flashlight, finally reading off the license numbers, asking for the 10–28, the ID, the check for wants and warrants.

Sam couldn't quite remember things in sequence after that, only scattered moments: himself saying to Merow, "That's Clare's car," feeling not so much frightened as befuddled, trying to see what the harmless reality of it could be, looking for some explanation from Merow, some dawn of understanding behind the thick lenses, and feeling an odd, embarrassed impulse to laugh. Then, at some later point, Merow reaching out to touch him, tentatively, the way one puts a hand out to an unfamiliar dog, and Merow talking inaudibly on the phone and over the two-way, the volume cranked down so that he could not hear what was said, and then himself sitting in the hallway at the hospital someone had driven him to, trying to sort out all he had been told by that time, trying to understand how to feel about Davy, about his struggle for life that went on all that night, and about Clare and Debbie, but not quite thinking clearly about them because he hadn't had to yet, not as long as Davy was in danger. And, sometime afterward, going back alone to the dark house where no one but he and Davy would live anymore.

The light was green at Grove and he went on through, not jogging north to Second Street to avoid the teenagers, but heading automatically for the newspaper. But he didn't stop there, of course. There was nothing left to do, nothing left to say to anyone, even Merow. He only glanced once at the lighted strip of windows on the third floor, passing by, thinking for a fleeting second of himself up there, looking down on the tops of the cars, and then turned his face again toward the river and home, feeling an irritable impatience with himself.

The cars around him—no more than dark hulks in the rain, twisted lights glaring against his smeared windshield—would not let him hurry. The ones coming toward him blinded him, kept him from seeing the rest of the world beyond, while those moving his way had their own rhythm, their own agenda, like animals passing nearby in the forest. He was swept under the railway bridge, the traffic splitting into twin streams to flow through the short tunnels, emerging into the heart of city light, the yellow street lamps in the rain, the scattered blear of neon, against which packs of young people, vaguely threatening, formed puzzling patterns of movement along the dark shop fronts, out of time with the discord arising from their boomboxes, the rattle of voices, the occasional drumbeat of challenge or greeting between car and sidewalk.

There were six blocks of this, of nighttime jostle and glare, dimly perceived, rising to a kind of crescendo at Broadway, the main intersection, and then falling away again quickly into a soft, rainy darkness in the last three blocks to the river, the dreary convention area presided over by the tall hotels and the bulk of Century II squatting by the terraced riverbank, the street itself turning to neat red brick that clicked beneath the tires. Most of the traffic turned back there, looping north and south, to head back the other way. Sam's car was one of two or three that emerged from the pack, running straight on ahead, like exiles, bound for the greater darkness beyond the river. At that moment, as the confusion of light and sound died away behind, he noticed a slight, solitary figure moving along the sidewalk, parallel to him, slightly bending against the rain, also bound away from the crowds. Something familiar in the shape, the posture, held his attention for a second longer than usual, and then he recognized Kelly Jo Greenleaf, the copy girl. As he watched, momentarily intrigued by this little mystery—why she would have come so far, on foot, she turned a corner and moved off into greater darkness, greater solitude.

He felt oddly apprehensive, and watched her in his rearview mirror as long as he could, then, on impulse, swung north at Water and took two more rights, coming back around onto Main, southbound, the way Kelly Jo had gone.

In the block where he had last seen her, he slowed, expecting to overtake her, but then he saw an unexpected island of light and movement taking shape ahead of him. As he drew near, he pulled over to the curb, ignoring signs, and got out, standing for a moment, squinting, and then walked toward the light, keeping to the night shadow of the building.

He was right upon the edge of the lighted area before he understood what it was. The front of Century II—its interior dark but its outside bright, emerged in the gap between the buildings, and between lay a kind of plaza that it seemed to him must not quite exist by day.

It was the downtown terminus of the city bus routes, where a wall of buses, nose to tail, sat always grumbling along the curving street that swept by the front of the convention center. In the elbow of the curve, nearest him, was a small parking lot that served the building whose shadow he stood in, as well as the city library beyond the little street, dwarfed by the bulk of its neighbor, Century II, though its larger windows were alive with light and movement inside. The other way, to his right, there was a tiny, rectangular park, squeezed into the cityscape and sunk below ground level, extending back along the row of buses to the main drag, with stair steps going down at the corners and benches scattered among banks of flowers and ornamental trees, all of it dripping now in the rain.

But inhabited, nevertheless. The bus drivers, many of them, stood outside their open doors, smoking and talking, but there were others there as well—passengers, he supposed, although many of them in fact seemed oblivious to the buses, seemed only to be enjoying the night, even the rain, scattered in small groups here and there, in the little park, in the half-deserted parking lot, beyond the curving street on the broad walkway that led to the library and to the steps of Century II, like picnickers in a Sunday park or students scattered across a quad between classes. Many wore raincoats and ponchos, but some wore ordinary suits and dresses, or the bright oversized shirts and shorts favored by teenagers, or jogging suits, all of them seemingly oblivious to the light rain, only wiping now and then at hair hanging down over foreheads, or brushing at their clothing as though to wipe away the weight of accumulated moisture. Sam ignored it, too; the city air was warm and still, the mist welcome and soothing.

Kelly Jo had disappeared into that loose throng, like a child joining her playmates. And that was what it reminded him of: childhood playgrounds where one ignored the rain or the heat or the snow to be with one's friends, leaving it to the adults to worry about such things. There was no sound of loud music from radios or tape decks, only a kind of murmuring, an occasional burst of soft laughter, a nearly subliminal sense of music drifting from somewhere nearby, gentle chords almost indistinguishable from the arrhythmic rattle of wind and rain.

He knew that it was time to go on home, to continue with what he had planned, but he found himself reluctant to move. It seemed to him that he recognized the place in some way that he did not quite understand, as though it were a place he had been looking for without knowing it, like the perfect house one dwells in sometimes in dreams. Standing in the dark at the border of light, he felt an ache building inside him—a sweet, incomprehensible pain he yearned to hold to him, to probe, to understand, as if, grasping it, he might then become oblivious to pain, to loss, to death, to everything that might touch him save the occasional raindrop kiss.

12

———

After he rang the bell, Loomis stood for a moment, rocking back and forth slightly on the balls of his feet, then rang it again. The night's rain had mostly passed, but the clouds remained, unusual for July, that felt as though it might be bringing with it a more serious storm, or even blowing in an early winter from Nebraska and the Dakotas. Leaving home, he had not thought to put on a jacket, and now wished he had. Inside, he could hear the roar of Edie's treadmill. He remembered a time when he wouldn't have had to ring at all because Marcie would have been at the window, watching for him. He did not resent the changes that were taking place—it seemed to him that the less intense relationship developing between him and his teenaged daughter was more normal, anyway—but he found that he missed that little girl intensely at times, as though she had died while he had been away somewhere.

When he rang a third time, the roar inside died, and a moment later the door opened, revealing Edie shaking her hair out around her face, one hand clutching the sweatband she had just pulled off. She wore a fluorescent yellow workout suit under baggy black sweatpants, and her forehead and arms glistened with sweat.

She had to push the screen door open, against the wind, then hang onto to it to keep it from snapping back. She blinked at the world outside as though astonished, then said, "Oh, L.J. Sorry. I heard the bell, but I thought it was some salesman or evangelist or something. Marcie didn't tell me you were coming. She's gone off to Towne East with her friends." She peered past him again at the dark day, gave a shiver, and then glanced back over her shoulder at the clock on top of the TV set. "What time did you tell her you'd be here?"

"Noon. I'm a little early."

"Well, she still ought to be back by now. She's got her head up her butt a lot these days. Come on in." She turned back toward the living room without waiting for a response.

Loomis pursed his lips and followed. The TV was on, but there was no sound. The titles of old '50s songs rolled across the screen above an 800 number. "It really pisses me off that she's not here," Edie said, coming back from the kitchen with a glass of water in her hand and tossing back a couple of pills of some kind. "And also not telling me you were coming."

Loomis shrugged, feeling himself slip easily into the role of mediator between mother and daughter. "She's a teenager," he said. "It's part of the package."

"Yeah, well, you don't have to live with that package every day." She paused and then winced and said, "Oh, shit. I didn't mean anything by that, L.J. You know me." She waved a hand in the air, erasing the remark, thought in fact it hadn't offended him. He did know her. "Can I get you something to drink?" she asked.

"Maybe a can of pop, if you've got one."

"You kidding? I'll see what's cold." She went back to the kitchen.

He never got over how the room felt strange and homelike all at the same time, a place he had never lived that was filled with small things he had lived with—photos and knickknacks, the mugs Edie had bought in Mexico, a plaster handprint Marcie had made in preschool. There were new things now, of course, things that didn't involve him, including a couple of items he knew had come from Guy Nyzer, the sociology professor Edie had been seeing for more than a year now. The clock, inside its glass cylinder, with the gold balls turning endlessly at the bottom, was one of those things, something he'd never have thought to buy for Edie himself, never could have imagined her wanting. He stared at it for a moment, as he sometimes did, wondering what it represented about her that he had never seen, that Guy had. Then he looked away from it, at the furniture, which was mostly the same, although he saw that Edie, since his last visit, had gotten rid of the recliner with the rip in back, replacing it with a bentwood rocker. When they had had a house with a rec room, the recliner had been the chair he had sat in, in front of the TV set, on football Sundays, a can of beer in his hand. And it had been where he sat when visiting Marcie here. He thought about sitting down in the new rocker, but it looked too delicate for him. Instead, he went and sat at one end of the old sofa, a place where he had rarely ever sat when the sofa had belonged to him, a place for visitors.

Edie brought him a can of diet Dr. Pepper. "It was either this or diet Sprite," she said, "and I know you don't like the white ones."

"This is fine." He clutched the cold can in both his hands in front of him, resting his elbows on his knees, and leaned forward slightly to peer at her.

"The exercise must be working," he said. "You're looking pretty good." It was something polite to say, but it was true, too.

She gave him a sharp look, then smiled. "For an old dame, you mean?" she said. "At least you didn't say 'well preserved.'"

He smiled. "No one would believe you're older than me," he said.

Edie gave him a crooked grin, her eyes narrowing. It was an old joke; she was eight days older. "So what's with you?" she asked. "You're in a funny mood."

"I am? What do you mean?"

"You're acting the way you do when you've got good news, or some story to tell, but you're shy about coming out with it."

He looked at her for a moment, surprised by the observation, surprised to find it was true, though she wasn't the one he wanted to tell the "good news" to. He thought fleetingly, irritably, of Haun, then said, "It's really nothing. I mean, it's just work."

"Not another promotion? You said you didn't want to go any higher."

"No. No promotion. Not even a raise." He took a drink of the pop, trying to think of some other topic.

She studied him for a second, then took a drink of her water. "Must be the Strangler," she said.

He blinked, surprised.

"I read the paper," Edie said. "This Munoz girl was another one, wasn't she? And I know you."

He made a wry face. "Sorry," he said. "I didn't mean to bring any of this up."

"You didn't bring it up. I did. What's going on?"

He shook his head, grimacing. "This is bad territory for us," he said.

She gazed at him for a moment, as though brought up short. Then gave a little nod and said, "That ought to be a long way behind us by now, L.J."

"I suppose so."

"But I do know what you mean," she said.

He sighed. "I always thought of the two things as being connected," he said. "I guess, because it happened at the same time."

She nodded. "Yeah, I know. But it wasn't the Strangler who broke us up. You know that. It was just us."

"You mean just me," Loomis said.

"No, I do not mean just you." Her anger surprised him. "I mean what I said. Us."

Loomis laughed nervously, wanting to calm her. "Okay," he said.

"Just like you to want the lion's share of the blame, too," she said, beginning to grin.

"Really? Was I that selfish?" he asked seriously.

She shook her head. "Shit, L.J., you weren't selfish at all. I was being sarcastic. Sometimes I think part of our problem was that you were never selfish enough."

"I don't understand that," he said.

"Never mind. I'm not sure I do either." She made a face at the glass of water, as though she wished it were something else.

"Look," Loomis said, "I seem to be upsetting you for some reason. I didn't mean to."

She gave him a blank, surprised look. "Do I seem upset?"

"Yes. Out of sorts. Something."

She considered that, gave an acknowledging shrug. "It has nothing to do with you," she said.

He waited to see whether she'd say more, and when she didn't he remained silent. These disjointed conversations were not unusual; they could still read each other, but the things they read were not always subjects for discussion between them, and there were gaps in what they knew.

"So what about the Strangler?" she asked like someone struggling to get back on track in a conversation. "Have you got him?"

Loomis made a deprecating gesture with his arms spread. "Nothing like that," he said. "It's just . . . there's this guy who looks pretty good, that's all. I have a good feeling about him. But all I've really got is a couple of small things that fit, and my feeling. Nothing to take to court."

"I'm surprised you're here."

He gave her a quick look, sensing an accusation, but saw none in her expression.

"I wouldn't break a date with Marcie," he said, then smiled sheepishly. "Besides, Binkley and Davidson are on it. I've got them out checking the places this guy lived before."

"Before what?"

"Before he came back. He was out of town during the period when the killings stopped, and he'd only been back a few months when the Munoz girl disappeared. So we're checking on the places he lived before he left town."

"Where did he go? Were there killings there?"

He shook his head. "He was in prison. Not for murder, for assault."

"What else?"

"What do you mean?"

"So the time period fits. What else have you got?" The question reminded him that Edie had once been a cop's wife, had even seemed to like it for a time.

"It's really almost nothing," he said. "Anyway, I shouldn't be talking about it. I . . ."

Her eyes widened, often a prelude to an argument. "You don't trust me?" she asked innocently.

"It's not that. It's . . ." But then he stopped because it was that—that he couldn't trust her not to say anything to Guy—or to other people he might not know about. She had new allegiances now. "Listen," he asked instead, "do you remember me ever saying anything about a peculiar pattern of evidence in this case?"

"You mean the flowers and stuff ? What was it? Underpants?"

He winced. "I told you all that?"

"No, L.J., you never told me shit about this case. Don't you remember? That's when we weren't talking much anymore. This case was like your secret hobby, like these guys who go down in the basement and lock the door and work on a model train."

He squinted at her, confused. "So how do you know about it?"

She shrugged. "I don't know. I heard it somewhere."

"Shit. Haun was right."

"Who?"

He shook his head. "Do you remember where you heard it?"

"Jesus. It's been a long time. Years. Back around the time of the last one."

"But you mean after we . . ."

"Yeah. After that."

"Maybe when you started going out to the university. Could you have heard it there?"

She thought. "Yeah, I think you're right," she said. "I have this vague memory of a bunch of people sitting around a table, talking, you know. Like in the student union. Something like that."

"You don't remember who?"

"Jesus, L.J. I mean, I probably wasn't paying that much attention. And it was probably like some friend of a classmate I hardly knew. Just people gathering around a table, you know. I didn't really know a lot of people there then. I was just on the fringes of things, trying to fit in."

Loomis was silent for a moment, then said, "Do you think it's something everybody knows, that you've heard other places? Or was it just around the university, mostly."

She shrugged. "I don't know. A university thing, I guess. Yeah, I'd say so. Why? It's important, huh?"

He gave a crooked smile. "It was supposed to be our big secret. The thing that only we and the killer know about. A guy I've been working with suggested that it might have gotten around the university because of the forensics stuff we had done there."

Edie nodded thoughtfully, then shook her head. "I'm sure I don't know anybody in that department," she said.

He shrugged. "It'd be tough to track it very closely after six years."

"Well . . . but if this guy you're investigating is the one, it doesn't matter, does it?"

"Not if he's the only one."

He saw the quick understanding in her eyes, no need of saying anything, and in that instant he remembered exactly how it had been between them once. Then Marcie came in the front door as though hurled by the wind, her stiff, moussed hair sticking out comically at one side.

"Daddy! Daddy! Am I late? I'm sorry." Then she was in his arms, not the sophisticated teenager at all, and his eyes held Edie's and they were for just that instant a family again, and he felt as though if he could hold on to Marcie he could hold on to that as well, but then she was pulling away again, and there was no reason for him to hold on to her. "I have to fix my hair and change clothes," she shouted back at him, disappearing into her bedroom. "Where we going?"

"Wherever you want," he said in a voice that was hardly more than a whisper, a voice she wouldn't be able to hear.

"She'll most likely want to go right back to Towne East," Edie said softly, and he wondered what that moment had meant to her, if anything. "That's where they all hang out now," she said dismissively. "They ride the buses, if you can believe that. Downtown, then back to Towne East again."

Loomis frowned. "Doesn't that bother you, not knowing exactly where she is?"

Edie chewed at a corner of her mouth for a moment. "It's part of the package, like you say," she said. "Anyway, she's with a mob of other girls. I don't worry too much."

He nodded, not wanting to slip into the old protective thing, to start thinking too much about the dangers out there.

"You know, it'd be okay to just stay here," Edie said. "I mean, the weather ... but of course, Marcie would be bored to tears."

"That's true," he said.

They were silent for a moment, and then she said, "L.J., there is something I need to tell you about."

He knew that this was what he had sensed in her earlier, the upset, the thing that had her off-balance, and he braced himself for it.

"Guy has asked me to move in with him, and I'm thinking about doing it," she said. "I thought you ought to know."

That was something like what he had been braced for, but it still made a wrenching down inside his gut, surprising him, reminding him that there was still a part of him that could be hurt.

"Not marriage?" he asked.

She shook her head. "No. Well, actually ... you're probably not going to believe this ... he did ask me to marry him, but I turned him down." She gave an odd little laugh.

That made him feel irrationally relieved. "Why?" he asked her.

She glanced in the direction of Marcie's bedroom, then lowered her voice and said, "To be blunt, I'm not really sure about Guy that way. I mean, he doesn't feel like my last stop, if you get my drift." She gave him a wry smile.

He smiled back, despite himself, not knowing what to say.

"So what do you think?" Edie asked.

He shrugged. "What difference does that make? I mean . . . I don't know what I think."

"What I mean is, how do you feel about it? I mean, Marcie and me, moving in with Guy?"

He shrugged, trying to be calm, neutral, the dispassionate friend. "Well, if that's what you want," he said.

She nodded slowly. "So that's the only thing I need to consider? What I want?"

She seemed angry again, and he wasn't sure why, or who at. "What else?" he asked.

As abruptly as she'd grown angry, she seemed to weary of the discussion, and turned away from him. Then, again abruptly, she turned back.

"What advice would you give Guy?" she asked. The look on her face put him on guard.

"I'd tell him he couldn't do better," he said.

She gave a harsh laugh. "Piss," she said, and then, "Men." She turned away as though he had just confirmed all her worst suspicions about him.

Before he could think of anything to say, Marcie came back into the room, her hair back in order, wearing baggy black shorts and a white sweatshirt with the arms pushed up above her elbows. "Ready," she announced.

"Shorts?" Edie asked in amazement. "Did you notice the weather when you were outside? You need jeans and a jacket."

"Mom, it's July!" Marcie gave him a conspiratorial look, rolling her eyes. "Can we go to the mall, Dad?"

He nodded, ignoring the pointed look Edie was giving him. "Sure," he said. "Whatever you want."

Sam awoke in the half-light of the bedroom, having heard one of the kids cry out. He was on his feet beside the bed, groping for the doorknob, before he remembered that there were no more kids in the house, that Debbie was dead, Davy one hundred miles away, that there was no one beside him in the bed, no one else there in the house with him at all.

It was cold. It had probably been that—and a full bladder—that had awakened him. He remembered cool wind coming through the open window at the foot of his bed, carrying the smell of rain, while he drifted in and out of sleep, visited by fitful, repetitive dreams he could not remember. But had that been tonight, or some other night, some other season? The wind from the window was cold now, and he knew he had been sleeping huddled in a ball beneath the lone sheet that covered him.

He padded down the hallway, shivering, finding the

bathroom door, remembering nights when he had gotten up to search for a lost pacifier or teddy bear, or to walk back and forth in the dimly lit living room, bouncing a tiny body softly up and down against his shoulder, while the small eyes stared wakefully, alert, unwilling to go back to sleep.

It was warmer in the bathroom because he had left the window there closed. Standing over the toilet, his head beside the little window overlooking the backyard, he squinted against the reflected glare, trying to see what the world was like outside, thinking now that it might have been his own cry that had awakened him. There had been times lately when he had awakened from dreams that left him weeping or trembling with fear, although he could not always remember what they were about.

Finished, he turned off the bathroom light and went back to the window. It was white everywhere, and for an instant he thought it had snowed during the night; he imagined the clean, cold air, the sky graying into early morning. But then he remembered that it was July, and saw that it was only a trick of the light trapped beneath earth and cloud, the grass gleaming eerily white in the suffused glow of the city.

From that light, he could not tell what time of day it was, but he didn't care much. Back in the cold bedroom he closed the window and burrowed back under the sheet, which had grown cold in his absence. He rolled himself up in it, waiting for warmth, remembering how Clare had slept on his side of the bed sometimes, when he was working nights, and how warm the bed had been when she rolled over, not quite waking, to make room for him.

But now one of his dreams began to come back to him, only fleetingly, obliquely, nothing he could quite grasp, and he opened his eyes wide, peering into the dusk of the bedroom, wanting to be sure that it was in fact dream and not memory. What he recalled was an aching sense of flesh against flesh, and of something shrinking and cracking beneath his encircling hands, the mingled tastes of desire and fear.

He sat up, agitated, still holding the sheet tight around him, searching for something more to grasp with his mind, some detail that would bring it all clear, prove to him, one way or the other, whether it had been dream or reality.

He swung his feet to the wooden floor and let the sheet go, standing up and taking a couple of steps in the near-darkness beside the bed. "Have I really done something?" he asked aloud, and his voice, seeming to come from somewhere else in the dark, made him shiver briefly with something like fear. He stared at the gray square of the window shade for a long moment, getting his bearings, then walked out into the hallway, feeling a need to turn on lights, look at a clock, reclaim a sense of the waking world.

The light helped. In the living room, even the tenuous grip he had on the memory began to fade, and with it the fear that it might have been anything but a dream. He went over in his mind the real things that had happened to him recently, the evening with Stosh and how he had left her there in her apartment, the visit to Rule's party, what he had seen and what he had said.

He was fully awake now, aware of the hums and creakings of the house. The numbers on the little digital clock of the VCR blinked at him, a remnant of some forgotten power failure, never reset, and he went to the TV and flicked it on, punching buttons until the local cable channel came on with the time in the corner: 2:10. He glanced at the window, saw it was, after all, too bright to be nighttime, must be afternoon, though gray like no July afternoon he could remember. He wondered briefly whether he could still be asleep, still dreaming, lost in some imaginary world that was neither dark nor light, filled with the distant roar of wind.

He shook his head, and went back to the bedroom, where he found some jeans and a T-shirt in the pile of clothing beside the bed. He put them on and returned to the living room, going on through and out the front door to the porch, barefoot but ignoring the chill. He slumped in the wooden chair beside the door, the accumulated dust on the broad flat arm tacky beneath his fingertips. The wind came up, tangled his hair, raised goose bumps on his face and arms, then died away again. He crossed his arms, not wanting to go back inside for a jacket or shoes.

He remembered suddenly that he had planned to kill himself the night before, had prepared the hose and the tape for his car. But then he had forgotten, because of the place he had stumbled onto downtown, the bus terminus by Century II. He shook his head, smiling. None of that made any sense to him now—either the planned suicide or the reason for letting it go. Most likely, he was a little crazy, as he had told Rule.

The old man who lived two doors down, across the street, had come out on his porch, wrapped in a brown sweater that hung far down below his waist, and was sipping coffee from a mug he held between his hands. He glanced Sam's way, and as their eyes met Sam gave him a wave. The man dipped his head slightly, acknowledging it, then looked away. It was the most contact Sam had had with any of his neighbors since Clare's death. Not that he had known any of them well before that. For the first time it occurred to him that they must all know what had happened. Should he feel bad now, belatedly, because none of them had ever come to call on him, brought him food and condolences, the way neighbors would have in Malden? He didn't feel that way; he preferred to believe they had sensed his desire to be left alone, and had respected it. He felt oddly grateful to them.

The wind came up strongly, lashing the trees momentarily, making him glance up at the gray sky beyond, and he remembered suddenly a terrible dream he had had, several times, in the weeks after Clare had died.

In the dream, at the beginning of the dream, he had been standing in a huge open area, a kind of plain, in exactly this same gray light, a grayness that filled the world, and in utter silence, although he remembered that it had also seemed that there was a hum of tension in the dream, as if some huge bell had chimed the instant before, so that its vibration still thinned out into the air all around.

Before him was a tiny caravan, two people and an

animal—a sort of man, a sort of woman, a sort of dog, all of them horribly unnatural in ways not easy to describe to himself later.

The man led, his face hidden in a darkness that moved with him, and he held a leash, attached not to the dog, but to the woman, who did not struggle against it, but simply moved along behind the man, accepting, acquiescent, as though the mere thought of escape, even protest, were unimaginable.

What was most horrible about the dream was the woman's face, which was not the face of a woman, but of an animal. He had described it to his counselor as a fox's face, knowing that that was not quite right, but that there was no true analogue in the waking world. What he knew somehow was that her original face had been sculpted into this new visage, perhaps by the man, a horrible work of art, some unimaginable surgery having produced the lengthened snout, the pointed ears, the brown liquid eyes.

The bad thing about the dog was that it needed no leash, that it followed along docilely, whipped, although its original function, he knew, had been to protect the woman from the man. He always thought too late to look at the face of the man, always found that he had moved past, into darkness, his face no longer visible. The man too was frightful, but not for anything Sam could name; his dark presence was terrible.

The dark man, he thought. But that had been months before the reappearance of the Strangler, before he had begun thinking about all that again. Could there have been some unconscious connection, even then, from that time six years before? It seemed incredible, and yet also somehow true, and for some reason it made him think of the bus interchange, the island of light in the darkness of the city, as though the figures from his own dream might dwell there.

He knew then that he would be going back there again, as soon as the darkness began to gather. He didn't know why, exactly. He only knew that he wanted to sit somewhere on the edge of the place, somewhere out of sight, and watch the comings and goings, see what it was all about. The thought gave him an odd, unsettling feeling, as though, down inside him somewhere, a second pair of eyes had just opened again, after years of sleep, and were blinking uncertainly in the strange, gray light.

Neither of them spoke during the ride, a ride that seemed longer to her than ever, for she had been feeling all day that tonight would be an important one in her life, bearing some kind of revelation to show her how things were to go from now on—a beginning or an ending. She had arrived at the mall uncharacteristically early, and then walked around, not really seeing the bright things inside the shops, waiting for Frank with impatience and also with a touch of that apprehension that always accompanied important things, crucial meetings, anticipated interviews, big things that might not go right after all. She felt that same familiar impulse to turn around and go home, hide in her bedroom, pull the covers over her head, give up the good to avoid the bad.

That was silly, of course, a kind of thing she'd learned to deal with a long time ago. She'd been thinking of this meeting, in fact, as though it were an important interview, had even been getting her questions ready, although, as was so often the case, she felt unable to formulate the most important ones, had to trust to her own ability to come up with them when the moment demanded them. It seemed to her now, thinking this way about meeting Frank, that it had always really been answers she needed from him—answers to questions that would have baffled him, had she tried to put them into words. There had been the sex, of course, and whatever else there was between them; for some reason, her mind shyed away from the word *love*. But always she had had this idea in the back of her mind that Frank, with his experience, his authority, had some special power to reveal to her something important about herself, something she would never learn otherwise. She had always felt—that very first time, and now—that she would be a different person after being with him, though she had never been sure, then or now, whether she was likely to be saved or damned by that.

But in his car, when he finally arrived and they were headed toward Eastborough, she felt tongue-tied. Perhaps he did, too, for neither of them spoke at all. By the time they reached the house, it was as though a pall settled over them, making talk impossible. The very silence of the big house seemed intimidating, almost frightening, as though they had been there together only the moment before, surrounded by the people they worked with, the people they hid from, and all those people had disappeared mysteriously, in the instant between. Or else it was a dream—but which? The party or this silence? She felt as though the words he had spoken to her on the staircase were still ringing in her ears. "Long enough to talk," he had said. But now the time seemed too long to talk in, lying there before her, as though whatever words she might find to say would be swallowed up in the expanse of it, the dismaying silence of the house.

She went ahead of him up the stairs, thinking that perhaps if they stopped there for a moment, reached back to that previous moment, when she had been on the verge of saying things to him, asking him things she could not imagine putting into words now . . . But they didn't stop. They went on up and then back along the hallway to the back guest bedroom—their bedroom. It was what they always did at this point.

Perhaps because of that familiarity, once they were inside the room, with the door closed and the bed in front of them, the tension she felt seemed to lift for a moment, and she was able to put her hand on his arm and say, "We were going to talk, to get things straight."

He flinched as though she had struck him or shouted in his ear. Indeed, the words echoed loudly in her own ears. The look he gave her convinced her that he had been feeling much like herself, filled with an irrational fear that language would destroy some balance between them, make it impossible for them ever to touch one another. It seemed impossible to her in that moment that they could ever have sat and talked, as other people did.

He seemed half out of breath, as though the walk up the stairs had winded him. "Afterward, please," he said, as though he could form the words and expel them only at great cost.

What's going on with us? she thought. But she turned away wordlessly, going to the little bathroom at the corner, as she always did. Indeed, she closed the door but did not turn on the light, not wanting to see herself, and began slipping out of her clothing with the same shrug of acquiescence she would have made at a doctor's office, draping them on the familiar surfaces, the vanity, the little chair, sliding her shoes off and setting them noiselessly on the tiny rug, not wanting to make a noise by dropping them.

Opening the door again, naked, she took a deep breath and found it more ragged than she had expected, as if the air had grown thin. Always, invariably, he was naked, too, by then, awaiting her. He might be stretched out on the bed, or sitting on the edge of it, his head cocked to one side, as though trying to see her more clearly than the dark would allow, or now and then standing between her and the door, his arms outspread to greet her. But his body would be white and luminous in the dark, like hers, making a welcoming community of their nakedness, to swallow up the shyness she could never shake, to make a warmth that replaced what she had left behind with her clothes, in the bathroom.

But this time he was still clothed. Expecting that whiteness in the dark, ready to zero in on it, she thought at first he was not even there, and came part way into the room before she realized he was standing near the head of the bed, looking down at the objects on the nightstand.

She knew what was there, and she thought then that she understood his state of mind. There was a photo of Susan and himself on the little table, and it was Frank's habit to turn it face down while Stosh was in the bathroom, undressing. But this time he only stood looking at it, as though unable to get beyond that point.

Her first feeling of embarrassment, seeing him clothed, gave way to something like relief. Still, she walked to him quickly, bringing herself close before he could turn and see her naked. When he did look at her, their eyes only a few inches apart, she thought she could see, openly for the first time, the regret that she had always believed he carried with him, that might be the thing she most admired in him, the thing that redeemed him.

She pressed herself against him, not lasciviously, but like a child needing a hug, wrapping her arms around his waist. "It's all right," she said. "We'll be all right. Just talk. Talk to me."

His hands rested on her back for a moment, and then he moved them to her shoulders, pushing her away again. She stepped back and waited.

"I want you . . ." he said brokenly, but then his eyes turned back toward the photo on the nightstand, as though it had spoken to him, interrupting him.

"You can tell me what you feel," she said. "Whatever it is, it's all right. I'll try to help you."

He looked back at her again, a puzzled look, as if he didn't quite understand what she had said, but then he reached out to her and she stepped into his arms.

He held her then a long time, not moving, not initiating anything, not talking either, until she began to feel uncomfortable pressing against the fabric of his suit. She tried to pull away gently, but he held her close, not letting her go, and instead she brought her hands around to the front, between them, and tugged his jacket open, trying to get at the buttons of his shirt. It seemed to her now that the physical part was something they needed to get past, to get through, to be able to talk.

"Take the jacket off," she whispered, her forehead pressing into his shoulder as she felt for the buttons, but he made no response, gave no sign even of having heard her. He seemed frozen, immobile. She got one hand inside his shirt and flattened it against his warm chest, then tilted her head slightly and kissed his neck. Still he did not respond, only continued to hold her close.

"Relax," she breathed. "Let it go."

His grip loosened. She freed herself gently, and then reached to his crotch, but what she found was that he was still small, still soft, beneath the fabric. Confused, she took a small step backward and studied him as well as she could in the dark. His eyes were hidden, unreadable.

"Do you want me to stay or go?" she asked. "You have to say something."

He blinked then, his eyes glistening for a second, and

then said, "Stay." He put out his hands again and gripped her shoulders, pulling her back to him, not embracing her this time, but pressing the length of her body against his, almost roughly, as if to abrade his body with her own, to force desire out of himself. He ran his hands down her back, cupping her buttocks for a moment and pressing their lower bodies together so that she could feel him growing hard now beneath the fabric.

She undid his belt buckle, slid down his zipper, but then he pushed her away again, not to finish undressing himself, as she expected, but only to gain access to her breasts, which he palmed for a moment, his fingers hard, unyielding, before resting his hands on top of her shoulders, on either side of her neck.

He stood looking at her for a moment then, squinting slightly as though trying to make out who she was, and she felt an odd glimmer of fear, of having suddenly found herself naked with a stranger. His hands moved closer to her throat, nearly encircling it, and she remembered without wanting to what Haun had told her, about the prostitute, about what the prostitute had said.

But he didn't close his hands around her throat. Instead, he began pressing firmly downward on her shoulders, making her bend, dip her head.

"Do me," he said, his voice oddly distant, matter-of-fact, as though he might be giving a casual direction at the office. She glanced up, saw his face turned not toward her but back toward the nightstand where the photo sat.

She tried tentatively to resist, but the pressure of his hands overcame her, forcing her further downward, until she knelt before him finally, not knowing what else to do.

13

___

He hung back at first, feeling uncharacteristically shy, like some novice reporter sent to interview the governor. He spent much of his first full evening just standing near the corner of the building nearest to his car, at the edge of the sidewalk, watching. He moved only gradually into the light; it was not until the next night that he began to explore the place.

He had been there often enough by daylight, but it seemed to him that he had never paid attention then, or that the true character of the place could only be seen as he was seeing it now. It was not really a single place, he saw—not to most of the people who came there—but a number of places abutting upon one another. There were the young people who parked briefly in the little blacktop lot beside the building where he stood, and leaned against their doors or perched on fenders to talk. They were like the few quiet exiles from the noisier mob along the main drag, and there were not many of them. Although they now and then greeted someone who emerged from a nearby bus, they seemed largely oblivious to the rest of the area.

The buses themselves sat in a long arc along the

sidewalk that formed the longest edge of the parking lot, making a quarter circle of it, and the benches along that curve were mostly populated by older people, passengers, who sat with packages on their laps, arms crossed, now and then flapping open a newspaper, now and then murmuring in low voices to one another and to the drivers standing beside the open doors, as though the parking lot behind them did not exist.

Beyond the street was the library—a wall of bright glass enclosing tall, endless rows of multicolored books and the people moving slowly among them—and the vast darkness of Century II, the concert hall and convention center. Those two buildings, with the street for a hypotenuse, formed a concave triangle fitting up against the convex parking lot, and the flat plaza between, from the long, low steps of the concert hall to the stone planters stretching alongside the library, boasted its own small communities—the readers carrying their books out to stone benches in the lamp-lit summer evening, and a ragtag mix of vaguely arty sorts, in the motley uniforms of the unconventional, meeting here and there along the steps and low flanking walls.

Finally, there was the little sunken park, a narrow, almost secret corridor running off from the sprawling square formed by the other parts, extruding itself all the way back, between buildings, to Douglas.

Searching for comparisons—other nighttime gathering spots he had seen in other cities—he came up short, understanding only gradually that it was not that sort of place, which was why it had no name that he knew of, and why there were no vendors selling hot dogs, pennants, icebox magnets. It was a place that was not quite defined yet, not quite aware of itself. He doubted that most of those who came there even thought of it as he did. They thought of themselves as going to the library, or going to catch a bus, or stopping in the parking lot, or meeting friends on the Century II steps, or visiting the little park. All the rest, going on around them, was incidental, like other shoppers who happened to be visiting other nearby stores.

It was only after he had finished his exploring and found a place to sit, atop the little wall that separated park from parking lot, close up against the building it abutted, a spot from which he could look out over the whole area and down into the park as well, that he began to notice other watchers like himself, perhaps the only ones who did have a unitary sense of this place, a notion that there was more to it than the random, individual purposes of the people out in the light.

Some of these others were clearly workmen, in nondescript gray, not quite uniforms—nighttime janitors, perhaps, from the surrounding buildings, or maybe city workers assigned here, though he didn't see any of them doing anything that looked like work. Mostly they sat, as Sam did, along the stone railings, or found places to stand at the back edges of the parking lot, in the shadow of the neighboring building, sometimes in pairs, mostly alone. Their presence sometimes could only be told by the flare of a match, the spark of a cigarette floating in the dark.

Twice, he had glimpsed a slender, well-dressed man standing in the deep shadows of the recess where the dumpsters for the office building sat, more truly hidden than the others. And there was a man who wore a baseball cap pulled low over his eyes, with seeming purpose, who parked his small, dark car in the street, not far from where Sam's usually sat, and leaned against one fender, his arms crossed, only occasionally shifting position. Still another man, tall, bearded and balding, arrived each night at the same time, on foot, dressed as a jogger, though he came walking slowly, not running. He did not always stand in the same place, but he always found a place that was dark, out of easy sight.

What distinguished them all was that they did not enter the light, were uninterested in the buses or the library or any of the other communities within the place, but only stayed on the edges and watched, appearing and disappearing silently, unobtrusively.

It was not clear to Sam whether these men—for they were all men, as far as he could see—were any more aware of themselves as a group than were the shifting crowds in the lighted areas. He could not tell whether they noticed one another, or himself. He studied them surreptitiously over a span of two or three evenings, but could not catch any of them looking back at him.

No doubt they all had innocent enough motives, but he could not escape the feeling that there was something sinister about them—and by extension about himself as well. He was reminded of the zoo—or a perverse image of it, as though it were the animals who sat outside the bars watching the oblivious humans mill around inside their vast cage, unaware of its existence. Sitting at what seemed to him the border of light and dark, studying both worlds, he sometimes felt edgy, filled with an unaccountable apprehension, an unfocused concern for those who moved so carelessly in his view, drifting with aimless purpose, smoking, chatting while the night breeze ruffled hair and skirts, blew cigarette smoke into thin wisps and then into nothing, carried soft laughter here and there, sometimes startlingly clear above the rumble of the panting buses. He felt sometimes as though he ought to be warning them of something, though he did not know what it was.

Stosh was surprised by the building where Loomis lived—its shabbiness and disrepair. It looked to her like the sort of place where one might live for a week or so, having just arrived in town, while looking for something better. Seeing it, she nearly changed her mind, afraid of embarrassing him.

But she moistened her lips, rapped on the wooden door. It was in a dark end of the second-floor hallway, only a few feet from the top of the wide staircase, a musty, comfortless place that she could not imagine had ever truly been home to anyone.

Loomis opened the door clad in white T-shirt and jeans, barefoot, his eyes round and bland with surprise, narrowing only when he recognized her.

"Stosh," he said.

"I'm sorry to bother you, L.J. I'm looking for Sam."

"Sam Haun? He's not here." He frowned. "Matter of fact, I haven't seen him in a week or so."

"He hasn't been at the newspaper, either. Nobody's seen him. Fred Cubbage thinks he's hanging out with you, not bothering to come by the office. A friend of Sam's, Stu Merow, said he went by Sam's place yesterday and his car was there, but no one answered the door when he knocked. Merow said he thought Sam was there, just not answering the door. He hasn't been answering the phone, either. I went by there myself, a little while ago, but his car was gone. I'm starting to get a little worried. That's why I came here."

Loomis nodded and stepped back. "Come on in," he said.

The apartment was even tinier than she'd expected; the living room was also the bedroom, and it appeared that the kitchen was the only other room. She didn't see a bathroom. It was like a room in a dowdy dormitory; she could no longer have lived in a place this small, and she didn't understand how someone as large as Loomis could. He waved her to a ragged armchair next to the window.

"Sorry about the clutter," he said, glancing around uneasily, as though not exactly sure what might be exposed to sight.

In fact, it seemed fairly neat, for a bachelor's place. The bed wasn't properly made, but the covers had been pulled up—probably he had done that hastily when she'd knocked—and there were no piles of dirty clothing on the floor, only a soiled towel hanging somewhat mysteriously on a metal rack beside the door she had come through. The floor appeared to have been swept recently.

"I've seen much worse," she told him. "I grew up with six brothers."

"Can I get you something? A beer? I don't have any soft drinks."

She started to shake her head, but then saw that that would leave him feeling awkward, nothing to do, so she smiled and said, "A beer would be good."

He went past her to the kitchen and returned quickly, carrying two cold cans and a wooden chair, which he positioned near the foot of the bed, facing her, and sat down on, crossing his ankles in front of him. She liked his unself-consciousness about staying barefoot, and had a sudden urge to take off her own shoes.

Instead, she took a swallow of the beer, too large a swallow, and felt it burn going down. Her armchair sat next to the apartment's only window, which stood open. There wasn't much of a view out there—only another equally shabby apartment building across the street, and the cars parked along the curb below, including her own—but there was an evening breeze coming through the screen, and she realized that she felt safe and cozy, glad to have ended up here. The only light, beside the deflected glare of the ceiling bulb in the kitchen, was the soft glow of the reading lamp beside the head of the bed. She saw a paperback novel lying spread open on the floor at its base, and realized that Loomis had been lying on the bed reading when she arrived.

"I didn't mean to barge in on you and interrupt what you're doing," she said.

Loomis grinned. "Don't worry," he said. "You didn't interrupt anything." He took a swallow of his own beer, wiped his mouth and asked, "What do you think's going on with Haun?"

She hesitated, wondering how much Loomis knew, how much it would be right for her to tell him. She really knew nothing about the relationship between the two men. Also, it occurred to her that she had come here under somewhat false pretenses, letting Loomis think she was searching for Haun because she was worried about him. That was true enough, but it wasn't the whole story—perhaps even not the main thing. She wanted to find Haun because she needed to talk to someone and he seemed to her the only one who would have any idea what she was talking about, how she felt, the only one she could trust to tell her the truth.

"Well, you know," she said at last, "Sam still has some emotional problems."

"You mean from losing his wife and daughter."

She nodded and raised the can to her lips again.

Loomis nodded in response. Then he said, "I've seen a lot of people who lost family members in auto accidents, that kind of thing. People handle it different ways. Some take longer to get over it." He paused. "Still," he said, "there's something different about Sam."

"What do you mean?"

Loomis thought about it. She had the impression he'd never really focused on this before. "In a way it's because he seems so unemotional," Loomis said. "But I think there's a lot of anger in him, a cold kind of anger. People are often angry at the dead, blaming them for leaving, you know. But that's not what it is with Sam. That's not who he's angry at."

Stosh looked out the window, avoiding his gaze. "No," she said. "It isn't."

She felt Loomis watching her, not saying anything. When she looked around at him, he took a long swallow of his beer, draining the can, then put it on the floor beside him and stood up. "Want another?" he asked her.

She shook her head, then held her own can out in front of her, indicating that it wasn't empty.

He went to the kitchen and got another for himself. When he came back he sat down straddling the wooden chair, the back toward her, and rested his forearms on its top.

"We've known each other awhile," he said, "but I don't really know anything about you. Six brothers, huh?"

"I was the only girl. And the youngest."

"Parents kept trying?"

"I guess so. They're Catholic, anyway."

"They are?" he said.

"We are," she said contritely, though it felt like a lie. She didn't know what she was anymore.

"So how'd you get to be a journalist? It run in the family?"

"Oh, no. My father works for the power company. Did. He's retired now. And my brothers . . ." She shrugged. "They're all in different things."

"Like what?"

"Oh, uh . . . Dennis is the only one still in Chicago. He sells computers. Stephen teaches European history at Illinois State. Rafe coaches high school basketball in a little town in Pennsylvania. George . . . uh . . . I don't know exactly. He manages some kind of business in Indianapolis. Something financial. And David . . ." She felt herself running down, suddenly not wanting to say anymore " . . . David's in seminary in New York," she said, making herself finish.

"That's only five," Loomis said.

She was dismayed to find tears welling up in her eyes. She blinked, trying to make them go away. "Danny," she said. "My oldest brother . . ."

"He's dead?" Loomis asked. He asked it neutrally, a cop's question, which somehow made it easier to answer.

She nodded, wiping at her eyes with a wrist. "He died," she agreed.

Loomis leaned back casually and reached into the top drawer of the little dresser that stood against the wall at the foot of the bed, then scooted his chair closer to hers and handed her a clean handkerchief. It struck her that it was a gesture she had only seen in movies.

She wiped her eyes and blew her nose, then laughed at herself. "I haven't cried about it in years, since it happened. I thought I was past that."

"Things come back and surprise you," Loomis said. "How did he die, if you don't mind my asking?"

She shook her head. "In Vietnam. He was a medic. His helicopter got shot down."

Loomis grunted. "I was there," he said. "That's how I got to be a cop. An MP."

"If Danny had come back, he'd have been a doctor," Stosh said, and gave a half-grin.

Neither one of them said anything for a moment. Finally, she let out a long breath and drained the last of her beer, putting the can down beside the chair, as he had.

"Got any more?" she asked. He started to rise, but she waved him down again. "I'll get it."

On the tiny table in the kitchen was a neat stack of dirty dishes, ready to be washed. She opened the half-size icebox and twisted a can from the plastic mesh that held it to its neighbors, noticing that the frost had built up so heavily in the freezing compartment that the little door wouldn't quite close. Apparently Loomis lacked one or two domestic skills. For some reason, she was glad to discover that.

He didn't say anything when she sat down in the armchair again; she had the impression he was waiting for her to speak.

"Did you know Sam back . . . before?" she asked him. "Did you know his wife, Clare?"

Loomis shook his head. "Never met her. I knew him then, but not well."

Stosh nodded, then said. "She was unfaithful to him, but Sam didn't know it. She kept diaries or something, all about the affair, and he found them and read them after she died. He had no idea before that."

"That's what he's angry about," Loomis said. "I wondered . . ."

"But I thought he was handling it," Stosh said. A touch of shrillness in her voice made Loomis look at her questioningly. She shook her head. "He didn't need me getting involved in his life."

"Why not?"

She made a face. "Clare Haun was having an affair with Frank Rule," she said quickly. "So am I."

Loomis pursed his lips, studying for her a moment. "Have you become involved with Sam some way?" he asked. "Why would that be a big problem for him?"

"Oh . . ." She wished now she'd never said anything. "I don't exactly understand it," she said. "Something happened between us, or almost did, but I don't know exactly what it was. It's something to do with Frank, I guess. And that can't be helping Sam. He's obsessed with Frank, I think. He studies him, knows all kinds of things about him, his background, stuff like that. It's kind of spooky. But, you know . . ." She hesitated, then said, "I don't really know Sam all that well, but there's a way in which I feel like he's one of my best friends in the world." She shook her head. "I don't understand that. Do you?"

Loomis smiled and shrugged. "I don't know," he said. "You're probably asking the wrong person. One thing I'd advise, though, is not giving yourself too much credit for Haun's problems. Or giving him too little credit." He frowned. "I would like to know what he's up to, though," he added.

He got up and went into the kitchen, where she heard him dialing the wall phone. She heard him give someone Haun's license number, which he apparently knew, and ask to be advised of the location if a patrol car spotted it. "That's about the best I can do," he told her, coming back and sitting down again.

"How long before you'll hear anything, you think?"

He shrugged. "No way to say. Could be ten minutes. Could be never. He might have gone to see his kid, you know. He might not even be in town."

She nodded. "I hadn't thought of that. But the door was open at his house. I think he must be around somewhere."

Loomis nodded. "We'll try giving him a call after a while. Right now I'm gonna have another beer."

He was beginning to get a sense of the patterns, the routes by which people came and went. The younger people came either in cars, in and out of the parking lot, or else on the buses. None of them stayed long, pausing only to see who was there, perhaps chat for awhile, before boarding another bus or taking off once again in a car, heading back toward the brighter lights of Douglas. The older people came mostly on foot, and often from the direction of the library. There was one gray-bearded man, for example, who walked over at just about the same time each evening, carrying a book and a brown paper lunch bag, and sat on the same bench, near the center of the sunken park, his lunch bag on the ground beneath him, read for a couple of hours and then got up and walked back toward the library, where his car was presumably parked.

There was some overlap, of course. A few older people arrived and departed by bus, but those were mostly the ones transferring, who waited on the wooden benches along the street, some clearly a bit apprehensive about the young people milling behind them in the parking lot. And there were young people who arrived on foot, usually from the direction of the main drag, often in groups, as though having gotten lost, been abandoned by their herd.

The concert hall hadn't been open during his sojourn there, but Sam guessed that when it was, that would change the quality of the crowd in the area as well.

This evening, in fact, there was a steady flow of younger people—not kids, but mostly couples and small groups in their early twenties—coming from the direction of downtown, all dressed as though they'd been to some performance.

He couldn't think of what they might have attended, unless there was some sort of dance being held at one of the big hotels, but that seemed unlikely, and, anyway, they weren't coming from that direction. As far as he knew, all the downtown movie theaters had closed long ago. When he'd been in high school, there'd been half a dozen within walking distance of where he sat, but now they were all out on the edges of the city, four and five screens to a building, with names like Cinemas East. In his youth, they'd all been single-screen theaters, some of them lavish in design, with names like the Orpheum, the Palace, the Crest. There'd been one a half-block from here, beside the old police station, called the Sandra, where on Saturday mornings there had been a kids' matinee—dozens of cartoons and serials and a couple of action features for ten cents. He remembered himself and his friends staggering back out into the noontime sun, after a Saturday morning in that air-conditioned darkness among hundreds of other kids, some of them now blinking as they looked for their parents' cars, others trailing in an attenuated stream toward Broadway and Douglas, the heart of town, where all the buses had then stopped. What was there for anyone to do downtown now? Who would send their children here for anything? It seemed to him that this place where he now sat was like a revenant of the town

that had once been. Had the watchers on the fringes always been there, unnoticed until he was one himself?

A couple passed close by him, talking, and he caught
a reference to a local musical group, the Fabulous
Shirtheads, whose name, before they'd become popular
enough to advertise in the mainstream media, had once
lacked an *r*. That told him where these young people
had been—to the downtown music bar, a small upstairs
hall which kept coming back under different guises,
with different tastes, under different names—now a
nightclub featuring jazz, next month a coffee shop with
folksingers—never quite prospering but never quite failing entirely. What was it called nowadays? It was on the
tip of his tongue.

"Roxy's." The name floated to him on the air, out of
a welter of conversation, as though on cue, and hearing
it he frowned at some unexpected association. Where
had he heard it lately, in what context that troubled him
now to think of it?

Then he remembered, and his head came up, other
associations suddenly clicking into place in his mind.
Roxy's had been where Karen Munoz had been, with
her girlfriends, the night she had disappeared. She had
vanished—how could he have not thought of this
already?—while on her way to catch a bus for home.

Sitting on his low wall, studying his surroundings, he
had half-remembered the other connections—Terry
Fillmore returning a book to the library, her car found
there the next day; Mosteller vanishing during intermission at a Century II concert, on an evening much like
this one, when the doors must have stood open, the

concert crowd mingling briefly with the others on the plaza outside. It was the connection to Roxy's that brought it all together for him suddenly. Marty Madsen's friends had said she'd disappeared on her way to Towne East, where she often went on the bus after work. But had she ever gotten to the bus?

He stood up, agitated, and began walking, his hands in his pockets, his head bent forward, not seeing any of the others now, lost in the logic of what was forming in his mind. A watering hole—he had thought of that himself once, the idea that there might be some place like this, where a predator could lie in wait, select the straggler from the herd. He took a quick look along the borders of the area, saw the man in the baseball cap by his dark car, his eyes hidden, saw others perched here and there, a workman smoking a cigarette, the man in the jogging suit leaning against a tree at the far corner of the parking lot, his arms crossed.

He turned and walked back toward the sidewalk, heading for his car. He didn't know where he was going, but he felt that he needed to drive, to get away from the place itself and examine what he was thinking. Did it all fit, or was it just a matter of crazy coincidence? What about Courter? No one knew anything about her disappearance. Suddenly it seemed significant to him that she had left her car at her apartment. The police assumed she'd gone off with someone else, but might she not have taken a bus instead? And was the terminus area not the sort of place that would have interested her, with her workshop stories about the dark places, the prostitutes and winos? How better to study it than by bus, to ride there with the others who came and went?

In the car, going south on Main, he found himself headed for Loomis's place, already rehearsing what he would say, how he would explain it. There were things Loomis could check on—whether anyone had actually seen Madsen board a bus, whether Munoz and her friends had arrived at the terminus in a group, whether Fillmore and Mosteller were familiar with the area. He wanted to look at Courter's notebooks. If she'd been working on something about the bus interchange, surely that would clinch it, fit all five pieces together, make it obvious.

The nearer he came to Loomis's place, however, passing out of the bright streets and into the dowdy neighborhood with its shabby buildings and unmown lawns, the less sure he began to feel of his ability to make Loomis see it as he would. He sat through two red lights at Lincoln, with no other cars around, going over it all again, feeling it begin to turn gossamer after all in his mind. Underneath it, there was still a certainty, a conviction, but it was like the hunch which was the starting point for a story, not the story itself, not anything you could sell to an editor until you'd found out more.

It occurred to him that he hadn't seen Loomis for several days, that he didn't even know whether he'd be welcome, whether he still had any right to be involved in the case. Probably Cubbage had sent someone else to replace him by now, or the whole project had fallen apart. He could imagine Loomis listening to him with cold politeness, then dismissing it all as coincidence, as the product of his own fancy. How could he describe the terminus area to anyone else, after all, to make them see it as he saw it, let alone make clear the connection he suddenly saw to the dark man? Would the men posted around the edges look as obvious, as menacing, to anyone else as they did to him?

Then he turned the corner into Loomis's block and saw Stosh's car parked at the curb near the front steps. He nodded to himself, realizing what should have been obvious, that it would be Stosh who was working with Loomis now, sharing the secrets of the hunt, the speculations. Glancing up at the light in Loomis's window, he wondered if there might not even be more to it than that. Maybe, after all, he had freed Stosh from Rule, not only doing what he had done at the party but making a new place for her with Loomis by removing himself.

It was a thought he liked. And it absolved him of further responsibility, he saw—for Stosh and for the Strangler. If Stosh was working with Loomis, then he was surely on his own again, as he had begun, the whole thing having been an interruption of his original four-week plan. But now there might be something to salvage, something he was uniquely positioned to discover.

He realized that he wanted to find the dark man after all, to see him, to know him, perhaps even to speak with him. He remembered how he and Loomis had talked about the hunter with the gun and the hunter with the camera, which he was, but it seemed to him now that he was neither, that there was a third thing which was very nearly like finding one's way home. If he could see the dark man, he thought, he might see the face of the man in his dream. Thinking of that man, and the dog, he remembered how he had thought, driving away from Rule's, the first night he had gone to the bus interchange, about humans raised as wolves, animals raised as humans. Maybe that was what was frightening about the dream, the way the man and the dog—was it really a dog?—had somehow switched characters. Maybe that was why the woman's face had needed to be changed, to fit the canine tastes of her master. He shook his head, coming back to himself in the car, finding himself going north again, on Broadway, back toward Century II, as though he had only now awakened from the dream.

Stosh knew she wouldn't be able to remember later all the things they talked about, though some of the things she told Loomis were things she wouldn't have been able to tell anyone but Danny, if he were still alive, and if she hadn't had so much beer. But Loomis told her some things, as well—mainly about still being in love with his wife, Edie, who was getting ready to move in with another man. He also tried to tell her how he had driven Edie away from him, though Stosh didn't really understand that part. Another time, she thought he was just about to tell her something secret about the Strangler, something that was happening in the case, but that he caught himself just in time.

She didn't mind; she'd decided she was glad to leave all that to Sam, if he was still interested in it. For the moment, she was just happy to be sitting here with

Loomis, feeling tipsy and sleepy and completely safe for the moment. She had not realized before that she had been looking for such a place to hide, if only for a few hours. The evening seemed to her an example of the unexpected grace of the God she had once believed in.

Once she thought she was going to be sick, that she had drunk too much beer, and Loomis led her out into the hall to show her where the bathroom was, and then stood beside her as she leaned over the toilet bowl, swaying, but nothing happened, except that then they took turns waiting in the hall for each other, as they both had to get rid of some of the beer.

Back in the armchair afterward, she felt herself drifting off, unable to keep up her end of the conversation, not wanting to go to sleep but doing it in spite of herself, until she awoke to find that he was carrying her to the bed, and he said something she didn't quite catch and in reply she nuzzled her head against his chest, knowing he'd know what she meant by it, and he put her down softly on the bed and pulled a cover over her and kissed her forehead and turned off the light that was shining on her face. When she awoke again sometime later, with a full bladder, the apartment was pitch-black and she felt confused for a moment, finding herself alone in a strange bed, and then she remembered where she was and got up somehow, feeling as though the room were spinning slowly, and found her way out the door and down the hall to the bathroom, where the light hurt her eyes, and when she came back it seemed even darker than before, and she had to stand inside the apartment door for a moment to remember exactly where the bed was, and when her eyes had adjusted to the dark again she saw Loomis slumped in the armchair, his feet on the kitchen chair, a sheet wadded up under his head for a pillow and the breeze from the open window ruffling his hair.

14

Someone screamed, and then whoever it was kept on screaming. He twisted in the chair, coming awake, not knowing where he was. Then his eyes snapped open and he saw the empty bed, remembered Stosh and barely had time to wonder where she was before the scream came again and he realized it was the telephone.

He pushed himself up, feeling achy and old, and picked up the receiver. "Loomis," he said, then remembered that that was what he said at work, not here. "Hello?" he added.

"You up yet?" Davidson asked.

Obviously, he thought, but he said, "Yeah, yeah. Now I am."

"We been running down the places Banks lived before he went to Colorado. There's a place on Gold where he lived for awhile. We already talked to the people that have been there since then . . ."

"Gold?" Loomis asked stupidly.

"Yeah. Gold Street. Over by the river, near Harry."

"I lived on Gold when I was a kid," Loomis said. "Sixteen-hundred block."

"No shit. Small world. Banks lived in the nineteen-hundred block. Anyhow, like I said, we already talked to the people who live there, but we didn't get much."

Davidson paused and Loomis waited, wondering what the point would be. You had to let Davidson spin his stories. What time was it? He couldn't see the clock in the kitchen from this angle. The warmth of the apartment suggested late morning.

"Anyhow," Davidson went on, "we went back out, just rechecking stuff, you know? And Binkley was talkin' to the guy, and he says something about a Mr. Fogerty. Binkley says, who? And the guys says, Mr. Fogerty, the guy that lived here before. Binkley says, no, it was Mr. Banks, that's who we been asking about, but the guy says, no, I bought the place from a Fogerty. We figured, maybe this is the name of the realtor, or maybe Kirby's landlord, 'cause most likely he was renting it, but the guy insists, no, he bought the house from a Fogerty and the guy was living here, with his family. This is the first we'd heard about any family. I mean, Kirby's got no family, not livin' with him. So we backed up and checked it out, and what do you know? There was a Fogerty family that moved in for a month, right after Kirby left for Colorado, and then they turned around and sold the place again. We just always figured . . ."

"Okay," Loomis said. "So where are they now? Have you talked to them?"

"It took some work," Davidson said, and his tone told Loomis that the story wasn't over yet. He hoped it was a good one. "We found 'em in Andover," Davidson said. "One of those big new developments out there. They got money, see? Not the kind of people to live on

Gold . . . " He hesitated, then said, "I mean, the way that area is nowadays, you know?"

"I know what you mean," Loomis said. "It's always been that way."

"Yeah, well, anyway . . . I talked to the woman on the phone. She says it was like a mistake, that they bought that house. Her husband got transferred here from someplace else, and he made the deal without ever seeing the place. Some realtor did a snow job on him. Right by the river, all that. Anyhow, soon as they got here, they saw it wasn't for them, so they put it up for sale."

"Okay," Loomis said. "So what else?"

"Just this," Davidson said. "The main thing Mrs. Fogerty remembers about the house is how bad the basement smelled. Said they had to get it fumigated before they could show it to anyone. She figured whoever lived there before must have had a lot of cats and kept 'em locked in the basement. But I never knew about Kirby having any cats. Did you?"

"No."

"I mean, Kirby uses basements to store his bike, right?"

"That's right," Loomis said, imagining the grin on Davidson's face. But it was hard to imagine what use could be made of this in court.

"One more thing," Davidson said with exaggerated offhandedness, and Loomis realized this was the punch line. "The lady mentioned that her little girl found some jewelry in the basement, after it was fumigated."

"Jewelry? What kind?"

"Costume jewelry, she said. Didn't seem to think it

was valuable. In fact, she made the kid throw it away. She didn't remember any of it specifically, but she said the little girl might. She said we could come out and talk to her when she gets home from school this afternoon."

Loomis thought about Marcie. Would she remember some treasure she had found, five years before, when she was that age? She might, especially if someone could jog her memory, give her examples. They'd have to be careful about that part, though. Kids could be too easy to coach sometimes, and defense attorneys knew it.

"It's worth a shot," he said. "I'd better go along."

"That's what I figured. That's why I called. You want us to come by?"

"What time is it?"

"Little after eleven."

Loomis blinked in surprise. It was later than he'd thought. He realized Davidson was being tactful.

"I'm coming in," he said. "You guys go get some lunch or whatever, and I'll meet you after that. Has forensics come up with anything from Banks's car?"

"Not that I've heard. Are we gonna bring him in today? I think we better do it soon, if we're gonna do it at all. He's gettin' hinky."

"I know. I'd just like to have a little something else. We'll see how it goes in Andover."

When he'd hung up, he stood for a moment, surveying the apartment, wondering how Stosh had managed to leave without awakening him, what the visit had really been all about. Sam, she'd said, but it had been just as much about her, too, he thought. Not that he was the one to give anyone advice about relationships. She'd just needed someone to listen, he guessed, and he'd been able to provide that. As he recalled, he'd done some talking himself. He hoped he hadn't said anything too embarrassing. He smiled then, realizing that Stosh Babicki had just spent the night with him in his apartment and how that would sound to anyone who heard it, to his colleagues, to Edie. The funny thing was, he'd never once thought of it that way himself, until just now.

He shook his head, thinking that he'd never received any response on his call about Haun's car. He picked up the phone again and dialed Haun's number, let it ring half a dozen times, then hung up again. If Haun didn't surface soon, he'd have to have a look, see what was going on.

The phone inside rang six times, then stopped. It was one of those phones that made a low, warbling ring, and it was turned way down. There was no sound of movement from inside, no answer when she knocked again. Still, the car was there, in the driveway toward the rear of the house. She turned around and surveyed the neighborhood. There was an old man sitting in a porch swing, not moving, on the other side of the street, two doors down. He had a newspaper spread wide in his lap, but he was staring at her, making no effort to conceal his curiosity. Maybe he was one of those old people who watched everything, who knew all the comings and goings, who would be able to tell her all about Sam. But she didn't walk over to him; instead, she stepped off the porch and went around the side of the house, heading for the gate at the back, where the little black Lynx was parked.

The rear door of the house was standing wide open. She gave another knock, listened to the silence again and then opened the screen and went in.

"Sam?" she called out timidly. "It's Stosh." She stepped through the little enclosed porch and into the kitchen. There were some scattered, unwashed dishes and utensils here and there, on the table, beside the sink, but they all looked old, as though no one had used the kitchen for a long time. She crossed the kitchen to the door that opened into the rest of the house, and found herself looking along a short hallway with two doors on one side and one on the other, all three standing open. In the room beyond the other end of the hallway, she could see a dining table and a tall glass cabinet.

"Sam?" she called out again, more loudly. This time, startling her, there was a responsive grunt from someplace nearby—one of the rooms along the hallway. She took a short, half-hearted step forward, feeling a little apprehensive now, and once more called out, "Sam? It's Stosh. I need to talk to you."

There was another grunt, this time something that sounded vaguely like her name, and then the creaking of springs and the rustling of clothing. "Just a minute," Sam called back to her, his speech slurred by sleep.

She bit her lip and retreated to the kitchen, beginning to feel uncertain about having come. The night at Loomis's apartment, without air conditioning, had allowed the hay fever to get to her; she'd awakened full of congestion, her eyes itchy, a dull ache in her sinuses, and had taken a decongestant. Now she was beginning to feel groggy from that, as though out of synch with her own body. She sat down at the table to wait for him, and heard him cross the hallway, go in one of the other doors and close it, then heard water running. When he came back out, his footsteps went the other way, toward the living room at the front of the house, then came back again. He appeared in the doorway, rubbing his eyes, barefoot but with his hair combed.

"I'm sorry," she said. "It's just that no one had heard anything from you, and we were all getting a little concerned."

He frowned, but then said, "I'm fine," and glanced at the open back door.

"It was open," she said. "I knocked several times."

He waved the matter away, and then ran his fingers through his hair, messing it up again. "No problem," he said. He looked around, seeming to see the kitchen for the first time, the dirty plates and glasses piled on the table. "Uh . . . you want to go in the living room? It's not so . . ." He gestured helplessly at the kitchen.

She got up and followed him through the hallway, past the dust-covered dining table and into the front of the house, where Sam sank into a battered leather recliner, waving her to a padded rocker nearby—Clare's rocker, she guessed, for both chairs faced the TV set in the front corner of the room. Along the opposite wall was a sofa, mostly covered with books, typing paper, manila envelopes, sections from the newspaper. There were heaps of paper everywhere, including what looked like stacks of unopened mail. She noticed the spiral notebooks sitting on the floor beside Sam's chair. Out in the middle of the floor sat a child-size version of the rocker she sat in.

"You . . . uh . . . you had breakfast?" Sam asked. "You want some coffee?"

She shook her head. "I just wanted to make sure you were okay," she said.

"Oh, yeah, I'm fine," he said distantly, without conviction. He glanced at the clock on top of the TV, his eyebrows going up slightly. "I . . . uh . . . I've been staying up late at night, working."

"On the Strangler case?"

He gave an odd, wary look. "No. Something else. I think I'm off the Strangler case, aren't I?"

She shrugged. "I don't know. You haven't been around much. I know Fred's been concerned. Loomis, too. He said he hadn't seen you recently."

He gave a little smile she could only have described as crafty. "You've talked to Loomis?"

"I saw him last night. I thought you might be at his place."

Sam pursed his lips and nodded. She had the odd impression he didn't believe her. "However they want to handle it's all right with me," he said. "The Strangler thing, I mean. I don't mind at all."

She didn't know what to say to that, and there was a small, awkward silence. She felt unresponsive from the decongestant, not quite able to pick up her cues. "You're working on something else?" she asked finally.

"An enterprise story," he said. "Cubbage doesn't know about it yet. I've got to look into it a little further, you know? Make sure there's something there. Anyway, it's supposed to be my vacation. I haven't had much of a vacation, up to now." He grinned.

She smiled back, feeling confused, partly by the drug but also by something in his manner that she couldn't pin down. Sam seemed perfectly rational on the surface; maybe it was her imagination, some kind of paranoia, that she felt he had some hidden agenda. Maybe it was just the old thing about Frank, which she supposed was always there between them. Still, she would have said he seemed like a man who had made his mind up about something, formed some plan, and was now following his own counsel, playing it close to the vest.

"Can you tell me anything about this story?" she asked. "The one you're working on."

He thought for a second, then shrugged. "It won't sound like much right now. Like I say, I've still got some spadework to do. But it's basically a transportation story. About buses." He smiled broadly, as though he'd made some kind of joke.

"Buses?"

"Yeah. Did you know there's a whole . . . kind of community of people who ride the buses? I mean, if you drive a car, you don't see those people, right? It's like a different world right beside us. I think there might be a story in it."

"Buses," she repeated, feeling that she wasn't tracking. "You mean you've been riding around on buses?" The image that brought, of Sam sitting by himself, riding all day among strangers, struck her as sad and bewildering.

He laughed. "No," he said. "I haven't been riding them. I should, I guess. But you know, they all pass by the same point. There's a common ... terminus ..." His voice faded away, as though he felt he might be giving away too much.

"Out at Towne East," she said.

He nodded eagerly. "That's right," he said. "And there's another one ... downtown. You can observe the people at those places. It's actually better than riding the buses because you can see more of them, a broader cross section."

He gave her a bland stare, as though daring her to say that it sounded absurd. She stared back, trying to look interested, persuaded. It sounded trivial to her, especially in contrast to the Strangler, but she had the impression that Sam felt somehow possessive about it, protective. She thought of asking him whether he'd seen his counselor lately, but decided not to. It was enough for now to know he was all right.

She remembered that she had intended to talk to him about her own situation, about what had happened with Frank, but now that seemed impossible, absurd. He seemed far more a stranger to her than Loomis had the night before. How had he changed, exactly? She couldn't say. Probably it had to do with the night at her place; he had erected some wall against her—maybe after all the whole bus thing was an invention, just to get rid of her. Or maybe it was all just the decongestant. She wished she hadn't taken it.

"I've been wanting to apologize," she said.

"For what?" He seemed genuinely mystified.

"The night at my place. I shouldn't have . . ."

"That wasn't your fault," he said. He started to say something else, but then shook his head. "It's not important," he said at last. "We'd both been drinking. One of those things." He shrugged dismissively. "Forget it."

For some reason, his casualness made her feel even worse.

"I don't want you to hold it against me," she said.

For a second, his eyes grew serious, and there was a glimpse in them of the Sam she had seen during that evening they had spent together, the Sam she had kissed. "Honest to God," he said. "I hold nothing against you."

She nodded, but there didn't seem to be anything to say to that. She realized it was time to leave. Her eye fell again on the miniature rocker in the middle of the floor.

"It must be about time to bring your son back," she said.

Sam frowned and looked at the rocker himself, as though surprised to find it there.

"Yes," he said, then shook his head. "I mean, no. I'll have to leave him there for awhile longer, I guess. I can't really have him here while I'm working on this . . . thing I'm working on." He pursed his lips, looking confused. "I'll have to . . . I'll just have to explain it to them," he said doubtfully.

Good luck, she thought. But she stood up and said, "I'd better be getting back. I'll go out the front." She went to the front door and opened it, then turned back to him, the way he had turned back to her, at the door of her apartment. The old man was still on his porch swing, still watching.

"Anything I can tell Cubbage?" she asked.

Sam shook his head. "I'll call him later, when I'm ready."

It was such an obvious lie, she only nodded. The dismay she felt seemed out of all proportion. If the decongestant hadn't dried her out so thoroughly, she might have been on the verge of tears.

"Are we still friends?" she asked, appalled by how hard it was to force the words out.

"Of course we are," he said, and smiled.

She swallowed and closed the door behind her, thinking she had heard a lie in that as well.

As soon as they were in the car, on their way back, Loomis got on the radio and ordered the warrant for Banks's arrest to be executed. Binkley, clutching the Baggie with the locket inside, hummed tunelessly to himself.

They'd come that close to not getting it at all. It made Loomis feel nearly dizzy to think about that. Davidson, driving, turned toward Andover, to pick up the turnpike and get them back to Wichita that much faster. The city wouldn't mind paying the extra dollar this time, Loomis guessed.

Right up until the end it had looked like a dead end. The girl, who'd been four when they'd moved into the house on Gold, and was now nine, had stood silently, her eyes wide, listening while they talked to her mother. The mother told them that she'd already questioned her daughter, and that she didn't remember the jewelry she'd found, only that she'd thrown it away, as instructed to at the time. The girl didn't contradict her, didn't say a word, and the mother wasn't inclined to encourage her to speak; she preferred to speak for her.

The mother talked at length about the odor of the basement in the house on Gold Street. "Cats," she'd said, making a face. Telling how her husband had made the deal for the house at long distance, Loomis had the distinct impression that she still blamed him for the incident, that it was still an issue of some kind between them.

The father had come in while they were there, arriving home from work. He'd been curious, but had kept quiet, letting his wife talk. The little girl had gone and perched on his lap. There, it appeared, she'd felt brave enough to loosen up a little, still not speaking but smiling shyly at Binkley. Kids always liked Binkley. Once she'd gotten up and left the room, then come back and climbed back onto her father's lap, whispering in his ear as she did so.

When they were ready to leave, having learned nothing important, the girl had gotten up and tugged at her father's hand, drawing him out of the room with her. The mother had given them a frown, but then quickly put a smile on again to say her good-byes.

It was after she had closed the door, when the three of them were out in the driveway about to get back in the car, that the father had come around the side of the house and beckoned to Loomis. When he'd stepped that way, the father had reached out and deposited the locket in his hand. His daughter had kept it, against her mother's orders, the father said, because it had her name on it. He pointed it out to Loomis, the name *Chris* in ornate script letters engraved on the back of a tiny gold heart.

Loomis hadn't had to refer to the list folded up in his pocket. Sarah Mosteller's boyfriend, the one who'd waited futilely for her to return from the intermission at Century II, was named Christopher Barclay, and when she'd disappeared she'd been wearing a heart-shaped pendant with his name engraved on it.

He'd hesitated, standing there in the driveway with the pendant in his hand, feeling as though he were touching Sarah herself for the first time. Looking up, he had seen Christine Fogerty and her mother watching them from different windows, and he'd suddenly felt himself on the verge of tears.

He made himself see that it still wasn't proof, that a chain had to be established, that there was a lot of questioning necessary, some of it no doubt tricky, given the dynamics of the Fogerty family, the span of time that had passed. They could do all that later, he decided. What he wanted to do now, what seemed urgent to him was to get Kirby Banks in custody, and then, maybe not today but sometime soon, to sit down in a room with him and dangle this pendant in front of him, tell him what it was, where it had come from.

"This is what Kirby's been waiting for," Loomis said now, in the car. "He wants to tell us all about it. This will let him do it."

"But will his lawyer?" Davidson asked.

"He won't ask for a lawyer until it's too late," Loomis said. "He's not that smart. He thinks it would look bad."

"What's all this?" Binkley asked.

Coming over the crest of a hill, they met a carnival of flashing lights: brown sheriff's cars and blue state trooper cars scattered like discarded toys along the shoulders and the median.

Davidson slowed, riding his brake to where a deputy tried to wave the unmarked car on. Instead he pulled onto the median, flashing his badge. They all climbed out, peering at the scene. Loomis slid his glasses on and moved along the strip of gravel between grass and blacktop, trying to make some sense of the welter of red and blue light twisting off of clustered car bodies. It was still daylight, but the setting sun rested atop one of the hills, casting long shadows through the little valley, seeming to alter color and perspective, to make it harder to see what had happened. It appeared to Loomis that at least three vehicles had been involved. Up ahead of him, a wheel stood high in the air, thrusting out of a tangle of green metal. It was a familiar shade of green. He frowned and moved nearer, and a burst of light exploded suddenly in his eyes.

He stopped and held up one hand, blinking at the photographer.

"What the fuck . . .?"

"Hey, sorry, captain. Just doing my job." The photographer faded back into the crowd.

"What did he take my picture for?" Loomis asked, but Binkley and Davidson had disappeared. He rubbed at his eyes, his fingertips sliding beneath his glasses, and then squinted at the wreck again.

The color and shape of the fender below the up-thrust wheel came together suddenly like an optical illusion resolving itself into a familiar face, and he took a step backward and looked around at the other cars and the uniform, beginning to understand, to feel the first tingle of panic.

"Evening, captain."

A highway patrolman he'd worked with once leaned toward him, his face made ghastly by the flicker of red and blue light. The man carried a clipboard and a flashlight, but didn't seem to be doing anything with them.

"Who is it?" Loomis made himself ask.

The trooper shook his head.

"Haven't got the names. Woman and a kid, that's all I know."

"Oh, Jesus," Loomis said. "Shit." He turned away from the patrolman, at an angle from the roadway, skirting the wreck, unable to approach it but unable to make himself walk away, feeling as though the photographer's flash were still blinding him.

His stomach churned and he sat down heavily on the slope of the median, catching himself on one arm, and then put his face in his hands, trying to clear his head.

"Loomis, what's the matter? You sick?"

It was the sheriff, Warren Raines.

Loomis shook his head, momentarily unable to speak, then began trying to climb to his feet. Raines automatically reached to help him.

"What's the matter?" he repeated.

"Warren," Loomis said. "It's them, isn't it?"

"Who?"

"Edie. Marcie. It's a green Vega . . ." He stopped and swallowed, feeling sick again, feeling as though he might scream.

Raines frowned at the wreck, then peered at Loomis again, still frowning. "It ain't green, L.J.," he said softly. "It's blue. And that's a Butler County plate."

Loomis looked again. Dazed, he saw that Raines was right. He felt his legs grow weak with relief and foolishness.

"They said it was a woman and a kid," he said.

"Yeah, a little boy. He's dead, but the mother's okay."

Loomis followed Raines's gaze and saw a woman sitting cross-legged in the grass, her arms wrapped around her as if she were cold. A brown shock-blanket lay unused on the ground beside her. The trooper with the clipboard was standing nearby, waiting for her to notice him.

Loomis swallowed, thinking that the sudden joy he felt was wrong, inappropriate, but unable to turn it away. An incongruous, comforting breeze moved along the turnpike, ruffling the jackets of the patrolmen and deputies, cooling the sweat on his face.

"I guess you think I'm nuts," Loomis said.

"Shit," Raines said. "Things get to a man, don't they? What about the Strangler? I heard something."

Loomis nodded. "I think we got him," he said, his voice hoarse with wonder and relief. He felt suddenly that everything was going to be all right—not just the case, but everything, as though he had somehow been reprieved.

Wheels crunched in the gravel beside the roadway behind them, and they both turned to see a highway patrol car pull in behind Loomis's car. A stocky man in a red windbreaker got out of the back and then clung to the side of the car for support. One of the troopers he was with took his elbow and urged him forward toward the lights and noise.

"The father," Raines said.

A moment ago, Loomis thought soberly, I looked just like that. They watched as the man made his way across the median toward his wife, stopping when she looked up at him, as if he'd run into a pane of glass. She gave a jerk when she saw him and then began moving away, scrambling awkwardly to her feet and limping off along the median, running away from him, the patrolman with the clipboard trotting awkwardly along behind her. The husband glanced at the two patrolmen flanking him, but they were talking to one another, and he didn't interrupt them. He put his hands in his pockets, obviously unsure whether to follow his wife or not, and took a furtive glance at the crushed cars. Then he peered along the roadway, where his wife and the trooper had gone.

I need to talk to Edie about this, Loomis thought.

"What?" Raines asked, and Loomis realized he'd spoken aloud.

He took a ragged breath. "Nothing," he said. "I've got to get out of here. I better find Davidson and Binkley."

The girl had come with a group of her friends, all of them very young, on one of the buses. Sam hadn't paid any particular attention until he'd noticed her standing by herself, looking perplexed. He'd thought for a second he recognized her, but then realized she wasn't anyone he knew, though there was something vaguely familiar about her face. Perhaps she was the daughter of someone at work, or he'd run into her during some past assignment, at some public gathering or while interviewing her parents. Now it appeared her friends had gone off without her, crowding onto one of the departing buses, not noticing they were missing one of their number.

He watched her as she walked over to one of the wooden benches to inspect the schedule taped to a metal light pole. She opened her purse and rummaged through it, poking into interior pockets, finally snapping it shut with a child's grimace of irritation. She had blonde hair, hanging long on either side of her round face, and she wore a black T-shirt so long it nearly hid her lime green shorts. The front of the T-shirt bore the negative image of a face, in yellow, which looked to him vaguely like Jimi Hendrix, although he supposed that was unlikely.

The girl stood and scanned the area, as though looking for a familiar face, or perhaps only a friendly one. Sam looked away as her gaze swept over him, though he doubted that she could see him in his perch on the stone wall, within the shadow of the building. She walked to the top of the steps leading down into the sunken park, and looked over the prospects there. At last, with a little shrug, she went down the steps and walked purposely toward the gray-bearded reader who sat in his usual place on one of the benches along the main walkway, his lunch bag tucked beneath his seat.

It interested Sam that she had picked this older, vaguely grandfatherly figure to approach, instead of one of the women in the area—although, now that he looked, he saw that there were no older women around at the moment, only some girls a few years older than herself, most of them gathered into bunches, or paired up with boys of the same age.

When she spoke to the man on the bench, who had not noticed her approach, his reaction was nearly comical. He started as though stuck with a pin, looked up at her, then looked quickly around, clearly suspicious of her intentions, no doubt expecting to find some crowd of young people preparing to taunt him.

The girl spoke again, but the man only shook his head and turned pointedly back to his book. She stood for a moment longer, nonplussed, then shrugged unhappily and turned away. As she did so, the man gave her one quick, shy glance and went back to his reading.

She came up out of the park only about ten yards from where Sam sat, and scanned the lot again, her mouth now set in a lopsided frown. She opened her purse again and studied the contents, then snapped it shut, chewed at her lips for a moment and began walking toward the sidewalk behind him, in the direction of the downtown area.

It was a route that would take her past the man in the baseball cap. Sam glanced that way and was surprised to see the man openly studying the girl, like himself, his head bent back a bit, so that his eyes were uncharacteristically visible. Sam felt a chill of apprehension and—oddly—another moment of near-recognition. His face, too, seen this clearly for the first time, was vaguely familiar. Sam associated it with Loomis, with the city building, and he thought of all the mug shots he had looked through, the photos of faces attached to rap sheets.

That caused something else to click, and he looked back at the girl in surprise, realizing it had been in a photo that he had seen her face before, and knowing in the same instant where it had been.

"Marcie?" he said, as she came abreast of him. "Marcie Loomis?"

She stopped, startled, her face first beginning to form a smile of recognition, then growing guarded as she peered at him.

"I know your father," he said. "I recognized you from the photo on his desk. You're older now."

She nodded, still uncertain.

"My name's Sam Haun," he told her. "I'm a reporter for the *Mid-American*. Did you get deserted by your friends?"

She gave a little sigh, relaxing all at once, accepting his words that easily. "Yeah," she said. "I guess they all went off without me. I thought I had money for the bus, but I don't."

"I could loan you some," he said. "Or I could give you a ride home. It's getting late, and I was about ready to leave anyway."

She glanced around, obviously wondering for a second what he was doing there at all. "I . . . uh . . . that would be great," she said, shrugging and grinning, leaving it up to him to decide which offer she meant.

He stood up. "My car's right over here."

He led her to the sidewalk, past the man in the baseball cap, who looked away as they approached, his face hidden again. As he was getting into his car, Sam looked back at him one more time and found the man staring not at Marcie but at him. It rattled him, not least because he once again felt a shock of near-recognition.

Neither of them spoke until they were on Kellogg, headed east. Sam was trying to pin down where he had seen the man's face before, trying to attach it to a particular photo, a name, but could no longer make it come clear in his mind.

"Have you known my dad a long time?" the girl asked then, apparently made nervous by his silence.

Sam looked at her, not quite hearing her for a second, then nodded.

"I've known him for several years," he said. "Not very well. It's only lately I've gotten to know him better because of . . . a case of his I've been covering."

She nodded. "I guess I should know your name," she said, "but I don't read the newspaper much."

"Most people don't notice bylines, anyway," he said. "You live somewhere around Towne East, don't you?"

"Oh, yeah. Sorry." She gave him the address, then asked timidly, "Why were you at the bus stop?"

He hesitated, then said, "It's just a pleasant place this time of night. A lot of people gather there."

"Really?" She frowned, confirming his judgment that

most of those who passed through the area didn't think of it as he did. "There's that little park," she said as though to support what he had said, which clearly struck her as doubtful.

She lived in a duplex on one of the side streets behind Eastgate, the old shopping center that had been nearly wiped out by the massive Towne East mall nearby, but was now reviving. He sat at the curb for a moment, after she'd gotten out, to watch her safely inside. The door opened as she was putting her key in it, and a woman looked out at him, her eyes narrowed in a frown. Marcie began talking to her mother, perhaps explaining who he was, why she had come home that way. He drove away.

Registering the concern on Edie Loomis's face, he thought for the first time how easy a victim Marcie would have been, and for the first time what he felt, thinking of the Strangler, was neither fascination nor professional interest, but something like revulsion. Debbie, had she lived, would not be as old as Marcie yet, but she would not be that much younger. She, too, would have been potential prey. And if Marcie had disappeared this evening, who would ever know what had become of her? Would the man in the baseball cap come forward, give a description of him and his car? Perhaps. But even so, it would be no help to the girl by then.

He realized that he had been spared something after all in the deaths of his wife and daughter—the apprehension that Edie must live with, and Loomis himself, watching their daughter go out into the world on her own, knowing as well as the two of them would what lurked out there. And of course it wasn't just Marcie, just young girls. It was Edie herself, even Stosh. They were all at risk. If not from the Strangler then from one of his many avatars. He remembered being surprised to see how many men there were who might conceivably be the Strangler, who had the potential for it. But for all the hundreds of them, there were thousands of women—tens of thousands—who might be his victim, for reasons having nothing to do with themselves. He could not quite understand why he had not seen that so clearly before; now that he did it seemed a far more overwhelming fact, and one that partook far less of fantasy.

For a second, he found himself mourning Clare as though she had been a victim of the Strangler, as though for that second he had forgotten how she really died. But then, remembering, it seemed to him that in some way he had not been wrong, that she had gone to the dark man, partly of her own free will. How many of them did that? he wondered. Not that they wanted to die, of course. What they wanted, he supposed, was something like what he wanted—to see, to know, to finally understand. They, too, had made the mistake of thinking of themselves as observers, not participants.

He drove by the bus interchange, but did not stop, only noticing that the car belonging to the man in the baseball cap was gone now. He thought of going to the city building, getting someone to let him look through the photos again. But what would it mean if he spotted that face there? What would he do or say about it?

And anyway, it couldn't be tomorrow. Tomorrow was the day he was expected back in Malden to pick up Davy. He still had to work out what he was going to do and say about that.

15

—————

When she got off the elevator, the first thing she saw was Frank, standing in his office, looking at her from behind the long glass window. She looked away with an effort and walked to her desk, feeling his eyes on her all the way. Still, she jumped when the telephone rang as she sat down.

"Could you come in here for a minute?" He hung up before waiting for her reply.

"Of course," she said to the dead receiver.

In Frank's office she closed the door behind her, as though that would shut out the rest of the newsroom, keep them from being seen there together. She sat down quickly, put her hands in her lap.

When she finally looked up at him, he was pecking at his VDT keyboard with two fingers, frowning at the screen. She realized that it had irritated her for a long time that he typed that way, that he had spent a lifetime in journalism without having learned to type properly. It struck her now as an obvious signal of disdain for those who did the writing. He finished and gave her an empty, speculative smile.

"You're still angry," he said.

She shook her head. "Not angry," she said. "Confused."

He put his hands together on the desktop and swiveled toward her. "I told you I was sorry about the other night."

He had. He had apologized in his car, all the way back to Towne East, but it had been clear, then and now, that he didn't understand what he was apologizing for. And she didn't seem able to tell him in terms that would make sense to him; she could not point to anything that had happened between them that night that had not happened before.

"I know it wasn't good for you," he said, lowering his voice to an intimate whisper. "I want you to understand that there's a reason. I've had other things on my mind."

She waited, and after a moment he gave a little grimace of distaste at being forced to admit it, and said, "It's Susan. She's going to leave me for another man."

Stosh swallowed a startling impulse to laugh. She stared at him, not knowing what to say.

"She told me all about it," he said gloomily. "All the details." He sighed. "Anyway, you can see why I'd be distracted, even . . . ambivalent."

"Ambivalent? About us, you mean?"

He nodded. "But it also means I need you more than ever now. I need you to stick with me, to overlook my ambivalence, all the rest of it."

She digested that, then asked, "Have you told Susan about us?"

He gave her a surprised look, shook his head, but then said, "Of course, in a way, I think she's always known. Not about you, specifically. But that there was someone."

"There's always been someone," Stosh said.

He started to say something, then simply shrugged and nodded.

"So are you going to tell her?"

He frowned. "I see what you're getting at," he said. "But I think it would just make things . . . more complicated right now."

"You're trying to talk her out of it," Stosh said. "You don't want her to leave."

"I've always told you I loved her."

She nodded. It was just that she hadn't really believed it, didn't quite believe it now.

He cleared his throat. "She's going off with this other man tomorrow," he said. "Not permanently, just for a few days, to talk things over with him. I've asked her to delay, to give us a chance to talk things over, and she needs to put him in the picture. They're meeting in Montreal." His voice faded away for a moment, and then he blinked and said, "I need you to be with me tomorrow night. It's going to be hard. I can't face being alone."

"You don't need me," she said. "You just need someone. It could be anyone."

"No. That's not true. I love Susan. I've always been honest about that. But you . . . you're special to me, too."

She looked away from him, out at the newsroom. Cubbage and Lueck were standing by the row of mailboxes, next to the elevator, talking animatedly, Lueck cradling a paper cup of coffee between his hands.

That's where I belong, she thought. Out there. Not in here.

"I'll be blunt," Frank said, his tone making her look back at him. "Things are going to be different from now on, one way or the other. In order to keep Susan, I may have to give you up. I don't want to, of course, but . . . anyway, this could be our last time together. On the other hand, if she does leave me, things could be very different between you and me, maybe more like you've always wanted them to be."

She stared at him, hearing the implied "and maybe not." It was nothing she could ever charge him with, or file a complaint about, but the threat was there, behind the hinted hope: If she didn't come through for him now, things could be different in other ways between them. He was, after all, her boss.

Perhaps seeing that she'd gotten the message, he waved a hand vaguely in front of him, as if to erase it. "We just need to talk everything out," he said. "None of us really knows what's going to happen."

"We were going to talk last time," she said.

"I know, I know," he said impatiently. "I've already apologized for that. I've explained about Susan. This time we have real issues to discuss."

She nodded. What they had to do, she thought, was work out a new contract, spell out everybody's rights and obligations in the light of this new development. He didn't even realize how casually he'd just dismissed the old issues—her issues—as the unreal ones. She also realized, with a distant sinking feeling, that the way he had put it, leaving all the eventual options open, made it impossible for her to refuse to see him, to be a party to the new contract, to find out how it would all come out. Her coming to see him was as inevitable as Susan's flying to Montreal. We all have to get our proposals on the table, she thought, try to make the best deal we can.

"Tomorrow night," she said. "What time?"

He looked at her for a second, perhaps surprised by her tone. "I'll be at Towne East at eight P.M."

She nodded. "Okay. I'll be there." She had the feeling she was arranging some clandestine interview with a source on an important story.

He smiled. "No maybe about it this time?"

She shook her head. "That's over with," she said.

He pursed his lips and nodded. "You won't be sorry."

On the highway, the city behind him, Sam thought for the first time in years of riding with his mother along this same road, just the two of them, singing incongruous songs he had learned in Sunday school or heard on the country station his grandmother listened to, singing loud in the rush of air from the open windows, the thin smoke of the cigarette his mother held against the steering wheel spiraling out into the night. He remembered wishing that those trips could go on forever, that it could always be just the two of them, but knowing that it would never happen, that it wasn't what she wanted. Sometimes, after she'd left him, after he'd been there awhile, he had begun to wish she'd never come back at all, that he could really live there with them, be a part of that world. What did Davy wish for now? The question answered itself: for Clare's return, as well as his. Sam sighed and turned on the radio.

The air was warming fast as the sun came up, and he rolled the windows down, letting the wind blow over his face and arms. With it came the first dry country smells, the pleasant stench of manure, the occasional sharp tang of grass and weeds being burned back. After awhile he found himself driving alone on a straight stretch of highway, no other cars anywhere, ahead or behind. From the radio came the hiss and rattle of synthesized music, some contemporary anthem of self-regard; he turned off the radio and began singing as loudly as he could into the wind, almost defiantly:

> *And he walks with me*
> *And he talks with me*
> *And he tells me I am his own . . .*

There was a hastily assembled press conference at the city building just after lunch, at which Lt. Ron Drake, the police PR officer, announced the arrest of a man named Kirby Banks in connection with the Karen Munoz murder. Drake wouldn't answer questions about Banks's possible connection to the Strangler murders six years before, but he acknowledged for the first time that those investigations were being actively pursued again. Loomis wasn't there, and neither was Haun. But Mickey Goodwin was.

Stosh noticed him standing to one side during the press conference, not writing anything down. Afterward, she caught up with him at the elevators, where they hung back while the TV and radio guys muscled for space for their equipment, in a hurry to get on the air.

"Why are you here?" she asked him bluntly.

He grinned. "Just a coincidence," he said. "I mean the press conference. Cubbage sent me over to try to pick up on Haun's project."

The elevator doors closed and they stood alone in the suddenly silent hallway.

"He sent you?" she asked, realizing too late how incredulous she sounded.

Goodwin's smile faded for a second, and his eyes turned cold, resentful, but then he smiled, punched the DOWN button, and said, "I guess Cubbage knew something was up, that they were getting close to an arrest. He needed someone quick." He shrugged. "I've been trying to get in to see Captain Loomis, but no luck so far."

She nodded, trying to imagine Loomis willingly working with Goodwin, as he had with Haun. It seemed unlikely. She wondered for a second if this was really Frank's doing, a second "message" sent to encourage her to keep their date.

"Maybe we could get together later," Goodwin said. "I mean, so you could fill me in on stuff. I've read the clips, but I'm coming in late."

His manner was eager, almost obsequious. She realized that he was always this way with her, the way he was with Cubbage, with Frank, with the other editors. She hadn't thought about it before, even noticing how unpleasant he often was with everyone else, the way he talked about his co-workers behind their backs. Probably he talked about her that way, too—about her and Frank. Once everyone knew that it was over between them, he would say the same things, make his taunting jokes, in her hearing, perhaps to her face.

"I don't think I could help you much," she said stiffly. "Sam and I weren't really working together. We were keeping separate to insulate the off-the-record stuff he was getting. So that if I got it, too, I could use it without compromising him."

Goodwin nodded sagely. "That was a good idea," he said. "I guess I'll just have to keep trying with Loomis. Or maybe get in touch with Haun. He's disappeared."

"He's on vacation," she said.

Goodwin gave her a sly look, but then smiled again and entered the elevator that had just opened in front of him. Stosh hung back, deciding not to ride down with him. The doors closed.

"Stosh."

She turned and saw Loomis leaning through an unmarked doorway, beckoning to her. She walked toward him and he stepped out into the hallway, keeping his hand in the door to wedge it open.

"I wanted to talk to you," he said, "but not while that jerk was around."

She knew she should defend her colleague, but couldn't find the words to do so. "What is it?" she asked.

He chewed at his lower lip for a second, looking uncharacteristically nervous, then took a quick glance along the hall before answering. "Edie and I are getting back together," he said.

She laughed, and he blinked at her in surprise.

"I'm sorry, L.J.," she said. "That's great. I just thought,

the way you called me over, like it was some big secret . . ."

"Oh." He smiled. "You thought it was going to be something about the case. Sorry."

"I'm not disappointed," she said. "I'm happy for you. I really am. I'm glad to hear things are going right for someone."

He cocked his head to one side. "I just went and told her straight out that I didn't want to give up on us, that I wanted to try again," he said. "That's all it took. It turned out she felt the same way. We'd just been going along assuming we knew how the other one felt. Sometimes you just have to take the bull by the horns . . ."

"I get the point," she said. "You're saying I should take control of my life, too. I agree. If I were dealing with someone like Edie . . . or like you, for that matter . . ."

"Maybe you should be," Loomis said. "Someone different, anyway."

"I know." She sighed and glanced back at the elevators, where a man and a very pregnant woman had gotten off and were studying the list of office numbers on the wall. "It's not that easy," she said.

"Yeah," Loomis said. "It's not going to be that easy for us. We realize that. There's a lot that's happened, a lot of practical things to deal with. Where we live, Marcie's school, all that. Hell, she had to break up with this other guy, and that's not easy. I mean, she was getting ready to move in with him. She cares about him, you know?"

"You feel sorry for him?" Stosh asked.

He thought for a second. "Yeah. In a way, I do." He

gave a grunt of laughter. "I guess I can afford to be magnanimous. But really, you know, it's almost as if nothing that happened while we were split up really happened, like it was all a dream or something. You know what I mean? Even the Strangler coming back . . . I know that doesn't make any sense."

She shrugged.

"I saw a wreck on the turnpike," he said, as though intent on making it clear. "A kid got killed, and I saw the parents starting to try to deal with it. That's when I knew I had to do something. I mean, that was for good, you know? That kid dying. I thought maybe we still had a chance to get things back while nothing like that had happened, nothing irreversible." He was silent a moment, then said, "It's funny how much things really are the same between us. Different, but the same."

"Like a changed, familiar tree," she said.

"What?"

She shook her head, feeling foolish. "It's from a poem I read in college, about love," she said. "Something about love." She frowned, gradually remembering a bit more of it: Like waves breaking, it may be, or like a changed, familiar tree . . .

"I like that," Loomis said. "A changed, familiar tree. Yeah. Guess I should have paid more attention in English class." He laughed.

She did, too, feeling suddenly uneasy as she remembered more of the poem, remembered that it hadn't been about love the way she'd been thinking, the way Loomis thought, that it had been about something else entirely.

He reached back and pushed the door open behind

him. "I just wanted to tell someone," he said. "I knew you'd be around somewhere. I hope you don't mind."

"I'm glad," she said. "I'm glad it was me you told."

He nodded and smiled, then stepped back and let the door close between them.

Going down in the elevator, she found the stanza going around in her mind, knew she'd be unable to get rid of it the rest of the day, a poem she hadn't even thought of in years. She spoke it aloud, alone in the elevator, frightened of the sound of her own voice; sometimes that worked. "Or like a stairway to the sea, where down the blind are driven." She was glad after all that she hadn't recited that part for Loomis.

From the front of his aunt and uncle's house, Sam could see all the way to the other end of town, where the road hooked sharply right, crossing the bridge to the cemetery. The flat, red pebbles rustled beneath his tires, now and then pinging off the bottom of the car, and he remembered how hot they were against bare feet in the sun, how cool they were in the shade, what a pleasure the one was after the other.

"Why do you play up in your room?" he asked Davy. "I used to be out here all the time, running around barefoot."

Davy, past his first excitement at Sam's return, beginning to be a little cranky now, looked out the window and shrugged. "There's nothing to do out here," he said.

Sam hadn't found a way yet to tell him that he planned to leave him here for a while longer. Maybe it would come at the cemetery, or this evening some time. He'd planned to go right back to Wichita, after seeing

Davy, but Harriet had persuaded him to stay overnight. He could tell that she was troubled, perhaps afraid that he intended some more permanent arrangement, that he was following in his own mother's footsteps.

Davy had shown him his room—the one Sam still thought of as his grandmother's room, so that it made him nervous to see all of Davy's toys, the little Fisher-Price people and their plastic buildings, spread out everywhere on the floor, a sprawling city. After that they'd gone out to Gerald's workshop, in what had once been a tractor shed, to see the small bookcase Davy had made under Gerald's supervision.

"Needs another coat of stain," Gerald had said. He was stripping the ancient paint off of a dresser they'd bought at an estate auction the day before. "You could take it with you, finish it at home."

Gerald had looked pointedly at Sam then, and Sam had wondered how Harriet had gotten the word to him so quickly. Or maybe it was just that Gerald had picked up on something in his own behavior.

Now he and Davy came to the single block of shops that constituted Malden's downtown area, and he took his foot off the gas, letting the engine pull the car along at walking speed. The stores were about as he remembered them, but most appeared to be closed now, except for the real estate office on the corner where the Rexall drugstore had been, where he and his cousins had bought cherry Cokes in conical white cups and dipped the ends of the straw papers in the syrupy liquid before blowing them at the ceiling, where they had sometimes stuck all summer. In its window now was the sign advertising the Ridgley estate sale, where Gerald and Harriet had made their purchase, and a half dozen others as well. No one was filling the emptying houses in the little town; there were no more crowds of summertime children for Davy to run barefoot with, as his father had.

On the opposite corner was the deserted telephone company building, probably the only three-story building within fifty miles. It had been vacated when Sam himself was small, when the town's switchboard had given way to dials, and it had stood empty since, as far as he knew. There had not been a phone in his grandmother's house until after she had died, when Gerald and Harriet had finally put one in. She had not believed that she needed one. Next to the telephone building was the post office—also looking deserted now, but he remembered how it had been inside, dark and cool, high-ceilinged, with the springy wooden floor and the rows of little glass-fronted boxes with numbers on the front and the tiny dials with their arrowhead pointers. His grandmother had sent him for her mail sometimes, trusted him with her combination. He remembered suddenly, vividly, the smell of the place— metallic tang and damp wood.

Somewhere along here there had been a "recreation parlor," with the sweet, exotic odor of beer bursting through the screen door as he and his cousins passed by outside, the sounds of laughter and an edgy kind of talk that could be heard nowhere else in the town, the shapes of men with long sticks in their hands circling the huge tables at the back, dimly visible through the dust-covered window with its neon beer signs and placards advertising rodeos and country singers. But there was nothing remotely like that now, and he could not even tell where it had been.

When they came to the turn, he accelerated again, putting the dead town behind them. Just ahead lay the river where he and Don had seen the snake. But as he approached he found the single-lane bridge blocked by a shoulder-high pile of gravel and a sign saying DANGER. STAY OFF.

"I guess we'll have to walk from here," he told Davy. "Either that or drive all the way out to the new highway."

Leaving the car in a patch of shade, they stepped around the gravel and out onto the oiled wooden planks that had once been the main way in and out of the town. Sam held tightly to Davy's hand; he had forgotten how scary the old bridge was, and he realized belatedly that the sign might have been meant for pedestrians as well as drivers. The twin rows of planks, like a railroad track for cars, lay across beams set every foot or so, the length of the bridge, so that anyone walking across seemed most of the time to be walking over empty air, suspended high above the brown, sun-speckled water.

"Wisht I had something to throw," Davy said.

"My cousins and I used to fish from here," Sam told him. "When the sun was in the right place, it made the water clear, and you could see the fish in the shallows along the bank. We used to throw rocks at them, but of course you couldn't hit them. They aren't exactly where you think they are, under the water." He thought about that for a moment, tempted to warn his son that everything was that way, once you grew up.

Davy stepped to the edge, putting a hand on the

rusted metal rail and leaning out far enough to look straight down. The movement brought a chill to Sam's heart, and he grabbed his son's wrist. "Be careful," he said. "It's a long way down."

"Would it kill me?"

Sam shook his head, smiling uneasily. "I doubt it," he said. "Not if you can swim."

"I don't know if I can swim," Davy said.

Sam realized he didn't know either. When would he have learned? He thought of what Harriet had said to him, back at the house, whispering it while Davy was up in his room, finding his sneakers: "In spite of everything, he's basically a happy little boy, Sammy. Don't do anything to make him melancholy, the way your mother did you." It had seemed to him she was telling him a secret about himself and his mother, something she had never intended to reveal, in order to save the boy.

He leaned his forehead against one of the metal braces and peered downward alongside Davy, imagining for a moment two other, slightly older boys, a snake, a circle of blinding sunlight. The sun was beginning to heat the tarred beams on the bridge, and the shadowed water moving sluggishly below looked cool, inviting. He remembered the Civil War story he had read in high school, about a soldier being hanged on a bridge like this, somehow falling instead into the water below and swimming to freedom. But then he remembered that the escape had turned out only to be a dream, in the instant before death.

"Let's go," he said. "It's getting hot."

The cemetery was no more than a hundred yards from the end of the bridge, though in his memory it had been much farther than that, as the town had been much larger, the river much wider. And he thought there had been a farmhouse between the bridge and the cemetery, though he saw no trace of one now, only a short stretch of high weeds backed by woods, bordering the road. Nearer the graveyard, he saw that a canopy was set up not far from the entrance with its cast-iron arch. A stack of folding chairs sat beneath the canopy, but there was no one in sight. He boosted Davy over the low wooden fence and then climbed over himself, and they zigzagged between the marble slabs, heading for the corner where the family graves were.

The canopy reminded him not of Clare's funeral, but of his grandmother's, when he had been in college. There had been a ceremony at the church she had attended in Fredonia, and then another, smaller ceremony here, at the graveside. At the church there had been an almost comical duet, two fat screechy sisters in tight black dresses belting out "How Great Thou Art," making it sound like a country song. When he'd mentioned them to Harriet, years later, laughing about it, she'd told him that the two sisters had been featured on a Sunday morning radio show from Independence that his grandmother had listened to every week.

He could not quite recapture the words of the song, though it seemed to him he had heard it at every funeral he had ever attended, except Clare's. "Oh Lord my God, when I in awesome wonder . . ." That was how it started, but he couldn't remember what the next word was, only that later on there was something about seeing the stars, hearing the rolling thunder. Such words meant no more to him now than they ever had, but he understood the pull of the soaring, triumphant chorus—"Then sings my soul"—which was the reason people like to hear it at funerals.

He felt momentarily disoriented, couldn't remember for a second how he had gotten off onto that track. In that second, it seemed unutterably strange to him that he was not attending his grandmother's funeral, but was walking with his own son toward the graves of his own wife and daughter, as if all of his adult life were only a story he had read, or something he had dreamed and did not remember clearly, as if he might awaken suddenly, as from a sullen teenage reverie, to find himself standing in the cemetery in Independence, beside his mother at his father's grave, itchy and yearning to be gone, to be back in the city—as indeed he felt now, unable to shake a strange anxiety about missing a night beneath the dark shadow of Century II. He gripped Davy's hand more tightly.

"Here they are," Davy said, as though someone they'd been waiting for were arriving late.

Looking down, he found Clare's grave at his feet, and found himself breathing heavily, swept by guilt. He groped within himself for the old anger, the old self-pity, as a counterbalance, but could no longer locate it.

"Dad," Davy asked. "Are you crying?"

The boy's tone was partly distressed, partly accusing. Sam looked at him in surprise, wondering what would make him ask such a question, but when he raised a hand to his cheek he found moisture beneath his fingertips.

"Hay fever," he said, bewildered, and rubbed at his eyes, drying them. He felt Davy watching him, anxious, as he blinked and looked down at the grave, biting his lip. To his dismay, more wetness welled up in the corners of his eyes, unbidden. The marble casket cover was a blur of gray. He thought of Clare lying beneath it, those few feet away from him, forever.

Why did you leave me? he asked her silently. Why didn't you tell me you were going away?

And then the tears poured out before he was able to stop them.

Loomis had come down to the forensics lab to go over the reports again, refresh his memory about the details of each crime scene before having another go at Banks.

Banks was stubborn, but he was getting ready to crack; Loomis could feel it. All he needed was the right push, the right lever. He had begun to talk about the murders in that speculative way they did sometimes, using the victims' first names, hinting at what they knew, letting you know they might be about ready to deal. Except there would be no deals this time. All Kirby would get was what he secretly wanted—a chance to tell his story at last, to reveal the greater, more interesting person concealed inside the slight, deferential man. "Maybe Marty never got on the bus," he'd said at one point. "She might have gotten a ride from somebody instead." And when they'd talked about the approach to Mosteller, the man at Century II who'd been asking someone to help him move something, he'd said, "It could have happened that way with Terry, too, over at the library. I mean the same kind of thing."

The one sore point was Courter. Whenever they brought her up, Banks shook his head, angrily, refused to talk, or flatly insisted he had nothing to do with her, never met her. It might mean he was telling the truth about her, was indignant about being falsely accused, even though it underlined his lack of such a response to the others. Or, turn it around, it could mean she was the only one he actually did, that he didn't mind talking about the others because he hadn't done them. Or it could be that he did them all, but that that one bothered him more, as it had bothered the police more, the savagery getting out of control. Maybe, with Courter, that other self had gotten away from him, more independent than usual, and he didn't like to admit that, even to himself.

But if Banks persisted in denying the Courter killing, even when he'd finally admitted the others, the flowers were going to be a problem. Because Munoz, one of the two they expected to nail him on, had been in sequence—five instead of the four she should have had if you took Courter out. It wouldn't be like Kirby, Loomis didn't think, to accept a copycat's work as his own. In fact, nobody had even mentioned the flowers yet; they wanted Banks to say something first.

"You're not going to find anything new in there," Kreider said. He was at one of the metal worktables, dropping tiny bits of some chemical into a series of test tubes, his glasses low on his nose as he peered over them at the results. Loomis sat at Kreider's old wooden desk, in the corner, the lab reports spread out in front of him.

"Never hurts to look again," he said distantly.

The fact was, it had been a while since he had really

looked at the reports, the itemized lists of what had been found and where. He had gotten used to thinking he knew it all by heart, or perhaps that he didn't need to see the descriptions because he could look at the things themselves.

Now he tried to make himself ignorant, new, to see the patterns—and the breaking of the patterns—for the first time. In every case, the flowers had been different from any growing in the area where the body was found, clearly brought there by the killer, but only in the Courter case had they been wildflowers that might have been picked somewhere nearby, on the spur of the moment. He flipped from one folder to the next, shuffling pages: Madsen, one white carnation, six feet from the body; Mosteller, two yellow tulips, cut close to the base, lying on a rock outcropping a dozen yards from where the body was found; Fillmore, three red roses, long-stemmed, arranged at the top of a ditch adjacent to the area where the body was found; Courter, four tubular wild scarlet flowers—*Lobelia cardinalis,* someone had written in—lying on the ground just below the body, which had been hanging from a tree limb; Munoz, four yellow lilies, found on the bank of a small gully twenty yards from where the body was found.

He remembered noticing before the gradual increase in distance between the flowers and the bodies—with the usual exception of Courter—but had made nothing of it. Now he went back over the reports, calculating in his mind the relative change in distance, trying to see if there was some constant factor, something that made some kind of sense. Lingering on the final report for a moment, he noticed something he hadn't before and looked up at Kreider.

"You got a typo here," he said.

"I don't think so," Kreider said. But he came over, pushing his glasses back up on his nose. He took the piece of paper Loomis held out to him and gave him a questioning look.

"Here," Loomis said, pointing. "It says 'four yellow lilies.' There were five."

Kreider pursed his lips. "That so?" he said. "Did you do the lab work on them?"

"No, but I saw them . . ." He stopped, puzzled by Kreider's attitude, then remembering how it had been. The petals had been flattened in the mud, broken. He remembered Sheriff Raines saying they might not have found them at all if they hadn't known what to look for. He hadn't counted them himself; he had simply asked Raines, and it had not even been a question, really. He had said something like. "There are five of them, aren't there?" and Raines had agreed. Had Raines counted them? Was it even possible to count them, really, as split and overlapped as they were?

"Where are they?" he asked.

Kreider left the room, came back in a moment with a transparent wax envelope. While Loomis hovered, he opened it carefully and used tweezers to extract the bits of petal and arrange them on a light table.

"Four stems, as you can see," Kreider said. "And just the right number of petals, once you put them back together. Nothing left over. Four lilies, like it says in the report."

"We saw five, out at the scene, Raines and I," Loomis said. He wasn't disputing Kreider.

"I guess you saw what you expected to see," Kreider told him, putting the lilies back in the envelope. "That's one of the reasons we have crime labs."

16

————

After supper, while Harriet watched something on television and Davy arranged his little wooden people around her feet, Sam went out and walked.

He didn't go far; you didn't have to go far in Malden to be completely alone, completely in darkness. There were no streetlights and only three or four scattered houses along the main road had lights shining from the windows. The rest, he supposed, were deserted now. It seemed odd to him to think of this handful of people gathered here in proximity, in this tiny town, still keeping separate from one another, huddling in their own houses, watching the television that connected them to the larger world outside. He never thought of Malden as having television; only with an effort could he remember its first appearance, his cousins' excitement. His grandmother had never had a television set, but Gerald and Harriet had bought one when he was in junior high, though as he recalled it had only picked up a couple of distant, grainy channels—one from Joplin, he supposed, and perhaps another from Oklahoma. Since then, the network affiliates had scattered translator stations around the state, so that now, while the rest of the world got cable, Malden was finally able to receive all three networks. One of the occupied houses, he now noticed, sported a round gray satellite antenna in the side yard, cocked toward the southern horizon.

He turned away from the main street and followed the rippling brick sidewalk past Gerald and Harriet's house, past the big two-story garage that housed Gerald's workshop, into the unpopulated dark behind the last row of houses. He walked slowly, feeling for the contours of the sidewalk with his toes. The last house on the side street, flanked by a weed-choked alleyway, sat behind a picket fence Sam remembered, its pointed upright slats once white, now gray, and he let his fingertips bump along the tops as he walked, feeling the ancient dust but remembering tacky new paint beneath smaller fingers. The humped sidewalk ended abruptly a dozen yards or so beyond the end of the fence, and ahead of him a half-mile of weeds ran down a long slope to the new bridge, a white expanse of concrete glowing dimly in the night, blotching the dark stain of the river that looped away from the town on that side.

Now there were only the weeds to one side of him and to the other the tarred surface of the road, frosted at its edge with chalky pebbles. A breeze came up the slope from the river, into his face, bearing a rattle of insects, the chirp of frogs. He stopped short of the bridge itself, not wanting to put a foot on it, wishing instead to find still the narrower wooden bridge he remembered. This new bridge, with its broad lanes, its railed walkways, was like an exit to all the rest of the world, to everything that was not Malden. Tomorrow he would drive across it, go back, but he wasn't ready for that yet.

He turned and went slowly back up the slope, realizing that he had not seen or heard any vehicle moving anywhere since he had left the house, not even a distant sound from the new highway, a half-mile beyond the bridge. The old highway, the one he and his mother had always come in on, lay three or four city blocks in the other direction, beyond the main street and the hump of the railroad tracks, parallel to both. He knew that weeds had grown up through the cracks in the old highway's concrete, and that the two filling stations which had once served as groceries and cafés—one of them having sported the town's only jukebox for a time—were black windowless hulks now whose drooping FOR SALE signs might have been older than himself.

His feet came back to the gravel of the main street, at the intersection where the house sat—the house he still thought of as his grandmother's. In the crossing, the hard surface of the road to the bridge, a county highway, mixed with the town gravel, shared its mottled texture for a space, then emerged clean and gray again on the other side, running on over the hump of the railroad bed, past the water tower.

"It's a pleasant evening," Gerald said. He was sitting at the corner of the big L-shaped porch, in a wooden armchair he'd made himself, his feet propped up on the porch railing. The radio—a tiny portable taped to a battery three times as large—stood on the floor beside him, and, as Sam noticed it, he heard for the first time its tiny voices, so familiar that he half-expected to recognize the names they called out, to hear them speak of Musial and Gibson.

"How're the Cards doing?" he asked.

"Not good. Down five to nothing, nine games out. It's all over. The Cubs have got it."

"The game?"

"The pennant."

"Really? The Cubs?"

"Surprising, ain' it?" Gerald said. "My dad used to talk about the days when the Cubs was good, back before my time. You wait long enough, everything turns around again."

For a fanciful second, Sam wondered whether the Cubs were really winning the pennant in the world on the other side of the white bridge, or only here in Malden, on Gerald's radio that brought him voices from cities and stadiums he had never seen. As far as Gerald really knew, all of it might be an elaborate fiction, like—as some believed—the moon landings.

Sam went up onto the porch and sank down on the wooden swing, spreading his arms along the top and letting it rock him gently back and forth, only now and then touching a toe to the porch to keep it moving. A pleasant night, Gerald had said, but that seemed to him a stunning understatement. It was a night, he thought, such as he had been missing his whole adult life without knowing it, as if he had spent all those newspaper nights roaming the city, or perched in the newsroom high above the circling lights, looking unconsciously, and in vain, for a time and place such as this, a lost childhood night with the wind moving in the ancient trees, swishing the long grass along the curbless road, and underneath it all a shrill insect noise so steady one took it for silence. Listening, he thought he heard a rumble somewhere far off that might have been a train, or only thunder somewhere out on the prairie, and he remembered with pleasure awakening to sounds like that as a child, or to the rustling of rain outside his window, and lying after that in an intermediate state between ache and ecstasy, not quite awake but not quite willing either to let go of the pleasure of the sound and fall fully asleep again.

Of course, it had never really been this quiet, this dark in Malden. The evenings he remembered had been filled with his cousins and their cousins—the strange relationships he had never quite grasped, of people who were kin to his kin but not to him—and the banging of screen doors, rectangles of light spilling out onto the black grass where fireflies blinked, the shouts of games in the darkness, flashlight beams illuminating tree trunks, cracked sidewalks, a footpath winding through an open field or down along the riverbank. And under and above it all, there had been the murmur of adult voices—younger then, most of them, than he was now—inside the houses, on the porches, no television then but the eternal radio music, the strum of guitar strings or an untuned piano from someone's parlor, and the occasional, envious barking of dogs from the farmsteads along the river.

Now, between silences in the ball game, he made out a sound from somewhere distant, faint music from one of the other occupied houses in the scattered darkness—a radio, maybe, but he thought more likely a record player, a ghostly voice singing of being on a beach "far from the twisted reach of crazy sorrow."

This night, this place, was the sort of thing he would never be able to write about for the newspaper, never be able to make clear to anyone else that way. What it needed was to bring someone here, to make that person sit and listen, but he could think of no one suitable. Thinking of Merow, of Loomis, of other friends from his job, he only felt sad, more alone than ever. But then he thought of Stosh and realized that he could imagine bringing her here, though in some ways she was more alien to this place than any of the others, more a product of the city. He could see the two of them walking down the slope to the river, himself bending now and then to pick up stones from the roadway, tossing them into the tall grass to hush the insect sounds for a moment while he spoke softly of what it all meant to him, finding, in this fantasy, the words. In his mind he could see the two of them walking slowly, in the dark, hardly needing their eyes, leaning into the wind coming up from the river as though being borne downward by it, as if ready to fly upon it, or to sink within it, into a safe place where neither eyes nor words were needed.

"Oh, Sammy. The news is coming on, if you want to watch." It was Harriet, leaning out through the screen door.

He shook his head, feeling foolish, as though his thoughts must be transparent to everyone. What was the point of thinking of Stosh this way? "No, thanks," he said. "I think I'm ready for bed."

She went back inside and turned down the TV. When he followed her in, Davy met him with out-stretched arms, a kiss good night. Upstairs, it was much warmer, but there was a breeze moving between the windows, across the narrow bed, in the corner room that had been his grandmother's storage closet. He lay awake for a time, imagining himself and Davy staying in the little town together, never going back. Considering the difficulties—How would he make a living? Where would Davy go to school?—and banishing them with fanciful solutions, he drifted off into dreams listening to the unintelligible crackle of Gerald's radio on the porch below, imagining it to be the fall of rain upon the city streets where the three of them—himself and Davy and Stosh (or was it Clare?)—stood waiting beside a curving sidewalk for the bus that would take them home, not quite knowing where that was.

He awoke to Davy's urgent whispering, just outside his door, and Harriet saying, "He'll be up soon enough. You just let him sleep," and then their steps going down the stairs.

He lay thinking, coming awake slowly, his fancy of living in Malden fresh in his mind, thinking for a moment by daylight that it might not be impossible. Gerald and Harriet lived here, after all; so did a few others. There were newspapers within driving distance, at Independence, at Parsons. Even apart from that there must be ways of making money, of paying for food and water and gas and electricity; certainly, there was no shortage of empty houses in Malden. There would be a school somewhere, too, in some nearby town, and the fact was that Davy had no more playmates in Wichita than he would have here. He could buy a computer, as Merow had so often urged, become a freelance writer. What would he write about, thus isolated? He didn't know, but it didn't seem a significant objection.

Harriet and Davy were sitting at the kitchen table

when he went down at last, mumbling a self-conscious response to their cheerful good mornings. A dish and cup sitting in the sink told him that Gerald had eaten and gone on out to his workshop. Perhaps he would try to get Gerald alone and sound him out before saying anything to Harriet or Davy about what he had been thinking.

"How long till you have to go?" Davy asked.

For some reason, that simple question—the answer he had to give to it—drove the fantasy out of his mind, made it seem far away after all. The daylight fact was that he had to leave Davy here, drive back to Wichita alone. Though it was his own choice, he felt put-upon, overwhelmed by the demands of the real world, the complexity of it.

"Sometime today," he said. "But I don't have to go right away."

"That's good."

Harriet slid a plate with scrambled eggs and bacon in front of him. "Do you drink coffee?" she asked. "I ought to remember."

"Cream and sugar," he said.

She went to get them, saying, "They caught that fella up in Wichita. It was on the news last night."

He looked up at her. "What fellow?"

"That Strangler. The one that's been killin' them girls. Thank God they got him. That was so terrible. I don't know how people live in such a place."

He sat for a moment, staring at her, unable to quite get his mind around what she had said, what it meant. "Did they give a name?"

"Yes . . . but I forget." She thought a moment. "It was

an unusual first name," she said. "More like a last name. Doby? Selby? Something like that."

"Kirby? Kirby Banks?"

"I believe that's it. Is that what you're working on for the newspaper?"

"Yes." Sam said, feeling unaccountably trapped. "That's what I've been working on."

"Then I guess you will have to be getting back to it," Harriet said resignedly.

Stosh kept hoping she'd run into Loomis again, but she didn't. She'd expected a lull in the flow of information, while they got their evidence together and the suspect settled on his own story, but she also had a sense of something else in the air, something unexpected, as though everyone had a secret they were not entirely pleased with. Jerry Majors, like Merow, was working nights now, so he wasn't around to talk to, and no one else in the dayroom would tell her anything, only shrug and smile and pretend to know nothing.

Not that she had much time to push it. There was plenty of other stuff happening—a drive-by shooting near Evergreen Park, a suspected arson at one of the local abortion clinics, a lawsuit filed against the county by a guy who'd been arrested at his job and led away in handcuffs on what turned out to be an erroneous bad-check warrant. It was one of those days when she seemed always to be running fifteen minutes late, not quite catching the people she needed in their offices, having to run them down in hallways, get a few muttered statements in an elevator or a stairwell. And Goodwin was still hanging around, trying to get an audience with Loomis, though apparently not having any luck. She had a sense of things in motion all around her, things changing, invisibly, just beyond her sight, out of her hearing, like a storm gathering somewhere far off, charging the air.

And the dark cloud hanging in the back of her mind was the promise she'd made to meet Frank, to meet him this evening. The feeling of inevitability, of needing to get things settled, that she'd felt in Frank's office had transformed itself into a kind of dread, though if she made an effort she could talk her way all the way around to looking forward to it, thinking positively, imagining that it might be the beginning of better times, the end of apprehension and confusion, like a cool rain following the lightning.

On her lunch hour she picked up some hamburgers and fries at the Sonic on north Broadway, and drove to Riverside Park, finding a shady spot to pull in along the narrow road by the riverbank. Sitting and eating, half-listening to music on the car radio, she watched as families with picnic lunches gathered around the green wooden tables in the park, women shepherding mobs of toddlers through the little zoo. Ahead of her and behind her, along the bank, were the cars of other solo people like herself, downtown workers grabbing a moment of tranquility, getting away from the sticky heat, the un-natural air conditioner chill, some of them stretched out on the mown grass of the bank, or sitting with their backs against tree trunks, a book in one hand, a cold drink in the other, or simply staring out over the water, where an occasional flock of jet skiers churned by, swooping and calling unintelligibly to one another, now and then pausing to sink quietly, as if exhausted or confused, only to roar up and out again before they and their machines had quite disappeared beneath the surface.

She had thought that she might be able to use this time to make a plan for the evening, establish a negotiating position, but it wasn't working out that way. All morning she had put off thinking about Frank, but now when she wanted to think about him her mind kept drifting off in other directions, her attention sliding out onto the surface of the brown water, following the antics of the jet skiers, tracing the crooked docks of the opposite bank, where her more affluent neighbors, in the pricier townhouse complex next to her own, kept their boats. Thinking of what to say to Frank, she found herself repeating the same phrase over and over to herself—"And then I naturally thought . . ."—unable to remember what had led to it or where she had expected it to go. "And then I naturally thought," she said aloud to herself.

It was all becoming wearying, like the ache of some physical, repetitive task she had worked at too long, could not face continuing, though she was bound for reasons beyond her comprehension to see the end of it. She tried thinking instead of her job, of Loomis, of the man they'd arrested, but where there should have been excitement, or at least interest, there was only another kind of weariness, something like boredom. Was she sinking into depression without quite knowing it? This was how it had felt for a time after Danny died—all the things that had normally filled her life seeming tedious, unexciting. She had been unable for a time to find reasons to get out of bed in the morning. Now she wished she were back in her apartment, hiding beneath the covers, not required to get up and do anything. Like Sam.

The thought of Sam brought a perverse quickening of interest. What was he up to, after all? Was he handling things, or just hiding out? She felt again the sense she had had the evening she wound up at Loomis's place— that Sam held some key for her, could tell her something, show her a way out of whatever it was she had wandered into. Maybe it was only that he was the only person she knew who might be unhappier, more confused than herself.

She stuffed half of her hamburger back into the sack and started the engine. There was a good half hour left to her, and Sam's house was only a few blocks away, in the old Oak Park neighborhood across the Nims Street bridge.

His driveway was empty, and so was the black hole of the garage. She sat in her car, the motor running, knowing she should leave, go back to work. But she turned off the engine and got out anyway, took a quick glance at the old man in his porch chair on the other side of the street, and then went along the side of the house, stepping carefully in the loose sand of the driveway, and through the gate.

The back door was unlocked, as she'd half-expected. She hesitated, then pushed the door open and stepped inside, feeling a mix of apprehension and something like sexual excitement, the tiny thrill of doing something improper.

She went straight through the kitchen and into the hallway, where she turned on the overhead light, stopping then, holding her breath and listening, thinking belatedly that his car might be in the shop, that he might be here. But there was only silence; the house felt as empty as any she had ever been in. Still, she had to take a breath and steel herself before going past the open bedroom doors, giving each a quick glance, not knowing what she would do if she found a face looking back at her—scream, perhaps, or burst into hysterical laughter. But there was no one there. She noticed that two of the beds looked as though they'd been slept in recently—the double bed in the master bedroom, and the smaller one in the room with bright birds on the wallpaper, three rag dolls sitting in a row on the little bureau. The thought of Sam sleeping in his daughter's bed, by himself in this house, brought tears to her eyes—tears partly for herself, thinking of her own lost room in her parents' home. In Sam's son's room, she saw the only made bed, its covers tucked in hastily, not quite square, the work of a child.

By the time she reached the living room, she wished she had not come. There was nothing here, after all, to instruct her, to make her own life make sense. Her presence here diminished her somehow, as if trying to see into Sam's loss trivialized her own pain and his as well. She wanted to try to explain to someone what she had meant, to justify herself, but there was no one to explain it to, and anyway she had nothing to say.

It was when she turned around, pointing herself back along what seemed the long, dark tunnel to the back door and sunlight, that her eye fell on the stack of spiral notebooks on the floor beside Sam's armchair.

Sometimes it seemed to him that Banks must be the one, that Loomis would never have arrested him without something substantial. But then when he thought of Banks, trying to make him fit the image of the dark man in his mind, he felt sure that some mistake had been made, and he felt an edgy need to get back, to figure out what had gone wrong, where they had made their mistake.

The edginess made Sam indecisive, kept him in Malden until late afternoon. Yet once he was in the car, driving back across the white concrete bridge toward the new highway, everything began to sort itself out in his mind, as if, back in the real world, he began to be more himself again.

From the radio accounts, he knew that Banks had been charged only with the Munoz and Mosteller murders so far. So there was something to link him to that one of the original four, but not perhaps the others. Still, it was troubling, because Mosteller was one of the two most strongly linked to the bus terminus. Could it be that Kirby himself was one of those who had hung around there, watching from the shadows? It wasn't hard to imagine.

Yet the more he did imagine it, the nearer he got to Wichita and that reality, the more convinced he grew that some fundamental error had been made, that the real dark man must still be out there. And feeling safe now, most likely. With Banks in custody, the dark man would assume that no one was watching. He might lay low for awhile longer, let events take their course, but surely he would begin to feel invincible, protected, powerful. And with that feeling would come the hightened desire to act, to show his power.

Sam had been thinking of calling Loomis when he got back—or even driving straight to the police department—but now he began to feel that he needed to be circumspect, find out by other channels what was happening. He would call Stosh instead. That thought pleased him; he wanted to talk to Stosh again, not only about the Strangler, but about . . . what? For a second, it seemed to him that he wanted to resume the talk they had had, though only in his fancy, the night before. He shook his head, smiling at himself, but the feeling did not go away.

The red sun on the horizon, off to his right and slightly behind, making a tall, oblique shadow of the car that slid along in the opposite lane just ahead of him, like a scythe for cutting down oncoming traffic. By the time he reached Wichita, it would be full dark. He would put off everything else—even calling Stosh—and go straight to the bus interchange, to see what effect the news had had there. He might be the only one who would be able to tell.

She pulled into the Towne East mall at 7:45, following the nameless frontage road that wound around the parking lot. She'd gone back to the newspaper finally, but hadn't gone in—had sat in her car in one of the pool slots, watching for Frank to come out and leave. But even then she hadn't gone in; instead she'd driven home and bathed and changed clothes, preparing herself resignedly, as though for an operation that might kill her or cure her.

It was not as dark now as it had been that first time she'd driven to the mall; that had been later in the year. She had felt apprehensive then, not knowing exactly what to expect. Now she felt only a kind of distant curiosity, as though her emotions had been dampened down by some drug. She was no longer even sure what she hoped for from this meeting, or from Frank himself. What had she started out wanting, that first time, when Frank had brought a bottle of wine and driven the two of them out into the countryside, not to a motel as she'd half-expected, and they'd parked behind an abandoned service station at a dark, untraveled intersection, and passed the wine back and forth, sparring nervously in silly double entendres until finally, somehow, maneuvering themselves into the back seat?

Reading Clare's journals had reminded her of that because it had been the same with her. Not just similar, the same. The same intersection, the same brand of wine, even some of the same conversation. Why did he begin that way? Clare had been ready to back out—or so she said—and maybe she would have, going to some motel, sitting in the car while he registered, seeing the sterile room they ended up in. But being in the car that way had made it harder to change directions, not only because of the sense of being trapped—which she observed, and Stosh agreed, nodding as she read, had added a dash of excitement to it, a tiny hint of danger, for neither of them had had any way of knowing what might happen, what sort of man he really was—but also because, in another way, it had made the whole thing seem more trivial, even innocent, a hot high-school date, transient and unimportant, almost unreal. That sense—of it having been so casual, of not having amounted to much after all the buildup—had made it easier to return the second time, had seemed to dispel all reasons for reconsidering.

Clare Haun had thought of it as an adventure, and that had been something she'd wanted at the time. Stosh didn't remember feeling that way about it, but could not decide how she would have characterized it. She was pretty sure she had not been looking only for sex, the physical connection, but the notion that she might have wanted anything else—love, for example— made her feel like blushing. Perhaps, even then, she had simply been caught up in the hope of something more, the fear of something less, in the relationship with Frank.

Now she swung past the Sears store, saw the black Mercury and Frank's form indistinct beyond the tinted windows. She didn't stop, not yet. She took the access road back toward the front of the mall, circling the shopping center, as if held in orbit by the mass of the place.

That first time, she remembered, she had parked at the front of the mall, clear on the other side from where Frank waited, and had walked through the sprawling building, pretending to be shopping. That had seemed pointless to her afterward, a waste of time, and she had not done it again. But now she pulled into a space near the entrance, and then sat for a time before getting out, as though she still might change her mind—finally reaching back for her purse, closing and locking the doors, wondering if it might, as Frank had half-promised, be morning before she came back for her car. The idea of it sitting there by itself in the vast lot made her feel unaccountably frightened, almost enough to change her mind and get back in.

But she didn't. She walked toward the bright entrance thinking of how Clare, an English major in college, probably a better student than herself, had written of understanding at last the linguistic connection between passion and passivity, had come to think of her involvement with Frank as a kind of drug to which she had somehow become addicted—how in the times between their meetings she would persuade herself that she must end it, get back to living her normal life, and then, when the time came, find herself once again unable to act on that decision, finding reasons to set it aside, to see him one more time, to persuade herself that things would somehow be different, be all right, or that it simply wasn't real, wouldn't matter.

What disappointed Stosh about Clare's journals— what she had read of them before growing suddenly disgusted with herself and leaving, slinking out the back door like a burglar—was that there was nothing in them she hadn't already known. As Sam said, no answers after all. To her, Frank wasn't the dark mystery at the center of things that he apparently was to Sam. Though, like Clare Haun, she had trouble seeing him clearly sometimes, at bottom she knew what he was: a relatively simple man who needed the physical attentions of women to reassure him, make him feel safe and in control, and who was frightened by the prospect of relying too much on any one woman. Most men were like that, in varying degrees. Maybe it was a part of Frank's attraction that he acted on that part of himself in a straightforward kind of way, was honest after his fashion. How much more complicated things would be, after all, if he were someone who really cared about her beyond the casual friendship that was real enough, that lay at the bottom of everything else. Certainly, any serious emotional involvement on his part would have made things much more difficult for Clare—though perhaps easier for Sam, who might have been able to understand that better, even accept it.

She could see how baffled Sam must have been, reading the journals. There was a sense in which Clare had turned to Frank in an effort to get Sam himself back—the Sam she felt she had lost touch with, through children and bills and jobs, imagining that someone like Frank might lead her back to the freer, more adventurous person she had been once, and that, thus recovered in herself, she might be able to find the Sam who had been that way himself, who had first become her partner. Stosh understood that, though she understood, too, how it would make no sense to Sam, would only seem crazy to him. What she didn't understand was what it meant to her—who or what it was that she had been trying to get back to, had been using Frank for.

She came to the sidewalk that ran along the front of Towne East and stopped to watch the flow of people there, mostly groups of boys and girls in riotous, punkish summer clothing, carrying cassette players and radios, a few with Day-Glo-wheeled roller skates slung over their shoulders, the laces tied together. The crowd

surged and scattered along the dazzling concrete corridor formed by the building on one side and the wall of
rumbling buses arriving and departing on the other.

It occurred to her that this was the area Sam had
been talking about—one node of the mysterious, improbable story he claimed to be working on. She
scanned the crowd, not expecting to see him, and
didn't. Yet she stood for a moment longer, letting the
young people move past her like a river, absorbing the
laughter and shouts and music, the underlying rumble
of the bus engines, trying to put Sam in this scene, understand what it might mean to him. A breeze moved
along the side of the long building, ruffling the sculpted
hair, billowing the oversized shirts. It was as if she had
suddenly found herself in the midst of a crowd of
rowdy vacationers about to embark on some adventure,
bound for foreign lands, though in fact, when she studied the movement around her, she saw that the identity
of the crowd itself was something of an illusion, that its
members slipped on and off the buses almost invisibly,
one by one, two by two, with the slightest wave of a
hand, the lift of an eyebrow, a murmur, simply stepping
up and stepping down, as though it were no more than
a single step from one side of town to the other, one
side of the world to the other, as if the buses were not
moving vehicles but fixed gateways.

As she watched, one bus pulled away and another
settled in behind it, its doors sighing open, the sign at
its front reading CENTURY II. That was the other terminus. Maybe Sam was there. She glance at the driver,
sitting high above, his face hidden by the dark glasses
despite the gathering dusk of evening, and then, as

though it were what she had come here for, she walked a half-dozen yards to the door and climbed the short steps into the bus, opening her purse to find the necessary change.

She found an empty seat behind a middle-aged woman whose lap was piled with small sacks from Penney's and Sears and Henry's. The bus lurched into motion, made its way through the parking lot in fits and starts, then finally roared out onto Kellogg, not quite keeping pace with the cars that streamed past. They swung south at Woodlawn, then back west again on Lincoln. Into the darker residential streets, the bus began to stop more often, letting off the dwindling handful of older people, the shoppers and shop workers. Refusing to wonder why she was doing this, Stosh thought instead of the first time she'd ridden a bus by herself, back in Chicago, going half a dozen blocks to a neighborhood pool for a swimming lesson, no more than six or seven; she recalled the sense she had had of embarking on something new and important, almost a new life.

They crossed Oliver, past the Parklane Shopping Center, and the woman beside her stretched to pull the cord that rang the bell up front. Stosh stood to let her out, then slid into her place by the window. She had forgotten how riding in a bus, sitting high up, not having to drive, made a place look different, and she craned her neck to look ahead at the dark place where Lincoln looped out and around the convent. Before they were quite there, however, the bus slowed and made a sharp turn onto Bluff, heading back toward Kellogg, and then, after a long wait at the light, where well-dressed couples went in and out of the expensive restaurant at the corner, they surged out onto the big road once more, the engine roaring as the bus picked up speed, while cars hurried by on either side, and rounding the curve toward downtown, she found the city center lying sprawled ahead of them, a montage of night lights and dark shapes rising against the prairie sky. She made out the beacon perched on the roof of the newspaper, and then the blue dome of Century II, huddled beside the river. Then the road dipped beneath the interstate and the arch of the viaduct hid the city from her sight.

When they turned finally into the curving street that ran past the convention center, she scanned the area like a passenger arriving in some exotic land. She didn't see Sam anywhere, but it was a complicated place—more complicated than she'd remembered—with curving sidewalks and sunken stairways, long shadows and arching trees scattered in planters along the expanse of concrete. She arose and followed the younger riders down the steps and out into the city night, finding a slightly different crowd from the one she had left at Towne East—a quieter, less flamboyant crowd, spread out over a larger area. Most of the people who had been on her bus headed immediately for others, to travel on; a few wandered off along the broad sidewalk, or into the parking lot, or crossed the street toward the library, all of them scanning the place, like her, as though expecting to meet someone there. A good place for meeting, she thought, though not the sort of place she and Frank would ever meet, a place to run into one's friends.

She hesitated, trying to imagine where Sam might position himself. Out of the flow of things, surely, but near enough to absorb it. Not the below-ground park, then, but perhaps somewhere across the street, on the steps of the convention center or along the planters beneath the library's bright windows.

She had decided to go that way when someone behind her cleared his throat. She turned, expecting Sam, but instead found herself facing a man with a baseball cap pulled low over his eyes, hiding most of his face. He was smiling broadly, almost mockingly.

"Beg pardon, lady," he said. "You looked lost. Can I help you?"

17

It was the touch of coolness in the air, like an early fall, that made him change his mind about going straight to the bus terminus. It was just the sort of night for cooking out in the backyard. He found the starter fluid under the sink. There was half a bag of charcoal there, too, probably several years old, but he didn't need it. He used the heaps of junk mail and old newspapers from the living room to get the blaze going, and then began carrying Clare's journals out in small stacks and feeding them in. He found it worked better if he tore the covers off first and fluttered the pages. Watching them, feeling the heat on his face and hands, he remembered how, when he had been a child, people had had incinerators in their backyards—big metal barrels they had used to burn the accumulated trash each week, until the ashes had nearly reached the top and they had hauled them to the dump, or paid someone to do so. He remembered standing in the snow, warmed by the fire, remembered the smell of the cold ash on other days. All that was illegal now, of course, but you could still barbecue.

The wind came up as it grew darker, and when he finally got to the parking lot across from Century II, the place was full of young people, moving here and there as though swept along the pavement like clustered leaves, their music and talk borne to him in snatches by the wind's ventriloquism.

He passed by the lot, going on around to the street where he usually parked, not far from the spot usually occupied by the man in the baseball cap. His spot was empty tonight, the man nowhere to be seen. Sam felt an instant's curiosity, then dismissed it. Since coming back to the city, he had felt increasingly that all the crazy time—his desire for revenge against Rule, his obsession with the dark man—was over, an illness survived.

His notion of the bus interchange as a watering hole where predators circled seemed remote and rather foolish to him now, an excuse his mind had manufactured to explain its attraction for him. Malden, he thought, had made that clear—made other things clear as well. Unexpectedly, it seemed to him, he had come to a place where the unresolvable questions that had driven him were resolving themselves, becoming unimportant. Somehow, because of what had happened at Rule's party and then at the cemetery in Malden, he had made his peace with Clare, with that part of himself, perhaps even with Rule; now it seemed likely that Kirby Banks's arrest had settled the rest of it for him.

He walked to his usual spot where the brick wall met the building and looked down into the park. A group of half a dozen boys and girls sat in a circle on the sidewalk, at one corner, like campers telling ghost stories, oblivious to the walkers who stepped around them. The bearded man sat in his usual spot, but he had been joined by a woman who spoke to him animatedly, as though she knew him. The man stared back at her, only nodding now and then, his book resting on his knee, unread. Sam could not tell from his expression whether he was annoyed or pleased by the intrusion.

He felt restless sitting there, no longer content with being the observer. Instead, he got up and began moving slowly out into the flow of things, making himself a part of the general crowd.

He walked along the wall itself to its end, where the park bordered the street, then went down the steps and along the lower walk to the park's far corner. Other walkers nodded to him as they passed. There was no wind down there, inside the ivied walls, only the motion in the tops of the little ornamental trees giving an indication of the hurly-burly above and outside. There were stone benches every dozen feet or so, inset into the banks of shrubbery along the walk, and he sat down at one for a few minutes, watching from his new perspective as people moved back and forth along the sidewalk, looking up at his own empty spot on the wall above, imagining himself there. The place was not so crowded that there were not moments when he was alone in an island of quiet, hearing only the general murmur of distant voices, like the unnoticed insect hum of Malden at night, a primer of steady sound prepared for the sharper, more distinct noises to be laid on top of it.

It was like the zoo. That was an odd observation, but for the first time he found that he no longer resented the presence of the others, no longer yearned to be completely alone. In fact, he regretted not having someone to whom he could show it, as he would have liked to show Malden to Stosh, to point out the regulars, the patterns of movement, the things he had learned by watching. He recognized it as a rebirth of the old need that had made a reporter of him, the need to share and tell. He felt also a deep regret that he had not found this place, or something like it, while Clare was alive. It seemed to him that such a simple discovery, his sharing it with her, might have saved her somehow, saved the two of them. Perhaps it had been something like that, after all, some similar yearning for what had been lost, that had led her to do what she did. The thought made him feel sad, not only for himself but for Clare, for the two of them who had been and were no more.

He got up and walked on, around the curve and along the wall that stretched between the office buildings, toward the corner where the young people still sat talking. The bearded man and his woman friend were gone. It was a night, apparently, for departures, for people being out of their usual places. He stepped carefully around the young people, and heard one of them talking with a regular rhythm, perhaps reciting a poem that was unfamiliar to him. He caught only the phrase "no need of stars," and it hung in his awareness for a few seconds like the too-familiar refrain of some song. He came to the corner of the park and mounted the steps that led back to the world above.

It was surprisingly good to be back in the wind and the larger night. The man in the cap still was not there, though a couple of the others he had thought of as watchers like himself were at their usual posts. Now they seemed to him not sinister, only solitary, drawn to the little world between the buildings but shy about entering it, like himself. Perhaps this was the perspective of those who inhabited the light; perhaps, unwitting, he had become one of them.

He crossed the parking lot and ducked between two of the buses, peering out at the traffic before crossing the street to the plaza fronting Century II. Here the crowd was more scattered, more stationary—couples and small groups dotting the benches, the edges of the planters, the convention center steps. He passed through them feeling self-conscious at his own movement, as though on display, wanting to seem as though he had someplace to go. He headed along the narrow service road that ran close beside the library, then looped around Century II to the big parking lot behind, and the loading docks beyond that, and, beyond it all, the terraced riverbank.

The road led him through a dark, empty stretch, as the lights fell away behind and then the softer glow of the lamps along the terraced riverbank began to emerge from around the building's curve. The vast convention center parking lot stretched into darkness to his left. Past the edge of that, he stepped onto the grass of the bank and found the steps that led down to the brick river walk meandering beside occasional benches and brick planters holding overflowing banks of flowers. He crossed the walk and stepped onto the grass again, to the edge of water, then sat down with his knees drawn up and leaned back against the slope, to look out over the black surface. Beyond it, above the opposite bank, were the lights of the west side, McLean Boulevard running past the big church at Douglas, and the movement of headlights on the thoroughfares and along the bridge.

He closed his eyes, feeling more content, more normal, than he had in a long time. What was necessary, he thought, was to simplify, to draw his life down to the handful of things that mattered to him. First, of course, there was Davy. And then what? His job? It was surrounded by questions now. Did he want to be a reporter again, no more late man? Did he have any choice in the matter, any job at all? How pissed off was Cubbage? What about Rule? The questions interested him but did not dismay him. There would be something for him, some way to go on. There always was, though he had gone a long time not remembering that.

Should he call Cubbage, or go see him in the morning, find out where things stood? He disliked thinking of that yet, and then remembered his plan to start by calling Stosh. That made him feel better, more optimistic, though he couldn't have said why. Certainly, there were things to be made up to her as well as to Cubbage, or Loomis, or any of the others who had relied on him. He felt ready now to make amends, particularly to Stosh. Doing that, he thought, would show him the way back to the rest of his life.

He rose to his feet, a bit stiff from sitting, and made his way back up the slope to the brick walk, where he paused for a moment to look at the nearest box of flowers, a thick, weedy spray of reds and yellows and greens. He didn't know much about flowers, but he recognized some of these as the same ones that grew wild along the riverbank at the foot of his own backyard. He supposed they had grown here, too, before the bank had been graded and landscaped, dotted with lanterns and benches. He liked the economy of cultivating and preserving them this way. Some would not like it, he knew, but the alternative was destruction; it was like the zoo in that way. These flowers, he thought, preserved a continuity between this place and himself, his own patch of it, and somehow, in his mind, it all wound on out through fields and roads and spaces, and back through memory, to connect to Malden and lost nights, lost lives that might exist yet, so long as he could make the connection.

He went on up the steps to the access road and back down the curving tunnel of dark sidewalk toward the lights of the plaza, thinking only of getting in his car, going home, getting some sleep, calling Stosh in the morning.

The first sharp sound might have been anything—a runner's foot striking the pavement, some indeterminate automobile noise, even the clap of a single wave raised by the wind on the river—but then it came again, and again, quickly, close by, drawing his startled attention, eyes following ears, to where two figures stood at a niche at the side of the huge convention center, inside the stretch of darkness. Focusing, he took it in in an instant—a man pressing a woman up against a recessed doorway, his arm moving back and forward rhythmically, inexorably, slapping her, her face twisting away, flushed, soundless.

"Hey," Sam said, the word only a startled breath of surprise, bewilderment. The man slapped the woman again, and Sam took a couple of steps in that direction as though pulled by the sound. "Hey," he said again, louder, the surprise turning to alarm and filling out his voice.

The man looked around now, peered at him, his head cocked sideways, the beard a splotch of gray against the darkness. The woman had her eyes closed, her lips pressed inward against her teeth. Her upper body shook spasmodically with dry, soundless weeping. Drawing nearer, Sam saw that the man held her by the throat with his left hand, the one that had not been doing the slapping.

"What's going on?" Sam asked, feeling now the dizzy tingle of adrenaline, hearing it crackle in his voice, as if he might be getting ready to cry himself.

"Who are you?" the bearded man said. "This is private."

The woman opened her eyes and looked at him, licked her lips. "Please," she said. "It's all right." Her face was red and wet with tears.

"He was hitting you," Sam said.

"Please. It was my fault." She sniffed and then suddenly was crying again, her eyes squeezed shut as if in embarrassment.

For a second, he hesitated. It was private, the man had said, and the woman seemed to agree. But when he tried to make himself turn away, he found that he couldn't. "I can't just go," he said, as much to himself as to them. He felt surprised by his own voice, the calmness in it.

The man half-turned his body and peered at him again out of the darkness, keeping his hold on the woman's throat.

"You'd better mind your own business," he said. But his voice shook, sounding more frightened that Sam's; Sam could hear in it that he was not as old as he had supposed, nor perhaps as harmless.

"If you have to hit someone," Sam said, riding with the unexpected calmness he still felt, refusing to acknowledge the other thing beneath it, the rising impulse to flee, "maybe you should try hitting me instead of her."

The man stared at him, blinking, his eyes as stunned and frightened as those of an animal surprised by light. It seemed to Sam that the world was filled with a thick smell of fear, his own and the other man's, and that a kind of silence sealed the three of them off there, locked to one another in a kind of stasis, separated from everything else. The lighted plaza, a few strides away, might have been on the far side of the world.

Sam took two steps forward, closing the ten feet or so between them, keeping himself just far enough away that the bearded man would have to release the woman to make good on his threat.

"Why don't we all walk back to the park?" Sam said quietly.

The other man shook his head. This close, he looked ill and also embarrassed, his eyes yellow and moist, like those of someone surprised in a toilet stall in the midst of some painful necessity. "This is our business," he said doggedly. "It doesn't concern you." His mouth worked soundlessly for a moment, and then in a lowered voice he said. "I'll kill you if you don't leave me alone." He spoke it as though it were an unpleasant secret he were being forced to confide.

Sam stared back at him, bemused, realizing with one part of himself that the softness of the threat made it sound real, meant, but at the same time he felt a tug of sympathy for the man, an identification with his fear and anger. Along with it came the first small eruption of his own fear, poking its way into his gut, penetrating the calm, making him swallow. It was hard, in that moment, to stay where he was, not take a step backward.

"I'll kill you," the man repeated sorrowfully, as though bound now by the words. He let go of the woman, who slumped backward against the locked doorway, her eyes coming open, not focusing, and turned fully toward Sam, crouching slightly.

For an instant, Sam felt like laughing. Then a voice from somewhere off to his right distracted him, a sharp cry that might have meant anything or nothing, nearly made him look that way. But he found that his eyes were fixed on the other man's; even when a clatter of voices arose from the direction of the plaza, he could not look away.

The man took a step toward him and then somehow, impossibly, he held a knife in his hand—a switchblade, it looked like. He held it between thumb and fingertips, almost delicately, the blade pointing slightly up, slightly to one side.

Sam was filled with astonishment, remembering this man who sat so quietly each evening, lost in a book, his lunch bag placed neatly beneath his bench, and now seeing him here in the half-darkness, hunched menacingly forward, the knife in his hand—a pose out of the movies, so familiar as to be nearly comic, unthreatening. Those scenes unwound in Sam's mind; he noted how it was that one stepped backward or to the side, arching one's body to avoid the thrust or the sweep, hands raised for balance like someone walking a tight-rope. But he could not imagine himself prancing that way; he only stood and stared at the blade and at the man, transfixed by wonder.

As he watched, the man took another quick step forward, dipping his shoulder suddenly, and jabbed. At the last second, still not quite believing it, Sam reacted, twisting awkwardly sideways, so that the point of the blade caught him not in the stomach but in the side. At first he didn't think he'd been cut, for he felt only the blow, the punch. It wasn't until he saw the ragged circle of blood staining his shirt that he felt the first dull pain.

The woman screamed then, something that might have been "Away! Go away!" But which of them was she screaming at? Perhaps both. It startled the bearded man, who looked once behind him, then off to the side where Sam saw from his expression, they had an audience now, people from the plaza beginning to notice and gather with a murmur of voices like the first tunings of an orchestra. I've been stabbed, he thought then, still amazed by it all, stabbed on the street by a man with a knife. It was the kind of thing he'd written about numberless times, working the late desk, and it filled him with something like joy, a kind of pleased excitement, as if all that he had feared from the world outside the high glass windows had turned out to be, after all, no more than this, nothing that could not be endured, survived. But then he saw that what he felt was not really joy but a kind of exuberant anger—a sweet kind of anger, like a long-sought physical release.

Now you've stabbed me, he thought; I can do anything I want to.

The bearded man was glancing from him to the growing crowd of spectators when Sam lowered his shoulder and lunged, wholeheartedly, inexorably, as though he would drive himself clear through the man and through the wall of the building itself and out the other side and into the night beyond. He caught the man in the stomach, carried him backward three or four staggering steps and slammed him into the brick wall. The man made a kind of gasping, heaving sound, as though about to vomit, but nothing came after it. Time seemed to Sam to have slowed down, as though he had as much of it as he needed, to plan, to proceed. He rolled slightly sideways, using his body to pin the arm that held the knife against the wall, and then brought his own forearm up hard beneath the man's chin, hearing the satisfying snap as the man's jaws came together.

A low, breathless moan seeped out beneath the man's closed teeth, and with it a trickle of blood that ran into his beard, staining it black. Sam groped for the wrist of the knife hand; the man made no attempt to evade him. When he had it, he pinned it against the brick surface and then took a half-step backward, pausing a moment, almost dispassionately, to calculate, and then drove his other fist deep into the man's flabby midsection.

He expected him to double over, bend forward, the way they did in the movies, but he didn't. The man's eyes rolled upward and he slumped heavily, his legs folding beneath him. For a second, Sam was holding him up only by the grip on his wrist, and then he let go of that, surprised, and stepped back to let the man fall. Was it that easy?

The woman screamed again. Someone came up beside Sam and pushed him away, making him stumble, then stepped to the bearded man and kicked the knife away from his hand. Sam had a glimpse of a gun, then a pair of eyes peering up at him from beneath the brim of a baseball cap. He felt a sudden tremor of fear, sharper than anything he had felt facing the bearded man.

"You're cut," the man in the cap said.

It was as if his saying it made it real for the first time, as if the man in the cap had stabbed him. He felt suddenly dizzy, felt the ache in his side, the coldness of the bloody fabric against his skin. Someone took hold of his arm and spoke his name.

He looked, blinked in wonder. "Stosh," he said. "What . . . ?"

"We heard people shouting."

"Who . . . ?"

"This is Jerry Majors. He's on stakeout here. You met him. You remember?"

He nodded. "At the dayroom," he said. "He's a cop." He felt light-headed.

"Come sit down," Stosh said.

The other people were pressing in closer now. Majors had put his gun away and was kneeling beside the bearded man, talking to him in a low voice. The man seemed to be responding, but not moving. From somewhere nearby came the shrill voice of the woman, complaining over and over about "sons of bitches fucking things up." Did she mean him?

He let Stosh lead him to the edge of the light, beyond the crowd, let her position him on the edge of one of the planters while she stood distractedly beside him, looking around.

"I've got to find someone to look at that wound," she said.

"It's okay," he told her, not knowing whether it was or not, but not wanting her to leave. He pressed one hand against his side, and found that that made it ache less. "I think the bleeding's stopped," he told her. He felt chilled and a little afraid but content to sit there with Stosh beside him. The beginnings of shock, some distant part of his mind observed. He reached out with his free hand for one of Stosh's, and pulled her down beside him. She resisted for a second, then sat, her tongue poking out of one corner of her mouth, studying him doubtfully. But she kept his hand in her own, holding it in her lap.

An ambulance came then, followed by police cars. Two attendants took the bearded man away in a stretcher, while a third came and knelt beside Sam, first cutting his shirt away so that a police photographer could snap a shot of the wound, then putting a blanket around his shoulders and swabbing the cut with alcohol, which surprisingly did not burn, finally taping gauze over it, never saying anything, only grunting from time to time, and then closing his kit and hurrying off to the ambulance as it pulled away.

The snug grasp of the bandage made him feel that everything would be okay. He even felt vaguely pleased with himself, watching the police come and go, the on-lookers who stole glances at himself and Stosh, then dipped their heads, murmuring to one another. He found that he wanted to say something to Stosh about Malden, about maybe showing it to her sometime, but then realized that that would sound silly, under the circumstances.

Two uniformed cops emerged from the darkness, escorting the woman, who was still talking, shaking her head as she walked. Loomis appeared behind them, holding the bearded man's book and lunch bag in one big hand. He looked around for a moment, spotted the two of them and walked over, not hurrying, looking as though he had just happened to be passing by, just happened to notice a couple of friends.

"Evening, Stosh," Loomis said, and then to Sam. "How you doing?"

"Fine," Sam said. "I'm fine." He meant it.

"I wanted to thank you for giving Marcie a ride home the other night."

Sam waved a hand in the air dismissively. "No problem," he said. It sounded to him like a silly kind of thing to say, and he felt like giggling but didn't.

Loomis sat down beside him, resting the book on his knee and putting the paper sack on top of it. The book, Sam saw, was *Riders of the Purple Sage*, by Zane Grey, a book his mother had once given him for a birthday, one he had liked. Lassiter, he remembered with an effort. The man in black. A burst of giddy laughter escaped him then, but he stifled it. Stosh squeezed his hand.

"The woman's a prostitute," Loomis said without preamble. "Not a streetwalker. She usually works the hotels around here. The guy—his name's Pelly—works at one of them as a deskman. He recognized her, or she recognized him—off-duty, as it were—and they got together, went back here to conduct some business. He was starting to get rough with her when you came along, but they do that sometimes. She's still more pissed at you for interfering than at him for slapping her. The knife surprised her, but she doesn't seem too concerned about it. He didn't threaten her with it."

Sam frowned, confused by what Loomis was telling him. "Did I do the wrong thing?" he asked.

Loomis studied him for a moment. "We don't normally advise civilians to confront armed assailants," he said. "But I'd say you did the right thing."

"He was slapping her," Sam said. "I couldn't just go on."

"Of course you couldn't," Stosh said.

Loomis put the book on the concrete beside him and began unfolding the top of the paper bag. "I want you to see something," he said.

Loomis opened the bag carefully and then tipped it up, shaking the contents out into his palm.

"Little sunflowers," he said.

"No," Stosh said. "They're black-eyed Susans."

"Six of them," Sam said, feeling a sense of renewed wonder rising in him, in his skin, as though he were sinking into cold water.

Loomis nodded, not quite smiling.

"What does it mean?" Stosh asked.

Sam looked at Loomis, then at her. "The Strangler,"

he said. "He always leaves flowers. The next victim would be the sixth."

She looked from him to Loomis, her eyes widening.

"That's assuming there's one guy," Loomis said. "Only there isn't. We've got Kirby on four of them, but not on Jeannie Courter. Turns out there were only four flowers with Munoz, so Courter was out of sequence. By Kirby's count, the next one would be five, not six. But the copycat would be counting them all."

Stosh shook her head, confused. "What do you mean? What are you saying? Is this him? The other one?"

Loomis shrugged. "Could be."

"Or maybe just a fantasy," Sam said. "I mean . . . just someone who . . . wants to think of himself that way."

"Yes," Loomis said. "There's a lot of that around." He stood up. "On the other hand," he said, more forcefully, "this Pelly guy took classes part-time at the university. And Courter was supposed to be a part-time hooker. He could have known her the way he knew this woman, could have run into her here."

"The flowers," Sam said. "They grow along the river back there."

"I know," Loomis said. "We had an idea this might be a likely spot, and there were connections to some of the other victims."

Sam laughed, shaking his head. "I thought I was the only one who saw that."

"That's why you've been coming here?"

He nodded, feeling foolish.

Stosh was still frowning, still trying to get it. "So this

may not be the guy," she said. "There might still be another one out there."

Loomis shrugged. "There's always another one out there," he said.

18

At Thanksgiving, they drove to Malden, the three of them, and Sam showed her the town, the river with its rusted bridge and the cemetery beyond. The leaves, lying in drifts across the curbless roads, were the same colors as the pebbles—the reddish clay color, mottled with mud brown and speckles of gold—as though the streets of the little town had put on a rough coat for the coming winter.

On their second evening, she and Davy took a walk by themselves, down along the main street to the dark business block. At the corner, a short flight of concrete steps led up to a sidewalk that ran beneath a wooden awning past the first half-dozen shops, most of them revealing only emptiness behind their unwashed windows. Davy stopped at each to press his face to the glass, his hands cupped around his eyes, and came away each time saying, "Nothing there," or, "Nothing there either," as though profoundly surprised.

On the way back, on the other side of the street, in a stretch of darkness in front of the tallest building, its windows long since boarded over, Davy took her hand in his, as though to lead her safely through it. When they emerged into the gray light at the end of the block, stepping back down to the gravel path that served as a sidewalk everywhere outside the main block, he stopped and asked her, "Why is your name Stosh?"

She hesitated only a second, and then told him, whispering in the half-dark, with the chill football breeze ruffling their hair, Davy's eyes staring up at her like pools of black light. She didn't tell him what she had told Sam, about it being Polish for Stan, her brothers' joke; instead she told him the other story, also true, that it was because of the old-world way her parents had pronounced her real name. He pronounced it that way himself several times—Ahna-stosh-ah—seeming to like the feel of it on his tongue.

"But it's a secret," she told him. "Just between you and me and your dad. Okay?"

He promised solemnly, but in the weeks after that, not quite breaking his promise, he took to calling her Annie, and before long Sam picked it up as well, though only in private.

She began to feel, oddly, that Annie was her "real" name, the name she had been meant to have all along, and it seemed almost incredible to her that no one in her family had ever called her that. She thought of going back to Chicago, taking Sam and Davy with her, telling everyone that this was who she was now, who they were. Sam and Annie, she whispered to herself, imagining that. Sam and Annie and Davy. She felt sometimes a happiness that was a kind of ache that frightened her, for she shared with Sam an apprehension that the universe harbored an ironic sense of humor.

But the months went on and nothing bad happened. They talked of going to Frank's Christmas party, doing something outrageous, but in the end they only stayed home, at the house by the river she was beginning to think of as home, though she kept the apartment, a hedge against the universe.

She continued on the police beat, as well, and Sam went back to days, on general assignment. They went out for supper once or twice with L.J. and Edie Loomis, and Marcie Loomis babysat with Davy a few times. Gradually, Debbie's old room became hers, the place where she kept her stuff at Sam's house, although she actually slept there less and less as it became obvious that it made no difference to Davy which door she emerged from in the morning.

As the weather grew warmer, Davy asked her to help move his own bed out onto the screened-in porch, and she did, the two of them ignoring Sam's doubtful frowns, his wondering aloud about how well Davy would like it out there when he woke up in the dark, his whispered, half-serious complaint that it would most likely mean they'd end up with Davy in their own bed half the time.

But Davy kept to the porch, only once coming in to join them, and that during a violent early-spring thunderstorm, at Sam's suggestion. Those same rains beat the straw-colored weeds in the backyard into a sort of woven mat. When the new grass began poking its way up, here and there, Sam decided to try mowing the yard, clearing away the dead stuff, to make room for it.

It took him most of a weekend, working in two-hour shifts with the mower and the weedeater, while she and

Davy helped by raking up the worst of it and stuffing it into huge plastic bags to be lugged out to the front curb.

On Sunday afternoon, when Sam was whittling away at the last thin rectangle of high weeds, back where the yard sloped down toward the river, spiraling around the edges and working his way in, a rabbit came bounding suddenly out of the strip of foliage, darting first toward the back wall of the garage, then making a sharp right turn, along and somehow under the fence, and disappearing into the underbrush along the bank.

Sam watched it go, pursed his lips, and seemed to mow more slowly after that, scanning the ground just ahead of him. At last he stopped and knelt to fold back some clumps of weeds, then beckoned to her and Davy.

"That's what I thought," he said, pointing. "That's why she waited so long to bolt, till I was almost there."

Davy was on his knees, peering at what looked like a writhing ball of gray fur just beneath the surface of the ground. Sam reached past him and carefully lifted out a single baby rabbit, its eyes still closed. He let Davy stroke it softly, round-eyed, then deposited it in Stosh's hand. It was nothing but a small, warm belly with long ears at one end and equally long feet at the other. She held it for a moment, feeling a chill of wonder, and then eased it back into the depression in the earth, where it quickly squirmed back into the intertwined mass of its brothers and sisters.

"Can we keep 'em, Dad?"

Sam looked down at Davy, shook his head. "No," he said. "They'd die."

Davy suddenly had tears in his eyes. "Will their mother come back?"

Sam hesitated, then said, "Probably. If we leave them alone. She'll probably come back and move them somewhere safer."

Davy looked relieved. The rest of the afternoon and into the evening, he sat inside the screened-in porch, watching. At bedtime, he got Stosh to help him move his bed slightly, so that he could see out the door from where his pillow was.

"She hasn't come yet, Annie," he said, his voice husky.

"She's probably waiting for dark. You might not be able to see her. Most likely, we'll get in the morning and they'll be gone." She hoped that turned out to be so.

Later that night, she awoke to the sound of Davy's voice, not crying out, but simply talking, as though there were someone with him on the porch.

She got up quietly and went along the hall and through the kitchen. Moonlight flooded the backyard and the porch itself, making a grill of light and dark across the floor and the bed where Davy lay, talking unintelligibly in his sleep. Looking out through the screen, she could see the dark hole in the ground, just at the edge of the unmown weeds, but could not tell whether it was empty or still full of baby rabbits.

"I will, Mom," Davy said. "I promise."

Stosh looked down at him for a moment, resisting the urge to touch him, to perhaps awaken him, and then went back to the kitchen and got a wooden chair. She carried it out to the porch and sat down, wrapping her bathrobe more tightly around her and putting her

feet up on the wooden box that held Davy's little
wooden people, his make-believe town.

She thought that there ought to be a special name
for the kind of dream Davy was having—the opposite of
a nightmare, a dream of the heart's deepest wish ful-
filled, from which one hoped never to awaken. It
seemed to her that she had felt, during these past few
months, that she had been living in such a dream herself, afraid of it ending. But there was no place for fear
in such a dream; if you awoke—when you awoke—you
dealt then with the world you found. To fear it beforehand only destroyed the dream itself.

A movement caught her eye, out in the moonlit yard,
and she saw that a small gray shape had appeared beside the darker spot where the hole was. She turned
her head slightly, trying to see it more clearly, but it
darted fluidly in the darkness, seemed to disappear,
then reappear. The third time it returned to the edge of
the hole, she was certain it was not some trick of the
moonlight.

She looked down at Davy and thought about waking
him up to see it, then shook her head. The noise of
awakening him might drive away both returned moth-
ers, and who knew if either would come again?

She lay her head back slightly, letting go of the effort
of trying to focus on the rabbit. Davy's eyelids fluttered
for a second, as though they might open, but then he
gave a long, pleasure-filled sigh and turned his face
away from her, toward the moonlight. She closed her
own eyes. there was no way she could keep the dream
for him—no more, really, than she could be certain of
hanging on to her own. But what she could do—the

most any of them could hope for, perhaps—was to stay here beside him, be here when he awoke, so that when he came back to the world that was not a dream, and remembered once more what was real and what was not, he would not be alone.